eye wuz here

STORIES
BY WOMEN WRITERS
UNDER 30

eye
wuz
here

EDITED BY
SHANNON COOLEY

DOUGLAS & McINTYRE

VANCOUVER / TORONTO

96 97 98 99 00 5 4 3 2

Douglas & McIntyre
1615 Venables Street
Vancouver, British Columbia
V5L 2H1

Canadian Cataloguing in Publication Data

Main entry under title:
Eye wuz here

   ISBN 1-55054-524-8

   1. Short stories, Canadian (English)—Women authors.* 2. Canadian fiction (English)—20th century.* I. Cooley, Shannon, 1969- II. Title:
I was here.
PS8235.W4E93 1996   C813'.01089287 C96-910439-1
PR9197.33.W65E93 1996

Editing by Barbara Pulling
Cover illustration by Barbara Klunder
Cover design by Michael Solomon
Typeset by Vancouver Desktop Publishing Centre
Printed and bound in Canada by Metropole Litho Inc.
Printed on acid-free paper

The publisher gratefully acknowledges the assistance of the Canada Council and of the British Columbia Ministry of Tourism, Small Business and Culture.

in loving memory of my grandmother,
J. Patricia "Tish" Guthrie

Contents

this is for real

you can go to sleep now, nana, I'm here

Acknowledgements

My love and gratitude to my parents, Julia and Jack Cooley, for bedtime stories and life without cable television. I would also like to thank my Gram, Arlene Hills Cooley.

Thank you contributors for your patience and enthusiasm, especially Judy MacInnes Jr. and Suzanne Buffam, support sources from day one. Thank you to the following readers for time and insight: Marion Bennett, Patrick Cooley, Carol Chavigny, Sheila Crossley, Andrea Galbraith, Ruth-Ann McColman, Erin Soros, Alissa York. My gratitude to the many writers, editors, coordinators and teachers who provided practical advice and support—special thanks to Jack Hodgins, Lorna Crozier, George Robertson, Sheri-D Wilson. Thanks also to Stephen Hendy (umpteen disk transfers), Tina MacLeod (emergency word processing) and Ken J. McLennan (original poster design).

I gratefully acknowledge the financial assistance of the Canada Council's Explorations Program.

Thank you Barbara Pulling for excellent editorial support and valuable guidance.

My love and thanks to old friends: Seanagh, Laurel, Jodi, Shannon, Tracy, Keitha, Rita, Christine, Suka, Karen, Taryn and many others. Without you, pals in the kookiness of life, the essentialness of this book would not have been recognized.

Thank you Ivan Iseppon, a wonderful writer and treasured friend.

The following stories have been previously published in book form: "Esmeralda" from *One Room in a Castle: Letters from Spain, France and Greece* by Karen Connelly, published by Turnstone Press, 1995, reprinted by permission of Turnstone Press; "The Peacock Hen" from the novel *When Fox Is a Thousand* by Larissa Lai, published by Press Gang Publishers, 1995, reprinted with the permission of Press Gang Publishers; "Living Dangerously" from *The Seasons Are Horses* by Bernice Friesen, published by Thistledown Press, 1995, reprinted with the permission of Thistledown Press; "The Air Between Us" by Gillian Roberts from *The Air Between Us*, published by Laughing Willow Books, 1994, reprinted with the permission of the author.

The following stories have been published in periodical form: "Yellow Sleeve Princess" by Lucy Ng in *Matrix* 45; "Cerberus and the Rain" by Shannon Cooley in *And Yet*, vol. 1, no. 1; "Saturday Night, August" by Janis McKenzie in *sub-TERRAIN*, vol. 2, no. 18; "in the red" by Suzanne Buffam in *Grain*, vol. 22, no. 3; and "Nosebleed" by Judy MacInnes Jr. in *Blood and Aphrodisiacs* 16.

The quote in "Particular Eyes: Mixed Messages from the Wall" is taken from *Heart of a Stranger* by Margaret Laurence (Toronto: McClelland & Stewart, 1976).

Shannon Cooley

Particular Eyes:
Mixed Messages from the Wall

> This is where my world began . . .
> A world which formed me, and continues to do so . . .
> A world which gave me my own lifework to do,
>   because it was here that
> I learned the sight of my own particular eyes.
> —Margaret Laurence, "Where the World Began"

This book is about being here and there. It is also about point of view. Margaret Laurence refers to Neepawa, Manitoba, as the place where her world began, "the strange . . . horrible and beautiful . . . never dull" prairie town she lived in as a girl, the place that gave her the sight of her very own eyes, that gave her a sense of "I". In this collection of short fiction, some of English Canada's most promising and provocative emerging women writers show us the world through their particular eyes. Commonly bundled under the label Generation X, Generation Y or twenty-somethings, these writers were thirty or younger at the time their stories were submitted. Some, such as Karen Connelly, Hiromi Goto and Larissa Lai, have already attained national and international recognition for their writing. Other writers are being published for the first time in this collection. Several of the writers are still in their teens, such as Amanda Hathaway Jernigan, who originally wrote her short story, "Card Games," at fourteen, and Jenna Newman, who at sixteen adapted her short story, "Duets," from a series of poems. Wherever here is for these writers—the road, the bar, the bedroom; the city or the small town—these short stories explore, and therefore acknowledge, the particularities of moment and place that compose the daily rhythms of young women's lives. Together, the women in this collection create a literature declaring young women to be present, insisting on their diverse ways of seeing. They write in a variety of prose styles, from the traditional to the fiercely original, and many of them also look for inspiration outside the established western-based literary canon. Ultimately, though, these stories explore a topic that concerns us all: the strange, beautiful, often repressive, never dull world we share with each other.

Young women today are the first generation of women to be born into a dominant culture influenced by feminism. While some of us already take our individual freedoms for granted, we also encounter conservative institutions, a backlash against women's rights, an accelerating technology explosion, an uncertain economic climate and a strident, often homogenizing pop culture propelled by mass communications. With our bodies caught up in the commerce of product and fantasy, we are frequently seen without being heard. The fact is that we rarely receive opportunities to present ourselves. Reacting to this world of mixed messages, young women have developed a sometimes contradictory, sometimes in-your-face culture of our own. Beyond the commercialism, convenient mythologies and lazy labelling are the stories of a generation of young women fully capable of identifying ourselves and our world.

I began collecting these stories in the spring of 1993. At first, I planned on editing a relatively small-scale book featuring young women writers I had encountered as a creative writing student at the University of Victoria. Soon, though, the project grew into something much larger, with a national focus. Starting with my own money, and then with the essential funding of a Canada Council Explorations grant, I coordinated a national call for submissions. Posters went to bookstores, mainstream and underground literary magazines, creative writing programs, writers' guilds, independent radio stations, and any group that would likely attract young women writers. I also contacted editors, teachers and writers across the country for recommendations. The selection process has been slow, gratifying and challenging. I ended up with a wide-reaching short list to narrow down to these twenty-eight stories. As editor, I chose what moved me, stimulated me, what I felt was the best and most intriguing of the writing I had to consider. *eye wuz here* is in no way a top-twenty-eight countdown, however. It does not encompass all the diverse and complex issues that face young women, and I read many stories that will find their way to the public's eye at a later date. I emphatically encourage everyone who undertakes the nerve-wracking adventure of writing, revising and submitting to keep writing and revising, keep submitting. Through sharing point of view comes empathy, and through empathy, the lessening of loneliness and isolation—a goal common to all art and literature—and an important facet in the process of working towards positive change.

magnifying the creases there

Bernice Friesen

Living Dangerously

Cam was doing his algebra at the back of the restaurant between taking orders. When he looked up, I could tell he was smiling at me, not at Marina, though she'd already claimed him as far as our group was concerned. She said it was because they were the same age, seventeen. She was with us in grade eleven only because she had flunked grade nine. Cam would look up and I'd get this feeling at the back of my head, the feeling you get when someone's playing with your hair. Jenny, his sister and my best friend, said he liked me, too.

I took some of the sweat from my Coke bottle and wiped it on the back of my hot neck. Marina said she liked him first and Marina is the kind of person who lights matches and throws them at you, even when she's not mad. Everybody knows my motto is "Live dangerously," but that was a little too dangerous for my taste. I hung around with Marina because she liked living dangerously too, seemed to have more guts and ideas than I had most of the time, and brought out the wildness in me. I took a peek at Cam and sighed. There was just no way. Marina was in a bizarre mood that evening, so I knew I had to be careful. She was nastier than usual to Jenny, who hadn't done anything, and sometimes she just stared off into space or over at Cam.

Even if you'd never talked to Marina, you'd know to be careful of her. Her hair is long and curly black and she plays up the whiteness of her skin with black eyeliner and red, red lipstick. She looks at you with brittle green eyes, and bites the corner of her lip. Guys she's used call her a witch instead of a bitch, maybe because they're scared of her. She likes that.

We were sitting in the best window booth at the Chinese on one of Jenny's days off, when she can sit with us and snap her fingers for

7

service from her brother. It was evening, August, and sweltering. My legs stuck to the red vinyl seat, which was worn out from the sliding of too many bums in blue jeans. In the middle of my seat, there was a rip only partly covered with masking tape, and the foam squished out like blubber from a slit whale. Jenny's dad, the owner, doesn't care about fixing things up. Pops spends his extra money on Chinese lanterns, wall hangings and homesickness in general. Otherwise, he's pretty cheap. He won't get new linoleum and it's starting to break in the high traffic areas, like around the bathroom doors, showing the black lino glue underneath. Guess he doesn't figure appearance is very important, because his is the only restaurant in town.

"Bet you anything she's pregnant, Georgie," Marina said, in the middle of some extra vicious, probably completely untrue gossip. She leaned across the table as if to whisper to me, but talked as loud as before. She didn't care who heard. "She's never disappeared for so long before, and you should have seen her in the clinic today, trying to think I didn't see her behind that *Seventeen* magazine. She was bigger—I swear—and white like she was going to have a nervous breakdown."

"You mean you didn't go right up and ask her if she had a full load? That's what I would have done," I said, and Marina eyed me with admiration. I twirled a curl of my blonde, newly permed hair around one finger and smiled at her, not sure whether I was lying. Cruelty bubbled out of my mouth so easily when I was with Marina, I was starting to get ashamed of myself.

"Yeah? You probably would have, you maniac. I would have, but I just didn't think of it." Her eyes narrowed. "Geez, as if her gut hanging out wasn't enough to prove it." She stabbed out her cigarette, sat back, and curled her upper lip into a sneer, as if I'd told her she wasn't trying hard enough to be nasty.

True, you'd notice if Carmen got bigger. She used to look like a dry corn stalk with wispy hair the colour of your old cigar-smoking grandma's teeth. When she filled out, it was like overnight. She stopped walking all hunched over since she didn't have a cave for a chest any more, but then she found that people didn't stop calling her names anyway. The names just changed because she had basketball boobs.

"Well, no wonder she's been gone," Jenny said. "Her parents would probably kill her if she was pregnant. I know mine would. And you've told us stories about her parents, Marina. Like that time when she was eight and had been playing boats down at the river with Arney Ratslaff. Didn't you say her dad beat her with a belt even though she hadn't done anything wrong?"

"Hey, Carmen didn't even know she *could* have been doing something wrong. She didn't know sex existed." Marina bit her drinking straw, spreading her red painted lips away from it to keep them beautiful.

"No wonder she keeps trying to run away," Jenny said, her voice slow and sad. She sprinkled some salt on the table and did a drawing in it. Jenny is artistic and quiet. She keeps me from doing a lot of things that are just too wild, which Marina calls "being a drag." When Marina wanted me to do something really awful, she usually had to figure out some way of leaving Jenny behind.

"Pregnant," Marina said again, and made like she was going to spit and enjoy it.

To Marina, like most people, getting pregnant is a sin even though sex isn't. I think that's crazy. It's like saying it's only stupid to play Russian roulette if you get shot, or saying you're a bad person if something bad happens to you. It's all very confusing to me because people say babies are good things, too, so why are you bad if you have one? People's mothers all had at least one kid, so maybe everyone should just shut up about the kids other people have. I'm a strictly logical-type person and maybe that's why this weird world confuses me.

Of course, everyone in Grassbank thinks me and Dad are a little strange, too. He's the art teacher at the high school. He wears an earring and he used to be a freaked-out hippie in the sixties. At first, I had a really rough time fitting in here with my city clothes and ideas, the wild earrings my mom sends me, and the fact that Dad and I don't go to any church. I was sort of going through a punk phase then, too, and I wore a lot of black, and one side of my hair was longer than the other, not the kind of style that works well in a small town. Hardly anybody here even has holes in their jeans. Everybody except Jenny said I must be a slut. It almost drove me nuts—until I developed what Dad calls my "attitude" and started hanging around with Marina. After that, if people wanted to talk about me, they had to do it very quietly. Probably they were more scared of Marina than of me.

"When the nurse said Carmen's name," Marina said, "she just sat there like she was thinking about how she couldn't hide from me any more. She dropped the magazine and walked past like she didn't even know me. Can you believe that?"

I couldn't believe it. Carmen was the kind of person who'd sooner hide behind a magazine forever than face Marina. There was the family thing, too. Carmen and Marina were cousins, children of brothers who may have tried to murder each other way back when they were teen-agers. Marina's uncle Stan went to the hospital with his knee shot up by a drunken bullet.

"She's disappeared lots of times before," I said, holding my face straight. I knew I was looking for trouble, but hey, it's in my nature. I felt a little like I did when I'd taken my dad's car to go jumping on the steep dune road out by the river. Play leapfrog with death. Question what Marina believed.

Marina looked at me as if she wanted to stuff my drinking straw up my nose, but she didn't do anything about it. She remembered everything, though, every little bit of disloyalty or doubt. It would swim around inside her like a swallowed goldfish until she could think up her revenge. I thought of what she'd done to Roberta. She'd dragged me through a whole rainy Tuesday to spy on Roberta, eventually catching her with Leo when she was supposed to be going out with Don. Roberta had begged and begged Marina not to tell, but the news was everywhere the next day. I knew it was revenge for something, but I didn't know what.

Out of the corner of my eye, I saw Cam get up and come towards us. He stopped right beside me. I combed my fingers through my hair. Jenny told me he liked it curly.

"So what do you want, Georgie?" He flipped the pages of his notepad with the end of a pencil and looked at me through his round John Lennon spectacles. I was too careful to look back for long. I looked down the neck of my Coke bottle at the frayed scum of foam at the bottom.

"I want fries and gravy," Marina said. I glanced up. She was smiling as if she was waiting for him to look at her, but I could tell from her eyes that he didn't. I was thrilled, and I couldn't help looking at him again. He was beautiful. His eyes were warm, dark as black coffee, and his face was strong-boned with skin smooth as china. Quickly, I looked away in case Marina saw.

The week before, I had gone to Jenny's to watch videos—not anything unusual, seeing as how the Chongs live above the restaurant and I live across the back alley. We lay on the brown flecked carpet, which smelled of feet and spilled beer, ate taco chips and talked about guys when *Night of the Living Dead* got too boring; we'd seen it three times before. Cam smuggled us a couple of chocolate whipped-cream milkshakes, right past his dad, and that was something pretty dangerous to do. He put them under a bag of garbage in a box he was supposed to throw away, then brought them up the back stairs. I held the cold-sweating metal cup, wishing Jenny would shut up and watch the movie so I could ignore both and think about Cam. I heard her slurp up the last foam of her shake, but my straw got stuck on a cherry. There were six maraschino cherries at the bottom of my cup. I tipped them into my mouth, one by one. Jenny never knew.

Cam was still waiting for me to order.

"I don't want anything, thanks," I told him, tasting the last acid of my Coke, but wanting cherries instead. He flipped his notepad closed.

"You sure?" he said. He sounded disappointed. I wanted to look up into his clear night eyes to thank him for last week's milkshake, but I didn't dare, and it made me ashamed.

Marina reached out and touched a billow of his sweatshirt.

"So, what are you doing after?"

"After what?"

Cam pretended he didn't know what she was getting at and walked over to turn up the drippy air conditioner above the door. Jenny clamped her mouth closed and looked at me with little laughs in her eyes. She knew exactly how much Cam couldn't stand Marina. On his way back to his homework, Cam turned on the old clover-leaf fan on top of the dented round-cornered ice cream cooler, and the Chinese lanterns that hung from the ceiling started to turn. The shadow of a dragon crossed Marina's face as she watched Cam sit down and turn away. She looked as if she'd had just about enough from life—definitely the wrong time to look at her.

"What?"

"Nothing, nothing," I said, and hoped she'd focus on something other than me if she was going to explode.

"Geez," she said under her breath, shaking her head as if I were the most stupid person she'd ever met. It reminded me of the way Mom talks about Dad when I go to visit her in Toronto. She left Dad to try to become a famous artist and said Dad didn't have the guts to do the same thing—that's why he became a teacher.

"I'm going to the can." Marina got up. "Well, you coming?"

I got up obediently. My friend Evan says it's weird how girls always have to take someone with them to the bathroom, or else a whole crowd of them go together. Usually it's to tell secrets and talk about guys, but you never knew with Marina, especially when she was in one of her puppy-strangling moods. In bathrooms, Marina always said things that made me uncomfortable and made me lie to her even more than usual. A year before, in that same bathroom, just about the time I'd started hanging around with her, she told me about the first time she did it with Andy Weins in the back of his dad's station wagon. I lied, and told her about the time I did it with my nonexistent cousin's nonexistent best friend Herbie, just so Marina wouldn't think I was a child.

She grabbed the key from beside the cash register and we went down the back hall, past the sign that said, "Our Bathrooms Are for Our Customers Only." She unlocked the door marked with a bleedy Jiffy marker "W." I headed for the mirror.

I fluffed my hair and swayed it forward, making some curls cover one eye. Seductive, wild . . . I hoped. Then I noticed the zit on the tip of my nose. Great. I leaned against the sink to get close to the mirror and check out my face. I stayed clear of the right side of the sink where the whole corner and a lot of the enamel had been whacked off. I used to tell Jenny someone had fallen, brained herself, and Pops had turned her into sweet and sour pork. I usually got a slap on the side of the head for that one.

"I think I know who it is," Marina said, after going into the cubicle and blowing her nose. I could hear her pull down her jean shorts, and then I heard pee spray into the toilet.

"Who who is?" I said, sounding like an owl and feeling stupid.

"Who do you think I'm talking about? Remember Carmen's baby? I know who the father is," Marina said through the partition. I heard her zip up her shorts.

"Who, then?" I mumbled, checking to see if my gold eye shadow really did go with my blue eyes, and rubbing a little foundation on my Rudolph the Red-nosed Reindeer zit. "What baby?" I thought. For all we knew, Carmen was just porking up.

"It's Mark Morin's."

Oh, shit. So that was it. She was on a man rampage.

Marina came out of the cubicle, and for a second, it looked like she was standing behind a storm-soaked window and her face was getting dragged down with the rain. Mark had dumped Marina months ago, even before he got a job with C.N. and moved to Rosthern. Everybody knew he was too sweet a guy for her, so she was the only one who was surprised. She took it bad—of course, she takes everything bad. She even stayed drunk for a while, but I thought she'd gotten over it. Her eyes were black as rat holes. "The slut, trapping him like that."

Carmen was dead meat.

"I've got my brother Larry's car in front of the post office. Come on—we don't need Jenny with us," she said, reading my thoughts.

We left the bathroom. Marina tossed the key back inside before slamming the "W" door; anybody who had to go pee really bad was out of luck. When we walked out of the restaurant, I felt as if I was being pulled along in an evil wind, too weak to go against it. I only had time to shrug my shoulders at Jenny—no time to see if Cam was back in the kitchen, or in the storeroom, or where he was.

I got into the old wrecked Nova. Marina revved the motor and squealed the car out of the parking spot, tearing some skin off the tires. I rode all the way across town with my feet on the dashboard because of the mousetrap on the floor. The piece of cheese in it was so petrified I figured the mice would more likely nibble on my bare ankles. Not that I'm afraid of mice or anything, just rabies. I would have much rather been driving Dad's car as usual, but it was my fault I couldn't. The week before, we'd been cruising in it and Marina dared me to go a hundred down Main. I did it, of course, right past Dad. I almost peed myself, but Marina told me I was the best.

Marina made me get out and come with her to the front door of Carmen's house.

"Aunt Tina!" Marina exclaimed to the frizzy-haired overweight woman who opened the door. "Long time no see. We were just wondering whether Carmen would like to go out to Saskatoon and see a movie or something." Marina craned her neck to see past the woman into the kitchen.

"A movie in Saskatoon? Getting a little late for that," Marina's aunt told her as she eyed the sunset. "Besides, Carmen isn't here." Her voice was stiff, suspicious, daring Marina to push her further.

"So where is she?" Marina's eyes shimmered deeply like pools of cold swamp water.

"If you can find her . . ." The woman's eyes narrowed with anger and she didn't finish the sentence. Her hand made a fist around the doorknob before she shut the door.

"Poor Aunt Tina," Marina said, and smiled.

It didn't take us long to get to Rosthern, speeding, the Nova rattling over every pothole. Marina knew exactly where Mark's house was. I was glad. I didn't really care if we found Carmen or not, but I wanted to get this over with. After twenty minutes of sitting in the car with flipped-out Marina, I wanted to go home, or hide in the ditch, or something.

The house was on Railway Avenue, and there was a beat-up cardboard sign that said, "Please use back door," so we went around. We rang the painted-over doorbell and waited. When the outside light flashed on, we saw the tall-grassed backyard, islanded with bits of old cars, and the tired, half-weeded strawberry patch on the edge of the dirt alley. Carmen opened the door and stepped back when she saw us. She was wearing shorts and a man's green work shirt, a darker green square over one of her breasts where the pocket had been torn off. Her legs were fat-white and pimpled with mosquito bites. She did look bigger—fatter, anyway. Marina pushed in and glared back for me to follow. It was better than standing in the doorway.

The kitchen was small and had just been painted with globby yellow paint. Turpentine stink hovered under the smell of garlic, and the leftover dishes on the counter still had a few reddened worms of spaghetti slithering over the edges. Carmen was leaning against the yellow wall and I thought she might stick to it, or walk away with a yellow swipe down to her backside. Nervously, she put one bare foot halfway on top of the other and gave Marina this hunted look, like an animal somewhere between running and attacking.

It always made me a little sick to see Marina turn someone into a quivering mound of Jell-O, even though I sometimes took part, but the feeling I was getting then was stranger. Carmen looked afraid, but she also looked careful. I felt like an invader—like a brainless Viking pirate who hung out making chit-chat with the farmer he'd captured, just before the farmer's wife dinged him over the head with her frying pan. If you're in the mood to pillage, Marina, I thought, do it and let's get out of here. I stood behind Marina with my back against the wall.

"What are you doing here?" Carmen said, her voice quiet, tense. She came out of the entrance way, sliding her feet over the dirty linoleum, and sat behind the table on the edge of a chair. In front of her, there was a pamphlet on childbirth that she tried to cover with a tea towel. I jabbed Marina in the elbow, making sure she saw it. We knew for sure. We could go now, I thought, but Marina started to wander around the kitchen, opening cupboards. It reminded me of Marina's mom going through Marina's gym bag and purse, right in front of me, looking for something to slap her for—the pill, condoms, whatever. Marina stuck her head in the living room doorway, then walked over to the sink and looked out the window into the black night; there was no more sunset. I saw her reflection before she turned around. She was smiling.

"Mark's not here." Carmen's voice wavered. "You going to tell Mum?"

Marina wet her lips.

"You're living in sin," she said, upright, like a TV evangelist. Carmen's mouth opened and she twisted a hangnail until the blood started coming. I thought of her with a tiny tiny baby lost somewhere inside her belly. Absently, Marina lit a match.

"You mean you don't want me to tell her you're pregnant?" Marina bit out, but just then, the screen door slammed open and Mark came in. Marina burned herself.

"Hey, look. It's a party, and I wasn't invited," he said, giving Marina a second look as if he couldn't believe she was there, then kissing Carmen. He walked over to the counter and let the chain of fish he was carrying slide like raw liver into the sink. Marina watched him open-mouthed, obviously still in love.

"I caught my limit, and Ted, he only caught four. How do you like that?" Mark stood uncertainly, looking from Marina to Carmen as if he expected a fight. Carmen smiled at him—this open kind of smile that I'd never seen before—and he smiled back, kind of relieved. "I'm going to run a couple of these jacks over to Dad. Won't be long." He took two fish off the chain, put them in a plastic bag and banged the door shut after him. Everything was quiet. Somehow the air had changed and it was cooler.

"Get out."

The words were soft, and at first, they didn't seem to be coming from Carmen at all—not Carmen the wimp.

"I don't want you in this house when he comes back." Carmen stood up and stepped forward, moving slowly, her thickening body steady as stone.

"We were just at your mum's. Any messages you want me to take back?" Marina said, unaware of her weak, lovestruck voice, sounding like she was falling into some hole. Her eyes flamed like dying fireflies.

"You'll tell or she'll find out anyway," Carmen said, and her eyes opened as if she'd heard the words from the angel of truth instead of having spoken them herself.

"I'm getting out of here," I said to Marina. When I got to the car, she was right behind me.

"She *is* pregnant. She is. You saw it," Marina said, desperately hating, and wanting me to do the same. She leaned forward in the dark street, and I backed away, afraid she'd touch me, hang on me, like I'm afraid of stepping on earthworms when they swim onto the sidewalk to die in a downpour.

She drove slowly, as if she didn't want to get home, as if she wanted to keep me in the car forever. I sat with my arms folded, the cool night air coming in the open window and splashing my face.

"He's going to be damn sorry. Wait until she has a couple more brats and gains about fifty pounds. This one probably isn't even his, you know. The fool. Just wait until I tell Rayleen and Lill about this."

Yeah. Right. Just wait until I tell Jenny and everybody else about this—about how Marina was ordered out of her ex-boyfriend's house by Carmen—Carmen the wimp. Ex-wimp.

Marina wanted to keep cruising, maybe catch a party somewhere if we could find one—anything to keep me around—but I made her drop me off at home. She wasn't impressed with me, but I didn't care. I went around to the back door. Over the fence I saw the back of the Chinese. The outside light went on and Cam came out to hoist a green garbage bag into the Loraas Disposal bin. I waited until he'd gone back inside, then crossed the alley. I said hi to Pops as I passed through the kitchen, then spied through one of the portholes of the swinging doors to see what Cam was up to. His head and arms were flopped all over his books and there was no one else in the restaurant. I went in quietly and sat down in front of him.

He looked up, his eyes very sleepy, and he stretched.

"So, what do you want, Georgie?"

"A chocolate whipped-cream milkshake. You know. The special."

I was smiling way too much—so much, my cheeks stung.

Bernice Friesen's work has appeared in Grain, CV2, The Dalhousie Review, Prairie Fire *and other magazines. The title story of her book of short fiction,* The Seasons Are Horses *(Thistledown, 1995), won the 1996 Vicky Metcalf Short Story Award.*

Amanda Hathaway Jernigan

Card Games

Clara always sleeps flat on her back, palms facing upwards, no pillow. Her theory is that she has more interesting dreams that way. She knows sometimes her mouth falls open and she snores, but she doesn't care.

This night, Clara falls asleep with her hands clasped behind her head, and wakes up to the horrible delight of total absence of sensation in her right hand. She moves it around in the darkness to feel its seeming nonexistence and touches it with her other hand, squeezing the dead fingers until the pain should be unbearable. Slowly the hand comes alive like fire.

Then Clara ducks under the blanket to hide from the sky and its eerie dark-light. Hidden in the musty black, she can't tell if her eyes are open or closed. She is losing control of her senses, one by one.

She tries to pinpoint the exact moment when she makes the transition to unconsciousness. Slowly, her mind slips into itself. She snaps it back once to think clearly, "I am still awake," then gives in, letting it go too gradually or too suddenly to keep track of.

When Clara wakes again at dawn, she lies there, her eyelids glowing red from the light that forces its way into her oblivion. She eases her eyes open, and the grey light slaps her fully awake.

A big-bodied spider swings from the dusty rafters of the cabin, half a metre or so above Clara's face. Clara has heard that you can drive a person insane by steadily dripping water on a spot in the middle of her forehead. She wonders if it would work. She likes to think that, no matter what is done to her physically, her mind will remain her own. Once she was having a bad day at school and a guy grinned at her and started chanting "P.M.S." She swung around and slugged him full force in the stomach. He'd gone off swearing, but they both knew he'd won.

Clara runs her hand through the air above the spider, grabbing at his invisible lifeline. She misses, but her finger brushes it, scaring the spider back up the vibrating cord. Strange, she thinks, that he goes up towards the danger, instead of down, away from it. She lets him go and flips over onto her side. The sky is grey with streaks of white clouds like torn Kleenex. A giddy wind blows in through the screen stapled to the wooden window frame. The corner staple is easing its way out. She reaches over and jams it in with her thumb.

Clara looks at the water. Big waves today. They claw the sand from the surface of the beach, arching down, frothing up, slipping over, kneading back, with a seething sound almost too dry for all that wetness.

Arching her back off the bed, she pulls the faded green army blanket around her, trapping her arms against the warmth of her sides. Then she disentangles one arm and moves the bedside table so she can see Shannon, asleep on the other cot. Shannon is curled up on her side, arms bent in front of her and crossed at the wrists.

Quietly, Clara stands up, letting the blanket fall to the floor. She goes through her duffel bag to find jeans, T-shirt and underwear, and then steals into the tiny bathroom to get changed. When she comes out, Shannon is still asleep.

The air, it seems, is flickering.

Andy is in the kitchen making Tang. His back is to Clara as she comes in. "Morning," she says, realizing too late how gruff her sleepy voice sounds. Oh well. Andy won't mind. She's known him since they were both two—they went to the same preschool. They used to spend hours together and tell each other everything, but when they were eleven their mothers decided they were too old to have sleepovers any more. Clara cried. Andy was embarrassed and didn't speak to Clara for days. Shades of Adam and Eve when they first knew they were naked.

Ever since, things haven't been quite the same between them. They still see each other when their parents get together, and occasionally speak in the halls at school if none of Andy's friends are around. And Andy phones her sometimes. Well, quite a bit, actually. To ask her advice about other girls. He never calls them girls, though. He calls them chicks if he likes them and bitches if he doesn't. Clara hates both words. But Clara isn't sure how she feels about Andy asking her advice. It flatters her that Andy values her opinion in these matters. She likes that he sees her as a kind of co-conspirator. She loves secrets.

But she also feels like a traitor, to her friends and to women in general. And it bothers her that Andy doesn't seem to see her as a real girl, as a chick. More like a relative or some sort of guy/girl. Definitely not as a romantic prospect in any case. But she keeps her mouth shut and plays the go-between. Andy isn't bad-looking. Even she can see that. He has longish black hair and pointed features. His eyes are almost black too. And he's tall. Girls like tall guys. Clara thinks he's a pretty good friend to have. The fact that she knows him well makes her semi-popular among the girls at school.

"Morning, Clara." Andy turns his head, but continues to stir the garish orange liquid. "You're up early. Too many marshmallows last night?"

"Shut up." Clara pulls two blue plastic cups off the shelf. Andy pours for himself and drinks it in three long swallows. Then he tosses the cup into the sink by the far wall. It clatters over the rim and spirals to the centre of the basin.

"Basket," he says. Clara smiles. She slips the pitcher into the fridge, sloshing some Tang over the side and onto the dusty wooden floor.

"Let's go for a walk," says Clara, glad that she hasn't woken Shannon.

"Where?"

"Just up the beach a ways."

"Where's Shannon?"

"She's still sleeping. I'll leave a note."

Andy shrugs and goes to open the door. He gestures towards Clara. "Ladies first."

"I'm not a lady."

"No guff. I was just being polite."

"Sure."

Andy goes out the door, letting it bang shut behind him. Clara hopes Shannon hasn't heard. She opens it again for herself and closes it quietly before she leaps down the stairs. She loses her balance as she lands on the scalloped sand and flops down flat on her back. She sticks a hand up towards Andy.

"What?" he asks.

"Help me up." He grips her hand and yanks so hard that she goes reeling forward. "You idiot," she gasps. They laugh. Clara shakes the sand out of her straight blonde hair, which is now beginning to curl. It's been at least two days since she washed it.

She walks beside Andy, about half a metre away from him. They move parallel to the surf. Once her arm brushes the sleeve of his windbreaker. "Sorry," she says. It is too humid out. Almost hard to breathe. She feels like the world has been bound and gagged. Andy walks with his hands in his back pockets. He kicks at the sand, and the wind won't let the dislodged particles come back to the ground.

"Andy," says Clara, "whenever I talk to you it's like I'm speaking through smoke." They stop. Andy looks at her; his eyes really are black.

"Let's run," he says. They run. The sand squeaks under their bare heels. Andy takes it easy so Clara can keep up. The wind blows their hair crazy. They swing closer to the water.

Clara zigzags, teasing the waves. She runs out through the wet sand that sucks at her feet as the foam drags back, defeated. Then she shies away as the challenge is returned, the waves growling and baring their teeth as they slap the beach at Clara's toes, splattering water berries up into the air. Dark stains creep up her jeans. "Let's go swimming," she yells through the wind.

Andy laughs. "You're a strange one, Clara."

"No, really. The water's warm."

"You gotta be kidding. I'm not going all the way back to get my suit."

"So. Go skinny-dipping."

"Sure."

"Yeah. Why not?"

Andy is getting embarrassed. They stop running. He stands on his heels and rubs the back of his neck. He laughs. "You are too much," he says. "Too much."

"I'm going in," yells Clara. She begins to take off her shirt. A look of absolute terror crosses Andy's face. Clara bursts out laughing.

Her shoulders shake, her mouth falls open, her voice is not her own. Gasping for breath, she throws her head forward and hides behind her hair.

"You're screwed," Andy says. Clara is still laughing. "I'm going back." Clara straightens. She holds her breath and purses her lips, trapping an awkward smile on her face.

As Andy turns away, she grabs his shoulders and jumps on his back, wrapping her legs around his midriff. Andy swears furiously and swings around. Arms flailing, he topples backwards into the swirling, ankle-deep water. Clara flies off to land on her bottom, her hands out behind her for support. She is laughing again. Andy is on his side, propped up by one elbow. He struggles to stand and pulls his wet windbreaker over his head.

"Bitch." Then he turns and walks back towards the cabin.

Clara stares at his receding shoulders. Abruptly she stops laughing. Bitch. Andy called her a bitch. Her eyes sting; she knows tears will fall if she blinks. She stands up to follow Andy, but instead spins around and charges out into the lake, hurling herself down on her stomach. She blows all her air out to let herself sink and tries to adjust to the growing pressure in her lungs. Her tears are part of the lake now. She opens her mouth and gulps water. She feels it move down her throat, sweet and cool and tasting faintly of rotting lake weed. It is as if she is dissolving, her molecules mixing with the water.

The pressure in her lungs is becoming unbearable. Her feet kick up milky clouds of sand as she digs her toes into the bottom, struggling to right herself. She wants to leap miles out of the water, hands outstretched, to tear the cords that hold the earth. She dives into the air, breathing it like candy. When she lands, she collapses to her knees, panting.

Eventually she rises and walks up the hard-packed, damp sand that forms the median between wet and dry. She spins and spins, water reeling from her clothes and hair. She stops. The drops form dark pellets where they hit the dry sand. She turns and walks straight back to the cabin. Absolutely straight.

Clara walks up the cabin steps and looks through the rusty, ballooning screen. Shannon is sitting at the kitchen table, her legs crossed at the ankles. She is flipping through the limp pages of *Seventeen*. She reads every issue cover to cover. Clara laughs at her. She thinks those magazines are stupid. Or so she says. But when she sleeps over at Shannon's house, she waits until Shannon is asleep and then digs through her bookshelves until she finds them. Then she guiltily scans the colourful pages to see what her new impossible standards should be. She also goes through Shannon's romance novels and reads the sex scenes until she knows them by heart.

Fascinated, Clara watches Shannon's hands. They are beautiful hands and turn each page uniformly, automatically. Shannon's curly brown hair is pulled back in a neat ponytail, every vagrant strand sprayed up. Clara runs her fingers through her own wet tangle of hair. Sometimes Clara fantasizes about Shannon coming down with a bizarre disease that makes her go bald and get acne. Clara loves Shannon. She just wishes her friend wasn't so good-looking.

Clara can hear Andy crashing around in the back bedroom, probably getting changed. Shannon looks up. "Hey," says Clara.

"Hey." Shannon doesn't seem to notice that Clara is dripping wet. Or at least she doesn't say anything. She looks at Clara, a slightly bemused half-smile on her face. Shannon is very good at this.

Clara is frustrated. Why can't Shannon just ask what happened and get it over with? Maybe she already knows. "All right," says Clara. "So I fell in the water." Shannon intently studies her fingernails. Clara shifts her weight to her right foot. "Well, I guess I actually jumped on Andy's back and he fell in the water and so did I." Shannon raises her left eyebrow slightly. Otherwise her expression doesn't change. Clara feels the tension like cold metal in her mouth. "Fine, fine. Andy and I went for a walk and I didn't wake you up on purpose 'cause I didn't really want you to come 'cause then Andy would have been all over you and I wanted to spend some time alone with him for once. Are you satisfied?" Her voice increases in volume as she speaks, then breaks off in a dry, cracked sob.

"Clara," says Shannon, drawing out the "a" sound. Clara hates that. She likes a purer vowel sound. Clara. Clarity. "Clara, I didn't ask you anything."

"But you wanted to know, didn't you?"

Shannon rolls her eyes. "Frankly, right now I couldn't care less."
She tugs at her ponytail and goes back to her magazine. Clara doesn't
move. Can't move. "So," Shannon croons, concentrating on keeping
her eyes on the magazine, "was it romantic?"

Clara kicks the table halfheartedly. "Shut up."

"Shut up," echoes Andy from the back room. Clara stomps into
her own room, water dripping from her clothes to leave a trail on
the floor behind her. Shannon sniffs back her laughter and reaches
her graceful fingers down to flip another page.

All day the humidity packs in around the cabin and the hot wind
bangs in through the screens. The wind slams the loosely hung porch
door again and again, an insanity of noise in Clara's head. It seems
too ominous to go outside, as if even so small an addition to the
atmosphere as her raspy breath will set it all off balance, things reeling
off the earth as it spins.

So they stay in and Clara and Shannon play cards, every game
they can remember: Go Fish, Crazy Eights, War. When these get
boring they move on to faster games—Pounce, Spit, Speed and
finally Slap Jack, until, in a flurry of flipping cards and slapping hands,
Shannon gouges Clara's knuckle with her fingernail, getting a blood
spot on the three of hearts.

Then they convince Andy to play Michigan with them. He's been
listening to Metallica on his Walkman. They use smooth beach stones
for poker chips. Clara loves their pearl-smooth weight in her hands.
She wants to put them into her mouth, to feel them on her tongue
and swallow the smoothness down her rough throat, so that their
cool weight can sit in her stomach.

"Clara, find some way to shut up that damn door," says Andy.
But it isn't the door. It's the wind.

"This is getting boring," says Shannon. "I'll go heat up a can of
beans for supper." She stands up and turns around. "Hey, Andy. Is
there any dust on my butt?" Andy is rubbing the back of his neck
again. Shannon doesn't wait for an answer. She strides into the
kitchen, her ponytail tossing back and forth as she walks. "Someone
had better put the storm shutters up," she calls after her. Andy grunts
a reply and plugs himself back into his Walkman.

Clara scoops the cards into a pile and begins to shuffle them, letting their gentle "pflap, pflap" sound, their hypnotic rising and falling, compensate for the absence of rain. Gradually, Clara's mind forms a pattern around the riffling cards and the continuing, seemingly erratic beat of the windblown door. "The weather's wrong," she thinks.

> Weather is wrong (bang)
> There should be rain (bang bang)
> Blood on a card (bang)
> There should be (bang) rain (bang bang)

Andy is beating the storm shutters into submission and swearing under his breath.

"Want some help?"

"Not now," he snaps. "Why don't you go help Shannon?" Clara can hear the clanking of a spoon against the metal camping cook pot her father lent them for the weekend. Shannon is being loud. She wants to make sure Clara and Andy are aware of her. Clara incorporates the clanking into her rhyme.

> Weather is wrong (crash bang)
> There should be (crash) rain (bang bang)
> Blood on a card (bang)
> And Shannon's a pain (crash bang)

As Clara rises to go set the table she slips a card into the back pocket of her jeans. She then calmly lets the deck fall from her hands. Fifty-one cards scatter at her feet.

Clara walks into the kitchen. Shannon glances at her and then goes back to stirring the beans. Clara swings open a cupboard and finds the silverware tray. She plops a clanking pile of assorted forks and spoons down on the cracked wooden table. "I wonder where Mum and Dad are right now."

Shannon shrugs. "Who gives? Probably in a fancy restaurant drinking something better than Tang. Tomorrow's Monday, right?"

"Yeah. Maybe they'll forget to come pick us up."

"Not likely. They weren't exactly thrilled about letting us have the cabin for the weekend."

"They probably figure I can do less damage here than I could if they left me in town." Clara searches through the dish rack. "Shannon, where'd you put the bowls?"

"What bowls? There were none."

"Oops. Oh well. We'll use mugs."

"Give me a break. You're such a blonde." Clara delivers a stack of metallic-tasting mugs to Shannon, who cringes as she touches their rough surfaces. "These things make me sick." She ladles beans into two of the cups.

"Aren't you having any?"

"I'm not hungry. Chop up some carrots, would ya?"

Andy comes into the kitchen. "Storm blinds are up."

"It looks pretty rough out there," says Clara. "Do they really work?"

"How the hell should I know?" Andy grabs a carrot off the cutting board and bites into it savagely. Shannon laughs.

They sit down. Andy seems to be sitting at the head of the table, which isn't really possible since the table is square. Maybe it's just his height, or the fact that the seat across from him is empty. Andy uses the remains of his carrot stick to rap on the table, presumably in time to the tape in his Walkman. Clara eats her beans one by one. Shannon watches them both. "Andy, quit it." Andy quickens the beat he drums out with his carrot. "Andy . . ."

Clara interrupts. "Andy, in polite society we generally do not come to the table with small black boxes sprouting from our ears." Shannon giggles. Clara grabs the carrot from Andy and puts one end in her mouth so that the other sticks straight out. She places the flat of her hand against it and pushes the carrot into her mouth, chomping her teeth up and down rapidly, so that the carrot is like a log moving down the conveyor belt to the sawmill.

"Clara, that's disgusting." Shannon wrinkles her nose. Andy laughs in spite of himself and sets his Walkman on the counter.

Clara looks out the window, and the hesitant storm meets and holds her gaze. She hears Shannon and Andy. They are talking about someone from school. Their voices become distant murmurs. Clara is transfixed by what she sees outside. She sees herself stretched out against the sky like an elastic band, vibrating with the tension in the air.

Andy's low voice slides back into her awareness, plucks the band. ". . . she's such a bitch." Elastics can only take so much. Clara snaps.

She stands up, knocking her chair over and spilling the cold remainder of her beans on the table. Shannon and Andy sit in shocked silence, which Clara fills with a scream that goes on for so long it seems to be coming from the wind itself. When the sound finally chokes to a stop, Clara tears out of the cabin and down the beach.

The wind rips at her hair and slams itself against her over and over. She runs in stuttering steps, tripped up by the sand. When she reaches the water's edge, she keeps going, knee-deep into the surf. Then she stops and looks around, trying to decide what to do next. The horizon is calling. She jerks her eyes away from it, wrenches her legs free from the grip of the water, and falls face down on the shore.

She presses her forehead against the sand and digs her fingers into it as far as she can, holding on tight. There are no tears, but after a few minutes she reaches into her pocket for Kleenex, out of habit. And her hand withdraws the three of hearts.

Clara stares at it, then tears it down the middle. She sets the pieces in the wet sand and watches until the waves pounce on them and drag them away.

"Clara!" It's Shannon, running down the beach, strands of her perfect ponytail blown out in all directions, her face red, sand in the cuffs of her tight blue jeans. "Clara, what the hell are you doing?"

"Laughing," says Clara. And suddenly, she is. She rolls over onto her back, laughing helplessly.

Shannon stares at her for a moment, her mouth half open, her left eyebrow raised. "Clara, what's so funny?"

Clara takes a shaky breath. "I'm," she gasps, "I'm a bitch." Laughter explodes out of her once again, and this time Shannon joins in and collapses on the sand beside her.

Andy stands at the base of the cabin steps, looking like a misplaced scarecrow. "What's so funny?" he shouts.

Clara glances at Shannon and they share a conspiratorial grin. "Andy," they yell, "you're a bitch!" More laughter, as the first drops of rain fall on the exposed palms of Clara's hands, magnifying the creases there.

Amanda Hathaway Jernigan was fourteen when she wrote this story, sixteen when she revised it, and will be going on eighteen when it comes out. She spent last year in Thailand and is now living and writing in Nithburg, Ontario.

Cathy Stonehouse

That's My Girl

It's dizzy, walking this close to a steep drop and pretending you just don't care. The path's dusty, full of loose rocks and dying weeds. My sandals slip and flap off my feet, skid on squashed whinberries. My hands are stained dark with juice.

"Paul Harris asked me out last night," says Joanne. "Of course, I told him where to go." We exchange looks; relief spreads over me. "He's a bit of alright, mind."

We carry on picking. I can see the remains of pink varnish on her long fingernails. Joanne spent the week at school chipping it off flake by flake beneath her desk. I spent the week watching.

"I've almost enough to make a pie. Let's go home."

"I could stay up here all day, it would be a brilliant place to snog, don't you think?" says Joanne. "Such a great view." We're up on the Edge. It's a clear sky and we can see far across the plain, pick out landmarks: school, home, the park, the post office tower, the satellite telescope curved like a bra cup on the green misty horizon.

"It's fab." I sit down and pick through my berries to check for worms. Once on a picnic Joanne found maggots in a chocolate biscuit. We took them back to the shop and got a refund, and free biscuits for a year.

"Let's go to your house," says Joanne. She has a secret crush on my brother Bobby. She has blonde hair and her mum lets her wear stretch jeans, but still Bobby isn't interested. It's a shame he prefers trains.

We pick up our bags and head down the slope to the road, stop at the corner shop for Orange Maids, then sit outside on the dry stone wall, licking the orange syrup that turns gooey as it melts and coats our hands.

We reach my house in the late afternoon, and I can tell before I walk up the path that something's terribly wrong.

"What's that noise?" asks Joanne.

"I think it's my dad," I say, listening to the muffled shouts coming through the half-open window. "He must be home from work early."

"Should I go?" asks Joanne.

"Okay." I'm looking up at Bobby's bedroom window with its stolen British Rail Cafeteria sign. Our house seems to have grown into a huge pulsating zit on the side of the road.

"See you tomorrow, then?" Joanne touches my shoulder briefly before she takes her basket of berries.

I wait for her to head off down the path. "Ta ra."

Inside, Mum's sitting on the settee. Her face is bruised and around her feet are bits of china. I recognize my Peter Rabbit cereal bowl. Peter's ears have broken off along with his head, one on each side of the room. Picking my way between the pieces, I watch Dad carefully. He's leaning up against the sliding doors. His fists are slack. His breath stinks of gin.

"Your mother and I were having a discussion."

Mum begins to sob into her sleeve. "You'd no need to break the china, Frank." Snot runs clear down her face. "Your dad's had a few too many." I look away.

Upstairs, I find a small bag on my bed, stuffed with knickers, socks, a cardigan, toothbrush and soap.

"Mum's taking you to Uncle Ron's," says Bobby, appearing in the doorway. "She wants to go away."

"Why do I have to go?"

"I dunno. At least you won't have to stay here." Dad and Bobby will be eating packet Smash and tinned meatballs for tea. Dad will smoke silently and fall asleep in front of the telly with his mouth open, snoring, until dawn. Bobby will stop speaking to me for a few days and walk around white-faced and manly, trying to take Dad's side. Then we will all start acting normal again. If only Mum would laugh, or Dad bring home a bag of chips.

"I'm thirteen in January, why can't she leave me alone?"

"Dad's angry with her."

We always end up taking sides.

"Tessie?" Mum's voice wobbles in that stupid fake sad way. She's heading up the stairs, dragging her cardigan, rearranging her hair.

"What?"

"We're going to Ron and Vera's for the night. Get your coat on."

"Where's Dad?" I whisper.

"He's out the back having a fag." Through the open doorway I can see her changing out of her laddered stockings, throwing lipsticks into her handbag at the same time.

"Are you okay, Mum?" asks Bobby. He is six inches taller than her, his ankles poking out the bottom of his jeans like pale mushroom stalks.

"Yes, love," sighs Mum.

"Why can't I stay at home?" I ask, already knowing the answer.

"Because your dad won't touch a man and I don't want you getting bruises."

Once Dad threw his glasses at me. I watched them shatter on the wall behind my head. I didn't run away.

We drive to the farm in silence until Mum starts singing old songs from the war, "It's a Long Way to Tipperary" and "The Siegfried Line," her eyes focussed on the sky. The light's hazy on the dried-up fields, the hedgerows thick with cow parsley, nettles, dandelion clocks broken in the breeze from cars. I think hard about my sailing trip, the one I'm going to take with Joanne when we'll go round the world in a boat and break world records. I imagine the foam lashing across the bows, me in a yellow oilskin telling her what to do. I hold my legs tight together, my shoulders hunched over the half-open bag. I don't want anyone to see me.

"Vera's taken the kids to the coast," says Mum, as we pull into the long familiar drive. "The kids" means the three youngest, Derek, Malcolm and Suzanne; Barbara doesn't count as a child any more.

"Your Uncle Ron and Barbara don't know why we're coming so just keep your mouth shut, pretend you're all right."

Mum slams the car door and motions to me to get out.

As we push the farmhouse door it opens. Barbara's on the other side, dressed like an old woman. "I was just coming to see who it was." I see her studying Mum's face. "Come into the kitchen."

"My, this is a surprise," says Uncle Ron, getting up from the table, mince and potatoes dripping onto the napkin he wears tucked into his collar like the bib of a child. "Sit down, sit down. Barbara, get a couple of plates."

Mum and I sit down at the big table, rustling the thin plastic cloth. "I hope you don't mind, Ron, but Tessie and I—"

"It's always nice to see Tessie."

"Tessie and I wondered if we could stay the night."

"I think we can manage that, can't we, Barbara? The wife and kids have gone off to your Aunt Chrissy's for the week. Give us a bit of peace. Busy time round here." Uncle Ron's face is very tanned and his hands are scarred and crusted with dirt. I try to avoid shaking them.

Uncle Ron tucks back into his dinner. We eat our mince and spuds in silence, Mum pushing it round her plate with a fork while I swallow without chewing, covering it all in butter and Daddy's Sauce. For afters we have blackberry and apple pie with custard.

"Are you still doing the Guides?" Mum asks Barbara politely.

"She held a camp on the farm last year. All them lasses gallivanting about in skirts—she's too busy to be fussing with that these days. Bringing home the bacon." Uncle Ron puts down his knife and fork and reaches across the table for Barbara's hand.

"Yes, I-I'm working at Renshaw's. Pick'n'Mix counter."

Uncle Ron runs his rough hand up Barbara's cheek. "That's my girl."

I think out loud. "You must get fat selling all them sweets."

"Tessie! Barbara's got a very nice figure." Mum dabs her open mouth with a napkin. We push our chairs away from the table. I offer to do the dishes.

I watch the sun set over the back fields from Uncle Ron's back door while the plates clunk against each other in the sink, bits of food floating to the surface. I pad softly to the fridge and open it, see the leftover crumble neatly wrapped in cellophane. I want to steal something. I'm about to peel back its transparent skin when I hear someone come into the kitchen behind me.

"You can have my room. Auntie June can sleep in Suzanne's room, and I'll sleep in the boys'." Barbara opens a drawer and takes out a stiffly folded tea towel with Birds of Britain on it, the blue print fading into white. "Shall I dry? I know where everything goes."

When I say good night to Mum, I pretend not to see her wince as my lips touch her swollen cheek. Uncle Ron nods to me from behind his paper. I go upstairs.

The clothes in Barbara's drawers smell of lavender. I prop the top drawer open against my hip, rifle daringly through it, fish out an unopened Marks and Spencer's three-pack of Ladies' Mini-briefs, "size 36–38 hip, sensuous jewel tones of ruby, turquoise and gold," peel back the crackling plastic, run my hands over the silky, brightly coloured cotton stretched around a cardboard band. Next I fish out a stately looking bra, well-worn, with half-moon tea-coloured sweat stains under its arms. Its cups are huge, unwieldy, stuffed with prickly nylon pads. I wonder how Barbara keeps it on. "Underwired," I whisper beneath my breath, "underwired, cup size 36B." Lastly I pull out a blue striped box labelled "Feminine Hygiene Products," squished and malformed at the very back of the drawer. Inside there's a diagram of a girl's body cut to reveal her insides, tubes even as a chemistry experiment. It's labelled "easy insertion," but I don't think I want to know. I close the drawer.

Barbara must have started ages ago. I wonder if she keeps Tampax with her other Girl Guide emergency supplies—notebook and pencil, piece of string, safety pins—her motto, "Be prepared." I remember her coming round to our house to practise for her House Orderly badge, polishing and polishing the legs on our dining room table as they had never been polished before, Bobby and I stuffing old banana skins into her prim little shoes that were waiting beside the door. We never stayed to watch her put them on. Perhaps she walked all the way back to the farm with her feet crushed up against the slimy skins, too much of a Girl Guide to complain.

Next I see her diary, one of those silk ones with a big fake lock.

What if I opened it? I touch the outside, rough flower shapes, a purple ink stain. No, really, better not.

Anyway, I'm tired. I get undressed, put my nightie on. It's nylon chiffon with a pink rosebud sewn on the top. I chose it myself, from the catalogue. I watch the summer night drape itself across the trees. Blue upon blue, branches placed behind each other meshing into a barrier of lace. A half moon swells between thin clouds, the lights of the next farm burning under it, sightless yellow eyes.

I am woken by a sound. The sound of creaking. The creaking is coming from my bed. It's still dark but the room is blue with moonlight. My bed is weighted down by a heavy sack, there's something in it, it's alive. I swoop outside myself, perch in a small projectionist's booth high above the padded headboard to watch a flat accident at the other end of a swirling beam of light—there's a man, I can see the curve of his bottom as he straddles her, teeth biting into her breasts as he pushes the nylon nightie up around her neck, feel something deeper, something like a lizard, no a fist, jamming in.

I'm back inside again, the pain so intense I see a burn blister weeping. I want to call out but his hand across my face presses me down hard into the pillow. "That's my girl. Oh yes, that's my little girl." Something familiar: I smell blackberry and apple pie, see Uncle Ron's face. Uncle Ron sees me, he knows I am slipping behind dark shapes, my eyes blinking without air.

"Barbara, Barbara?" he whispers, and the weight of him is suddenly gone.

I try to be silent but the breaths shudder through me like trains. My neck hurts. I breathe into the pile of the carpet. It smells like sick. Propelled into action, I pull my nightie off, roll it into a ball under the bed, and lie back down.

The light strengthens slowly. When Uncle Ron gets up again I hear him leaving his room, descending the stairs to make himself breakfast. It's 5:30 A.M. by the clock beside Barbara's bed. I watch the numbers change until Barbara gets up at six, creeping along the landing in her mule slippers, her dressing gown swishing the floor as she clips to and fro.

I slide out of her bed, moving as little as possible, stifle the sobs surfacing like hiccups—"that's my girl"—begin stripping the sheets, place my rolled-up nightie inside. It's easy now. All I have to do is get dressed.

Mum isn't even stirring. She likes to sleep in. There's a Girl Guide voice inside telling me what to do next: walk across the landing, wake her up and tell her what happened. But I can't.

Renshaw's Sweets opens at eight to catch the children on their way to school. I sit motionless on the edge of the bed counting the furry seams in Barbara's pink candlewick bedspread until seven-thirty. When I hear Barbara starting her tinny car I carry the bundle of sheets downstairs and put them in the rubbish bin, pushing them deep into bacon fat, tea bags, mouldy bread, a bag of grass clippings and another of chopped liver. I hope that somebody will just dump the lot.

I'm so thirsty. I drink a few sips from the kitchen tap, then realize I have to go. In the downstairs loo I take my knickers down and see a brownish stain on them, wipe myself and there's a long string of blood. I wind yards of toilet paper off the roll and bunch them up into a kind of bandage, strapping it to the gusset of my knickers with another strip. Pull up my knickers, wash my hands.

Mum wouldn't know what to do.

I leave a note on the kitchen table saying, "Gone home. Took the bus. Thank you, Tess."

We've always been taught that guests should say "thank you for having me."

I decide to walk across the fields, careful to cross the road first and leave Uncle Ron's land. My bag is heavy, and I hurry. I don't want anyone to see me. Sun hot on my back, dark berries squished between my legs, what if i am dying dying? Over the stile through the hedge i slide down by the river muddy loose soil water low i run run breathe breathe branches caught between my teeth teeth at my neck rope of nylon blue fields yellow weeping eye a dream barbara's dream monsters in her bed i slide from beneath it and cross the road.

When I reach home it's two in the afternoon. The car's outside.

Mum must be back, cleaning the house from top to bottom. Dad's at work. Bobby's up in his room playing the radio loudly. Piles of washing are stacked up in the kitchen as I come in.

"Hello, Mum." I feel tears deep in my chest but can't speak.

I can't find the words to explain myself with. Instead, I pull childishly at my knickers. "Bleeding—"

Her eyes are hidden behind dark sunglasses. "Get those clothes off at once, go on, get in the bath. I'll fetch you a towel."

I go upstairs. Bobby opens his door, looking at me, a stranger from a previous life. "Don't," I say, before he can speak. He puts his hands up as if to say "don't shoot," and goes back inside his room.

In the bathroom, wrenching off the smelliness of my clothes, the white curves of enamel slide onto me, cradling the skin I didn't think I had. So hot, sticky in here, sweatlike beads of moisture form on the vinyl wallpaper then drip back into the bath.

"Can I come in?" Before I have a chance to reply, Mum opens the door. She stares at my breasts, their naked skin cooked pink by the heat, kneels down beside the tub and takes the old loofah, begins to rub my skin so hard I'm praying it peels off.

"Women must always wash a lot this time of the month." Her face is unreadable, puffy and swollen beneath the dark lenses of her special crying specs. "I've left you some supplies. When you need more let me know. Please put the old ones in the incinerator. Don't leave them in the waste bin, your dad doesn't like it, and please don't flush them down the toilet or it'll block. We don't want to call the plumber for that." She leaves the bathroom abruptly, the bruises on her cheek turning bluish-green as the heat wipes her make-up off.

I close my eyes and imagine her bending down and lifting me out of the bath, onto her knee again. She hums quietly, bouncing me on her wool-skirted lap while a white towel flaps around my shoulders, shooting plumes of talc into the steamy air. I reach for her sweaty hand that marks time softly against my knee but find myself holding onto the cold water tap. I let go.

My mother isn't here any more. My body so much bigger, so much stronger now. I lie still, watching my fingertips wrinkle, remember there are berries downstairs, fresh ones, ready to make a pie. The bathwater slowly turns cold. Outside, I can hear each glassy smack as Mum throws Dad's empties away. I don't want to touch it, that vast hole surrounded by thin hairs, but I can't help it. When I open my legs gently, a thread of dark red escapes.

Cathy Stonehouse immigrated to Canada from Britain in 1988. Her first book of poetry, The Words I Know, *was published by Press Gang in 1994. "That's My Girl" is her first published piece of prose.*

Tonja Gunvaldsen Klaassen

The Nest

She never talks about it. She pussyfoots around it, jumping from bale to bale. Fernie would like to say it out loud. She wants to know what Joy thinks kissing would feel like, but Joy is only seven, she would tell their mother, so Fernie keeps it to herself.

They play the game Joy likes the most, although Fernie is in grade four and feels too old for it. Joy is the damsel in distress and Fernie must be the pirate trying to capture her. If Fernie catches Joy, the game ends and starts from the beginning again. The pirate and the damsel never kiss or fight or anything. Just run. The aching in Fernie's thighs makes her wish Joy would fall down. She wants to stop running, to push Joy over, but then she would cry and stop playing the game.

"Hey!" Joy's voice rings clear in the overcast sky. Fernie looks up in time to see her sister's head before she ducks behind a bale. Joy is lucky. She has long yellow hair and their mother ties it back in smooth braids. Once, Fernie tried to tie Joy's braids herself, but the hair kept falling out of place and getting snarled. Then she felt guilty because her hands were dirty, so she gave one braid a good yank. Fernie's hair is dull and brown. Mousy brown. It has to be kept short because she used to chew the ends and it tangled easily. Now Fernie chews her fingernails, which is just as bad. She tries to hide her hands from her mother, but her mother always sees.

"Yoo-hoo. Ferrrnie. Come and find me." Fernie is hot and sweaty from running, but the cold winter air hurts her lungs. Creeping slowly and close to the bales, she peeks around the stack. Joy is looking around the next corner, her back to Fernie. She is close enough. Fernie holds her breath and pounces. They both trip and fall. Fernie clamps her hand over Joy's mouth.

"Gotcha!" Fernie yells, face down in the straw.

"Helmph. Hhhelmph," Joy mumbles, her cheeks soft and wet with drool under Fernie's hand. Fernie wipes her hand on her jeans and they both burst out laughing, mouths wide open like baby birds. Happy and relieved, Fernie laughs until she can't catch her breath and her ribs hurt under her arms. Through her wet eyes, Joy looks pink from the laughing and the cold. Fernie loves Joy. She is warm and good, always always good.

"Eeeeeek. Gross gross gross," Joy screams, jumping up and shaking off the straw.

"What!" The laughter tightens into a fist in Fernie's stomach as Joy claws at her braids. "What what?" Fernie cries, shaking the sleeve of Joy's parka.

"Get it off my hair!" she shrieks. "It's on my hair—get it off!"

Fernie is taller than Joy, so she can see to the top of Joy's head. She brushes straw off Joy's scarf. "What is it? There's nothing there now."

"A mouse." Joy shudders.

Fernie looks around at the straw. There is no mouse—Joy's screams would have scared it to death. But off to the side there is a hole.

"Look," says Fernie.

The nest is a small dark hole in the balestack, and Fernie longs to reach out, to uncover it and cradle it in her palm. She touches a cold hand to the straw.

"Don't touch it, Fernie." Joy's voice is high and insistent. "Don't, don't! Please." Joy's face, clouded with worry, frightens Fernie. Joy runs to the house. Fernie watches, wanting to follow, but she's unable to turn away from the dark nest.

Behind her, Fernie feels the nest hole growing deeper and blacker. She pictures the mouse in a small dark bedroom, very much like her own.

"Mousie, mousie," she whispers to soothe herself, but her heart is thudding with apprehension. The pleasure of so small a thing, smooth fur, warm, alive and trembling in her hands tempts Fernie. Her legs, no longer heavy and tired, are weak with excitement. But it would be wrong to touch the mouse, wrong to touch its nest. She falls to her knees. She wants to—needs to—see this mouse. Surely it would not be wrong to look at it?

Fernie bends over the nest, but she can only see darkness. Hands stiff with cold, she brushes aside some straw. There is no mouse. Only tiny sacks of bare, pink flesh. Pink like Joy. Pink like Fernie's own hands and face scrubbed clean before she goes to bed. She touches the baby mice quickly, before anyone can see her do it, and they feel warm against her cold fingers. When she closes her eyes she remembers the warmth of her own body and the softness of her flannelette nightie pilling in her fingers as she touched herself. A horrible dread falls over her. It is too late. She couldn't hide her hands from her mother in the morning, and afterwards, her mother's suspicion hung over the breakfast table while Fernie ate her cold cereal.

The sky hangs over Fernie, and over her house. What has she done? The mother mouse might never come home now. Fernie is scared. She stands and mews to herself before pushing a knuckle in her mouth. Her hands are dirty and taste like salt. What will her mother see if she checks Fernie's hands now? She will know. She will know that Fernie has touched these baby mice and ruined them with her cold, poking fingers.

Tonja Gunvaldsen Klaassen's poems and stories have been published in several Canadian journals and in the anthology Breathing Fire: Canada's New Poets. *Her first book of poetry,* Clay Birds, *is published by Coteau. She lives in Saskatoon.*

Elaine Littmann

Bad Reputation

When Louise thinks of making love with Ray, she sees no picture at all. She tries to imagine the two of them twisted together on the big bed, as if she's looking in the window, but she can't. She can't see her own face, or any other part of her body. She's too close, there's no focus. She can hear breathing and moaning, feel sweat and the way she trembled when he touched her.

This is the place she fought for years to reach. To let go so completely that she could not pull back and watch herself perform. She thought this would free her. Instead, it's obliterated her. Because before Ray left, he said, *when we make love it's like you're not really there.* As if he was still remembering her at the beginning, her careful tableaus, the way she arranged her body on the bed knowing how the light would outline the curve of her thigh. Is it possible, she wonders, to fall too far? He could have said, I feel like I'm drowning; he could have said, I don't love you that much. *You're not really there.* She mourns this, as if, perhaps, all she has is not enough.

Nothing used to bother her. It was a kind of innocence, for her, but for the guys as well. *You want to get raped?* they used to ask, grinning. And Louise would laugh, seeing only their desire. Because she always said yes. Even when they pinned her arms, snatched at her clothes, squirmed on top as if they were trying to grind her into the earth, they seemed like desperate children. Those were the moments she felt most in control. Not because she could stop what was happening; she never tried to. But because they needed her so badly.

It was like watching a movie. Even now, she can close her eyes and imagine how her own body looked. The thin bow of her back, the ripple of ribs, how soft the skin must have felt inside her thighs. She believed it was this, the exact curve of a leg, the fall of her hair across her face, that excited them. She cannot remember, often, how it felt. She remembers things like the evening the light came in the window to turn her skin the colour of white wine.

The first time she didn't know anything. The closest she could get to saying she was a virgin was, "I'm not on the pill." Chris said he'd use a rubber, but Louise had only the haziest idea of how that would work, didn't know how she could tell if he had put it on. She didn't know enough to touch his cock, guide it into her. She didn't even know she should hold him. She just spread her legs and braced her feet, tried to will her cunt open. When he finally squeezed inside she felt relieved, relaxed enough to slowly, curiously, put her arms around him. She remembers the knobs of his spine, his ribs, thinking how skinny he was, this boy everyone said was so tough. Afterwards, she didn't see him for months. He didn't have her phone number, he didn't go to her school. She didn't expect to hear from him. What happened had nothing to do with him being her boyfriend. Even the very first time, she knew that.

Brian was her first real boyfriend. That surprised her, but Brian did things the right way. He reminded her of the fifties, the way it was shown on TV, high school rings and letter jackets and going steady. Louise met him at a jock party. She and Katie had climbed into a car full of beer and football players, just to see what would happen. Those boys seemed harmless to Louise, overgrown children, clean and polite. She sat on their laps in the back seat and laughed when they slid hands between her thighs, because she could tell they thought they were scaring her. "Let's go up that road, there," one of them said as they sped past a logging road. A single streetlamp flooded the intersection with white light for a second, then darkness stamped down like a foot. "Forget it," Louise said. "You told us there was a party."

After the party, Brian drove her home. He was high, and she thought he was cute, and so serious. He was angry about something that had happened that night, a fight he had almost got into. He kept talking about it, he wouldn't stop. Then he asked if she wanted to smoke a joint. When they parked near the playground he almost jumped on her. He was clumsy, his breath harsh and smothered, as if he was about to cry. "Slow down," she said, "take it easy." Her jeans were so tight he had to work them down, it hurt, he wouldn't let her do it. He grabbed her hips and pulled her flat on the seat. She saw the sky through the windshield, then his shoulders covered everything.

On the way home Louise stared at the window and watched herself not crying in the glass. She felt fragile, and brave, and very alone. There was a tight, hard little stone rattling around inside her, a star come loose from the sky. Brian kissed her good night, and in the morning he came to take her for a drive. And then they were going out, it was that simple.

Reggie was the line she crossed. She thought she was safe because he didn't go to her school, Brian wouldn't see them together. Reggie had a big black Chevelle, too hot and shiny, too perfect. Maybe because Reggie was so not-perfect, it seemed like a joke on him. His own joke, but not intended.

"Does that feel like a big dick between your legs?" he asked once when he revved the motor. Louise said no, but it did. And despite the faintly ridiculous car, he excited her. He called her whiteman, one word. As if her colour even wiped out her being a girl, anything desirable or sexy about her. *Why are you so mean*, she always asked. *I'm just bugging you*, he said, *can't you take it?*

Brian and his buddies, spread across the hall on the way to the smoking yard. They parted to let her pass, closed up again like water over her head. She was too afraid to breathe.

"Hey, Louise, don't you fuck white men any more?" The sound of a zipper sliding down. She didn't look back.

Louise in the back seat, pushed up against the door, her whole body rocking with the thrusts, her thighs trembling, on the edge of coming, as close as she ever got.

Reggie took her to visit his mother. When he went out to get stove wood, his mother leaned across the table and said, "He's doing real good. You're keeping him out of trouble." Later, all of them at the kitchen table: "So, Reginald, when are you going to marry her?"

"When she asks me."

Ray is out at his place on the Gulf Islands, as far as Louise knows. It's an old float house dragged up on the beach, with fine, hand-carved doors, the high tide washing around the pilings. One night they saw a falling star that seemed to come down between islands and land in the water. Louise remembers the bed with its blue sheets, the sun on the floor. She has a hard time picturing Ray's face, sometimes. Other memories are acute, surprising. Last week she sat behind a woman on the bus and looked at her hair, coarse, wavy, glinting red and blonde in the sun. After a while she realized she was imagining how strong and springy the hair would feel under her fingers. Like Ray's. She got up and moved her seat so she couldn't see the woman any more. That's how she gets through the days, by moving, looking at something else.

Does Ray remember such things about her? She can't imagine it, thinks he must have carved her cleanly from his life, leaving no trace. There was, after all, nothing memorable in the way she ran her tongue down his chest and belly and into the hot nest of hair and cock, how she kissed the hard curly hairs on the insides of his thighs. Her body is the same as any woman's, and so, probably, are the things that she did with it.

She had a hard time breaking up with Reggie. He phoned, he drove by her house late at night and parked out on the road, leaving the motor running. The big V8 sounded like a heartbeat, some great slow beast lurking out behind the spruce hedge. She began letting her mother answer the phone and say, *my daughter is not home, and don't call here again.* Her mother swelled with virtuous rage, doing this. *What do you want to go out with an Indian for?* she asked, pretending it was only Reggie who wasn't good enough for Louise.

At school something shifted. Brian was behind it, she thought, and his new girlfriend. The popular girls hadn't liked Louise dating Brian, but they couldn't say much while she was with him. Now there was graffiti in the bathroom. *Louise the sleaze.* Three grade eight boys hanging on the parking lot fence jumped down around her like little commandos. They spread their legs, stuck out their chests, faces hard with contempt and yearning. "Hey, Louise, why don't you wear a bra?" One of them was Reggie's cousin. She went home and cried. She knew about sneak attacks, knew there would never be anyone to confront, even if she had the courage.

Mark was twenty-four years old. He told her he thought she was "nineteen, at least, wow," when they met at the bar. Mark didn't know anything that went on at her school and didn't care. He had a sixth-floor loft downtown, with a floor-to-ceiling window where she could see the lights on the water, polished floorboards, four-foot stereo speakers, a red and white Fender electric poised delicately in a corner. They made love by the window with the lights off, and Louise could see their faint white reflections in the glass, and the city beyond them. That was what she watched while they fucked: the wavery coloured ribbons of light, the circling sea planes blinking, the high white walls of the apartment, cleansed and bare and untouched.

There was a big window in the Gulf Island house, too, looking over the sun deck. There were no curtains because there was no one to look in, only the deer that picked their silent way out of the bush, making the dogs whine and bark. She remembers the bed wide and blue as the sky; Ray is pressing his leg between hers and she's grinding herself down so hard on his thigh it aches between her legs, deep in her belly, in her teeth. The top of her skull is about to open like a hinge, her body turn inside out, so the lightest touch, a breath, contracts her. It's brain surgery. He's probing for the place that will make her scream. She thrusts towards it as if she's swimming.

Ray's kissing her neck, biting, burrowing, she can hear him breathing. She slides her hand inside his shorts and his cock springs into her fingers, hot and compact, like a little animal. She slithers further down until she's lying beneath him. He sinks down and into her like a tide.

The water begins to wash out again. It cleans the beach, taking back the small shells and cedar and bull kelp. Out there with the sunken boat engines and fallen stars. Louise forgot to hold on, and in the morning there was only sand. And here's her body: folded on the shore, one arm flung towards the water as if reaching in her sleep across an empty bed. Her skin is dry and warm, and it tastes of salt.

Elaine Littmann lives in Vancouver and works as a graphic designer. Her fiction has been published in several journals and in the 1996 Journey Prize Anthology.

Kathleen Oliver

Pool

Annie breaks and sinks a solid, so I'm striped and swimming in this green sea of felt, her eyes, and the sudden preposterous memory of Cindy Waters handing me a made-up "Personality Test" in grade nine, where you're given eight shapes and have to draw something on each one, then choose a word to describe it. I was being fairly inventive, deliberately unconventional: on a shape like a peanut shell I drew some diagonal lines and wrote "striped" next to it. Afterwards Cindy took the paper back and used my words to fill in a stock set of blanks: Your personality is (blank), your dreams are (blank), and my favourite: "Your sex life is striped." Even then I suspected it was true.

If it's striped, so far most of it's been stuck in the blanks between the lines, like the prim white edges of the balls I'm trying to sink. More like the cue ball, even: intact and round and hard in its self-protective whiteness. And so when Annie asks me things like how come I've never played pool before, what do I do with my time, the only answers I can pull from my crowded days are blanks. Your pastimes are (suddenly) blank.

This afternoon on the Seabus, her first time, Annie was surprised that we weren't allowed to sit up on deck. Down east a lot of the people can't swim, she said, even though some of them spend their whole lives on boats. There were a few disdainful looks from the commuters when she jumped up to look out the window at the water. I stayed in my seat, but moved to the edge of it, to be closer to her.

Later, we compared journals: her hard, ornate cover, my coil-ring notebook. I have to have lined paper, she needs blank. We were waiting for the bus, eating the plums we'd bought, and Annie said she felt like we should be hitchhiking. Something about the mountains reminded her of other times, but I had to admit sheepishly that I've never hitchhiked.

And yes, really never played pool, until today. The click of the balls is perfect punctuation for the sappy country songs on the radio. And now, every time we pass the cue back and forth, sometimes pirouetting around each other, as she does a one-person waltz and keeps commenting on what perfect music this is for dancing, I can't help thinking about the water. When we got off the bus, Annie gave me her coat to carry and just plunged in, dancing in the rain. She said it felt good, like when you're diving and the water gets into your wetsuit and warms you up. I've never gone diving, either, so I could only nod blankly, round and agreeable as a white cue ball that jostles all the colours but is never supposed to sink. Whenever one of my shots takes it dangerously close, she puts her hand over the hole to stop it.

Now there's this whole wet country between us, and suddenly this vessel that's been carrying me all my life is shot full of holes. I can bail and bail and not move one lap of wave closer to her. I think about my journal, pulled from its rulered life into her blank sea of words. What would she write—no margins but her own—about this afternoon? About the cues we take, don't take, the cue that dances from her hand to mine, this dance of round shapes on a felt sea green as her eyes, now the hard snap and slow shuddering thump of another striped one, sinking.

Kathleen Oliver has published poetry in Contemporary Verse 2 *and features and reviews in* Kinesis *and other publications. Her verse play,* Swollen Tongues, *was read at the 1996 Women in View Festival. She lives in Vancouver.*

Shannon Cooley

Cerberus and the Rain

b oing dit boing dit boing dit boing dit boing dit boing dit

Head 1 jumps away on the brown floral duvet, rapping her fingernails against the plaster ceiling: up and down   up and down   up and down boing dit boing dit boing dit. She faces the window. It's pissing outside.

We 3. We 3: Head 1, Head 2 and Head 3 are skipping school. AC/DC sing small, tinny, removed. It's raining hard.

Head 3 is an angle leaning towards her reflection, flicking at her hair.

flick-flick flick-flick *disappear-disappear*

She always does this. Weak glasses, practically blind and beautiful eyes—brown triangles smiling shy and blind. *disappear-disappear* She yacks at herself as if she were some bozo dude joshing around. She goes to the mirror, lowers her voice, "Nice Head." She goes, "Nice Head, where'd ya pick it up? At a third-hand store?" She always does this, shaking her head to fling free.

"Look at this," she says to Mick Jagger.

"Look at this!" she says to Head 1's older sister framed in a cap and gown. Maybe the photos can see.

And then she turns to me.

"LOOK AT THIS!!"

She does this all the time.

"You've got a nice head, Head, for sure." Here's me. I'm tracing a happy face into the shit-brown rug. If I could perma-grind this face into the rug.

Head 3 makes a sound, a canary firing a semi-automatic rifle. This is totally Head 3. This is her way of talking: clicks, whirrs and twickers. It's nuance? Cracked-sounding, sad, as if Tweety Bird has decided to end everything once and for all. (Sometimes I don't know who is victim and who is evil, Tweety or Sylvester—I don't know who to feel sorry for. Both, I guess. Those cartoons always made me edgy and confused.)

yuppa Head 3 talks her own way. Head 1 and I sort of borrow her sounds, adding a few words and squickers here and there.

Head 3's talk makes most folks edgy.

"You're a honey." She wide smiles.

"You're the honey." She needs me to say it back to her.

"You're a honey." Head 3 is a sweetheart. I've said hurting Head 3 would be like booting the underbelly of a puppy. Makes me think about Head 1 telling about what her sister has seen in bars. Guys with metal cleats on, booting the crap out of some poor gweeb.

Anyways, guys like Head 3, slim in her Levi's, and sometimes she wears pumps to match her sweater. I think her smile, her words, confuse guys. They never know what to make of her.

Hell, she is confusing.

But she listens to AC/DC and she puts out. THAT they understand. Other girls call her a ditz. And they don't understand, either.

Head 1 turns away from the rain, pulls up her Southern Comfort T-shirt and exposes her smooth middle. She looks down at her stomach with her huge hazel eyes. "Do you think I'm thick? I feel thick, Heads." She tugs at a pull of flesh as if it will slide free from her spine.

"No, Head. Don't be a nerd. You're skinny," I go, half telling her off.

"I feel thick."

"You're skinny!"

"You're a honey."

"You're a honey."

"A honey."

"A honey."

"YOU'RE BOTH HONEYS!!" bellows Head 3.

Head 1 squirks with a grin and bounces some more   bounce
bounce bounce bounce bounce bounce

The guys like Head 1 since she CRAVES SEX. And laughs at their
jokes. Any stupid joke. Should see Head 1 laughing around guys. I
think she's laughing cuz she's smarter than all them. And she is.
Mmmyup. She's only five foot two and for as long as I've known
her she's been into her body, keeping it toned, keeping it strong,
keeping it perfect. Other girls don't know how to deal with her—

So they call her a SLUT. But not to her face. They barely say two
words to her.

I am her friend. I know she's smart. She always skips school,
sometimes on her own, sometimes to meet some guy at Burger King,
sometimes with us, Head 3 and me. But whenever she puts her Head
to it SNAP—amazing grades.

Head 1, Head 2, Head 3. It just started one day. Head, Head and
Head. Laughing did it to us. We were upsidedown squatting, our
backs pressed into the sofa seat, our Heads hanging over the edge,
bloating with blood. We were laughing. Our shirts crumpled into
our armpits, baring our bellies and bras. We laughed so hard, laughing
away.

NICE HEADS!!

hiccup

Mmmyup

Head 1, Head 3. They have sex and I get to hear all about it. Head
1 lost her virginity when she was fourteen. To a friend of her older
sister's. He was twenty-four. Head 1 told me necking with guys
who've been drinking tastes good.

I don't know

Head 3 crawls over to me and head-butts me like a goat. She wants
a head rub. My fingers swirl around in her shiny dark hair, messing
up what is usually hair-brush PERFECT.

Head 1 twirls a 180 to face us   up and down   up and down
bounce   bounce   bounce "IT" bounce "MIGHT" bounce
"FLOOD" bounce   bounce   She stops jumping. She twists around

to look at the rain that hides the mountains. "With the snow runoff and everything, this could be it," she says. "The dikes might not hold this one and everything will get flooded again."

Rain
   I don't mind rain any more than I mind mountains. Here mountains and rain are the backdrops of my eyes. The mountains are strong and not moving. Always here. Beautiful. Still I constantly what if. I wonder what's behind the mountains—another town, the island, the Pacific, Hawaii, Japan . . . round again round . . . then here again.
   or maybe there's nothing out there
   Sometimes I'm convinced. Sometimes I wonder if the mountains are supposed to keep everything from flooding in, in or out. Sometimes it's like nothing can enter this valley. Except clouds that travel everywhere *disappear-disappear*

"He went NORTH," Head 1 told me. Her father left when she was seven. So her mum took Head and her sister SOUTH.
   "And then she met UGLY," Head 1 explained, holding her face as if numb with dentist freezing. UGLY became her mother's new boyfriend and they moved here to manage the Eagle. It's the oldest bar in town, supposed to be really gundgy. The Eagle still has separate entrances for Men and Ladies with Escorts glowing neon red in the rain until 2:00 A.M.
   "I want to HUMP you," Head 3 leans over and squickers in my ear. It doesn't mean anything, she says that kind of thing all the time. She just wants attention.
   When Head 3 and I get our spare class together, we go to the library and hide cross-legged between the short shelves. Just the two of us singing Dr. Hook soft enough so we don't get booted out.
   She has a beautiful voice   really

Head 1 looks bored. She boings off the bed and turns behind the hallway wall. What's she thinking?
   "HEADS," through the wall she says, "HEADS ya wanna have a nip? UGLY doesn't get back 'til after closing tonight."
   "GAGS and GOOGS," Head 3 boomerangs, "gags and googs and

googs and gags and gags and googs and gags and gags and gags."
Head 3 talks this way when something sounds neato to her: a song
on CXRZ, a stick of gum, trading shirts, skipping school. So down
the hall, tracing our fingers on latex and velvet, down the stairs
thump   thump   thump   and around the corner, past the bile
glass wall and then we are there. UGLY's BAR.

Head 1 scoots behind the counter that comes up to her shoulders,
ducks underneath and then pops up three glasses and down and up
and crème de menthe and gin and rye and Amaretto. Sounds pretty.

"You know my mum buys all the groceries for this fucking house,
she pays hydro and oil. So WHAT the hell? All UGLY ever spends ITS
money on is this bar and he owns the house. Everything is separate."
Head 1 snaps her gum against her teeth. Pissed off.

This room is a shrine to who knows what. It has a twenty-six-inch
TV in the corner, (they have another twenty-sixer upstairs), and
mantels lined with German beer steins and spittoons and empty
forty-pounder bottles. There's this Scotch bottle half the size of Head
1. "You can't get those in Canada," she told me. Mirrors everywhere.
Head 3 spins on her Naugahyde stool, stares at her reflection in the
ceiling. "Hey! HOLY SNAPPIN' ARSEHOLES!! NICE HEAD!!"

Freaky room.

"Look at this," goes Head 3, "it's got a little doober." She's
pressing down on this little yellow plastic man who squirts all over
the counter. We laugh. Head 1 wipes away all the pee.

"Want a hot cross bun? I thought I saw some." And Head 1
disappears behind the counter and pulls out a styrofoam tray of
squashed-looking buns. Head 1 pierces the plastic with her nails and
rips one out. She holds it above her head drops it bounce bounce
bounce on the counter. Laughter hard against my stomach. Head
3 grabs the bun and aims at her mirrored head above us. Gravity
works, the bun rebounds into Head's drink, knocking it over. All
sticky on the counter and on the floor. Stains dot our arms, our laps
and the carpet behind us.

"Move it! IT's going to kill me." Head 1 yanks forward, panicked
and serious, sanding the light-blue carpet with a drooling J-cloth.
She's acting like he knows. Like UGLY's gonna be on his hands and
knees snorting rug and going after her with one of those pink plastic
mini-swords, or a corkscrew. Head 3 stands near looks startled doesn't

know what to do . . . what to do. "Sorry," she goes, "I'm so sorry, Head. Sorry-sorry. Head? Sorry."

Head 1 looks less freaked out and more peeved. "Don't say sorry so much. You just say it over and over again. You don't need to. Don't say it."

"Sorry."

Head 1 goes from snappish to grim. "It's okay, Head, it's not your fault. It's mine, I brought you down here, I started off."

"Sorry, Head."

Head 1 reaches over, gives Head 3's bangs a flick. "It's okay, I said it's okay. All right, Head? Look at it out there. I bet it's going to really flood." Head 1 walks heavily to the La-Z-Boy and collapses into it. Flops her arms. Seals us off with her eyes.

"How's it hanging, Head?" I ask quietly. She wants it quiet.

No answer.

"What's the prob, Head?" I ask.

"I hate it. I just HATE IT. I don't GET my mother. I can't handle IT any more. IT'S SO UGLY . . ." Head 1 opens her hazel eyes. Tears? "Last Thursday I was taking a shower after my workout. And why should IT be home? IT'S never home then and we never talk anyway so how am I supposed to know IT'S home? So I was standing in my room naked, drying off and UGLY is standing in the doorway watching me and I didn't know that and IT'S standing there staring at me. And IT'S UGLY, GOD IT'S ugly. And IT'S STARING. So I rush to the door and slam it shut. And IT starts laughing but this is not a joke and IT knows this isn't a joke and IT'S laughing at me. AT ME. And I didn't leave my room until IT left for afternoon shift the next day. I can't, you know. I just can't handle."

"Tell your mum?" I ask.

"Yeah, I told her."

"What'd she say?"

"She said. She said life is not a bowl full of cherries."

"What's THAT supposed to mean?" Head 3's cross-legged at Head 1's feet.

"She said I didn't know what it is like to be alone. She said I had to learn to make do pahh."

"Fuck that," I said.

"So what am I supposed to do?"

"Well, what do you want to do?"

"Move out. I want Mum to come with me. We DON'T NEED IT."

"Well tell her then, tell her how you're scared of him. She'll listen, she's your mother."

"I don't know."

"Come on, Head. She's your mum. Tell her, Head."

"I heard there are vacancies at the Alpine Crest Apartments."

"How's it hanging, Honey?" Head 3 squeezes Head 1's foot. Head 1 goes quiet. Her neck starts to turn red but then she breathes in. "Yeah, I'll talk to her. I'll talk to her, Heads."

Head 1 told me that her older sister was sixteen when she moved out, moved to the city. "She made a living hustling old men at pool," Head 1 said with a grin. "She went to University and then she became a YUPPIE for god's sakes, lives in freaking Kitsilano with a Porsche and a Boyfriend."

Every few Christmases UGLY would be left at the Eagle and the three women would gather in the city for dinner.

"We aren't close at all," went Head 1.

Her grin gone.

"Rain, Rain, Rain."

Head 3 is lying on her back with her calves folded underneath her thighs. "I bet all the ditches are plugged with drowned worms."

Head 1 snaps her gum against her teeth as if keeping time.

"Can I have some?"

"Gum? Supstairs. Hang on." And Head 1 thump thumps up the stairs.

Head 3 stands up, stretching like pulled licorice, giving off a twicker. She walks lazy-legged to the rawhide pulled taut across a wall. Some wallpaper. All of UGLY's friends have signed this hide, mostly in green felt pen. The three Heads are on there too, and all those other names and gunk or whatever. (The Canucks Suck KOKANEE RULES JF wuz here All little girls want this # BIG Ben Jensen Fran's Love Machine Right Karl? YOU AIN'T DONE TIL YOU DONE EM ALL)

Head 3 traces over the marks on the dead skin with her finger.

Stops. Pulls off the felt-pen cap in her mouth. Crosses out her name.
Rewrites   HEAD 3 WUZ HERE   Encircles it with a heart. Underlines
it.

"Have you signed the new guest book in the downstairs can,
Head?"

"Gags and Googs!" Head 3 takes exaggerated steps towards the
bathroom, felt pen plunked in her mouth like a smoke.

So I'm standing here. By myself. In this freaky old barroom, this
freaky IT'S A FRIGGIN' ZOO OF DEAD ANIMALS: an Owl, a Chip-
munk, a Salmon, a Hawk, the mounted heads of a Moose, a Deer.
All stiff with the shape of life. Staring, but not staring. I walk over
to the Deer and tap its eye. Glass, dark glass.

I'm wishing the life back into that head.

Head 3 showed me where she was raped. We were walking on a
sunny Sunday, walking to the river for something to do; we moseyed
on down No-Name Road to the trail that winds through the bush
to the river, people party there sometimes. Near the white fence
moulding green, about three posts along, Clea stopped and her
triangle eyes went smaller. She said, "It was there." I knew what she
meant and looked. The grass was growing so tall and healthy and I
wondered why it wasn't dead yellow. The grass wasn't even bent

> NECK
> ARM SQUEEZES NECK YANKS
> DOWN
> PUSHES MY MOUTH GO FINGERS PRY SHOVE FORCE TASTE
> NO
> BOOZE MINT

Head 1 has me crammed in one of her headlocks, her fingers
kneading at my lips; she's trying to force a piece of her chewed-up
gum into my mouth.

"HEAD! What the fuck!" I spit out. I fall back, my wrist jams—a
shooting pain. My head barely misses the jutting corner of the coffee
table. A gross burn starts in my gut, rushes a sweaty chill all over
me.

Head 1 stands over me, reaches into her mouth, stretches out a string of green gum and casually twines it around her index finger. "The last piece, thought I'd share."

"You're a nerd, Head 1, a real nerd." Head 3's hair falls forward as she looks down, studying me.

I glare at Head 1, quickly flipping my wrist back and forth. "Could have really hurt me, Head. Don't you ever do anything like that again."

"Come on, Head, you can take it. I was only joshin'. Fun."

"Yeah, right, fuck you. I thought I was gonna choke."

"Jeeze Louise, Head, get off it."

She can be such a bossy cow sometimes, the only one with problems that count. I look at her, almost too choked to speak. "How'd you like someone to do that to you?"

Head 1 rolls her eyes. "Get off it."

"I'm still way bigger than you."

Head 1 tosses me a grin like I'm Gweebus 2. I grab for her legs. She hops back from my reach. Knees, I stand up. Lunge—

I've got her by the stomach and force-push her against the couch. She grabs onto my shoulders, trying to shove back. She's looking at me scared and I'm looking at her scared. Head 3 ricochets around us, against the wall, over to the doorway, then over towards us, skreeking the hell out of her head—Raccoon. "NERDS NERDS NERDS NERDS NERDS"

I see Head 3 winging her head about, freaked.

disappear-disappear   fling-free

Then the quietness. Then the laughter.

Air. Laughter.

Breath.

"What heure is it?" I ask.

"Five-thirty I think."

"Gadzooks!" Head 3 yipes, still panting.

"Ah shitster, I gotta get home before Dad, Mum'll kill me." I think of my mother's voice and chicken with rice.

Head 1 mumbles into her elbow.

"What's that?"

"I said, at least you've got a home to go to."

"Come on, Jen, don't talk that way."
"It's true."
"Talk to your mum."
"Guess so." Head 1 rolls over onto her back.
"Head."
"Yeah. You okay walking home?"
"Yuppa, hasn't flooded out there yet." I go over to the fogged window. "I don't think it's even raining as hard." I look back at Head 3 trying to touch her nose with her tongue. She crosses her eyes, breathes in her tongue. "Reeeooooo," she says, "how's it hangin'?"
"You're a honey."
"A honey," she says back to me.

Outside the clouds are lifting
    and the mountains stand dark behind

Shannon Cooley graduated from Howe Sound Secondary School in 1987, and later earned her BFA in Creative Writing from the University of Victoria. Her work has appeared in several Canadian journals and in the anthology Chasing Halley's Comet *(Laughing Willow Books).*

Suzette Mayr

Glass Anatomy

The Fiat travels in the wrong direction.

Lethbridge
NEXT EXIT

"Wrong way," she says, and pokes an orange potato chip into her mouth. Salt and artificial barbecue flavour sting the wet corners of her mouth. Bum rests comfortably in the plush bowl of her seat, plush the colour of concrete. She crumples the empty chip bag, salty foil thrown among rolling cans of pop.

"I can see that," he says, irritated. The insides of his cheeks hungry for the salty cut of another chip, he turns the steering wheel quickly, God Bless Power Steering, and they do a U-ey, the swirl of their heads and necks and arms in the car's doughnut. He could go for a doughnut right about now too. A kruller, with a regular, no, make that a large, coffee. But an apple fritter might be better. With raisins.

In the back seat, the daughter Jez listens to Blondie's "Heart of Glass" over and over again. The small Walkman whir between her hands, between her thighs, she pops out the cassette, inserts a pencil into the right cassette hole and spins the cassette around and around. Must save batteries, it's already been an hour and they haven't even left the city yet. Her own heart made of glass, she has found her theme song and she likes the look of Deborah Harry's legs on the cassette cover. She is hungry and would have liked a chip but wouldn't ever risk getting crumby food inside her Walkman. She eats warm yogurt instead, licks the spoon clean and can smell her own breath, sweet and dairy.

Parked at a hotel in Medicine Hat, Karen lights up a cigarette and Jack sucks at his pipe, their room small, dark, and the floor covered with blue-green shag. Room cloudy with smoke, Karen tugs at the window facing the parking lot, remembers the days when there was no such thing as smoking and non-smoking hotel rooms, just how much money you wanted to spend. Karen hits the window frame with the heel of a hiking boot.

He sucks at the pipe, vanilla-flavoured tobacco, Jack's favourite thank you very much, would rather have flavoured pipe smoke than cigarette smoke any day of the week, and he presses his thumb on the ON button of the remote control. The blank screen stays blank. Tries different angles with his thumb pressed on the button, watches her bang around the window glass with his shoe. The grey screen of the TV reflects her vigorous at the window, his body relaxed on the queen-sized bed, luggage and coats piled in the corner of the room.

Chlorine seeps in under the door. Jez has a view of the foothills and the parking lot. Beats the hell out of the pigeonhole smoker's room they got, but the chlorine smell is almost worse. Loneliness tickles the front of her skull. She quickly combs her hair in case there are any good-looking men out in the hallway and closes the door too loudly.

"Can I have a drag, Karen?" Jez asks. She picks up the burning cigarette perched on the edge of the hotel ashtray. Holds it in front of pursed lips between V-shaped fingers.

"Like hell," her mother answers, their usual game, Jezzie is getting just a bit too fresh, sweeps away the burning butt and pops the filtered end into her own mouth. She lies back on the bed under the bedspread. Watches TV shows flicker back and forth on the screen until she lets her eyes close and dozes, a light purr from her nose.

Jez considers Jack's pipe warm and smoky in his mouth. But he would miss the point and let her try it. Put that in your pipe and smoke it, Jack. Ha ha ha. Gives up and appraises the touristy cars in the parking lot.

Karen wakes up, a snort chokes her awake, and they decide on the Black Angus for dinner. Five-thirty P.M. Before the dinner rush, they hope. He hopes. He hates standing in line for anything.

He has Black Forest cheesecake, a hint of kirsch but not too much, and she lights a cigarette for dessert.

"I need an ashtray," says Karen and Jez nicks one from a table two tables down. Karen sets the cigarette in the glass ashtray and takes another sip of water. Sip sip. He shouldn't eat so many sweets, diabetes runs in his family, damned if I'm looking after any bloody invalid. Her ass on the verge of going numb from so much goddamn sitting. Shifts her seat backwards.

"Where's the bill?" and since when did Jezzie start taking her coffee black?

Dumb colourless people here, thinks Jez. God what a crone and how can she wear curlers in public like that? Oh he's not bad.

VISA's gotta be somewhere, somewhere. Accidentally shoved in next to the driver's licence. Tomorrow they'll hike the foothills. Can't wait, the skin on his face itches for the smell of trails.

"How much," he asks the daughter, she was a waitress once and it gives him an excuse to overtip and not have to fight with Karen.

"Five bucks."

"No way five bucks. You think we're made of money?" She taps her cigarette on the glass edge.

Five dollars, he scribbles in, signs his name large with a tail at the end of the last letter. Such a long day, he's ready to crash and burn.

He sucks at his pipe, legs and arms sprawled easily in the easy chair in front of the easy TV. She butts out her cigarette, reaches over from where she is on the bed and puts her left hand between his legs.

"Let me finish my pipe first," he says and there isn't even time to pull off the top blanket, God Bless Tubal Ligations, they breathe into each other's mouths no longer just hints of kirsch and nicotine. Stains on her pink slip, he falls asleep, sweat gleams in the small of her back and in the crack of his round and furry butt. She had her nap this afternoon. She flicks on the TV. Pats the back of her hair, crosses her feet, two humps turned into one hump under the hotel covers.

She remembers the days when she was younger, less cautious, the

days when she would pick her nose until it bled. Pick anything until
it bled.

Pink frilly bikini, her legs were dark brown, dark and shiny with
sea water, his skin was bumpy with heat rash, a green pair of trunks,
legs itchy with dried salt. They lay back on the sand. They lay back
like actors did in the movies.

What am I doing, she thought, reached around him, slid her hands
under his trunks and clutched his butt, round and furry as a peach.
How can I do this, she wondered and pulled him in, bikini bottom
slid away easily, she pulled him into her body, strained with her
pelvis, the stretched muscles in her thighs. Shameless, she grabbed
viciously, shameless I am so shameless, a rip no a tear a bloody rip
tear of skin away apart the skin like the skin inside her nose torn
out for the snotty pleasure of blood.

So this is what it's all about. She opened her eyes. Thought about
how much blood.

So this is what it's all about, he thought. She was his first virgin.
His legs were itchy.

How ugly you are, she whispered and masked her words with a
groan, his eyelids wide open, she masked her words with a moan
like the ones she heard in the movies. Her womb was see-through.
Like glass.

Jez dips her incisors into his nipples, Bob from down the hall, picked
him up at the ice machine by the pop dispenser and they picked her
room with the single, oversized bed. He has some zits and his breath
smells of stale Coke and Black Angus french fries, better than chlorine
though, his skin warm and smooth as eggshells. She sends him off
to his room at 3:00 A.M., the dry skin scales on the soles of her feet
scratch against the sheets' smooth fabric. She doesn't believe in
premarital sex, straightens the sheets and pulls them up around her
head. She'll do everything but. Her insides are made of glass and
snow. She coughs. A pubic hair caught in her throat.

Welcome to ELK WATER

"Way off," Karen says, scratches her nose. He clenches his teeth and
they circle back to the general store they just passed. He fingers maps

and talks to the sales clerk, she buys a pin, Elk Water Alberta, with the picture of a wild turkey above it, and a T-shirt for the nephew back home.

Jez's head dips forward then sideways, eyes open then close, slowly the lashes on her eyelids descend, head rattled from the cold car window glass, hollowed by the smell of chlorine. What a dumb name, Bob. He's gone with his family back to Toronto, their encounter short and salty and the muscles inside her thighs unusually tight and what would Karen say if she knew? Uptight. Drowsy she croons along with Debbie Harry.

Once they reach Cypress Hills they slog through mud and horse shit, could be cow shit, does it really matter what kind? He's been on better trails than this. He is disappointed, but refuses to show it.

"How you guys doing back there?" Animated. Snow pellets bounce off the ground in front of him, collect in the hoof marks churned in the mud. The trail is flat, the trail is boring, the trail is smelly, he veers off into the bushes for a piss. Bright orange anorak signals his piss stop through the trees. Wife and daughter toil past.

They eat dinner at Denny's stinking of horse shit and mud. The waitress brings them their orders in under ten minutes and Karen is impressed with the service but not the food.

"This is atrocious," she says, picks the bacon out of her clubhouse sandwich, what a dump. "What an all-round crapper of a day."

"What's for dessert," he jabs. He agrees with her but won't admit it. The trip his idea after all.

The gravy's aftertaste reminds Jez of Bob.

"This is it?"

Jack pays the entrance fee and Jez separates from them almost at once, lingers at the souvenir shop for a little bit then walks past concrete walls, slide displays, bison skeletons. Head-Smashed-in Buffalo Jump. She relishes the sound of brain juice and blood broken through skulls. Presses coloured buttons on displays, she is too old for this kind of shit but she enjoys it anyway, she likes the reconstructed skeletons the most. Too many children.

"Head-Smashed-in Buffalo Jump," she hears through slide presentations, guides, beeps of computer displays.

"Head-Smashed-in-and-a-Broken-Leg Buffalo Jump. Head-

Smashed-in-Arm-Twisted-off-Bum-Screwed-up Buffalo Jump," a very small girl says.

"Yasmina!" exclaims her mother.

"Yasmina!" exclaims Jez and Yasmina runs silent to her mother.

From behind the killing-floor re-creation, Bob watches Jez in front of a bison skeleton. The Walkman in her hands, headphones around her neck, she stares at the lit-up bones. He lied about Toronto, really he's from Bowden, thought he'd be home yesterday. Slicked-back hair. She turns around and does she see him yes she sees him and, hello, he is about to say when she smoothly reaches her fingers under his shirt and stretches out his heart, puts it into her mouth and chews, his heart no more than just a medium-sized wad of gum. She is the first woman to ever have oral sex with him. He will have to remember her forever now. Jez turns away her head angrily, then is stopped by the sight of a blonde woman standing a few feet away.

My god it's her.

My god it's her.

My god it's Deborah Harry, I'm standing next to Deborah Harry, and Jez's stomach implodes, a chatter clatter of panic, light sweat peppered across a pale and bloodless forehead.

Look at the legs on that one, Jack thinks and stares at the pale double length of leg standing next to his daughter's scuffed-up jeans. Nice ankles! Wonders if there's a Coke machine anywhere nearby, checks out the souvenir shop instead.

Karen notices the black roots first. She sees Jezzie staring rudely, then she sees the woman. Why would anyone let their hair go to hell like that? Obviously bottle-blonde. Aside from that she's certainly well-kept, smooth curve of expensive fabric over a still young bosom, a bosom of forty or so, a woman my age in fact, she wonders why the woman's face looks so familiar, the legs in particular. Karen notices gold flecks in the scarf around the woman's throat. How attractive, fingers the identical scarf around the skin on her own suddenly heated throat. Hurry to the bathroom, she is sweating so much. She picks at the corner of her lips, long strips of lipstick-stained skin torn away.

No. Debbie Harry can't be that old. Close though, so close, and she puts her headphones on. Doesn't push PLAY.

Creak of a cubicle door and

"Nice scarf," says Bottle-Blonde, she shows her teeth grey around the edges, smiles laugh lines around her mouth.

"Where did you get yours?" Karen asks politely. She is the mother of a teen-aged practically adult daughter, married for going on fifteen years. "I bought mine in Banff."

"Oh, the States," says Bottle-Blonde. "I like the way you wear yours. I should try mine like that." She lifts her arms to readjust the scarf and Karen suddenly swims in a cloud of Boucheron perfume. Very expensive. Karen wears her Boucheron only on special occasions. "Can you help me?" asks Bottle-Blonde. "I can't seem to get it quite right," and Karen touches skin and silk arranged loosely with two tails in the back. "Thank you."

Karen touches skin and gold-flecked silk, smells her own perfume.

"Thank you very much."

"Oh, you're welcome." Karen's ripped lips smoothed over with fresh red lipstick.

Thank you. Oh you're welcome. Suddenly there are too many mirrors for one room. For one woman.

Back at the Black Angus for dinner, Karen pokes at creamy pasta with the outside tine of her fork, remembers she's lactose intolerant and drinks glass after bitter glass of Black Angus's lousy house white. Thank god she ain't booze intolerant. She puts her hand on Jack her husband's thigh and begins to stroke, then knead.

"Saw a woman wearing the exact same scarf as me today."

"Oh yeah, well I thought I saw Debbie Harry, can you believe it. Thought I was losing my mind." Thought I was losing my mind, he said he was going back to Toronto, her nipples suddenly cold under her jersey. "Can I please have a drag, Mum?"

"Why the hell not."

His body rocks slightly from the pressure of her hand on his thigh. Now what, he would like to ask but knows it'll just get him into really deep shit. A drunk Karen snoring the night away. He asks the waitress for another carafe and pours his glass full.

Welcome to CALGARY

"Yeeahoo," snorts Jez.

In the car Karen digs in her nose with a Kleenex.

"Why do you bother using a Kleenex?" says Jez, "it's just as gross as watching you pick with a finger."

"Because my fingernails would make my nose bleed. And that's more gross."

Jack tries to remember the last time his nose bled. Once when he was at the beach. He was hungover that day too.

Suzette Mayr recently published her first novel, Moon Honey *(NeWest Press), and is the author of* Zebra Talk, *a poetry chapbook (disOrientation Press). Her poetry and fiction have appeared in a number of literary magazines, including* Open Letter, West Coast Line *and* Fireweed. *She currently lives and works in Calgary.*

and here we are now
_____

Judy MacInnes Jr.

Nosebleed

Can you go and get some help? Red current, stream, huckle-berries. Mrs. Spears runs from the warmth of the orange staffroom, coffee cup still in hand, and out into the playing field where Enid stands with her feet slightly apart, the wind touching her pleated skirt, the skirt touching her knee. Dandelion, quick grass, stinging nettle. Blood rushing from her nose. The game of California kick-ball slows, someone yells for the blue ball to be pitched. Were her arms out and palms open? Were they opening out to me?

+

I see Gus in the Bank of Nova Scotia while I'm in the express line-up. He tries to convince a teller with a tidy beehive to cash a personal cheque. He advises the four people behind him in line to switch banks when she closes the wicket, slides a "Closed" sign across her window. Then he notices me.

"Isobel, hey, Bella. How's it going?"

"Good. Not bad," I say and then "Are you living here again?"

"Nah, I'm just visiting my dad. Thinks he might be able to get me on at the waterfront. Longshoring. It's shift work, but anything's better than being in Lashburn. It's such a nothing place."

"And how's Enid doing?"

He's wearing a gabardine sports coat, and he tugs on the right collar. He had been talking loud, so I'm relieved he's suddenly silent when I ask him about his sister. His eyes are closer together than I remember. When we step outside the bank, I ask about Enid again. He tells me she is still living in the same place, a block and a half from my old house, with her partner, Caren. He boots gravel onto Pear Street. Stones, rocks, dirt. The teller's beehive unravels behind the glass.

+

Enid and I are in her brother's room looking through his stuff: chewed pens, athletic socks, a pack of Craven A smokes jammed into the sleeve of a sweater, food wrappers, a jockstrap. I find the plastic gold plaque I gave him for his fifteenth birthday in his underwear drawer:

ANGUS GILBERT
Confident, Kingly, Obstinate
Sometimes theatrical in behaviour

Then Enid shows me what we have been looking for:
July, 1979.
Penthouse.
She shoves Gus's magazine down her jeans and pulls on one of his sweatshirts, hiding the rectangular outline against her body.

+

Mrs. Spears teaches us fractions. Common denominators. $3/10 + 6/5 =$ and Enid gets another nosebleed. Enid keeps a spare blouse in the cloakroom. She's allowed to leave her desk, go to the cloakroom and then to the toilet, without asking permission.

+

This is how Lashburn is remembered:
Gus, my neighbour, pushes me and his younger sister down Clark Avenue in a wheelbarrow. Enid and me are freshly cut tulips. Stiff and bright and standing. We pass disoriented bees who lick purple gummy plum heather. They whirr and wheeze, dizzily. Buffalo beans, fenceposts, streamlet. Then it's me and Enid leaning back, arms dragging, disturbing rock piles on the side of the road. Gus stops pushing, reaches his arm up over his head, blocks out the sunlight. Enid gets out of the wheelbarrow to run around. Pebbles ricochet from her toes. The bottoms of my feet rest on each handle. Legs together and apart. Together and apart. Still lying down, wanting Gus to see my middle.

+

A nothing place?

+

"Well, how about dinner tonight, Isobel? Do you have plans? Have you gotten rid of that boyfriend of yours?"

"He moved out two months ago."

"So, are you free?"

We walk away from the bank, up Crest Avenue.

+

Blood. Does Gus remember the sound I made when he first went inside me? A sound from my mouth, like a fist bumping a hollow wall. Was Enid in her room? I'll ask him about her tonight.

+

We wear matching purple and white checkered ponchos. Climbing over the chainlink fence, into the neighbour's yard, holding back the brambles. Looking for insects and sticks. Enid holds a dead grasshopper in her palm. "Isobel, let's get married and live in a pink apartment and buy lots of long-haired cats and designer pillows and scented candles and scatter them all over the place."

We can't stop laughing.

+

"Do you want a baked potato, rice or fries?" Gus asks before the waiter approaches the table. He always does this.

+

I make Gus's best friend call Enid one night while she is baby-sitting.

"Hey, Enid. It's Robert. How's it going?"

"Not too bad. What are ya doing?"

I prepared Robert before the call. My voice, mechanical, giving instructions: "Tell her you like her. Just to see what she says. I know, tell her you want to take her to grad. Say that you've been thinking about her. Say that you think she's a babe." I listen on the upstairs phone in Rob's parents' room. Purple curtains, cream shag rug. Gus lies beside me and we listen together. He tugs on the phone, pulls the skin on my elbow.

"Uh, I don't know, Rob. Our family is going away that weekend. Family reunion."

"What a liar," Gus mouths as I cover the extension with my hands. He sprints downstairs into the rec room and whispers into Rob's ear: "She's frigid, she's a virgin, I bet she's gay. Go ahead, ask her."

"What are you?" Rob says. "A lez? Frigidaire?"

Did I find out like that? It was a joke. How long had you been that way?

+

"Do you want some juice, Sugar?" Mrs. Gilbert asks. She sews crooked pillows with her white hands. Slippery pillows, hard to lean on. Mrs. Gilbert in her worn-out, almost transparent terry-cloth housecoat. Near the sliding glass door, her girdle and her thick longline brassiere are noticeable. I take my juice over to the breakfast table and wait for Enid to get off the phone, long distance, with her dad. Enid thinks it's cool when she sees my dad in the backyard mowing grass or rooting up mushrooms. My smiling dad holding an ice-cream bucket of weeds against the bed of sweet williams. I picture her long-distance dad, smiling, staring at the numbers on the dial: 1 2 (ABC) 3 (DEF) 4 (GHI) 5.

+

In certain light. My seventeen-year-old handprints above Gus's bed. I don't want to remember the marks I made in Enid's room. Another kind of light?

+

Enid is in Vancouver, visiting her dad, so my mom sends me to Joanna's place while she shops for groceries. All the pieces of cardboard furniture (a stove with a yellow turkey cooking in the oven; a freezer with a rectangular handle; the light blue bed big enough to hold three Barbies comfortably; a vanity with a silvered paper mirror attached) are placed on the basement floor. It's hot July and the cement cools us. We take turns choosing items that will fill our separate houses. Joanna gets to pick first because we are in her basement, where her father makes dandelion wine, and because this is all her stuff. There isn't a choice about the dolls. I get the plain one with brown hair and the blurred features, bought by Joanna's Aunty Jean for her ninth birthday. She plays with the Bride Barbie who has fussy blonde hair and white plastic high-heels. We decide to play with Ken this time, but he is shared. The vanity is the most revered item and is Joanna's first pick.

+

Enid and me and Joanna are in the can. We are skipping gym class. "I refuse to play war-ball," Joanna says. And we agree. Skins vs. Shirts. Good gawd, it's vulgar. Enid and me climb on top of the toilets and begin flushing with our feet. Motorbikes. Like Charlie's Angels without their van. Our hands form into fists. Turning, revving. Joanna disapproves of our behaviour and instead scratches messages into the metal cubical door:

SWEET COCK

LONG SHLONG DONGS CAN DO NO WRONG

J. LOVES GLEN

+

"Isobel, what is the common denominator in this equation?"
Mrs. Spears
lady hair, navy-blue pumps, lettuce on upper lip from sandwich

+

Enid's mom
housecoat, OceanSprayCranberryJuice, a new boyfriend

+

Joanna
sweet cocks, shaven armpits, a ranch-style home
=
?
Who was the number/below the line/in our fraction?

+

Bloodstains, the shape of hands, pattern her beige bedspread, her nightclothes. Enid's mom likes to cover the stains with Holly Hobby patches. Enid says the patches are like medals. Her dad used to call them war wounds. Thick curtains, sewing machine, canopy bed. Silvery pictures of Saint Sebastian, begging limbs out and open, in a drugstore frame. Matching white furniture with gold trim. Giant Shaun Cassidy poster covering the off-pink wall.

+

"What's with all the questions about Enid?" Gus says as we eat. "Why don't you ask her yourself? You've got a telephone, don't you?"

"Yeah, sure," I say.

"You've got a piece of potato on your chin."

"Is it gone?"

+

I haven't finished doing my math problems. Mrs. Spears won't let me go outside. Everyone's playing soccer. Almost half of the lunch hour is over. $1/2$. Two being the bottom number. I know this much.

"Isobel? Haven't you finished? You should be enjoying the weather. Go ahead outside. But make sure you finish up by tomorrow. I will be checking notebooks on Friday, young lady."

I run out to the soccer field and Joanna grabs me just before my feet touch gravel. We swerve into the back bush. I think she is trying to make me smoke again. She pushes me in further and there stands Enid:

her corduroy knickers pulled down
her ponytail loose, red bobble on ground
three fingertips on Glen's waist
her floral underwear
(cotton)
still on

She sees me, my pushed body jerked into seeing her. Joanna behind me, hand on hip. Only the smell of juniper bushes. She sees me watching her. The taste of red on her face. Left arm reaching out.

+

"She makes her nose bleed to get attention. It's so sick."
Joanna is my new best friend
this week.
48 pencil crayons, sharpened, in her desk.

+

I rename my Barbie doll Eileen after the older girl Enid swims with
at Hjorth Road Park. Joanna doesn't believe in swimming, so both
of us stare at them through the chainlink fence. Eileen has hair
growing out of her armpits.

+

Page 47:
A woman's whole mouth is sucking and pinching a brown breast.
    Camera click.
    Nipple, hair, click.
    The next page:
    One woman
    Over another woman
    Click.
    "I feel like I have to pee."
    "Me too."

+

Alone, between the sweet williams and the rock garden, with my Barbie,
Eileen. I use a maxi-pad for her bed. When she wakes up, she strolls
across the lawn. In her plastic pink hand she carries a beach towel made
from scraps of old underwear. I bury her in the soil like Enid used to
bury my shins in the warm sand of the playbox at school.

+

Why did I let things happen between us? I should have stopped
myself from looking
stopped you from playing wheelbarrow with me
my hands walking on the school lawn
your arms holding my ankles into the air
looking down my skirt
Shouldn't I be thinking this way?

+

I sit up on Enid's bed. A fresh stain? Blood, from me? Now I'm bleeding? Mrs. Gilbert directs me to the bathroom. Mr. Clean, maxi-pad, a new patch.

+

"I would invite you inside for a drink, but I work in the morning. Thanks for the dinner invitation."
    "Well, I could stay the night."
    "No, please, I'd rather not get into this," I say.
    He's playing with his keys. And he wants to sleep with me. After six years of not seeing him, not seeing Enid.

+

I'm pushing my nose with my palm. Hard. As usual, nothing happens.

Judy MacInnes Jr. was born in 1970. She has written a chapbook entitled Super Socco and Other Super Stories *(Ga Press) and is currently working on a self-titled collection. Her poetry was included in* Breathing Fire *(Harbour Publishing). She lives in Vancouver with screenwriter Andrew McEvoy.*

Hiromi Goto

Canadian Culture 201

1. Two young women are driving in a convertible, eastbound, on Highway 1. They are travelling at 125 km/hr. If they are wearing black bikini tops,

a) how long will it take before they are stopped?

b) who will stop them?

c) If you thought they were blonde, move on to the next question.

"We should stop. My tits are freezing." The sun edged out of today and into tomorrow, the wind ceaseless through my sandpaper hair, giving me a headache. I was also sick of driving.

"Let's just keep going until we find a decent motel. There's too much stuff in the car to put the top up without having to take some out. Especially with my crutches. Just turn on the heat full blast and it'll be warm enough until we stop."

I turned up the heater, full blast.

"Burning my knees," I muttered. "Look at the map. How far did we come?"

"Not very." Ivy shifted her legs again, her surgeried knee stiff inside the garbage-tossed confines of the car. Not to mention all the luggage.

I never thought of her as ivy, as in vine, but more like IV, like in drip.

"We should have stopped in Regina, I suppose," she sighed. "Nothing but little shit towns for miles."

"What's the next town?" I asked, trying to be the patient older one.

"Balgonie."

"No shit?" I laughed.

"Yeah, Balgonie, Saskatchewan."

"Jesus, what a great name! Let's stay there."

"I don't know." IV squinted down at the map, wanting to go on as far as possible but not wanting to impose too much because she couldn't drive with her bum knee. "It's only a circle on the map. You know, those small circles without another circle inside it? Just a single circle without a dot or anything. Think they'd have a motel?"

"They must." Tired and fed up. Sick of driving a car I wasn't used to, and my tits were still cold. "When do I turn off?"

"Must be pretty soon. There! Turn left! Turn left!" IV yelled.

Welcome to the village of
BALGONIE, SASKATCHEWAN

"Jesus, what a dump." Even I was slightly dismayed. The motel beside the highway all peeled paint and sagging steps.

"Yeah," my sister puffed around a cigarette. "Drive downtown. Maybe there'll be something else."

We drove two blocks and found a downtown that was all of one hotel and one grocery/post office/drugstore combined.

"Balgonie Hotel, huh. It's worse than the motel." IV flicked her cigarette butt out the open top. "Want to go to the next town?"

"Naw, I'm sick of driving. I want a beer, too. Let's check into that motel by the highway and get a good night's sleep. Get on the road earlier tomorrow," I said importantly.

"All right."

The woman behind the counter looked at us askance-like. Us in our bikini tops and goose bumps and cutoff jeans. IV with a fat scar down her knee, bright red from the heater blowing on it full blast. She looked at us all up and down, but she didn't ask for any ID, like I thought she would. I don't suppose you can afford to be too picky about your guests in Balgonie, Saskatchewan.

"Make sure you park in the spot marked 3. Like your door, huh," the woman nudged with her chin.

IV and I looked at each other. There were all of two cars in the otherwise hugely empty parking lot.

"Sure, sure. No problem."

I carried our luggage, a half bottle of Evian and a package of Reese's Peanut Butter Cups with two discs left in it. IV grabbed the camera bag. Limping a little.

"Your leg sore?"

"Not too bad. But I'm a bit tired. Do you still want to go out for a beer?"

"Yeah, you mind?" Not so selfish that I couldn't ask.

"No. Just let me take a shower or something."

IV took a shower and I jotted some notes in my journal, got my tape recorder set up for my before-going-to-sleep oral commentary.

"Testing! Testing! 1, 2, 3. Pfffffffft. Pfffffffft."

"That's really helpful!"

"Shhhh! It's recording!

"Wewe?"

"Shhh! Uhhh—August, uh—What day is it?"

"Wednesday."

"No, idiot. The date."

"It's the seventeenth, asshole."

"Uhhh August seventeenth and we're in, uhhh, Balgonie, Saskatchewan. We're staying in the Bluebird Motel, here. It's been very hot, and didn't make much time today. We're planning to get up early tomorrow and haul our butts. Uhhh, nothing too exciting happened. Oh, when we decided to go out for a beer, at first we were nervous. It being a small town and all. I mean, you never know where there are small pockets of Ku Klux Klan around and all that. Anyways, we decided there were two of us, so we'd be okay. And went to the small café right next to the motel. And the owner was a Chinese Canadian and it was immediately all right. He felt like a father of a friend we had at home or something. I mean, he didn't beam at us or give us free food or anything. It was because we could see that we weren't the only Asians around. And when I realized that, it made me wonder what it meant about how I felt about the country I lived in. That's it for today. Oh. Do you have anything to add?"

"No. That was really deep, Jenny."

"Oh, fuck off."

"No, really. I'm being serious."

"Oh. Thanks. Uhhh, that's it for today."

2. Two Japanese Canadian sisters drive eastward in a white convertible. One sister is five years older than the other. The younger sister is being driven to Montreal by her older sister because of recent knee surgery. When they arrive, the older sister will fly home on the airplane.

a) Is this an example of a traditional travel story, and if so, how many kilometres will it journey?

b) If you still think they are blonde, just hand in the exam without bothering to read the rest.

We had the music going full blast so we could hear it above the wind roaring over the open space above our heads. The sun tight on our burning shoulders, and I smoked more cigarettes than I usually do because I felt extra cool. I wasn't so cool as to recognize what my younger sister was listening to, but even I can bob my head to a bass backbeat that's loud enough to burst veins.

"Will any of your friends be back in town yet?" I yelled above the blur of wind and highway.

IV popped the tape out with her toe.

"What?"

"I asked if I'll get to meet any of your friends."

"No, they won't be coming back for another week or so. Besides, you wouldn't like them. They're all white." IV rolled her eyes.

"That's not fair." I glanced at her. Eyes met, shifted away. "I have white friends too!"

We both burst out laughing.

"That's really *bad*," I cringed. "I mean, I don't dislike or avoid Caucasian people, it's just that so many of them haven't done their homework."

"Yah, yah, but hardly anyone does. No one gives a shit. And the people who do just look like fanatics," IV yawned.

"Do I look like a fanatic?" I asked. Curious.

"Sometimes. But it's okay because you're my sister."

"I'm so relieved," I simpered. "I would hate for you to think I'm a fanatic and alienate you from my life."

"Fuck off." IV punched me in the arm.

LARGEST MOOSE IN THE WORLD
10 km ahead

"Hey, look! The largest moose in the world! Do you think we'll be able to see it from the highway?" I pointed an excited finger, signage blurring by.

"It's just a fiberglass thing," IV smirked.

"Oh." Disappointed. I had imagined an enormous, ancient, primordial creature housed in a resplendent game farm. "It's funny how a lot of these small towns want to have the largest of *something* to make them famous. Why do you suppose?"

"Because bigger the better. It's the ol' size game. Big gun wins. Big prick. Big bucks. Big boobs," IV grimaced, clutching her breasts like they were missiles.

"You're gross."

"Testing, testing . . .

"Uhh, it's been a couple days. Prairie, prairie land and see. The weather's been holding out. We power-drove through the night. IV's driving now, too, even though her leg gets sore when she has to shift gears. Says I'm too slow. A cop pulled us over yesterday and yah, he had a moustache. Said he clocked us at one-forty but he'd let us off for one-ten, because he hadn't ever seen such cute Oriental girls before. IV really played it up, downcast-eyes shit and tilting her head to one side. When he drove off, she crumpled up the ticket and flipped it out the open top, stood on the car seat and pushed her tits together to make juicy cleavage. Bent over and stuck out her tongue in that gross way, like she was turned on or something.

"I was laughing so hard I really kind of peed my pants!

"We actually drove by the creep an hour later! He was hassling two dykes on a bike. Virago, that is."

"Did you see that!" IV yelped.

"A bear. Big deal. I've seen tons in Alberta."

"Let's stop!"

"Are you crazy? It was a bear *cub*! That means there's a big fucking bear *mother* around to protect it!" I rolled my eyes at my sister's wildlife ignorance.

"I've never seen a natural bear before," IV said happily.

"As opposed to an unnatural one?" I asked.

"Spare me your sarcasm. I wanted to take a picture."

"There's this *Bear Attacks!* book that deconstructs the myth-making around bear so-called attacks. And one of the stories," I gulped in air, excited, "one of the stories describes how this kid was attacked by this cub in a national park. But listen, the incredible thing is about this kid's mom!"

"Did she fight off the bear?" IV blinked.

"No!" I crowed, laughing. "She stopped the car to get a picture of the cute bear cub, right, then she gets this brain wave to smear her kid's face with honey so she can get a picture of the bear licking his face!"

"Jesus."

"Can you believe it?" I laughed, clutched gut in spasmic gasps. "Isn't it fucked?"

"I don't think it's *funny*," IV muttered.

"I'm not laughing at the mauled kid! It's just the whole mentality of this culture! I mean, it's the epitome of twentieth-century ignorance. It's so pathetic, all you can do is laugh." I weakly wiped some tears from my sun-creased eyes.

"Like that cop yesterday," I added. "He had this pretty doll/geisha thing in his head and you played it out for him. Like honey. And if you had claws, sharper teeth, you would have licked his face like any nice 'Oriental' girl would, I'm sure."

"Yah, you have a point."

"That's all I'm saying." I grinned.

"This life is fucked." IV lit up a cigarette.

"Tell me something I don't know."

3. SURPRISE BONUS QUESTIONS worth an extra 15 per cent of your test results.

    a) What do *you* think is Canadian Culture?

    b) Does it matter?

c) Both a and b are correct.
d) A, b and c are incorrect.
e) All of the above
f) None of the above

"Jesus, what time is it?" I scrubbed my eyes with my forearm. A crick in my neck and thighs sticking to sweat-wet vinyl.

"Almost nine." IV had bags beneath her eyes.

I toed the empty Evian bottles, nacho chip bag, chocolate bar wrappers crinkled into balls.

"We should get some real food."

"No fucking chance. There's nothing around here for eons. Except polluted swamp grass," IV scowled.

"Where are we?" I peered out at the dim countryside blur of highway nothingness.

"Armpit, Ontario."

I started snorting.

"We might have to sleep in the car, you know." IV glanced over. "There really is nothing on this highway. When Sherry and I drove it last year, we slept on the side of the road until the sun rose. It's warm enough for a while, with the top down, but it's freezing in the morning."

"Can't we put it up?"

"There's too much stuff. We'd have to unload half of it on the side of the road and someone might take it while we're sleeping," IV explained, having gone through this trip three times already.

"Maybe we'll get picked up by aliens," I said hopefully. Summer stars rose from the east like dying fireflies.

"You and your aliens. More like picked up by gross truck drivers." IV, the perpetual optimist. "I can't drive any more," she said. Pulled off the highway in a spray of gravel, into a tiny lane that went nowhere, just an edge of short, dense trees.

"I can't either. My eyes are crossed, I'm so tired." I stretched, then slumped forward on the dusty dash.

We stared blankly at the ugly trees.

"Are you going to do your tape recording thing tonight too?" IV asked. "What's it *for*, anyways?"

"I don't know. It was a whim. Making historical, yours and mine, in present place and time. Something like that."

"Hey, that kinda rhymed," IV grinned. "And so sublime!"

"Shut up." I punched her in the arm. "Do you have any water left?"

"No, I drank the last bit while you were sleeping. I can hear frogs, though. There's probably a whole swamp out there, stretching for miles."

"Drop the sarcasm. I'm too tired to play." I shut my eyes. Nudged my head into the head rest for a comfortable place that wasn't there.

"Jenny?"

"Yeah, what?"

"Did you like university?" she asked.

I crossed my arms, head still back and eyes still shut. "No," I said. Silent space.

"But I don't regret it," I qualified.

"I'm thinking of quitting school," IV softly said.

I sat up. "How come?"

"It's fucked. Me, taking East Asian studies, in Canada. Being taught by white professors about Japan, how people live there, their customs, being *corrected* by white *teachers* when I offer my opinion. It's fucked. I don't know what I'm doing there any more."

"Well," I said slowly, "maybe you're there to learn what you *shouldn't* be learning. If that makes any sense."

"And *paying* for it?" IV incredulous.

"Nothing's free," I smirked. "I think the process is important. Look how far you've come even recognizing that what you're paying for, to learn, is tainted."

"Jenny, don't patronize me."

"Sorry." I was sincere. For a change. Patted her on the arm, signs of true affection as rare in our family as sarcasm was overabundant. "Well, think about it some more, huh?"

"Yeah, I will," IV sighed. "Don't tell Mom and Dad! They'll shit if they find out."

"Huh! Like I want to deal with their hysterics. Go to sleep." I shut my eyes again. "We have one more province to drive through." I leaned back, smacking my unbrushed teeth with a furry tongue, hating the stink of vinyl stained sweat. Wished there was room to tilt my seat back, even a couple inches.

"Yeah."

Croak of frogs larger than any found in Alberta. Wondered how long it would take the mosquitoes to smell our sweaty blood. Eyes sticky closed. My head spun so dizzy-tired I only wanted to tip into the mud of sleep.

"Jenny?"

"*What?!*"

"I think you'll like Montreal."

"I'm sure I will. *Good night.*" I scrunched a sweatshirt beneath my neck and chin, signed heavily. Undid the top button of my cutoffs but it didn't make any difference. Breathed slow, even, the breath of sleep, to inspire it in myself and telepathically will IV to leave me alone. Please, leave me alone!

"Jenny?" IV whispered.

"I can't *hear* you because I'm sleeping," I mimicked, like childhood.

"I'm glad we did this trip together."

"Me-too," I whispered quickly, eyes furiously shut.

"Jenny?"

"Je*susssss!*" I hissed, patience when overtired not being my strong point.

"There's-a-moose-standing-right-beside-your-window."

I slowly turned my head to my right. Immense prehistoric nostrils blasted two circles of steam, eye-level. Huge rubber lips drooped, chewing a wad of soggy weeds.

I screamed.

Moose panic snot splatter glass, me screaming, IV screaming, hug each other death grip, scream thud/splash of hooves through sludge, scream/laughing hysterically, gasp gasping tears running down our faces. The splash of hooves bigger than pie plates. They squelched farther from us and frogs bigger than the ones in Alberta started croaking once more. IV and me, whined and dined upon by mosquitoes bigger than house flies.

All we could do was giggle in spurts and gasps, hold on for dear life, still. Until swirling in exhaustion, between slow hiccups of dimming adrenalin laughter, we fell asleep in each others' arms.

Examiner's Note: There is no mark assigned upon completion of this examination because completion is not possible. You will, in some way or form, enact and (re)configure Canadian Culture for the rest of your life.

Thank you for your participation.

Hiromi Goto is a Japanese Canadian feminist writer. Her novel, Chorus of Mushrooms, *was the 1995 Canada/Caribbean winner for Best First Book of the Commonwealth Writers' Prize. She is on the editorial collective of* absinthe *magazine and is currently finishing her second novel.*

Jo-Anne Berman

The Catwalk

Cold night and they're stompin' into the Bovine. Gotta know the doorman, Frank the Crank. He's so cool standin' in the cold, lets the regulars past Saturday-night gawkers from Scarberian burbs. Into the room, long and narrow. Dark walls, neon designs. Smells like laundry a week overdue. A sea of black leather biker jackets all worn in and personalized. Clips and studs and buttons and patches burst on the scene with long hair flying, cowboy boots, leather tits, and asses crammed into stonewashed Levi's.

Where the dark lights and the neon sun shines. Search the open with your face in a shadow. Faces, pasty with shining health, beckon to the freedom of the merry-go-round. Hip young women tarted up, heated up. Looking for love where once no nice girl could be found. Nice girls and nasty girls, side by side, looking for fun in roach rooms with a view. The Bovine's the coolest; gets all kinds. Sift through the poison to come up with a shiny dime. All the trolls lookin' for love or drinks for free. Sue, Debbie, Katya, Cindy and Steph revvin' on a girls' night out. They head to the low-slung bar. Boho bartenders with ripped tights and pinned-together velvet outfits serve drinks from the Bovine beer fridge. Grab a piece of the bar to make home base. Look around. Pass over five bucks for the beer. Light a butt, drink the beer, check out the scene.

Steph's looking around with Canadian-drinking Katya by her side. Trollin' the area for a masculine eyeball to hook. Steph gets one fast, this time out. Her secret for picking up men is to have the steady grind. If not, the capital D for "Desperate" starts to show, tattooed on your forehead. She's the luckiest troll at gettin' lucky, 'cause nothing ever happens when you want it to. Stephanie, dark and dangerous. Slippery tricky. Already has a man at home waitin' around for her to decide which way's up. He doesn't like to party. He's a good guy, but only wants to play cards. Won't stomp around town causing bad-ass trouble. Smoking doobs, biding his time, waiting for life. Mellow dude who means no harm. Steph doesn't know what she wants. She dreams of lots of men and money. She has no plan. Never tries too hard at anything to get the everything she wants. Likes them young and lean. Likes to teach them tricks.

Steph checks him out again. This one's got long brown curly hair. Not young, but actually just right. His shoulders are the highest wave in the sea of leather. He can cruise above all the other heads. That's how Steph caught his eye—her height. Coulda-woulda-shoulda been a model but just didn't get around to getting her portfolio together. Now she's twenty-four and too old to get a start. She looks down. She's just there for a good time—to flirt, not to fuck.

The sea is five leathers thick. Clumping groups clot the skinny barroom. Downtown bar scene of hazy-dazy familiar faces. Steph sneaks a look back up at him and sure enough, he's still there checking out her scene. She gives him a little smile, then looks away. What to do with her hands? Elbows angle in every direction gangly-geek. Her left fingernail's already scratched away the gooey gluey paper shreds from Blue bottle.

"Hey, any of you guys gotta light?" Steph tries to keep busy so he'll know she's cool.

Katya, staying beside her, lights Steph's butt. Steph takes a big haul and looks out across the leather sea in His direction. Gone. Shit! Anything that easy couldn't be all that great anyway. Quick and easy Steph believes in love at first sight. She can feel one of the trolls tapping her on the shoulder. She turns to see . . . Him. If she'd known, she would've put a mint in her mouth. Now she has beer 'n' butt breath.

"I noticed you from across the room. Thought I'd buy you a drink—unless your boyfriend would object to that." His voice is deep, steady, together. Smooth.

"Would I be flirting with you if I had a boyfriend?"

His mouth curves up at both ends. Those brown puppy-dog eyes of his sparkle. His jeans hang low on his hips. As he leans in, his slouch brings him close to her ear. "Would you?"

"Maybe." Her eyes dare him to tease back. To maintain the game she looks away in a hurry. "Bingo," she says in her buddy Katya's ear. "I got one hooked. Free drinks for me tonight!"

"All right! That's a good excuse for a shot if I ever heard one." Leaning on the bar, home base for hot trolls out for a night of vamping, Katya orders two shots.

They clink their glasses. "To Jägermeister," they toast, giggle, do their shots, then knock glasses back down to bar. Real cool, yeah, that's them. Wannabe cool Steph ignores him.

"Did you check out his ass? Bay-bay! How'd you like to grab ahold a that one, Katya? But I'm jus' lookin' tonight, not touchin'. Gotta man of my own home all alone."

Primed with margaritas at Katya's place before they hit the Bovine, and Katya's head starts to loll on her shoulders as her mouth puckers. "Love this song. Less dance," she yells in her friend's ear to beat the speaker's beat. Without waiting, Katya's prancing beside Steph with Deb and Sue. Stephanie's ear stings from Katya's shrill yell. She sticks her finger in it to stop the sting. She smiles at Him. He's watching the trolls groove to the Chili Pepper sound. Let him gawk. Watch while they undulate. Steph wants his stare. Wants to show him what she means.

But Cindy, man, she doesn't dance, gotta be good and drunk for that crap. Cindy, brown curls, leathery skin, dilettante waitress workin' on degree a class at a time. She'll never finish, keeps changing her major. Economics to Philosophy to Comp Sci—that's the latest. Smart girl wears glasses to bars, giving the guys new flavour. Insecure babe, wannabe rich bitch. Every guy she meets. "Now this is IT, the ONE." Losin' every time they catch a line. "I'm an actress, you know, yeah, I'm really an actress. Gonna make it someday. Get my big break."

Cindy holds down home base while trolls trawl.

"Another Tom Collins, 'nuther one." She tips glass up for bartender magic. Tart lime discharge to taste-bud sensation. Perky barstool butt perch, shoulder slouch, sexy legs. Coy glance flit to calf to make sure muscles shapely styled. Peek through curly hair to check out action in smoke-filled haze. Smile, smile, I'm-so-cool smile. Red alert—nerd smile interception. Not-for-you-buddy smile turns scowl. Dream on buddy. Yeah, dream on.

Cindy's gettin' nervous sittin' there all alone. Naked, solo. What if someone thinks she has no friends? Look busy, purse fumble for cigarettes. Find one, light it, arch head back to exhale. Sophistication. Wait for trawling trolls.

"C'mon, Katya, let's drink." Steph pulls Katya to home base. Gotta pass Him with two buddies on the way back to Cindy. One guy has stringy blond hair and John Lennon glasses. Too skinny. The other one is short with mousy Q-Tip hair and freckles. Tough sell on troll market.

"Wass yer name, anyway?" Steph asks him.

Smiles. "I'm John, not anyway." Thinks he's funny. Points to friends, first glasses, then Q-tip. "This is Alex and Dave."

Coy Steph. "Aren't you cute? This is Katya, I'm Steph and that over there's Cindy. We're gonna join her, if you wanna come."

The guys follow. Hey, man, how's it goin'. Hey. Hey. Nice to meet yah.

"You ladies want to party after?" John leans over to Steph. Long brown curls mingle with her black to tickle back bare from bustier. She shivers, turns to catch his eye. "Maybe." Leaves eye on face long enough to tease and cocks the left side of her mouth. Grabs her beer bottle to give him silhouette of real woman, one who knows how to drink, who can keep up. Then she turns her back on him, shows a little ass, wants to make him want it. She wants it but doesn't think she will with him.

"Katya, my little mer-friend." She strokes Katya's long blonde hair, leans her face close to Katya's ear. "They wanna party after."

"Make sure they have booze first. I don't wanna get stuck there with nothin' to drink."

"Smart thinkin'." Good old Katya's never one to let her down. Good troll. They're all leanin' against the bar. His friends seem cool. She smells the musk of man. He asks, "What are you ladies drinking?"

"Jägermeister."

"Jä-ger-meister?"

"Don't you know what that is? You won't have a hangover if you stick to Jäger and beer . . . oh yeah, and tequila."

"Why don't you order six of them? My treat."

"Thanks, man. Hey, you guys got booze back at your place?"

"Yeah."

"Watcha got?"

"We got a full bar. Lots of beer, tequila, gin, vodka . . . no Jägermeister, though. But I'll be there."

She raises her eyebrows and smiles. "Sounds good. I just gotta talk to the girls. It's girls' night out and we stick together, you know."

"That's cool." He smiles down on her.

Steph trollops over to Debbie, who's loomin' large and carryin' on with a friend of a friend's cousin who used to know Frank the Crank in high school and says Frank just got outta jail a year ago for smashin' a guy's head in with a brick at a bar brawl in Nipissing or Kapuskasing or one of the two. Scary guy. Frank told them there's this booze can over at one-ten Spadina. Should be cool. Debbie decides that's where the trolls wanna go.

Steph says, "I don't wanna go there. I don't wanna party with Crank or any of his cronies. He's a freak, man. A real creep, coke fiend, pothead, weirdo. You know? I wanna party with that guy I met."

"Where is this guy? What's his name?" Debbie demands. She marches over to home base where he stands with his friends. "We're goin' to a booze can. Why don't you guys come along?"

"No," he says. "We don't want to party all night tonight. We're just gonna hang out after."

"Well, suit yourself," swings the Debbie boom. With hands on hips, "But if you're takin' my friend with you then I need to see some ID." Finger motions demand he show his wallet. "Come on now. Cough it up."

"Here." He smiles patiently while he hands her his wallet. His eyes twinkle with amusement. Stephanie watches. She's happy Debbie cares enough to make sure she's safe.

"Well, that's more like it now. Hey . . . John Stomper . . . cool name."

"John Songma."

"Oh well, as if I'd remember it anyway. You take care of my friend or you'll have to answer to me. And remember I'm only half as drunk as you think I am." Debbie stomps off again.

Cindy, sitting pretty, spies an eye in John's friend Dave. Got glasses, must be smart. Not so cute, but gotta have some guy to hang onto. One man's just like any other.

"Hey, Dave, wanna drink? My treat." Simper, Cindy, simper. Buy 'em a drink then they gotta talk to you—any gentleman would. Get him drunk and he won't have a chance.

Hey, this guy is skinny, but he's still cool. Lucky girl, it's not yet twelve. Maybe this is fate. Everything she says, he says, yeah, I do that too. Too good to be true. Could this be IT? She loves him already. She'll let him ask her out. This is no one-night stand. Keep him here as long as she can. "Hey, want another drink? A cocktail? My treat!" Mind-expanding man, bespectacled knight, take her away on his horse. On a smart man's arm you'll get respect. Fills her brain with new refrain. "Wow, cool, I never thought of that before!"

Cindy looks down at his fingernails, too long. When he loves her, in a month or so, she'll make him cut those ugly devil claws. She shivers.

Dave stands up from the barstool. "I'm going to the bathroom. Be back soon."

Cindy smiles at him, admires. He'll be back soon. Drapes back on bar.

Heart pounds a thought of new, desirable object. Stay cool, style pose for his return. Ready. Now, vacant gaze around room, neon designs on far wall, leather sea of black with dracula faces peering out from behind beer-bottle suckers, the trolls trottin' around and . . . him, Dave, kissing big-boobed blonde bomb in corner roost. Indignant stare. "I bought him two drinks!" Dave sees her, waves, winks, and turns his back forever on watchful, waiting Cindy. Cindy wonders, Man, why does this keep happening to me?

Katya turns to John and Alex. With Steph they stand together. "Do you guys smoke?"

"Smoke what?"

"Well, obviously not cigarettes."

"Why, you have some stuff?"

"We can pop a squab later if you want."

"Pop a what?"

"You know . . . smoke a joint, burn some fern."

"Sounds good. Let's go!"

Stephanie can't believe it. "Before las' call?! What time is it?"

"Quarter to one."

"We can't leave before las' call!! One more shot, then I wanna finish my beer, and then I have to go to the washroom, and I have to check in with the girls. Then I'll be ready. Okay? Get me a beer and a Jäger. I'm gonna go find Debbie and Sue so they don't miss last call."

Sue sees this drunk chick who's weavin' around bump bang and past the pickin'-up stage in her plaid dress dribbling puke stains. Guys are gawkin', guys are laughin', "Ha, ha, look at that drunk chick." But in comes Sue for the rescue. "Haven't you guys ever been drunk before?" She starts following the girl, who's wandering around downtown with a crowd that's one step ahead of her.

Stephie's like, "Hey Sue, wait up. You gotta get las' call!"

But Sue keeps going. "Gotta find this girl's friends. She belongs home in bed."

Sue's the mom. You see, she just wants to have a kid. Just lookin' for the right guy's genes to pass along. Tonight she took her temperature and knows she's cooking. Only wants a sperm and then move along. Wants one kid, not two. Wants to answer only to herself. Bad relationships ending dreams of suburbia, nine to five, house and swing set. She's solid, smart. Went to college. Gets lucky breaks and good jobs 'cause she's quick. Short dark hair mushrooms around her pixie face and tiny red puckered lips.

Steph waits while Sue meanders through the crowd on the drunk chick's heels. Bump like a bowling ball, the drunk chick busts up a group of posers. Sue's all, "Is this your friend?" Posers nod affirmative. "You should take her home, you know. She's much too cute to be lookin' so sad."

Everything's all right when Sue's around.

There's Debbie in the back room. Debbie, just trying to get by. Doesn't wanna work too hard, just party, party, party. Rich mom and dad got her a house and car. No big deal. Easy way to travel. Why work hard? They'll just give her less money. She's a big-mouth bossy full-of-love dog lover who just keeps having to give those dogs away 'cause she never stays still long enough. Heavy-metal rockin' brown-haired bodybuilder. Tough, solid, tanned babe. Don't mess with Debbie.

Steph and Sue find Debbie talkin' to pretty cleancut gaggle of

jocks in their rugged leathers. Bunch of small-town guys lookin' for
a fun night out in the big city. Looks like a couple of good physical
specimens for Sue. Gotta have brains, though.

Turns out one of the guys is an ex of Debbie's. Ditched her. This
is the one who broke her heart. Can't pick that one, Sue. One of
his friends here's a ba-a-ad choice too. Debbie's starting. She gets
into her hands-on-hips stance. "You still hangin' around with him?"
Looks at her ex-love and points to one of the jock friends.

Guys start to shuffle, cast eyes down to ground.

Push, Debbie, push. "Oh, yeah." Points to ex-true love's friend.
"I know you, don't I? I picked you up that night at the Corral. You
kiss and tell." Finger-pointin' Debbie's goin' all out now, ready for
her sweet revenge. "Betcha didn't tell your buddies the whole story,
eh?"

"We-e-e-ell, it was a long time ago. I don't really remember what
you're talking about."

"Sure you do."

"I didn't say anything."

"Oh yes you did, big shot." Debbie laughs at her own joke. Her
voice begins to rise. "Listen, this guy here's braggin' about gettin'
me in bed. Well, he's got nothin' to brag about. He can't go the
distance. Not a heavyweight, that's for sure. You guys shower with
him, I don' need to say more." Deb takes a breath deep inside.
Everyone's quiet. Calm and cool after blowing her load. Turns to
Steph and Sue. "C'mon, girls, let's get last call. There's nothin' worth
havin' in that bunch."

Debbie's strutting back to the trolls' home base. Sue and Steph
are proud of their buddy's bravado. Way to go, Deb. You were right.
Lousy bunch of double-standardizing louts. You told them. Cool.

Spy Katya's long blonde locks dancing to the beat. Neon blonde
mer-hair a beacon for the bar. Her man, she left him at home. He's
too busy with the TV. Hockey game to baseball to football then
basketball and endlessly around again. Hockey night tonight! Go on
out, honey. I'll see you in the morn.

Good. Katya's keeping the meat simmering at home base. John
sees Steph, Deb and Sue. He grasps Stephanie's hips to steer her
towards the bar beside Cindy's stool.

Steph grabs her shot, passes the others to his friends and the girls.

They clink glasses. Stephanie aims her glass at him: "To new friends." She winks and downs her shot.

The trolls are lookin' high and droopy. They're finishing up and gettin' ready to start the day with a night of partying. Ecstasy, idolatry, whatever you want. Your thing's her thing the high thing anything as long as it knocks you down. They all hang and laugh and joke and chide. Gotta leave before the lights go on and the true light under the fluorescent stars shows the hag bags of the eyes. Vampire girls gotta go. Once a guy yelled out when the lights went on, "I've been wasting my time trying to pick up ugly chicks all night."

John's hanging at the door with his buddies. "Ready to go?"

Steph wants to go to the booze can now. "Come for a while, John. Promise it won't be long. You only live once." Steph pleads with her eyes widely innocent. Poor guy doesn't have a chance.

Steph guzzles that last gulp from her beer bottle and zips up her leather. She wraps her scarf around Sue's neck. She needs Sue to last as long as she does tonight. To be her conscience. They head to the door. Outside it's all bye, see yuh.

Hail a cab. Come on, man, we'll squish in the back, sneak so the cops won't know there's eight. Dave's in the front, or is it Alex? Debbie's on her throne up there directing traffic. The other one's in the back with tiny Sue on his lap. Beside them there's Katya, Cindy and then, against the other door, him, John. Steph sits on his lap. She can smell his curls—apple pectin—and his breath—beer. She sniffs near his lips and puts a light kiss on their soft sponge. They touch tongues. She shuts her eyes or maybe she doesn't, but all of a sudden they are there.

They pile out of the cab. Head into the lobby. Oh no—bright lights, lots of hip leather Queen Street chics, to long hall. Five bucks for admission and a beer. Dark room smothered with heavy bass beat. Smell of pot swirls in the air, long stripes dancing to staccato beat.

Plop perches Steph in nest of a beanbag chair. "Got any rolling papers? Who's good at rollin'? Nobody? I'll do it then. Thanks, man!"

Find a lounge area to make home base. Deb runs off to join the swirling, swarming crowd out on the floor.

Good doob pass around, suck on beer. Move to flea-bitten couch next to him. Curl up. It's gettin' pretty foggy in here. Permanently dilated pupils blur the details. Ha ha, that's so funny. What? Can't remember. Steph's necking on that old couch next to a bunch of mellow partiers. Hoping nobody knows her or can see. She forgets that thought as his tasty lips move her soul. She's gettin' electric inside, wanting more. Let's go to the can, man. Let's head for the door.

Both of them behind the door of the can, he's breathing in her ear. "You can trust me, honey. You can, you can."

Alarm bells ring in Stephanie's head. Did somebody say that once and she knew it was a lie, or was she the one who couldn't be trusted? So, condom or not, they do the deed in that dirty old bathroom with cockroach and spider eggs beside them bursting in birth. With needles and cigarette butts littering the floor. Where no orgasm of wheat fields or sunflowers by van Gogh could ever moan. Stephanie's boyfriend lies slumbering at home. All alone.

Back to the party goes Stephanie. Trolls are waiting. Where the hell . . .? Gotta go, says he. But gone is the magic in this guy's smile as she kisses him good night. Her kiss he endures despite the sharp-bitter breath from her nostril flair. As he goes tra-la-la out the door, alcohol and tobacco ferment to combine garlic reek that wafts and lingers. Adios. Cold morning waits.

Jo-Anne Berman grew up in London, Ontario, and is a graduate of York University's creative writing program. Recently married, she lives with her husband and her many pets in Toronto, where she works as a freelance writer and editor.

Alissa York

A Real Present

U p the front of the bus there's an old man dozing. He's several
seats away but I can smell the liquor in his body, like liquor
soaked up in a rag and left in the sink, turning sour and sad.

I can smell him as if he's close enough to tell me a secret. As if
I'm sitting on his knee.

Roy Philipchuk was so good to us.

He was the first in that Alberta town to welcome us when we
came from across the sea, my parents with their strange voices, like
Brits lying on their backs and yawning. Their stories of the sun, the
sharks and the kangaroos. And their two small children.

Roy was so good to us, helped us find a house and fill it with
furniture, sold my parents his old Ford pickup for too cheap, told
us now we had a truck we could come out to his cabin on the lake.
And we did, my brother and me riding in the back, our noses to
the wind, happy like dogs.

Roy was so good to us on those afternoons, gave us white bread
with strawberry jam and Kool-Aid the colour of flowers. We stuffed
ourselves, my brother and I, and my parents drank beer with Roy,
though he had three to their one, and we all lay on our backs,
surrounded by trees so tall, water so dark, and flies as fat as the berries
that grew wild in the underbrush, the ones we had to learn names
for. There were no poisonous spiders any more, only ones that gave
us welts. And welts were good for getting love.

My father was the first to try water-skiing, his face hitting the
water again and again; he had to be Canadian, more Canadian than
Roy, or even Roy's two sons, who piloted the boat like gods, with
the sun in their limbs and beer in their hands. I remember loving

one of them, his windswept hair at the helm of the boat, his cruel smile. But it can't be true, I was only six.

My father learned to ski in time. He and Roy's two sons tore up the lake's back like men with whips, while Roy sat drinking in the shade, while I played with my brother in the slime and shadow of the underdock. My mother watched us all from the shallows, closing her fingers round the drowning roots of a birch, the one that grew too close to the lake.

Later, the men would build a fire and Roy would send my brother and me for sticks, green ones, mind, or they'll catch and burn. We'd have contests to see who could get their marshmallow the brownest without setting it alight, but mine always caught in the end. I couldn't keep far enough from the flame.

Later still the mosquitoes came, and then the dark. Roy would kick at a beer can with his boot, heavy farming boots he wore no matter what the heat. He'd kick at a can until it rolled away into the blackness and then he'd ask me to sit on his knee. And even though my parents were right there, I felt afraid of his old man's hand, his calloused hand on my skin, turned golden and amphibious by the lake, and his sad, sugary breath, the smell of hops and loneliness in my face.

The bus lurches, the old man lifts his head and looks at me, but my eyes slip away like foxes to the hole in my jeans.

I wish this bus ride were done.

The only reason I ever take the number eleven to this suburb, to the end of the earth, is to see my father. And his wife. In their new house that my father's fixing up and getting just right.

When we all still lived together, the four of us in that small Alberta town, my father fixed up our house until it was a dream. A dream any woman would've died to live in. Any woman except my mother.

A couple of months ago she and I were looking through pictures of that life, the life before I turned ten and we came to the coast and split apart. We found frame after frame of that house, documented, the best a man could do. Cedar shingles like feathers outside and everything warm and lovely within, stained glass, wood and plants. In the yard two cats, two dogs, a treehouse with a swing. All by his hand. Look at that house, my mother said, holding out a photo. It's perfect.

The pictures of that life had been locked away in a trunk, left with my mother because my father couldn't bear the pain. No one had looked at them for a dozen years, as though the four of us were partners in a heinous crime that none would mention and all hoped to forget. So I was surprised at how well I remembered things: the layout of that cedar house, the garden I weeded with my brother, the cats both dead of distemper, the dogs, one left with Roy at the lake because it barked too much, the other brought along, kept by my father in the split, a flesh and fur memory of our life together. I remembered everything right, my mother like a mermaid, braided hair touching the lake alongside her golden arms, my father with a wilder beard, crouched by the fire with smoke in his eyes and an arm around his small son. And me on old Roy's lap, his eyes half shut with drink, his hard hot hand on my knee.

The old man's whispering sad secrets to his chest, reminding me of the last time I came out this way. My father drank one beer after another, as though the bottles were tied to a long, invisible thread. By the time we'd finished our ice cream, he was ready to cry about my mother. He looked into his empty bowl and told me he'd never love another like her, she was the one he'd had his children with, she was the one who knew him for what he was. No, he'd never love another like her, and his wife made noise in the kitchen, clattering the plates into the dishwasher, banging the pots in the sink so she couldn't hear.

The bus doors sigh. The old man lumbers down the steps, and I watch his broad, bewildered face through the glass, the face of a dog left off at the side of the road. I try to imagine he's going to his daughter's home. She'll be angry he's drunk, but she'll give him something to eat and put him to bed all the same.

Tonight it's my father's birthday, so maybe he'll be in better spirits.
   Or maybe he'll have an excuse to drink even more.
   In any case, I've brought a real present, the first one in years. It's a wooden frame with six spaces. I've chosen and pasted six photos

with care, three of myself, two of my brother, one of my father and
the two of us standing at the edge of Roy's lake. All taken before
the split. None of my mother, though she's there in all of them, like
a shadow. No matter how drunk he gets, I'll tell him, look, there
we were. And here we are now.

---

*Alissa York was conceived in Australia and born eighty miles north of
Edmonton. She is currently working on a collection of short stories, as well
as her first novel. She lives with her husband in various British Columbian
settings.*

T. J. Bryan

Sista to Sista

A Story from the Rainbow Side of tha Dark

She's . . . on my face again . . . i'm struggling . . . to lap her up . . . remember to breathe . . . hands . . . grip her so tight she's . . . cryin' out . . . shit . . . her hips are . . . bucking . . . there's juice . . . from pussy smeared over me . . . she's making these little . . . grunting noises . . . she . . . makes me stop . . . just for a second . . . wants to switch positions . . . now she's . . . clamping thighs around my head . . . diving head first . . . down . . . into my hole . . . i'm so fucked up . . . i hear ringing . . . in my . . . ears . . . got two big hand . . . fuls of butt . . . a phone . . . it's ringing . . . tongue flicking . . . sucking . . . under the hood . . . makes my clit . . . jump . . . but phone's ringing . . . ringing . . . she's . . . riding me . . . telephone's . . . ringing . . . she's . . . i'm . . . ringing . . . riiiinnnging . . .

I bolted straight up outta the dream. She's not here. Never was. "*Damn!* It was just starting to get *good*, too." I crawled in the direction of the telephone's ring. It wasn't easy. With all the lights off, my basement was so dark that I couldn't even see my hand in front of my face. There were a few annoying seconds when the sleep in my eyes had me stumbling over unidentifiable pieces of furniture with only the direction of the sound to show me the way.

"Yeah . . . hello." It was Her. I knew it. "Mmmm . . . after last night, you should be tired. What are you doin' callin' me at this hour?"

"I know it's early, but I couldn't wait. You got any more of that sweet stuff you dished out last night?" Her voice was full of laughter.

"Well, I think that could be arranged . . . for the right fee. Think you can handle it?"

"Humm . . . we'll see." Her deep, smooth voice erupted into rich laughter. "Don't shower and don't get outta bed. I'll be right over. And Zeena?"

"Yeah?"

"Make sure you're wet."

I hung up the phone and scrunched back down under the covers to catch a few more zzz's but then I realized there would be no sleeping. Even over the phone her words were getting under my skin. "*Make sure you're wet.*"

Smiling at the thought of last night and salivating with anticipation of what I was gonna be gettin' *real* soon, I wrapped my legs around a pillow and started to rock my hips back and forth. "Yeah, I'll make sure." I rolled over onto my belly cocooning myself more securely in the warmth of the blankets. Thoughts of our first meeting surfaced, sending waves of pleasure over me, cradling me, renewing my memory, leading me back, back to a not-so-distant past. . .

About a year ago I was cursing myself. Promisin' to never attend another wimmin's conference, consciousness-raising session or workshop series again. Helen, one of my co-workers, was supposed to be the shelter's delegate this time round. But she broke her leg the week before the conference was scheduled to begin. And boy did she *evah* work that crutch and cast for all they were worth. Hobbling around, looking miserable and sighing over in my direction at LEAST ten times a day. It drove me crazy the way she was always saying, "God, ain't this just tha fuckin' pits. I wish SOMEONE could take my place at the National Women's Health Awareness Symposium. Gee, I wonder WHO would have the time."

Bold, hunh? Asking ME for favours like we're tight. Her mayonnaise-coloured self was always hovering around my work station. And you can be sure she *never* missed an opportunity to remind me that I was new on the job *and* at twenty-seven, the youngest woman in the place. Her ageist shit is *so* tired. How many times have I heard, "But that was way before your time—" or "When you're older you'll understand—"? *Most* of the wimmin at work get off on treating me like I'm just fresh outta diapers. Like I'm new to adulthood or somethin' and therefore in need of their guidance and advice ALL THA TIME.

I listened to the same lines over and over and over again for

DAYS and the wheels began to turn. "Soooo . . . things are going crazy and she's asking for MY help? What, pray tell, can I do to make her life easier?" Now, it wasn't that I felt *sorry* for her. Noooo. According to my law of the universe, "sorry" was something you felt for three-legged puppies with mange or flat-chested wimmin who buy padded underwire bras. NOT. Helen's a big girl.

I was thinking more about my own silent, slowly simmering case of Strong Black Woman Burnout. I was dreaming about a few days away from work and the fast pace of the city. The thought of five days in the States complete with shopping and new sights started to put me in the conferencing mood. That's when my mouth opened up and I heard myself say, "Enuff with the sad heifer eyes, okay? Let's make a deal: you take on my caseload and I'll give you what you want."

Helen got this crafty look on her face. But before she could make me lose my patience by trying to bargain, I said, "Shut it. This deal is not negotiable. And all sales are final. So take it or leave it." She took it.

And that's how I ended up in another country, well, across the Canada/U.S. border, anyhow, in a hotel with all expenses paid. Sounds great, right? But it wasn't. Girl, I was miserable. Had it up to my eyeballs with the doublespeak and courteous good girls too tight-assed to get upset. How could I have for one second thought that going to a wimmin's health conference would give me a breather?

Girl, *can* you spell b-o-r-e-d? Bored to tears? Bored by the drone of yet another well-meaning presenter's voice? *So* bored my mind was wandering? Helen *must* have known it would be bad. Yeah . . . maybe she did. Since my body couldn't leave, my mind took off instead. I made up this psuedo-James Bond story. Only James was on vacation and I was the star. I've got a whole heap of gadgets and a customized fuchsia BMW that I drive at high speeds. My hands and mouth are busy with a crew of statuesque, dangerous sistas in skin-tight spandex sporting Angela Davis-in-the-seventies 'fros out to HERE. My girls are offing anyone who gets in their way. And Helen? Helen's a double agent for this European drug cartel who had in fact *thrown* herself down the stairs of her own house, *just* so

I would end up being a delegate at this year's conference and die a slow, painful death from chronic boredom.

Back in real time, I felt a twinge of guilt. Monotony aside, I had to admit that this work *was* instrumental to life in wimmin's communities. It's just that I could have done without the long speeches, snail's-pace workshops and power breakfasts where community bigwigs met over vitamin supplements, herbal teas and rice cakes to strategize and drop names. But I just kept repeating Gloria's famous line: "I will survive. I will SURVIVE. I WILL SURVIVE." And so I did.

By the last night, I was starting to feel like a hardened veteran. So I decided to get adventurous. Mistake. Attended a wine and cheese "party" back at the hotel. Second mistake. Well, it *seemed* like a mistake at first. With a full day of films, meetings and note-taking behind me, the sight and sound of schmoozing gone overboard *killed* my appetite. After saying a few polite but extremely brief hellos to some of the women, I located a chair in the far corner of the room and sat myself down.

"Zeena?" I heard my name and looked up to see who was speaking in such luscious tones. "Uh, you don't know me. I . . . was in the Women, Health and Self-Recovery workshop this morning?"

"Sorry, I don't think I remember you . . ." But I wanted to. Sweetness. How could I have missed this? With numerous broad, shoulder-length plaits framing the unblemished chocolate-brown skin of her face and huge, piercing eyes rivalled only by the generous ruby red of her lips, this woman was unforgettable. And I had no shame. I stared and gaped and ogled. Objectifying, eroticizing and yesss, sexualizing, I ate her UP, consuming every detail of this stranger's body, my mind creating unspeakable fantasies as my eyes roamed.

The other woman didn't seem to notice, though. She was trying not to spill the contents of a plastic cup she was holding in one hand while dragging a chair over with the other. "Mind if I join you?

All I could squeeze out was, "Unh—"

She interrupted with, "My feet are killin' me. And where's the food? Crackers and cheese is NOT food." She grinned conspiratorially and added, "I passed a West Indian food place on the way here this morning. It's over on 6th Street. Wanna come?"

"Uh—" I *wanted* to ask her name. But my tongue took this

moment to go on strike. Seems it was stuck to the roof of my mouth with no future plans of forming thoughts into coherent words.

Not to worry, though. The woman—I soon found out her name was Nia—sat next to me and started talking up a *STORM*. She was definitely capable of making enough conversation for both of us. Which was just fine by me.

"So, are you coming?"

Caught off guard, I blurted out the first thought that came into my head: "Not yet." Too late, I realized what I had said and how it must sound.

"Pardon me?" That devilishly sweet smile spreading slowly over Nia's whole face showed she knew *exactly* what I meant. Her eyes toyed with me, offering me a time I wouldn't forget. If things worked out, that is.

Despite Nia's flirtatious ways, there were some things I couldn't quite figure out. For one thing, it wasn't clear if she was a dyke or not. It's not that easy to tell, y'know. My one real friend at work, Leslie, a short blue-Black woman with serious granola-lesbian leanings and reddish locks reaching halfway down her back, always looks for natural hair and sensible footwear. "When you are *confused*, check out girlfriend's *do* and her *shoes*," she always says.

The party gyals have their own methods. You know them. The bar rats. Social butterflies (I prefer to call them social cockroaches). Take my friend Mony, for instance. She's been at it for ten years. She's a predator (her word, not mine). Her territory includes but is not limited to bars, after-hours booze cans and wimmin's dances. I mean, I could be away from the scene for a *serious* amount of time. Weeks. *Months.* Yet when I finally surface she's around. Manoeuvring and bumping off the competition. Spouting the same cheesy lines. Scoping the available selection of potential poonani and possible fuckmates.

This will not do for the activist, community organizing set at *all*. I've seen them putting the moves on sweet thangs at poetry readings and wimmin's marches. Talking about the political but really wanting to explore the *clitoral*. Support groups, collective meetings, I.W.D. marches. It don't matter. For some sista lovas these are the ONLY places to turn up suitable girlfriend material.

And as for me? Lesbians, demos, locks and Birkenstocks don't necessarily add up to a hot time in *my* mind. It's not about places or lines. It's about intuition. Mine is strong, exciting and unpredictable. I've got the power of GAYdar on my side.

You know GAYdar. It's sorta like radar, only it's less mechanical, more biological. Well, actually it's . . . instinctual. GAYdar is everywhere and in everyone. Only it seems to work best for lezzies, bi-people and gay men. GAYdar is about seeing and being seen. It's about knockin' boots and about the hunt for the juice! With it I take in every little detail of a sister's being—the sass in her walk, the roll of her eyes, the flick of her wrist and the cock of her ass. Like a one-hundred-and-eighty-pound flesh, bone and clit computer I collect, compare and collate the information passed on by my GAYdar. And soon I KNOW. If the woman is gay, straight or dancing to her *own* tune. If she's rigid or bending. If she really wants to have it, or somehow can't stand to face it. If she'd welcome it with legs spread wide or run from it eyes squeezed shut in fear. All that knowledge is mine in the wink of an eye.

And chile, it could happen *anywhere*. I could be in a public washroom drying my hands after a good dump or walking down the street surrounded by thousands of people with my head stuck in a book. And all of a sudden GAYdar would be all over me. Raising the hairs at the back of my neck. Freezing my legs in mid-stride. Yanking my head up and around just in time to meet the gaze of the most perfect woman I had *ever* seen. You get the picture, don't you?

The night I met Nia, however, it *seemed* something was jamming the signal. Maybe it was the late hour or the wet throb between my thighs. Whatever it was, my lesbo-finding instincts were seriously outta whack. No matter how hard I tried, Nia remained an enigma, a riddle without an easy answer, a puzzle with a few missing pieces. Which left me with the same unanswered question: if she wasn't into wimmin, why was she being so friendly? Did it really matter? Here she was, bright smile definitely making my day. Talking so fast and sweet just so we could spend some time together. Come to think of it, when *was* the last time a woman, gay, het or bi, paid me any mind? As if in reply to my unvoiced questions, Nia slid out of her chair, saying, "Well, I won't be long. Just gotta go upstairs and change outta these shoes. So . . . meet you in the front foyer?"

The restaurant was only about three blocks away, so we walked instead of cabbing it. Ten minutes later I was comfortably tucked away in one of the restaurant's corner booths with Nia by my side. Our surroundings put me in mind of one of my favourite after-work hangouts in T.O. Same familiar smells, same warm atmosphere, same juke box at the back pumping out Dance Hall tunes. What it lacked in spaciousness it definitely made up for with the food and the people. After four straight days in the company of white wimmin at the conference, I was happy just SEEING some Black wimmin and men. In the restaurant I didn't have to be a lesbian feminist conference delegate. I could be ME. A Black gyal. Even if they didn't know me here, we were all Black people. We would *always* know each other.

For starters there was our waitress, Ce Ce. The two of us hit it off almost immediately. While she was taking our orders, she kept up a steady flow of friendly chatter. With almost no encouragement she spoke quite a bit about her life. Seems she was the seventh daughter from a long line of seventh daughters. They could find lost things. Jewellery. Pets. Unfaithful husbands. She, her mother and her mother before her all received messages in dreams or got *feelings* that just turned out to be right.

Ce Ce didn't give our orders in to the kitchen right away. She stuck around until a tall, brown-skinned man with a scruffy beard and bright smiling eyes came up and wrapped his arms around her from behind. This must be her man, Delroy. We already knew about *him*. He was probably coming from the candy factory where he worked the late shift. We looked on as they hugged and kissed enthusiastically. He greeted Nia and me, then seated himself at a nearby table. Ce Ce left to check on our orders.

"Oh yeah. . ." I could feel myself letting go of all the tension and discomfort that had been accumulating over the past four days. Not meaning to start the violins playing or anything, but I began to get the feeling that Nia was someone I already knew from sometime or somewhere else. Of course we were two of maybe a handful of Black wimmin attending yet another majority white girl conference. But there was more to it than that.

Our conversation went *everywhere*. We huddled over the table, talking like two best friends meeting for our weekly gossip session. You know . . . whose doctor did the most skillful pap smear. Whose parents were divorced or should be. Favourite films. Most hated enemy. Best and worst dates. Most memorable fuck. I took that moment to throw in the "L" word, watching carefully of course to gauge Nia's reaction.

But she was cool. "And? Is this where I run from the room, screaming 'LESBIAN! LESBIAN!' Stopping on the way, of course, to warn Ce Ce *and* her man? Get REAL, Miss Thang!" Seems *her* GAYdar was in excellent condition. She had me pegged back at the hotel. "Seen it, been there, had it. Done *DAT!*"

My lesbian ego was shaken. Here I had thought I was gonna slowly entice Nia over to the rainbow side of the DARK. And lo and behold, she tells me she HAD her first lesbian, a butchy tomboy, at fifteen.

"Her name was Rachel. She was real short. But she had these SHOULDERS. Wide and *strong*. And the butt? The butt was *much*. It had a will of its own! I was addicted to it. Because of the butt, I sent her notes in homeroom for two weeks. I got that butt in the storage room of Home Ec *class* and *BAAMM!* We were all over each other."

"*No!*" I was jealous, wishing I had some teen-aged lesbian story I could drag out for those times when friends start dishing first-experience tall tales.

"Yeah! We did it right there on a pile of scrap cloth and half-finished sewing projects. Was damn uncomfortable with all those needles jabbing us. But we managed. It was just fine. If you know what I'm sayin'. She met me there a few more times. It didn't last long, though. Her family left town later that year. Never saw her again. But *I'm* not a lesbian. I don't put labels on myself like that." Then she says, "I mean, both wimmin and men are attracted to me. You know what I'm saying?"

I bit back a few smart-assed comebacks. My political lesbian alarms were going off, though. What does she *mean* it's just a bedroom issue? Doesn't she know? Doesn't she care that we're fighting for our lives? My inner feminist was goin' crazy. The slogans were flying fast and furious.YOUR SILENCE WILL NOT PROTECT YOU, GIRL-FRIEND. YOU'RE HERE, YOU'RE QUEER. SO WHY WON'T YOU GET USED TO IT? And give me some while you're at it?!

Oh my GOD! Did I say something out loud? I just decided to play it cool, ignore the alarms for the time being and just go with the flow. "Unh . . ." I reached out to stroke her plaits. "I wanted to know . . . who did your braids, anyhow? Looks expensive."

It worked. She relaxed a little and said, "Oh, did it m'self."

"God, I thought I was the only Black woman still into braiding hair these days. Most wimmin seem more interested in puttin' all the hairdressers' kids through university 'cuz they forgot how to do their *own* hair. Hmph." She nodded in agreement. And I exhaled, glad we still had hair in common.

Now, there is no place that Black wimmin, gay or straight, gather that hair don't just come up. Favourite pastime and cursed obsession, we pull it, cry over it, cuss at it, try to forget it and against all odds learn to love it. It's hard, though. What with all those oppressive TV commercials about flowing blonde, brown and red hair and hair so soft, hair so permed, hair so conditioned and easy to curl, we can't *really* be blamed for deluding ourselves with lies about processed hair. How it's so manageable and softer to the touch. *Oooo . . . Alberto. You need to be put out of your misery!* Then of course the Diasporic lesbian feminist layer mixes the story up even more for me. It ain't bad enuff that sistas gotta work out whether to straighten, dread, weave, extend, blow out or *crop*. Noooope. In political circles Black gay gyals are agonizing over *WHY*. Biting their nails down to the QUICK over the pan-African-socio-politico-historical significance of our nappy naps. "Sally straightened her hair last week. D'you think she's having problems decolonizing?" Or: "Rhona's really got her internalized shit together. Have you seen those cute little baby locks she's cultivatin' these days?" AnyWAYS . . . hair is a real BIG thang . . .

Back in *real* time my hair was a *mess*; to call it bed-head would be puttin' it mildly. I yawned and glanced over at my clock radio. Eight fifteen. Well she *said* she'd be right over, but girlfriend runs on G.B.G.T.—Gay Black Gyal Time. I'd be lucky if she got here before one or two. That would give me some time to wake up, comb the hair and get my shit together.

I ran my hands roughly over my nipples one last time. Then I untangled myself from the sheets and went to look for a comb. The naps were feelin' a little brittle so I made a mental note to take some time this evening to oil my tips and roots. With the comb I began to draw a careful path down the middle of my scalp. "Two schoolgirl pigtails will do for now," I said through a mouthful of plastic clips and coloured elastics.

I set to work in front of the bathroom mirror, fingers flyin' at the speed of light. Forming patterns and shapes in my hair that I learned as a child from my mother and aunts. Lost in the rhythmic act of combing and plaiting I smiled in anticipation of Nia's visit. We've been through so much trauma and drama that we could write, produce and star in our own *soap*. Somethin' like, "As the Dyke Tongues Untie," "Dykes of Our Lives" or "The Young, the Flirtatious and the *Lesbian*." Yet, we've survived. Which is a lot more than I can say for some of the *other* dyke duos I know. And we're still here. Still respecting each other's space and feelings. *Still* hot and bothered when we cum together.

I put the finishing touches on the do I created, brushed the teeth and washed the gunk out from the corners of my eyes, all the while chuckling wickedly. Knowing Mistress Nia had *expressly* ordered me to wait for her in bed. Unwashed and undressed. When she sees how *disobedient* and *defiant* I've been . . . chile, sweet *hell* is gonna break loose. And I can't *wait*.

T. J. Bryan is a twenty-eight-year-old Barbadian-born Wicca woman and artist/writer. She's part of De Poonani Posse, a Black dyke cultural production house with a new magazine—DA JUICE! She's also a Fireweed editorial collective member. "Sista to Sista—A Story from the Rainbow Side of tha Dark" is an excerpt from an unpublished book-length work of fiction in progress.

Taien Ng-Chan

Write Me Sometime

Whenever I think of my father, I think of food. I think of the years we spent eating at McDonald's and the Old Spaghetti Factory and pizza parlours galore. From as far back as I can remember, I saw my dad only once a week, when he picked me up every Saturday afternoon to go out for lunch. I'd get to choose which restaurant we'd go to, and then he'd ask me about school, my mother and assorted things that I can't remember now. I was probably too busy eating. My mother did come along with us at first, mainly to keep an eye on me, but she eventually stopped because she didn't want to deal with my father. I don't blame her.

When I turned ten, my six-year-old half sister started joining our Saturday excursions. Suddenly, I had a weekend sibling, which was strange because I had always thought I was an only child. The three of us would argue about where to go for lunch, but as my sister liked the same things I did, it wouldn't take too long for us to decide. Every now and then we'd let Dad choose, but we knew he'd just want to go for dim sum, which we thought was boring.

I used to look forward to these Saturdays because I could eat anything I wanted. As I got older, we started going out for steak and seafood, but for the longest time, I just wanted pizza. My mother never made pizza, or even spaghetti. Sometimes she made pork chops or shepherd's pie or soya sauce chicken and rice, which I liked well enough. But I loved my pizza. Thin crust with extra sauce, sometimes ham and pineapple, sometimes all dressed but no olives. My dad and I were harsh pizza critics: the sauce had to be spicy, and the vegetables cut and arranged just right. An abundance of pineapple was a must, and the cheese had to pull away into long, thin strands between the slices. One particular restaurant failed abysmally to meet our standards and was forever dubbed "The Yucky House of Pizza," which we'd shout every time we drove past it.

After lunch, we'd go bowling, or to the dinosaur park at the zoo, or paddle boating at Prince's Island in the summer, or skating and tobogganing in the winter. Sometimes, Dad would take us to Ikea and spend an hour pretending to look at furniture while we jumped around in the room full of blue and red plastic balls. Other times, we'd go to the bakery at the mall and each pick out two slices of cake, plus a couple for my mom. Chocolate cheesecake, fruit tarts, danishes. We'd make a pot of tea and pretend to have a party. Then, just before dinnertime, my dad and my sister would go home.

The images I have in my head of these Saturdays are blurry, happy pictures that go with my dad's stories like illustrations. There was the time he ate two slices of a pizza and I ate the rest. I must have been only six or seven at the time, and I see myself sitting small in the corner of a restaurant booth with dark brown vinyl seats, a huge pizza in front of me. "The whole pizza!" my dad exclaims every time he brings up that story.

Or the time we went for spaghetti, and the top fell off the container as I was shaking out some parmesan over the spicy meat sauce, spilling a ton of cheese like a snowfall over the entire plate. That's the picture I have, me with the container still in my hand, the lid in the spaghetti. From then on, we made a great ritual of checking the lids every time.

If I could look just at these pictures, I'd think that my childhood was made up of fifty-two happy lunches a year. But somewhere along the way, I stopped looking forward to Saturdays. I'd listen to my sister talk about playing basketball with Dad after supper, or the way they both called grilled cheese sandwiches "grouchy" sand-wiches. Or notice how my sister knew all the songs on the tape of Chinese opera that my dad liked to play in the car. It left me with the taste of something sharp and grey under my tongue, like a tiny piece of rock had slipped into my food. If I wasn't careful, I'd break my teeth on it. Once I told him not to bother coming any more, that I had lots of friends and needed more time to play with them. But I felt sad about it afterwards, remembering how his face had changed. After that, I seemed to go into automatic cheer whenever

I saw him. Our Saturday lunch rituals continued right up until the time I moved out to go to university.

We live in different cities now, and I only see my father once or twice a year, when I come home to Calgary for Christmas or if he happens to come by Vancouver on business. I see my half sister even less, and I'm still apt to think of myself as an only child. I think she feels the same way, because we've never tried to stay in touch.

I don't know why I feel the need to keep in touch with my father, when he wasn't much more in my life than lunch once a week. But somehow I think that the lines have to be kept open. My mom thinks so too, oddly enough.

"Have you heard from your dad lately?" she says every time she phones. "What did he say? You should write him."

And I do write him. I write him longer letters than I write my friends. I write him about what I've been doing, how my classes are going, what projects I've been working on. I sent him the entire movie script that I had gotten funding to write, and the last essay I researched about the effects of Darwinism on Victorian literature. I tell him about newspaper articles I've been reading on the controversy over the age of the universe, and what I've been thinking about our last conversation on artificial intelligence.

My father, you see, is a scientist. More precisely, a geophysicist. When I was younger, he used to tell me he sat at a desk and drank lots of coffee for a living. When I found out that he flew all over the world to look at rocks and stuff, I wanted to be a scientist too. Or an artist. "A scientist or an artist, I haven't made up my mind yet," I used to tell people who asked what I wanted to be when I grew up. In my letters to my dad, I guess I try to be both.

He hardly ever writes back to me, but every so often he calls. Every time we talk, we say that we should write more often, get to know each other better. And then I won't hear from him for another year. I feel as if I'm trying to communicate with outer-space life-forms, my satellite dish sending out signals just in case.

The last time I saw my father was about a year ago, when he was in Vancouver for a business meeting. He called me just before noon and wanted to take me out for lunch. I had already eaten an avocado and tomato sandwich.

"That's okay," Dad said. "You can eat more!"

"Well, maybe we can go for a walk instead," I suggested. "We could go to Stanley Park."

"I can't do too much walking," he said. "I've been having a little trouble with my feet lately. Your dad's getting old, you know . . ."

"Oh, Dad, you're not getting old," I said, as cheerfully as I could. "We can do something else. Maybe we can go to the art gallery. Or what else do you want to see?"

"I don't have too much time," he said. "Why don't we go have lunch anyway? We can go a little later if you like."

So I gave up and let him take me out for lunch. We ended up at a trendy restaurant on Robson Street, since it was close by, and Dad tried to order me everything on the menu.

"How about an appetizer?" he said, poking his finger at the description of the liver paté. "This sounds good. Or how about a salad? That's good for you. How are you eating these days? You should have some soup, too."

"I'm really not that hungry," I said. "I can't eat like I used to. What about you? What are you going to have?"

"I'm not too hungry either. I'll just have a beer," he said. I'd never seen him have a drink before. "Maybe we should've gone to the pub," I said jokingly.

The waiter came over and waited.

"I guess I'll have the spinach salad," I said, handing him my menu. "And a glass of white wine, please."

"I'll have a beer," Dad said. "Any kind."

The waiter nodded and smiled and went away. Dad looked at me funny for a second, probably because he'd never seen me drink before, either.

"Is that all you're having?" he said. "You should have an entrée. The veal looked very good."

"Veal . . .," I said, screwing up my nose. "Dad, I'm a vegetarian."

"Oh. That's right." He scratched his head.

I could see him wanting to debate the issue, just as he had when I first explained to him why I was a vegetarian. I was back in Calgary for Christmas. I hadn't seen my dad or my sister in quite a while, and we were about to go out for lunch when I told them the big news.

"So," he had said, "that means you don't eat meat any more."
My sister looked at me as if I was crazy.

"What about chicken?" Dad asked. "Do you eat chicken?
Seafood?"

"No, Dad, chickens aren't vegetables. Fish aren't vegetables
either."

"What's your reason for not eating meat? It's not just because you
have to kill animals, is it? After all, death is a part of life."

"I know. If you went out and killed your own animal and ate it,
that'd be fine with me."

I had launched into the whole thing about battery cages and
steroids and how you could feed the world with the grain that goes
to feeding cows and how the rainforests of Brazil were being
destroyed for hamburgers. Dad countered each point. We ended by
discussing the impact individuals could make, and why Buddhists
didn't eat meat. My sister just looked on.

Finally, Dad asked us what we wanted for lunch. My sister
suggested pizza.

"Uh," I said, "actually, I don't eat pizza much any more. I try to
stay away from dairy products. Hard to digest."

But there weren't too many places to go to in Calgary, so I
compromised. "Wow," my sister said after lunch. "I never had a
pizza without meat before."

When the waiter came back with our drinks and my spinach salad,
there were bacon bits that I had to pick out. My dad watched me
for a while and fiddled with his beer glass. Then he started what had
become our usual routine.

"So," he began, "what do you think of what's been happening
in the news lately?"

We had an ongoing discussion about politics and the economy
and the state of the world—it gave us something to talk about. These
talks always started and ended the same way. He would ask me what
I thought about recent events, and then we would talk about the
future, the need to adapt to change, the impact of technology. Dad
always got very animated when talking about technology. I would
bring up the need for human responsibility in science, and he would
agree with me wholeheartedly. They were good conversations.

My father likes to debate things, to argue for the sake of argument. My mother said he had wanted to be a philosopher when he was young and idealistic. A lot like you, she said. That was when she first met him. That was before he decided there was no living to be made in philosophy and went into the oil industry.

"Arts," he said to me once, "are for the weekends."

I told him then that I wanted to be a writer.

"Journalism?" he said.

"No, writing," I said. "Stories and plays and stuff."

"Write for the newspapers," he said. "That's what you should do if you like writing."

I told him I would think about it.

But he never did ask me what I wrote about. And I never asked what he thought of the things I sent him, either. Except once, about the Darwin essay.

"Interesting," he said. "Very interesting. Why don't you write a book about the relationship between science and the arts?"

I said I might do that. And we haven't mentioned it since.

By the time I had finished my salad, Dad had convinced me to have dessert. I mulled over the menu, torn between the chocolate hazelnut torte and the blueberry apple flan.

"Aren't you going to have any?" I asked, hoping we could swap bites. Dad shook his head.

"Why don't you get both anyway?" he said. "After all, how often do you get to have lunch with your dad?"

I settled for the flan.

The rest of lunch was spent in polite enquiry. We had run out of politics and technology, so I asked him how his work was, and how my sister was. He asked me how my work was, and how my mother was. She's fine, we both said. Things are going fine.

After I had finished eating, we walked up Robson Street. We passed chocolate shops and pizza joints, and every time I looked in the window of a store, Dad would ask me if I wanted anything. When we passed a frozen yogurt shop he wanted to buy a tub of frozen yogurt for me.

"Yogurt's very healthy," he said. "I want you to eat right."

"But I just ate."

"You can eat it later," he said. "You're a growing girl!"

"Not any more," I said. "I haven't grown an inch in years."

"Remember that time you ate a whole pizza?"

"I was seven years old, Dad."

"A whole pizza! How about getting some pizza now? You can bring it home for dinner."

"That's okay."

"You don't eat much any more. Are you getting enough protein? You have to be careful, being vegetarian."

I nodded and smiled. "Yes, Dad."

We went on like this all the way up the street, with Dad ducking into a store every now and then despite my protests. By the time we reached my apartment, my arms were laden with bags of food. I invited him in, but he said he had had only a couple of hours to spare.

"Write me sometime," he said. "Let me know if there's anything you need."

I closed the door behind him, my insides feeling forlorn and empty. I went into the kitchen to put the pizza in the fridge, the frozen yogurt in the freezer, the chocolate in the cupboard. But I didn't feel like eating again for days.

When I told my mother about Dad's visit, she wanted to know all the details. Where we ate, what we talked about, what he had bought me.

"Did he give you any spending money?" she said. "Well, he should have. He's your father. And he can afford it."

"I don't want him to," I said.

I could hear her clucking her tongue over the phone. "You're his *daughter*," she said. "You shouldn't even have to *ask*."

I haven't seen my father since that lunch, although he did call me a couple of weeks ago. I was out at the time. When I came home, I found my father's voice on my answering machine, sounding almost querulous. He said that he'd call back some other time. I called him a few days later. The phone rang twice before he picked it up.

"Hi, Dad," I said, only to be greeted enthusiastically with my sister's name. "Uh, no," I said. I felt almost apologetic. "It's your other daughter."

"Oh," Dad said. There was a moment's silence, then he cleared his throat. "You sound very much alike."

"Well," I said, as cheerfully as I could. "We are sisters, after all."
The conversation went downhill from there.

"Are you in town?" my father asked.

"No, I just called to say hi. And to return your call."

"Ah," he said.

I asked him how his work was, and how my sister was; he asked me how my work was, and how my mother was. She's fine, we both said. Things are going fine.

Taien Ng-Chan has had poetry and fiction published in several magazines and anthologies, including Out of Place *(Coteau Books),* blue buffalo, Corridors *and* The Orange Coast Review. *She's a good egg, say her friends. Presently she lives in Montreal.*

Mina Kumar

How I Made Love to a Negro

I read a few chapters of Dany Laferrière. You might think I already knew how to make love to a Negro, but I was tired, so very tired, so obviously there was something I was not getting right. My stomach turned and turned.

The first time I read Laferrière, I was sixteen. I found the novel at an alternative bookstore on Queen Street. I was still a virgin. My experiences consisted of two white boys who kissed me and a Sikh who ate my pussy badly. I loved the book. What *profondeur*, what glamour it had, what wisdom about interracial sex. So long surrounded by whites, I saw my dark self easily in Laferrière. I forgot my other selves: my eleven-year-old self getting beaten up by white trash Angel and enormous, West Indian Jasmine; my pussy self of labyrinthine crimson and brown folds so easily crushed; my woman self who would one day feel so culpable because I had inveighed against Driss for having a white wife, and then he left her six-and-a-half months pregnant for a Brazilian from Bahia.

I loved the book because our hero satirizes the white women he sleeps with for their submissiveness, to him and to their illusions. Their desire for him is only a version of imperialist fantasy, and so our hero punishes them with ridicule, sniggering as they do his dishes. I understood how he felt: I was everyone's first Indian girl. One man in Florence while kissing me in a hotel stairwell paused to discuss his passion for Sanskrit philosophy, someone else pulled away from my mouth to ask me why Indian women wear dots on their foreheads. These things happened afterwards, but they are the best examples of what always happened. Except with the Sikh, I guess, but that was too lousy to matter, and he liked me with too much hysteria. By the time I read the book, I was almost wondering if I was subconsciously racist because there were few black men I was attracted to. There had been one Nigerian with incredibly good bone structure who had said, not two feet away from me, that as a rule he didn't like black girls. And even though there were plenty of Indian-black couples at school, the girls were either impossibly fair like Sukhinder or mixed beauties from the West Indies like Anne Mohan, and I knew that for the Nigerian, I was one of the black girls. So you see Laferrière's charm.

Claude, too, called me black. When I protested, he accused me of wanting to be white, so there was nothing left to say. He was the kind of black man whom white women fawned upon, so I was puzzled by his interest in me. He was very "downtown" and hip, had spent half his life in clubs, and whatever I looked like, or however I had lived, I was still a gauche and pudgy middle-class girl awed by the chic I did not have. I was amazed he wanted me, so glamorous did he seem. O.K., also dissolute, but I wasn't going to marry him.

Claude called me black because I wasn't white or yellow, but he differentiated me from the dark-dark-skinned girls. "If I am with a girl that dark," he said, "it's only fucking." I smoothed my pillow, my head turned away; I wasn't used to this side of the fence. "It's not prejudice," he said. "I like black women. I just don't need to lie down next to a jet-black girl who will scare me when I wake up in the morning." I nodded absently. But when I told him I didn't like flat noses, he turned his flattish-nosed face away from me, he said I had been brainwashed by white people.

I met Claude with Joyce at a Japanese bar in the Village. It turned out that this bar was a famed den of iniquity, and everyone we ever mentioned it to knew that it was a hangout for drug dealers. A friend of Joyce's had even moved out of a nearby apartment because of their preponderance. It was common knowledge, only we didn't know it yet. The place was empty except for us, and Claude.

I had never seen anyone quite like him. I had seen dreads on Rastas (and sants) before but his were different: thick, neat locks that fell to his jaw. He didn't have his beard then, and I wasn't sure how attractive I found him. He spent a long time talking in a low voice to Joyce, who was quite tipsy from all the sake she was drinking. I sat making an airplane out of the napkin of Joyce's drink. On the stereo system, Barrington Levy sang, "Two months later, she said come and get your son, because I don't want your baby to tie me down, because you are old, and I am young, and while I'm young, I want to have some fun." Except it was thirteen months later, and I said what are we going to do, because you are an illiterate, unemployed drug dealer and I am young, and while I'm young, I want to have some fun.

I was surprised when he wanted me to write my number on the airplane, and Joyce slurringly told me he liked me. Neither of us thought he would ever call. Whenever I blame Joyce for taking me to the bar, she reminds me that she told me not to go out with him. He was too ornery and too horny, she said. But he was an adventure I was determined to embark upon.

Meeting him for our first date, I eyed another man and the hurt look in his round, brown eyes peeking through his dreads thoroughly seduced me. He is vulnerable, I thought, and I blanched only slightly when his pale, feline friend talked openly about selling drugs as I sat between them in his friend's red jeep. How exotic it was, not the dreads but the clubs and the drugs, like a story I had read in *Christopher Street*, like Henry Miller, like the girls I had despised and admired in high school who wore leopard coats and short-shorts to go dancing all night with strangers, and with eyes half-closed like gay Paris with absinthe and debauchs. Within a certain circumference, I wanted to be debauched.

I was amazed to discover myself pregnant. First of all, I was almost religious in my use of condoms, I wasn't promiscuous and I didn't like babies. I had always said that my womb would reject the idea. But I soon discovered my womb held six millimetres of risk, stupidity, hunger and lust, six millimetres of us. My days were spent in my bed, staring at the ceiling, anxious, stomach churning, nauseated. My head felt dull and heavy, but my senses were filed sharp. The salsa played by people in the building opposite mine seemed to come from speakers built into my pillow. Fire engines screamed up my legs. In the distance, I could hear what simply could not have been—a man saying, "Allahu Akbar," over and over again. And smell! Paint varnish and chicken soup and my own juices skewered me with their odor. I was nauseated and dizzy from the smell of toothpaste and orange soda and exhaust fumes. Almost any food made my stomach turn, but I dreamt helplessly of garlic rasam and porichche kute, helplessly and hopelessly.

I remembered Barbara Pym as innocuous, but reading *Quartet in Autumn* was depressing. It hardly distracted me from my anxiety about death. Before I was certain I was pregnant, I thought I was going insane. I was obsessed with death, the snuffing out of my bright, beautiful consciousness, the uncertainty of every day. I picked out therapists from the phone book and begged them to tell me what was wrong with me. They took my money and asked about my childhood. I sat immobilized in restaurants over plates of jerk chicken, wondering about a chicken's consciousness. I prayed—not to God, since I had no faith—but prayed Claude would come and save me.

Finally, I took a taxi to the Japanese bar he still hung out at, though he had long since stopped working there. I clutched the seatbelt sure that the car would veer off the road, sure that I would die, sure that the headlights of cars passing in the opposite direction were turning towards me and coming closer and closer. I wanted to tell the driver to slow down, but that was so out of character that I simply couldn't do it. The orange paper lantern outside the bar grew brighter and larger. I paid the driver, and lurched out into the rain, skidding in my heels.

I had known Claude for slightly over a year by then. He had left me in the spring, a week before he was supposed to return the three hundred dollars he had borrowed (but not used) to pay off his suspended driver's licence, and a month and a half after he had hit me with my telephone until my lips and nose were bloody. To tell the truth, months earlier I had kicked him in the face in a fit of rage, and a few days after he hit me, he was mugged and those thick lips of his were bloodier than he had made mine. I took him back when he called me at 6:00 A.M. after the mugging mostly to see how badly off he was. "You don't care, do you?" he said, sinking into my bed. I sat on the futon, laughing. "I care about as much as you cared when you hit me," I said, which of course was far from the truth.

When he tried to come home in the fall, it was easy to forgive the beating which was not foreshadowed or repeated, and which was punished by karma in seemly haste. I could turn a blind eye to the unpaid debt because he so often said he would repay it—"I wouldn't talk to you if I didn't mean to repay it," he would say—I could dismiss it as merely irresponsible. I could think around anything that I didn't like because I wanted him to take me in his arms. Claude had a genius for cuddling, and the equipment to match: broad shoulders, strong arms, a hard, flat chest with tiny little nipples like brown dots. I loved sleeping next to him, my arm tightly wound around his waist, head on his chest, leg over his leg, rubbing my mound against his thigh for comfort or raking my hand through his dreads.

It wasn't just cuddling—there were memories I could summon up which tempted me with their warmth. Claude bringing me ginger ale and Fisherman's Friend cough drops when I was sick. The time I told him about someone else's lovely eyes, and he said in his butterscotch voice, "I have nice eyes." Once, I was drunk and bawling that I knew he would rather be with a white girl, I apologized through drunken sobs for not being white, and he said, drawing me to him, that the girl he wanted was a beautiful Indian.

Claude said plainly what could have been the lines in a song. "You make me feel hurt," he once said, "and you know I love you." And artlessly, he uttered clichés which were fresh in his mouth. When I asked him why he came to my house only to sink wordlessly into slumber—or rather I screamed, "You don't come here for me at all. All you want is a bed to sleep in. Why are you in my house?"—he said, simply, "You do something to me." Claude made me feel, finally, understood. When I was helplessly hungry, he cooked rice and vegetables, saying, "I'm your Daddy, and I'm going to take care of you." The time after we broke up when Michelle and I ran into him at the coffee shop, he said hello, and he left, only to return to me sitting at the counter, only to leave, only to return again. He did this dance five times before he finally asked if he could come home with me.

Yes, eventually, in the fall, the leaves fell to the ground, and he tried to come home again. He claimed he had never left. I let him into my bed, but I would turn his lines onto him, this Laferrière hero, his skinny black dick his access to the world, who said to me when I asked why I should wash his clothes or buy him presents or why he never took me out, "I fuck you, don't I?" So for weeks, I told him I couldn't afford his sex. At any kind gesture, caress, I moved away, explaining I had no money to buy it. He held me close to him all night, rubbing my hip as I had once longed for him to do, but I declined to be his girlfriend. I told him about every handsome man I knew until he clasped his hand over my mouth. But finally, he said, "I'm lonely, I miss you" and kissed the top of my head and I opened myself. He came hurtling in, telling me how tight I was and how he knew I had been faithful to him—which I had been, somewhat accidentally—and he told me he wouldn't come inside me and he called out my name. Over and over again. And then he came.

It was the first time anyone had come inside me, and not being in love, I was repulsed by his semen, but I felt too languorous for a fight, and besides it was all over. Of course, it had also just begun.

I took up the fight days later. I screamed and screamed until my throat was raw, naming his every wrongdoing. All I wanted was for him to pull me to that chest, sponge up my rage, but instead he put on his shirt and left, wordlessly.

For weeks I heard nothing from him. I was sure he would call, but he didn't. That accoutrement of drug dealers, his beeper, was no longer in service even before that night. I didn't know how to reach him when the time came except to stand out in front of the bar, pregnant, in the pouring rain like in some hokey country song. He stood under the awning.

He waited impatiently for me to start and finish what I had to say. He didn't have the beard which made him look as old-fashioned and kindly as his name. "I think I'm pregnant," I said. He shook his head. It's not possible because he used a condom. It's not possible because he no longer wanted me and I was using it as a ruse to win him back. He told me he wouldn't talk to me unless I paid the gas for his car. I gave him what money I had and he drove me home, on his way to another bar. I abased myself because of my new reason and all the old reasons, but he wouldn't stop, wouldn't talk, wouldn't stay the night. That was it, I thought, but what was it?

Often, I missed him, like when I watched a video with Bobby Brown entwined with a lovely girl on a beach. "If it's not good enough, I can work harder," he sang. It's not good enough, and he's not working at all. I watched the video enviously, yearning for that embrace, flesh against flesh, the warmth and womblike comfort of Claude lying between my thighs, and until I remembered the jab of the needle inside me.

I rose, restless. I called just about everyone I knew, on the other coast, in other countries, to engage them in a conversation about death. "It could strike so suddenly and the spark of life is extinguished," I said. I was often afraid to go to sleep. When my stomach turned, I didn't know whether it was my fear or some physical problem. My fear became a physical problem. "I don't want to die," I would say. I calmed the panic partially by realizing that I wouldn't know, that it would be like fainting, or being knocked unconscious. I was anxious, waiting for the blow to be struck.

Other times, I talked about Claude. It took days but he had called me eventually. He said he wanted me to have the baby and give it to his grandmother. When I had elicited his comment that night in the rain, he had snarled, "What should I say? Let's go buy a ring?" I had put my hand out to touch the glass wall of the bar. He had continued, his voice more gentle, "Are you going to have an abortion? You are a child and not ready to have a child, and I'm not ready to take care of a woman and a child." By the time he called me, he had decided it was about time some woman had a kid for him. I no longer cared. He was calling from a pay phone, and was about to get cut off. "I'll call you back," he said. He did. The next night. I hung up on him. In the morning, I went to New Haven, to stay with Michelle, to try to put an end to the problem we had caused.

The abortion was more pain than I had ever experienced, the injection to numb me was like a drill thrust into my vagina. The doctor hushed my screams, saying I'd frighten the other patients. I vomited and wept and went home. My skin boiled until I was dizzy. I stumbled into the Emergency Room, waited all day with my fever, whimpering. The other women stroked my forehead, brought me cups of water. I went back to the clinic to have my womb scraped again. I sat in the recovery lounge afterwards, bleeding, Ashford and Simpson cooing on the radio, thinking of my last conversation with him. I had raged, "You hit me, you took my money, you made me pregnant and you gave me a disease. What's next? Are you going to murder me?"

He had paused. "You couldn't wait to yell at me, could you?"

"I don't ever need to hear from you again," I had replied, banging the phone down.

My friends cheered when I told them about it, as if it was the end of the story. But before returning to New Haven for another abortion, I left Michelle's number on my answering machine message and asked him to call. Michelle was quite displeased at all the phone calls I got. None of them were from him.

"Forget him!" Michelle cried out, worn from the demands I was making on our friendship: more days of staying with her, the nursing I demanded, the wretched conversations about dying, how it felt to be in his arms, loving Claude, the neediness I felt. I fell silent. I didn't explain why I talked, because she knew why, and she didn't explain why she was fatigued of listening, because I knew why.

My body, that instrument of pleasure we had played, Claude and I, had become a fragile, crumbling, mortal case for a queasy stomach and liquid shit and a heavy head. I couldn't read or watch television for fear of coming across death and so I stuck to romantic videos and felt my buzzing anxiety compounded by dull aches. All I wanted to assuage my fears of death was his love, as illogical as that may seem.

I hadn't seen him since that night he drove me home and he hadn't slept next to me since the night we had fought. I wanted him in that desperate, ashamed way that a starving person wants someone else's leftovers in a garbage can. I wanted him the way a baby wants to feel strong loving arms. Only thinking of him and the sadness it brought to the back of my throat stopped me from thinking about dying.

I thought of Dany Laferrière. I had found Claude exotic. Because of him, I had read Jacques Roumain, and the lines had meant something: *Vers vous je suis venu avec mon grand coeur rouge, et mes bras lourds de brass es d'amour.* I bought Claude a mustard shirt and made countless pots of spaghetti and bought bottles of wine. I had sucked his cock, well, and he wouldn't even kiss my breasts unless I whimpered and begged. I had been impressed by certain of his pronouncements and I had asked him if I was disturbing him when I clanked his dirty dishes as I washed them. I had liked his dreads.

At the end of our first date, we sat in a diner, eating hot bagels with melting, salty butter, and I, for the first time, touched his hair. I raked my fingers through the woolly locks and massaged his head. He was uncomfortable at first, because he was used to women—white women—liking his dreads. I understood how he felt, I was weary of compliments on my eyes, long hair. Soon, he shifted his legs, because the way I was touching him was making him hard.

Sometimes he would say that I was using him for sex. "Sex we have, where you come and I don't?" I would respond. But other times, he would say that he wouldn't go out with white women because they couldn't love him. But he treated me not much differently than Laferrière's hero treated his white girls. And reading the book again, I wonder which of the white women were listening attentively because they were impressed a black man could speak intelligently, and which were genuinely interested, which didn't want to disturb him because the sight of a black man reading was a colonialist exemplar, and which didn't want to disturb him because they were polite, which were using him for the sexual skill they presumed him to have, and which loved him. It's all very to well to tell us, *Comment faire l'amour avec un nègre sans se fatiguer*, but that is only half the story. I took such a long time to come to this, but I am no longer sixteen, and I need more than to know how to make love to a Negro. How do you make a Negro make love to you back?

Mina Kumar was born in Madras, and came to Canada at the age of ten. She is the author of HOLE.

this is for real

Eufemia Fantetti

The Curse

My house is cursed.

There was this man, a young man, but older than me, I guess maybe even a teen-ager, and he hung himself in the bathroom, my mamma tells me. She's seen him. When she comes in to say *buonanotte* sometimes she says, "Truth or lie?" and I always say Truth. She says I can read the lies by myself anyway in this book my godmother Luisa gave me, *My Book of Fairy Tales and Fables*. My dad says it's all stupid, what my mamma's telling me is all lies, but I've seen him too.

One night Anna came to sleep over and we sat in the hallway and stared into the bathroom, daring him to come out. Anna screamed first but I saw him when she started screaming. Then my dad yelled at us both for waking him up when he had to go to work early the next day.

But we saw him.

We agreed that he had blond hair and was really kinda cute except for the blue tongue hanging out.

Sometimes when Anna stays over she goes, "Truth! Truth!" too, but when we're alone she says, "I bet that was a lie." I know she's just scared.

Anna's dad came to our house once and yelled at my mom when she was putting up the laundry. He said Mamma was upsetting Anna and Anna was having nightmares from the stories she told. When he left Mamma said, "*Va bene*. They Portuguese they donno nothing."

My mamma knows a lot of things. The kinds of things no one else knows about, or maybe they just don't care. My dad says it's crazy. But Mamma knows someone's spying on our family. When she finds them, they'll be sorry. Mamma says she's gonna put them in the hospital if they don't watch out. You better believe she'll do it too.

My neighbourhood is cursed.

Angela Frazzano died at the swimming pool on Saturday and she was only a year older than me and Anna. She wasn't even running or nothing and no one even saw her till she was already dead.

"Doing the Dead Man's Float," Anna says.

I'm not allowed to go swimming, which Anna thinks is funny because I don't know how to swim anyways but I just wanna go hang out with everybody, otherwise there's nothing to do. I'm not even supposed to go sit near the pool and watch them have fun.

I went to see Angela, though, because Mamma made me. She thinks it's important I learn about life from looking at Angela's dead body. My dad got mad. He thought it was stupid and I would have bad dreams. They were fighting about it until Mamma broke some dishes on the floor to show how important it was to her. Dad gave up. I guess he knew I'd already seen worse in our own bathroom.

They put her in her first Communion dress, which I didn't think was such a good idea. Angela Frazzano sat right beside me for Communion Mass when we got the body and everything of Christ, and I didn't want to remember her sticking her tongue out for Jesus and dead both in the same dress.

I had to kiss her hand and she felt more like plastic than Anna's new birthday Barbie.

Angela's big brother Luciano grabbed the coffin at one point and his dad had to pull him away. He was trying to get in the coffin with her. He blames himself, everybody says, because he almost went to the pool with her but changed his mind at the very last minute.

"Did she look gross?" Anna's all jealous she didn't get to see a real dead body, specially of someone she knew.

"Nope." I can't tell her that Angela felt like plastic. I don't think she'd believe me anyways and then she'd go home and tell her dad and I bet he'd come back. His face was pinker than Barbie's car.

"Barbie's pregnant," Anna says.

She pulls off all of Barbie's clothes and has her sitting with her legs out in front and her arms too. It's like Barbie's trying to hold her stomach but she can't so she just hugs the air in front of her.

"How did she get pregnant?"

"How do you think, stupid?"

"You left Barbie and Ken alone and naked when I wasn't there?" I didn't care to see Angela dead, but I did wanna see what happened with Ken and Barbie naked.

"Because you're a retard when it comes to this stuff." Anna's still mad at me from when she gave me *The Happy Hooker Goes Wild* and I gave it back to her after reading only ten pages. She had to go to all the trouble of getting it from her brother and then I didn't even get to the part about the German shepherd. Her brother Carlos wanted to know if I liked the book and he kept bugging me about it. But I figure if Carlos won't explain why he puts french fries on his vanilla ice cream, I don't have to explain how the book made me feel.

"*Ma che fai?*"

Anna kicks Barbie under my bed but too late. My mamma saw her naked and I'm sure she knew she is pregnant too. Since Ken and Barbie aren't even married yet, well it looks bad. Anna and me playing with sinners.

"*E pronto da mangiare.*"

Mamma stands in the doorway. When I walk past her I can feel the heat from the kitchen. She always smells like pasta and lemon-scented Pledge.

Anna screams, and I turn around expecting to see the guy from the bathroom. But it's Mamma.

She's choking Anna.

Then I can't hear Anna scream any more so I start screaming and my dad comes running.

Mamma joins in the screaming, yelling, "*Figlia di puttana!*"

Dad hits Mamma so hard I can feel it in my feet. Anna falls down coughing and wheezing.

"Are you okay? What happened?"

"You—" Anna's breathing okay again. "Your mother's crazy!

Everybody says so!" And she gets up and runs outta my house. I go after her for a bit saying stop! wait up! but I know I can't go all the way. I'm afraid if I go to her house her father and brother and maybe even her mother will choke me back.

I want to go anyway, to explain to Anna's family what I know really happened. I've heard enough truths to know it was possession. Maybe Angela's mad because Anna didn't go pay her respects. Or maybe it was the guy in the bathroom. I think he gets lonely.

I'm cursed.

Two times actually, but I pray to God and say thank you it's not three times, because that would be very bad luck. This lady my mother took me to see says one time isn't even a curse at all, just bad luck, but I still count it.

The first curse is no one will talk to me at school any more. Anna told everyone that my mother was an insane murderer type of mother and she had the marks to prove it.

The second one my mamma calls the big curse. I was supposed to tell Anna when I got it, but I can't now because she won't talk to me at all. She doesn't even want her pregnant Barbie back.

This lady, Olga, tried to help with the big curse. My mamma told her I was in too much pain. Olga gave me a hard-boiled egg and told me I had to bury it in the backyard. We don't really have a yard, though, just one giant tomato garden. She freaked out a little when she heard that and yelled at us as if we were deaf or old people, "NO! NOWHERE NEAR THE TOMATOES! CAPITO?" Mamma said we could put it near the parsley and plant it for the next full moon. Then she begged Olga to pray for me and to give me some charm. My mamma says the spirits of the dead have been following people since Angela Frazzano died. She says they're following all the girls but she's specially worried for me. Mamma thinks Angela herself is following me.

Sometimes I pretend Angela is right behind me, like a guardian angel you can't see even when you make yourself dizzy from turning around so fast. At night I move my bed away from the wall so she won't feel squished just in case she really is there.

But there's definitely another spirit following me around, the mean spirit of Brenda MacDonald. Ever since she and Anna became new best friends from teaming up for murder-ball in gym, I can't walk home slowly any more. I kinda run the whole way. Brenda failed grade four last year, so she's bigger and faster, and sometimes I end up in the ditch. When I get home my mom's always waiting for me at the door.

"*Ma che è successo?*"

I can't really tell her because if she goes and chokes Brenda and kills her, then I'll never have another friend for as long as I'm alive. I tell her that I fell, that it felt like someone pushed me but when I looked behind me no one was there.

She knows I'm lying.

I can tell from the way she looks at me when she thanks Olga for the charm. It's a crucifix I have to wear over my heart. Olga said nothing could be done about the big curse if the egg didn't work but the bad spirits wouldn't bother me any more.

Some nights I can hear him, swinging and struggling. And then there's this noise like someone cutting him down and he falls.

I wake up when he calls my name, but I can't get into the bathroom. I push against the door, imagining his body on the other side. When I do get it open a bit, I can see Mamma lying stretched out on the tiles. He is standing guard over her.

My dad calls the ambulance and we wait in the front hallway. My dad says it's probably demon possession, but I know he's just trying to make me feel better. He doesn't believe in any of that stuff, even though he says this is a special case.

"... *è malata*," he says.

Mamma has to go to Saint Joseph's and she won't be back in time for Easter. On Good Friday she won't even wake up in her own home. We can go visit on nameless Saturday.

She's in this part of the hospital where no one walks, they all shuffle. If Mrs. Cox were there I can imagine she'd be yelling, "No shuffling! Walk like ladies and gentlemen!" Mrs. Cox is nuts about turning the grade five class into polite little ladies and gentlemen. She says it's a thankless task.

It's stuffy hot in Mamma's room and smells like somebody peed their pants but the window only opens three inches. My dad moves like Hot Potato from one foot to the other. If there was a breeze he'd fall over. My mother just looks old.

She wakes up and looks right at me. I try to stop my brain from thinking anything because I know she can read my mind.

"*Mi hai rovinata*," she says. She starts to cry and she won't stop. Then she starts to curse everybody and everything. She curses our house and my dad for taking her away from Italy. She curses Christopher Columbus for discovering America. She means Canada too.

"But the Vikings were here first," I say, thinking she should know. We just learned about it in Social Studies, I tell her.

She says get out. And don't come back.

At church the next day I want to light a candle for Mamma's soul, even though Dad says I can't. She's not dead, he says, and he gets on his knees to pray. He wants to talk to Father Michele about coming to bless our house. It would make her happy, he says, and maybe bring us some peace. But it's too busy with everyone trying to wish Father Michele a Happy Easter. Father Michele says, Yes! Thank you! God go with you and I'll see you at Christmas!

He's very funny for a priest.

That night, like I knew he would, the man from the bathroom comes to me. I wake up and he is standing at the edge of my bed, staring at me. His head is completely on his stiff left shoulder, but he uses his free arm to show me I should go with him.

I feel weird in front of him in just my nightgown. I know if my dad wakes up he'll kill me for having a guy in my room, dead or not. I'm not even allowed to have a boyfriend until I'm eighteen. The guy smiles at me like he knows. And from the way his head tilts I can almost pretend he's checking me out, which is more than any guy alive has ever done.

I follow him slowly down the hallway. I follow him right to the backyard. When he reaches the section where the tomatoes are, he turns around and looks at me, all lonely. I'm thinking if only he had met me in time some things would be different.

"What's your name?" I ask him. "I'm Mia. How come you killed yourself?"

He looks at the ground, right where we buried the egg. He smiles at me and then he fades out till I can't see him any more. I know he's not coming back.

I stare at the empty garden.

When the tomatoes are ready, later in the summer, maybe I can take one and spread it over our door like the lamb's blood in the Ten Commandments.

Maybe that would protect us.

I asked my dad if he thought Mamma had broken a commandment, did she try and kill Anna. He said he didn't know. Things are not going to be like before, when my mamma knew everything. Because when she gets back, Dad says, things are going to be different around here.

As a young girl Eufemia Fantetti got the idea that writers made a lot of money because her father bought her so many books. This story is for him. Previous publications include "The Last Moon" in Concrete Daisy *and* Contours.

Lucy Ng

Yellow Sleeve Princess

My mother always declared that she had come from a good family in China. She did not remember the family home—they had moved from the village to the city when she was very young—but she said that someone had once shown her a picture of it, and that it had a gently curving rooftop and a courtyard in the middle. At one time, long before my mother's birth, the Chans had been a banking family with extensive estates.

When she spoke of this past, I imagined a house with rooms and rooms furnished with rigid, lacquered, hardwood furniture, walls hung with silk. In the courtyard, I saw a pond filled with shimmery, gold-skinned carp. If I strained, I could hear the bright laughter of the servant girls in the summer, smell the faint perfume of peach blossom in the air.

Ever since I could remember, my mother kept a small black and white photograph of herself on her bedroom dressing table. It was a picture taken of her, at age twenty, a few months before her marriage to my father. Even though she was the sole subject, the photograph was an engagement picture of sorts, my mother explained to me, one that was sent to her future in-laws in Vancouver, my paternal grandparents, for inspection and approval.

The young woman in the picture had shoulder-length hair that curved softly around her face and a shy smile. Despite the girlish hesitancy of her expression, she looked out at the camera with bright, steady eyes. It was an image of my mother that I held close to my heart, one of her before the disappointment she felt at my father's death had extinguished the light in her eyes.

In the photograph, she was wearing an elegantly styled jacket with a short skirt and high-heeled pumps that showed off her slim ankles.

The outfit was a new one, purchased with some of the money her father had given her for a trousseau. Their family did not have much money by that time, my mother said, but an elderly aunt had persuaded my maternal grandfather that the trousseau was an absolute necessity. An auspicious event such as a wedding came only once in a lifetime, the old woman said, and thus the occasion ought to be celebrated in a manner that reflected most favourably upon my family's honour and standing.

Last summer, at the last moment, I was invited to the wedding of an old high school friend. My mother offered to lend me something to wear since most of my clothes were still in my apartment in Toronto. When she brought the jacket and skirt out from her battered brown suitcase with the rusting hinges, I recognized it immediately as the suit she had worn in that photograph of long ago. It was made of a fine, lightweight wool, a pale robin's egg blue with a band of cream around the lapels and sleeves of the jacket. The label on the inside said that it was designed and sewn by Regency Tailors, Kowloon, Hong Kong. The suit was impeccably cut and stitched, something I could picture the young Jacqueline Kennedy wearing, a costume fit for a modern-day princess.

I slipped on the jacket and buttoned it up. It was too tight for me under the arms. I managed to zip up the skirt, but then I couldn't button the waistband.

"How did you fit this, Ma?" I asked her suspiciously. "How much did you weigh when you married?"

"About seventy-five pounds, I think."

I groaned. "No wonder. I'm a good twenty pounds heavier than you were then."

"Well," my mother said, miffed. "I was only trying to help you. I don't know why you didn't bring more of your clothes home with you. How much longer do you expect to stay out there in Toronto? How many years does it take to do a Master's degree, anyhow? It's costing a fortune in airfare and long distance phone calls."

I bit my lip. I considered reminding her that when I called her during the school term, we would only talk for about five or ten minutes at a time. "I called to see how you are," I would say when she picked up the phone.

"Good, what about you, are you eating regular meals? Do you

have rice once in a while? How's school?" Then, after a bit, she would get flustered and say, "We should get off the phone soon. This must be costing you a fortune. You know the telephone company charges by the minute, Rose."

I would feel annoyed then, and get off the phone with a curt good-bye. Usually, afterwards, I would regret my hasty action. It was silly of me to let her anxiety about money get in the way of our conversation. I knew that she missed me. Every now and then I received care packages—Chinese sausages, dried mushrooms, almond cookies, even plums from the fruit tree in our back yard. I had learned, long ago, that in Chinese families, mothers and fathers gave candy and cookies instead of kisses and hugs.

I stared at my reflection in the mirror. I felt a little depressed that the suit did not fit me. It was a beautiful colour—perfect for the wedding. Yet, somehow it seemed appropriate—the past and the present never fit together so neatly. I was always having to make revisions.

When I was young, I had difficulty connecting the pretty young woman in that photograph with the woman I called my mother. The woman I knew never wore dresses, only shapeless sweaters and polyester pants with elasticized waistbands plucked from the clearance tables of the Army and Navy Discount Department Store on East Hastings in Vancouver. Her hair was cut short and permed into frizzy curls; her hands were rough and red from washing dishes and scrubbing down the counters at the restaurant where she worked at the corner of Pender and Main in Chinatown.

Sometimes I went to visit her at the Maple Leaf Cafe during recess at Chinese school. The air in the restaurant was always thick with steam and smoke. The smoke came from the brown-suited old men who belonged to the benevolent societies in the surrounding buildings. They sat smoking cigarette after cigarette, calling out to each other across the room while the waitresses moved in and out of the clouds of smoke, plunking down fresh pots of tea, egg custard tarts and dishes of shrimp and pork dumplings.

My mother presided over the front counter with its row of red vinyl bar stools kept warm by a host of regulars. There was Mr. Chan, the balding morose barber from across the street, Mrs. Jung, the old woman who sold Chinese newspapers at the corner of Pender and Gore, two brisk lady social workers who walked over from Hastings Street, and a whole group of others, the youngish clerks from the banks and stores in the area.

She kept busy—pouring coffee, filling orders, wiping down the counters and the glass display case filled with apple, Boston cream and lemon meringue pies, chocolate eclairs and parfait glasses filled with cubes of red Jell-O topped with whipped cream. Every hour or so, the red-faced owner, Mr. Lee, emerged from the kitchen with steaming trays of buns. Some of them were filled with minced barbecued pork, others with a mixture of pork, chicken, preserved duck egg, mushrooms and bamboo shoots. There were sweet buns as well, filled with black lotus seed paste. It was my mother's job to transfer the buns from the trays to the gleaming metal drawers behind the counter to keep them warm. The customers trooped in all day, ordering a dozen at a time. My mother filled the cardboard boxes, then tied them with red string. The customers had no idea, and she did nothing to suggest, that once she had been something else.

My mother's family left the village for the city of Canton when she was five or six. Then, a few years later, in the late fifties, they moved again. First to Macao and then Hong Kong. With the Communist "Liberation" it had become dangerous to be a member or a former member of the bourgeoisie. They had escaped with only a suitcase or two and my grandmother's marriage gold sewn inside the linings of the children's coats.

Over the years the jewellery was sold off piece by piece so that there was enough money for food and rent during the times my grandfather was late in sending money home. He had gone to Lima, Peru, to work in a restaurant. My grandmother found a job sewing men's shirts in a textile factory on Kowloon Road. Even the children worked. My mother and her sister called on the clothing factories after school, asking for piece work, odds and ends. They went home loaded down with bundles of cloth coats. Late at night, after they had finished their school work, they stayed up and worked on the coats, snipping off stray threads and sewing on buttons. They were paid a few pennies for each bundle. Their brother had a job making deliveries for an herbalist and tea store owner. He was paid hardly anything at all, but sometimes the customers gave him tips. For amusement, my mother and her siblings made up stories, played cards and mahjong for melon seeds.

"Your grandmother wept after the last gold ring was sold," my mother said. "She said it was wrong to leave nothing for the children, to have no dowry for us when we married. Then she regretted that we had not brought more with us when we left. She said that we had left so many things behind."

"What did you leave behind?" I asked.

"Oh—I don't know. Some pieces of jade and ivory. A few pictures. Silk. Linens—embroidered sheets, pillowcases, quilt covers."

"What happened to them?"

My mother shrugged. "I suppose the house was looted after we left."

I did not like this story as much as the one about their escape from China. That one was full of intrigue, mystery, triumph. I was dismayed that my mother had given it all up so easily, trading precious rings of jade and ivory for a handful of melon seeds. I wanted to bury my face in the folds of those embroidered sheets, to trace my fingers over each sculpted flower petal, each bird feather. I wanted to lie beneath a quilt on which dragons danced.

Instead of battling in the waters of the Middle Kingdom, the dragons of my imagination were harnessed to decorate the red pillars of the Dragon and Phoenix Food Store, or Yuen Fung Foods, in Chinatown. Pronounced in English, all the shop names were ugly monosyllables—Hing Loong, Sun Wah, Gum Fa. The clanging sounds of these words echoed in my ears, hard and sharp like the word "Chink."

I had only been called that name once before, when I got into a scuffle with a group of three girls on the way home from school. I had been walking with my head bent down because I was busy skimming the back of the new paperback I had just borrowed from the school library. I did not pay much attention to the trio of girls smoking cigarettes and walking towards me with their black leather purses slung over their thin arms. I was not sure if I actually bumped into them or not, but the next thing I knew I was lying on the sidewalk and they were punching me. "Watch where you're going stupid Chink or next time you won't be so lucky." Their blows were not hard enough to really hurt me, but I felt stunned that I, with no effort at all, had moved them to such hatred.

Often, while waiting for my mother when she was shopping inside Yuen Fung, I would lean against the dragon pillars, my back pressed to the peeling gilt scales. I learned to be patient. My mother was not a careless shopper. She took her time sorting through the piles of snow peas for the youngest, most tender pods. She weighted each mud-covered preserved duck egg gently in the palm of her hand before putting it in the bag. She boasted that none of the butchers would dare parcel up a piece of meat for her that had too much fat or bone. They knew that she had sharp eyes.

Once, when I was leaning against these pillars, I saw one of my classmates walking towards me. Her name was Melanie Stewart. She sat two seats in front of me in our grade four class, but I had never really spoken to her before. I thought she was beautiful with her pale hair and freckles. In my opinion, the freckles looked like little flecks of gold dust against her white skin. She always wore lacy white blouses and jumpers or wool sweaters with pleated skirts. Even her underwear matched—white cotton camisoles and panties with a pink rosebud motif. When I saw her changing during gym class, I felt doubly ashamed of my own underwear. I always sat on the bench of the girls' changing room, keeping my blouse or sweater on until I had pulled on my shorts. My underpants were cut and sewn from the rough printed cotton of fifty-pound rice bags. "Couldn't we just go out and buy some?" I pleaded, when my mother was bent over her sewing machine stitching them up. She only clicked her tongue and said, "Why waste perfectly good fabric? These will be fine. What difference will it make—who will see them? They are only worn on the inside."

The rice bag underwear did make a difference to me, but I did not know how to explain it to her without sounding frivolous, petty and ungrateful. As a young girl, my mother had survived civil war, food shortages, the death of a parent. How could I tell her that I could not bear the scratchy feeling of the rough cotton against my bare skin?

I darted behind the pillar and pretended not to see Melanie, but she had already seen me. She waved at me.

"Hi, Rose."

"Hi."

"What are you doing down here?"

I flushed and stared down at my sneakers. "My mother's shopping."

She scanned the entrance of the store as if to look for my mother. A clerk had just unpacked a crate of dried salt fish. "*Dai kam ka, dai kam ka,* big reduction!" he shouted. Several women crowded around him, grabbing at the fish. My mother pushed her way to the front of the crowd.

"You can't see her," I said. "She's inside." I looked down and pulled at the drawstring of my jacket. I prayed fervently that my mother would not call me over to help her with her packages when she went inside to pay for the fish.

"Oh!" Melanie seemed disappointed. "Well—this is my mother."

"Hello," I said.

Mrs. Stewart frowned. "What's all the commotion about? Why is everyone crowding in?" She wrinkled her nose in distaste.

"There's a big sale on salt fish."

Melanie made a face. "Yuck."

Mrs. Stewart tapped her daughter's arm. "Now, Melanie, don't make fun. Everyone has a different opinion about what tastes good."

"My mother and I came down here for lunch," Melanie said. "I just love wonton soup and egg rolls. It's a special treat for doing so well at my recital."

"Recital?"

"Yes—you know—for piano," she said a little impatiently. "I came in second overall in my group."

"Oh," I said. "That's wonderful."

I knew that Melanie took piano lessons. During choir practice, she turned the pages for the music teacher. I tried to focus on what Melanie was saying, but from the corner of my eye I saw my mother waving at me.

"Do you like wonton soup?"

"Mmm—yeah." I felt bewildered by this conversation. Melanie was saying more to me than she had said to me all of last year when I sat directly behind her.

"But I guess it's nothing special for you—you must have it all the time."

I didn't have a chance to answer.

"Mui-Gui, Mui-Gui!" My mother's voice was shrill with annoyance. "Didn't you see me waving at you? Take these while I go in to pay for the salt fish." She thrust several bags, crammed full with vegetables and canned goods, at my feet. A tin of straw mushrooms spilled out of the bag and Melanie made a little move forward, as if to catch it. I quickly shoved the offending tin back into the bag.

My mother glanced at Melanie. "Oh—ha-lo. Who are you? You friend of Rosie's?" she said brightly in English.

I winced. "Yes, we're in the same class at school." My mother waved the salt fish like a baton in front of Mrs. Stewart. "Look at this—best quality fish. Not every day they have it at this price," she said. I wondered why she was telling this to Melanie's mother. I didn't think it was because she thought that Mrs. Stewart enjoyed salt fish.

"That's lovely. We must be going," Mrs. Stewart said. "If you want you can invite your young friend over to our house sometime, Melanie."

Melanie shrugged. "Sure. Do you want to come over tomorrow?"

I hesitated. I could tell from Melanie's peevish expression that she did not really want me to come. "I have Chinese classes after school."

"Well, then, what about Tuesday afternoon?" Mrs. Stewart offered.

"I have to go to Chinese school every day," I said.

"Surely—not every day?" Mrs. Stewart asked.

"No—no," my mother said. "Rosie only go Monday to Friday. I want her to get a good Chinese education. Not like her mother. I have to teach myself. She can get better job with two languages."

"Well, your mother certainly plans things well in advance," Mrs. Stewart said. She flashed me a brief smile. There was something else in her eyes too—pity, perhaps. "I'm sorry you won't be able to visit with us, Rose." She turned and took her daughter by the hand.

"Bye, Rose," Melanie said. "I'll see you at school."

"Don't walk so close to the stalls, Melanie, you'll make your dress smell," her mother admonished. I lifted my hand to wave good-bye to them, but they had already disappeared into the throng of people moving down the street.

My mother frowned. "What did that woman say to me at the end?" she asked in Cantonese. "She sounded as though she disapproved of me."

"Nothing much," I said.

"Tell me what she said, then."

I looked at my mother. She was doing her best to sound nonchalant, but I detected a note of uncertainty in her voice.

"She just said that you were a good mother to consider your daughter's future so far in advance."

"Really?" My mother's face brightened visibly. "Then she must understand how difficult it is to be a parent herself."

At school my favourite stories were Grimm's fairy tales. In these stories the beautiful maidens were clothed in silks so fine that the fabric could be pulled through the circle of a gold ring or tucked into the curved hollow of a walnut shell. All the princesses had hair the golden colour of corn silk or sunbeams. The only one who did not was Snow White, whose hair was as black as ebony. However, her skin was as white and pure as snow.

Whenever I looked at myself in the mirror I saw the stain of yellow on my skin. In Chinese school, we practised writing the word for yellow—*wong*. It was the same as my family name. As I drew the black ink in strokes across the white paper, I remembered thinking that I was yellow through and through. Yet the word for yellow also sounded like the word for emperor or king. Yellow was the colour reserved for the emperor, the teacher told us. All his ceremonial robes and gowns were lined with yellow silk.

I once had a dream in which my mother was serving her customers at the Maple Leaf Cafe. Everything was the same as it usually was, except that my mother was wearing a delicate high-necked gown of rose-coloured silk instead of her brown and white uniform. The customers did not seem to notice her changed appearance. I sat at the counter as well, but I did not notice either. It was only when she bent her wrist to pour tea for me that I saw the pale yellow lining of her sleeve.

It was the first day of my second term in Chinese school. During the break I went to visit my mother at the Maple Leaf Cafe.

"School okay?" my mother asked.

"Yes," I said.

"What characters did you learn today?" She always wanted to

know what words I was learning. She was proud of her reading ability. She had never finished high school in China because her mother had died when she was young, but somehow, over the years, she had acquired enough of a vocabulary to read Chinese novels and newspapers.

"Blue, sky, high, mountain, river, boat," I told her.

A balding man with a brown moustache came in and sat down two bar stools over. I knew he was a salesman because his black leather shoes were polished to a high shine. My mother always said that the shoes were a giveaway. "The regular, Annie," the man said to my mother. Annie was the name the white customers gave to her.

My mother went to the display case, took out the apple pie and cut a large wedge from it. She topped it with a dollop of whipped cream. She set the plate in front of the man with a fork and napkin.

"Here you go, George," she said. "Busy today?" The English words rolled off her tongue easily, but to my ears they sounded artificial. She poured him a cup of coffee.

"Not bad. Got a nice commission from this older couple who are going to redo their living room. Their kids just moved out. Premium aquamarine saxony."

I realized then that George was the carpet salesman from Woodward's Department Store my mother had told us about. My mother always said that if we ever needed new carpet, we could go to him. He would give us a good deal.

"Oh? Sounds good," my mother said. I knew that she didn't know what colour aquamarine was. I took a napkin from the metal dispenser and wrote in Chinese: blue of water. It was a phrase from my reader.

"Here," I said. "Aquamarine is the blue colour of water." I pushed the napkin in front of her. My mother pursed her lips and studied the characters.

"Hmm—you missed a stroke here," she said, pointing to the word "blue."

George leaned over to look too. "Don't you read English, Annie?"

"No," my mother said. "Too old."

He laughed. "You sure know how to add up a column of numbers. A real Jew under the skin, I'd say."

"Yes, sure," my mother said, although neither of us understood this comment.

That evening, after she had washed the dishes and I had finished drying them, my mother said that she wanted me to teach her how to read.

"Are you sure?" I asked her doubtfully. "I don't know if I can teach you."

"Why not?" my mother asked. "You always have your nose in books. It can't be that difficult a task. Or do you think your mother is too stupid to learn?"

I brought her the simplest book I had. It was an illustrated book of fairy tales I had bought for ten cents at the school bazaar a few years before.

I also brought a pencil and a sheet of paper. I printed out the alphabet neatly in upper and lower case letters. She knew the alphabet. When my mother first came to Canada, she had briefly attended language classes. Then I printed out a list of simple words. We practised sounding them out: cat, hat, fat, row, bow, flow, old, gold, hold. I made her repeat them again and again.

"Can we try the book?" my mother said finally.

"I think it's too hard for you," I said.

My mother shrugged. She began to flip through the pages slowly. She pointed to the first illustration in the book. "What is this story about?"

The picture showed a bed piled high with mattresses and a young girl lying on top of them. It was "The Princess and the Pea."

I told her the story in Chinese: "There is an old king and queen who are searching for a royal bride for their son. One day a stranger arrives at the palace during a storm and asks to spend the night. She claims to be a princess. The old queen decides to find out whether or not she is a true princess by placing a pea beneath twenty mattresses."

My mother interrupted. "What kind of pea? A fresh one or a dried one? A fresh one would be flattened right away."

"I don't know—a dried one then, I guess." I felt a flash of annoyance but I continued. "In the morning when the young woman wakes up and is asked how she slept, she answers that she had a terrible night and that her body is bruised and sore. The king and queen rejoice at her answer and begin to plan the wedding of the princess and their son."

My mother was perplexed. "That was her reward for answering her hostess so rudely?"

"No—no," I said. "It was the pea. It was because she was sensitive enough to feel the pea through all those layers."

"But why did they put it there in the first place?"

"They wanted to know if she was a true princess or a false one. They were looking for a bride for the prince."

My mother frowned. "Why didn't they ask her to recite the court history, to solve a riddle, or to sing a song? That was the test—to detect a lump in her bed?"

"Her sensitivity revealed that she was a true princess," I insisted. "It was something inside her that distinguished her from the common people."

"Ah," my mother said. She did not sound at all convinced. "All those mattresses. What a waste. In China we slept on boards mostly. So many mattresses. Crazy, don't you think?"

I thought I would laugh when she said that, yet somehow I did not want to.

"So crazy," she said again.

"I guess so." I mumbled the words.

"What?"

"I guess so," I said sullenly.

Several emotions seemed to flit across her face all at once—confusion, annoyance, hurt. She held my glance a moment longer, and then turned the page.

Much later, when I was in university, I told stories about my immigrant childhood over coffee in the student lounge of the English faculty. Everyone talked that way, as if they wanted to disown everything, their whole history. It did not matter if their fathers and mothers were doctors or teachers or union people. I told stories about Chinatown, the Maple Leaf Cafe and the people—the characters—who ate there. It pleased me to know that I could survey my past that way.

"But Chinatown's changing now. The new grocery stores are

more like supermarkets nowadays with their parkades built over top, their shopping carts and scanners and vegetables prewrapped in plastic. My mother can't stand those places," I said. "She says that they wrap the vegetables in plastic so that they can hide the spotty leaves in the middle. Just another way to cheat the customer, she tells me."

I knew that I talked as if I mourned the old Chinatown unequivocally, even though I did not. When I came home from school in the summers to live with my mother, life did not seem so different. She barely acknowledged that I had grown up, even though I had already completed a Bachelor's degree in English and had lived on my own in Toronto for three years while working on my Master's.

Every summer I returned to the same job—shelving books at the main library on Burrard Street in downtown Vancouver. On the weekends, I went out with friends, but on the weeknights I usually stayed at home. On these evenings, I often lounged around in my bedroom and read. Sometimes my mother would come in, unbidden, and attempt to tidy the mess of papers on my desk or to do my laundry.

"What a mess," she said one evening as she sorted through the crumpled clothes at the bottom of my closet. "If you don't have time to do your own laundry . . . at least bring it downstairs so that I can do it for you."

"No—leave it," I told her. "I'll do it myself. Most of those things need to be hand-washed anyhow."

"Do it yourself? Sure! When?" she snorted. "You're so busy. Always coming and going. You come home for the summers and I hardly see anything of you."

"Don't worry, Mom," I said. "I manage to do my own laundry all the time in Toronto."

I realized, a moment too late, that I had given her the perfect cue to launch into an attack.

"Toronto . . . I don't know why you must go thousands of miles away for school when there's a perfectly good university on our doorstep. What is it you do at school? You study literature . . . you read books. Can't you do it just as well here? It would be different if you were studying something else. Winnie Lee is studying to be an optometrist. Her mother tells me that there are only two schools in Canada and so she has to leave home. That I can understand. Sometimes one has to make sacrifices. But what can I tell Mrs. Lee about my daughter? That she does not want to live with her family?"

"That's not true," I protested.

"Then tell me, what is it? Are you ashamed of your mother?"

Her question caught me off guard. I would never admit to being ashamed. Embarrassed, uncomfortable perhaps, but didn't most people feel that way about their parents?

"No, of course not."

"You're so educated, so refined. You think that you're too good for your own mother." There was a note of bitterness, of self-pity in her voice.

"I don't understand you. At home you have a mother to do your laundry and make nutritious soups for you and yet you insist on going away for school. You have no heart. If it weren't for all those soups I fed you when you were a girl, do you think you would have the mental strength, the fortitude to do so well in school? I know that you don't believe in such things now, but how could they not work when I had such good intentions?"

"Yes, I know," I said, "I am grateful. I know that you have always tried your best for me."

My mother looked at me searchingly as if she wanted to believe me but was not sure of my sincerity. I looked back at her with steady eyes. I knew that I meant what I said.

And yet I was aware of a sense of duplicity creeping over me, too. How could I tell her that I would have preferred pretty clothes and piano lessons to herbal soups that steadied the heart and mind? Would she tell me, scathingly, that I was foolish to want beautiful illusions instead of wisdom? In the end, I didn't have to say any more, because my mother retreated from the room, appeased, for the moment, by my answer.

Lucy Ng lives in New Westminster, British Columbia. She has had her fiction and poetry published in various journals and anthologies. "Yellow Sleeve Princess" is the title story of a short fiction collection in progress.

Theresa Smalec

Uncertain Angles

There are degrees of safety, that's sure. The table is stiff, not long enough. He whispers, "Wiggle your bum to the edge," while the nurse looks through a wall. Legs spread, heels clamped, sweat at my back but—safer, now?—yes, that must be the word. So why is it safer, no, why does it seem more safe inside this narrow room? Not only that, but safer still when I shut my eyes, when I listen to his voice. A ribboned voice, unfurling at exactly the right pitch of urgency. But there you go, degrees again. Manic measures for everything.

Really, though, listen. Shut your eyes. Squeeze down the lids with your fingertips. Orange, dark green, red. A pattern of spots always there. In darkness it's easy to hear things, easy to feel almost everything. Crusts of dust, of dirt; flecks land like shrapnel on the skin, and they burrow below. A rubber-glove hand at my thigh. The latex sticks, snakes trails towards inside where skin is soft and damp. Easy to feel—feel everything. Sensitive, the nurses note. Press down my eyes for the safety of spots. Pretend to be blind; the reason I'm here.

"Try to relax," the doctor says.

"Okay."

And I do unclench the jaw, slacken the wrists. Just breathe, that's all; he does the rest. The worrying, he does for me. "Not quite entirely clear yet. A new wart near the labia." New wart, old wart. How do they know? I guess he checks his chart, the one that spills my history since that first visit. The double-take, why are you here? The sweater I wore must have fooled him; silver-blue cardigan, pure virgin wool. Or the dimples and shoulder-length hair? "You look like my daughter," he said.

Waiting, I wonder her name. Margaret Katherine Marie. Jennifer

Heather Kimberly. Cervical cancer sterility. Jane? Orange, dark green, red. Does he think of her when he sprays liquid nitrogen inside me? "This stings," his promise that first time while rubber-glove hands pried my thighs. Rough. Abrasive, I thought.

Thinks I'm a slut.

Stop, he's a doctor; what does he care?

I look like his daughter.

You looked like. Now, he knows what you've got.

Vaginal warts. The diagnosis disappointed me. After so many visits and tests, I expected something more dramatic. Clots, or tumorous lumps. Bloody-legged insects crawling my flesh, prying at the folds. And HIV: even for that my fears didn't count. Not gay no intravenous drugs not prostitute not promiscuous not into kinky sex. Not pale enough or gaunt enough no open sores my glossy hair. "A healthy heterosexual girl," he said.

"ANXIETY," the doctor scrawled. ANXIETY: his letters looming stark, neurotic, even a bit hysterical. "We can't run tests without a valid reason," he explained.

"Why don't you write that I'm concerned?"

"Anyone who's engaged in sexual intercourse might be concerned."

"But they're not getting tested, right? Which means I'm more than just concerned."

His labcoat eyes read, "You said it, not me."

ANXIETY like AMBULANCE, reeling the streets, screaming my name. The oily way his thumbs press. The smear of them. Don't open your eyes, don't look till he's gone. Does he think you like these visits? Does he make the new warts up? At home when I check with my pink plastic mirror, nothing seems abnormal. But my bathroom lacks angles, lacks harsh metal glow. My bedroom lacks his tilted table acute so as to probe at anything. At home, I don't probe long enough. I panic, assume things. Hard little lumps, or gristle and burns. "All in your head," he declares. "Just one more spray; you'll be clean." Inside, pinned to these paper sheets, I actually believe him. Heels locked, knees bent, hiss of the gas and hiss of his voice like a spring with the sting between my

should be more uncomfortable, what's wrong with you?

Perhaps I've grown addicted now to lying here, waiting for the slow sizzle against pink acid lacerations burns blisters when he sprays too long and yes I do. I like to lie, feel safe, hear him say, "Just one more spray. I'll see you in a month." The truth? The truth is I don't want the warts to go. Degrees of safety, yes? Incalculable. As long as he insists that I return, lie flat so they can look, well, this assures that things are right. I'm in my place. My ritual.

The clinic hides behind tacit peach awning, sits pushed back on a corner of the road. The woman at reception always asks if I would have a seat and so I do, scour magazines while from a cornered eye I scan who else is there. The game's to guess what others have. Sometimes it's hard to miss, the large purple lesions leeched to the neck, or the runny red rashes and scars, or the gouges that trail from elbows to wrists, or bright scalding burns and vicious cysts. What catches me, though, are traceless faces, their silky-smooth ovals of flesh. I've grown good at uncovering things. Often, sleeves betray: thick cotton rims hiked over wrists, or shiny gold brooches holding the material too tight around the neck. How they sit with spines drawn back from wall. To stand, they arch like cats. And faces, these pinch, compose. They march stiffly when they're called.

Just past the waiting room, delay again. Inside the cubicles the nurse leaves gowns starched white, as sterile as the gap between my thighs. Does she think white soothes? Electric lights and cotton balls, the glare of paper sheets. Things have to be disposable. The clinic checks that nothing's left when treatment is complete. I once forgot a sock and a nurse chased me out to my bike. "Please take it back," she said.

That's understandable.

What bothers me is how, within a week, my panic mounts again, with nothing to see or touch or grab, but with softness inside like pumpkin rot. And slow steady burning, the pulp near a flame. ANXIETY, no doubt—he was right all along. "Really," the doctor insists, "there's nothing much to worry about. Your progress is clear. You'll be fine." The progress is obvious, is evident. Is evidently obvious. Why can't I tell?

He barely checks, just skims the surface while my skin lies safe. But what about where flesh lurks subversive? Where cells grow treacherous? He doesn't believe that my body is a threat. "The pap smear will detect any abnormalities."

I always test negative, always. I wait, hold my breath while I dial for results. This time, this time for sure the truth will be out. Each call takes hours. The receptionist finds a nurse who finds the file that files my fate that claims I'm well.

"Number one fifty-one?"

"That's right."

"All negative again."

"You're sure?" I ask.

"Quite positive."

"It's my results you're looking at?"

There are degrees of safety.

Just close the eyes, press the lids. Katherine Marie. Orange green angles of certainty. If there's only one new; if there's only one left. If this curse disappears, I will not lust again.

"You think you deserve this," she said. Her voice, its gentleness surprising me. An older voice of crow's feet, flaked mascara, a voice whose edge is not as soft as the ears might first suspect.

"Of course not. I made a mistake, that's all."

"Now you're so careful that you call up to three times for each set of test results."

"Just want to be safe."

"I know," she whispered back.

Silence then, and memory of the imprints on my neck. How fingers squeeze down and down and down—for glands, for growths, for swollen nodes. Memory of nights I didn't sleep for fear of soaking wet sheets; night sweats mark the body's urge to clean itself. First sign of full-blown AIDS. A memory of needles sucking blood, the expectation of taint.

"Don't put yourself through hell."

"I know. I wasn't bad."

You were good. Very good.

And wanted, always wanted. You hungry bitch.

   Hold back!

Why didn't you? That summer you uncovered hinge of hips, of thighs. The plush of your own waist.

Shoulder bone, the curve of bird bone. Scared to touch pipe-glass neck might break. So fragile all their eyes.

   "Such a nice young girl."

Sick is what you grew of that.

"I do, though. I deserve it."

"Why do you say that?" Her asking doesn't make me feel I have to answer, doesn't make me ashamed or sick.

Not like the time he smiled that prim smile. "Have you considered counselling, dear?"

"For what?"

"Perhaps," he purred, "to find out why you feel this way."

Guilty? You mean how I'm to blame? Because I wanted. Want. I'm wanton—let-things-happen-far-too-easy. Rhymes with sleazy. Not your daughter, hey?

And his voice: flatly soothing, never angry, never shifting tones. The sound of someone who has never been irrational. Yes, yes; you're right, I'm ill. Twisted, contorted, fucked. I'm fucked. So fix me, please, I beg you now. I'm crying, see? ANXIETY like AMBULANCE—might need one—too exhausted to imagine, to arrive at the way things might turn out.

"I need to find out if I'm sick or not," I tell her.

"Do you feel sick?"

Do I feel the way his thumbs squeeze hot and greasy, smearing trails along my thighs? Do I feel eyes inside the room, like mine, inspecting who is clean and who has sinned, who has suffered and who is well? Whose penance is due and whose penance is paid? My monthly offerings: the warts I bring. My eyes turned down, I can't meet his stare.

"I feel sick when I go there for the tests, yes," I answer.

"Why do it, then?"

"For health."

"The tests say you're fine."

"But warts? The tests don't check for those."

"They disappear, eventually."

"How soon is that?"

"It all depends. Each person's different, right?"

A different paper gown for each.

"What's your name?" she asks me now.

The first time someone at the clinic has ever asked that. They usually hand out numbers: 150 162 381. You get a card to stick inside your wallet. I always worry that I'll lose mine and have some stranger call, "Is this one forty-five?" Real names are dangerous, perhaps more dangerous than warts. What if this woman knows me, or my mother, or a friend of mine? What if she tells? What could she say? Excuse me, dear, do you know your daughter suffers from . . . Degrees of safety, that's sure. Incalculable. No idea why I trust her but I hear my shaky whisper, "It's Krystyna. Why?"

She laughs a bit. "When someone calls non-stop you start to wonder things. Like what her name is. What she looks like. If she knows these things work out."

It is funny how her wondering doesn't bug me. With him, each time he pulls on a glove I sense a smirk: *She doesn't look at all like Kate. Like Margaret. Katherine Marie. Jennifer Heather Kimberly. Jane. Not at all.* Her wondering strikes me as the kind I do while waiting, watching others like me. There are times I've wondered how my body grows so sure of its disease. Or patterns of safety—squeezing for the spots—orange, dark green, red. Don't look. Don't touch. Don't want too much.

"You had warts too?" I finally ask.

"At twenty-one."

"I'm twenty-two."

"Forgive yourself."

"Just one more test," I say.

Theresa Smalec is a graduate student in English at the University of Western Ontario. She publishes her poetry in Grain, Fiddlehead, Fireweed, absinthe *and other Canadian journals. She is writing her Ph.D. thesis on women's discourses of* HIV *and* AIDS. *She wishes to thank the English Department at the University of Calgary for all that she knows about writing and dis/ease.*

Suzanne Buffam

in the red

1. in the red:

You wear a red skirt to school today, dark & to the knee, terrified
something might leak, or slip out of place. Would the other kids
laugh like they did when it happened to Emily? You asked me about
it then, a shocked look on your face when I said it'll happen to you.
(You can't stand even the *idea* of blood, place bandaids over bruises
to hide the bleeding that goes on under the skin.) Your shifting
eleven-year-old body that insists on changing, on pushing at your
clothes, although you try to hide it in baggy jeans & loose T-shirts.
Not today. Today, the red skirt, scratchy & stiff, gift from some thin
aunt back east. You swore never to put it on. Ugly. Ugly. Skirt.
Today it's a bandaid. A thin disguise.

Mr. Bringham, grade six teacher & after-school soccer coach, tells
you to go put on your gym shorts & start warming up with the
other girls. He looks at you funny when you tell him you're not
feeling well. He knows. You want to die. You wish the earth would
swallow you up. But all he says is okay, then why don't you just sit
out today & watch.

- & Angela, you look nice today, dear. You should wear skirts
more often.

Why is there this twisting in your stomach? This slow shredding
of flesh.

: the condition of being in debt or operating at a loss

158

2. red light:

- baby! baby! yur nothin but a girl!
- am not!
- yes you are. & girls can't do anything.

prove it prove it prove it—Peter & Richard & Daniel from down the street, with their go-carts & hockey sticks, thick socks, baseball cards, watch me climb tree branch to rooftop Richard throws rocks at my feet bare feet thick-skinned summer toes gripping shingles & slivers slipping, falling, falling down rooftop, down branches, my apple knees skinned & bleeding down to the ground (without being caught).

: a signal of danger; a warning

3. red-handed:

My big sister, Nadine, is in the girl's washroom at recess, locked in a stall. Her friends are outside, smoking behind the tenth grade portable, trying to look bored in pencil-thin skirts and dark make-up too heavily applied. (They haven't learned yet that the trick is to look as though you're wearing none at all.) They leave plum-coloured rings on the filters of cigarettes. On purpose.

Inside the stall, Nadine's skirt is up around her waist. She peels off blood-soaked underwear, trying to stem the flow between her legs with handfuls of balled-up toilet paper. Unbearable pain, like flesh tearing apart inside her. Nothing like the usual, like what she's learned to get used to. (Later, much later, she will tell me it was like fire inside her. Great balls of fire, she will say, the words rising like smoke from her subtly painted lips.)

She curls her legs tight to her chest, as if to ward off the pain, praying to God to forgive her, to stop punishing her & she promises to never let it happen again. All she can think is that somewhere inside her a life has been growing like a weed & now a hand is reaching down & tearing it out at the root. She's in too much pain to be relieved.

Later that morning the school nurse calls our mother to come get Nadine. Says Nadine's having some trouble with her monthly & it might be a good idea for her to see a doctor. (Nadine was found half-conscious on the washroom floor, a pool of blood between her legs, smeared on her arms & her hands.) Nadine has stopped crying by the time my mother arrives & insists she is fine, just tired.

I hear about it at lunch & am confused by this story. Nadine told me about missing her period, what it might mean. But not this. She didn't say anything about this part. I decide Nadine must have made some mistake, must have got her facts wrong. Facts are facts, after all, I'm learning these days.

In the back of the grade six science lab, posters show diagrams of a man's & a woman's naked bodies, stripped clean of their flesh. Reproductive systems on display beneath bundles of muscle, cages of bone. Everything transparent & brought to the surface. & the shelves lined with jars of clear liquid, unborn bodies floating like planets in their galaxies of glass. Nothing more opaque than these absolute transparencies, these silences no one can fill.

My mother starts washing Nadine's laundry by hand at the sink with hot water & vinegar, makes Nadine scrub every night in the tub. At first my father is angry. There is screaming & yelling at first. But soon he grows quiet, acts like Nadine's disappeared. Like she no longer exists.

: caught in the very act of committing a crime, wrongdoing, etc. . . . or in possession of self-incriminating evidence

4. red-letter:

- o baby, baby, I want you . . . please baby . . .

faint whirring of streetlights, the sound of a cat
(it seems all my life I am called this, regardless of age)

hands fumbling at my skirt, at my nylons nylons ripping ripping panties the feel of breath on my neck hot & quick eyes shut & squeezed—red sparks against the back of my head, against my eyes

& then the roof of his car, above me, over his shoulder more real than his face, more precise—the ripped upholstery, chipped paint, peeling vinyl—

—a sound from my throat hollow & strange a sound to make the air shudder cold & retreating from my lungs—

does he notice, under the weight of him, I am forgetting to breathe

the penny-size circle of blood on my panties, the light in the bathroom, hospital-white, paperclean, the silence of hallways,

filling the bathtub, soaking & soaking. skin, hair, bones, blood. scrubbing flesh, the colour of salmon eggs, pink & raw,

my mother, her soapwhite hands, always soaking. dishes, laundry, stained napkins, bedsheets. Nadine's clothes in the sink—
          boiling & scrubbing

: *memorable, especially important or happy (a red-letter day)*

5. *red herring:*

We're in Nadine's room, listening to records. Our mother's in the living room (dusting & waxing & scrubbing). The air smells like a forest after a storm. Pine-scented purity wafts through the house as she moves. There's a bruise on my mother's cheek & one on her arm that happened when she walked into the open fridge door late last night. All day they've opened & reddened, blossomed like roses against her pale skin.

  Nadine says she heard fighting, behind their closed bedroom door. & later, Mum crying, alone in the kitchen. Nadine whispered into the darkness & there was silence. She lay awake all night with the light turned off, watching the moon move through the trees slow as a cruise ship. Tells me she could see herself there, light years away from this house, orbiting Earth from such a great distance, the rest of us smaller than dust.

- fucking bastard, she says.

I can't imagine. Nadine started swearing when she met Greg. Climbs in & out the window at all hours of the night. Feels like Holly Golightly in her little black dress with a knife in her boot & a flask. She won't let me french-braid her hair any more but sometimes if I choose the right moment she'll still take the time to do mine. I love her fingers in my hair. I close my eyes & everything else disappears, goes back to the way it was . . . the way I want to remember it.

My father threatens Nadine with his fist in the air, nails shut her window but she pries it loose. She can't wait till June to get outta here but a girl needs a good education, she says. *Elope* is a word that looks like chocolate on her lips, the way she tastes it, smug & not willing to share.

This is what I want, more than anything, something like this, all mine. How this word has become a place for Nadine to escape to, not big enough for the two of us.

My mother, with her cleaning & bleaching, seems out of reach. Untouchable. Her cupboards crowded with bottles of Javex & rags. Everything about her white & remote. Lily white, of the valley. Perfumed & cleaner than snow. Her feet don't touch the ground. When I was little, I thought she was an angel.

- they're both fucking crazy, says Nadine.

I want to ask her if she loves them anyway, like I do, but I'm afraid of the way she might look at me, the way she's begun looking at people, like they're out of their minds, or like she is.

The doorbell rings & my mother's voice chirps when she opens the door. She cradles longstemmed red roses tied in white ribbon, stripped clean of thorns.

- look what your father did! she exclaims, waving a hand through the air. It flutters, butterfly-quick, & lands on her own blooming cheek.

: something intended to divert attention from the real problems, from the matter at hand

6. red alert:

- hey, baby, how're ya doin' tonight?

thick hand on my ass. smell of beer in my face. on my neck. fingers tighten on my carton of ice cream. my wallet. eyes locked ahead.

- don't fucking touch me. my voice hard through my teeth.

- ooh baby, aren't you a bitch!

thin smile from the man behind the counter, as I pay him & leave. the other man follows, keeps talking.

- yur a bitch, y'know. bet you never even get laid. what you need is a good fuck. that's what you need, isn't it, toots? huh? bitch, I'm talking to you.

key in car door. eyes ahead. *ignore him. ignore him.*

- did you hear me, bitch?
- fuck you.

driving home, the red sports car behind me red sports car gleaming in my rearview mirror. bearing down on me like a nightmare. weaving & darting. cutting me off. bastard. son of a bitch.

please don't kill me. God, I don't want to die.

for weeks I dream of owning a gun. under my pillow. alone in my apartment. my room. in my bed. shooting dark shadows of men as they come through my door.

but at the last minute,
          their faces turn into people I love.

: the most urgent form of alert, signalling that an enemy attack is imminent

7. red rag:

My lover & I are lying in bed. Early Sunday morning, light through
the blinds streaks the wall, the bedspread, our faces, the air full of
heat, clings to our skin. I want to make love, now, in daylight, not
strangers at night, in the dark under mountains of sheets. Slowly, I
begin rubbing his thighs, chest, with my body.

  – want some breakfast? he asks. My stomach tightens, body stops
moving, ashamed of itself.

  – do you still find me attractive? plaintive, hating the need for
reassurance I've begun to hear in my voice.

  – what? irritation edging his.

  – you heard what I said. I don't feel attractive any more.

  – oh, not this again. Please, Nora. I *find* you at*tract*ive.

  – but the way you touch me . . . don't touch me . . . I don't feel
desirable. My voice growing softer.

  What comes next is the thing:

  – Nora, he says, please don't take offence to this, because I don't
mean it in a bad way at all, it's more of an observation than a criticism,
I guess, but what I was noticing is that you seem to get really sensitive,
like more so than usual I mean, around your, you know, time of
the month. You know, like when you're on the rag.

  Does he have any idea what he's saying. What this does to me.
& how can I tell him without sounding *hysterical* (my father's word
for my mother).

  My uterus guiding my head like a beacon, my mind draining out
with the discarded flesh, with the blood, my common sense pouring
out from between my legs. Tie me down to the bed for a week
every month, ignore my childlike ramblings. Tie my tongue in a
knot.

  nora's on the rag nora's on the rag baby baby nora's on the rag
on the rag on the rage

  Like a red flag to a bull.

  : something that arouses anger; a provocation

8. *re(d)ress:*

Now you stand in front of the full-length mirror in the bathroom, trying on sweaters, skirts, blouses, nylons you've taken from my drawer without my permission. My daughter, playing dress-up as me. Your shifting eleven- almost twelve-year-old body looking more & more like my own. You put on a red dress, cotton & to the knee, gift from my sister Nadine. Brilliant, the colour of raspberries in thick June heat. Since when did you start wearing dresses?

And suddenly, I'm afraid for you. This fear catching like a stone, a silence in my throat. I see things, my own life, stretching out before you. My mother's voice kicking in inside my head: Young Girls Should Not Wear Red.

In a flash (as thin & bright as the lips you have carefully painted) I understand her need to clothe us, to veil us, in white. As if somehow this cleaning, this bleaching of our skins & our minds could keep us from discovering the dangers alive in us.

I know this is wrong, that I can't protect you, that I shouldn't try. You're beginning to understand freedom & it's a colourful thing.

- how 'bout the brown one, honey? I say, in spite of myself. Brown is nice. (Brown is neutral).

- oh, Mum! Brown's disgusting. Don't you like the red one, Mum? Red's my favourite. It reminds me of a celebration, y'know?

I look at you, your bright smile, giving me answers I don't even know the questions to. & I see the warm colour hugged to your body. Your arms held out in the air like banners, like people celebrating.

- yeah, I know, Angela. Red's my favourite colour, too.

Today I'm wearing the dress we picked out together at Leslie's Petites. Well, you picked it out. Were you testing me by choosing the only size six left in pomegranate red? That's what the kohl-eyed saleswoman called it & I must admit, the sound of the name on her lips was tempting enough in itself. A perfect fit, a rare occasion. You wouldn't let me leave the store without buying it.

I'm at the Fairview cemetary, with lily-of-the-valley for my mother's birthday. (Her favourite flower, the whitest blossom she could find.) I mean no disrespect, standing here in my bright red dress, no matter how it may seem to anyone looking on. & I know it's too late for this, for her. I'm not even sure she would have understood, even if I *could* have tried to explain. The truth is, I'm not sure who I'm doing this for.

: a setting right of what was wrong.

Suzanne Buffam's fiction and poetry have appeared in various journals, the chapbook Mouth to Mouth *(Panarky Press, 1994) and the anthology* Breathing Fire *(Harbour Publishing, 1995). She lives in Vancouver.*

Lesley-Anne Bourne

Junction

Her whole life Imogene had loved Benny. She thought about this while lying next to him in the bed he shared with his wife, Martha. Martha was at Goodmart where she worked as a cashier. An express cashier, she'd correct people when they described her position.

Martha wouldn't be home until four.

Benny had only recently come back into Imogene's life. She'd had car trouble. Specifically, her car was billowing white smoke one afternoon during rush hour, well, what was considered to be rush hour in a place like Willow Junction. And what kind of a name was Willow Junction? she thought as it passed her as a bus headline. Once when the bus roared towards her, the first three letters had disappeared or burned out or fallen back behind where the destination or route was supposed to be spelled out. The junction sounded even worse then, if that was possible. The sad thing was, it perfectly described the area she was born in and which she'd never left.

Rush hour meant about twenty more cars than usual passed through the main highway intersection. This happened precisely at 5:10. Ten minutes allowing for the drive from town, from the city, Bay Lake. And, thought Imogene, that was another dumb name! Was it a bay? Or a lake? Couldn't the city also be called Lake Bay? Leave it to city folk to screw up like that, she'd reasoned when she was a kid; they couldn't make up their minds.

Imogene figured her car was about number twelve through the intersection. Or it would have been, that Tuesday, when the car started smoking. Then it died. Cars angrily swerved around her as if she'd planned the scene, as if she'd always wanted that kind of power and had worked and worked to develop the moment. She rested her head on the wheel. Sun burned her left arm. Her hair completely hid her face and she thought, I'm not Imogene, I'm Imagine.

She'd done this since she was a kid. Since her mother had told her one day that they named her after the actress Imogene Coca. An actress, said her mother, a film star. Someone who pretends to be someone else, and gets paid for it.

Imagine, her mother had said one afternoon long ago when Imogene was crying, actually wailing by the side of the sink. Imagine you are someplace you really want to be, and you are doing something you really want to do.

Imogene was standing above the sink, on the bathroom counter, naked. Her mother had been washing Imogene's feet or something, and had lifted her daughter from the soapy water. Imogene thought of her mother as lifting her with the hands of a swan. Or, more precisely, the wings of a swan. She'd just recently seen the white birds while on a car trip with her cousins. They'd all driven five hours south to a theatre town. Culture, her mother had said as they ate cheezies in the back seat on the long hot drive there. Imogene thought her mother said vulture, and from then on the drive seemed to be headed straight into dread. So when the vultures turned out to be swans, Imogene was more than relieved. Still, she didn't venture that close to the birds floating in the river or standing on the grass. Melanie, a city cousin, went right up to one, her fat hands out to pet it, of course.

Melanie's mother had screamed first, just before Melanie. Sure enough, the bird grabbed on for a second. From then on, Imogene thought of her cousin as Meal. Instead of Mel, as the little girl wanted to be called, Imogene would say, Meal.

Imagine, Imogene told herself in the hot Mustang, you are on a beach, Silver Beach, say, behind the Bamboo Garden, with Benny. Okay, she thought as someone honked behind her, that takes care of the where. Now what am I doing that I want to do?

She pictured Benny, his round tanned face, the cluster of red bumps that seemed always to circle his chin. She thought they were like the strawberry patch they'd stretched out in that time he'd asked to see what was under her T-shirt.

Nothing is under my T-shirt, she said, not getting it.

But Benny, a year older, had persevered, and they had seen each other without clothes on. The strawberries had squished in places and so they wrote their names on each other with the juice. Benny had written his right across her chest. An "n" landed on each developing breast. There was a nice balance to that, she thought, scrunching her chin to look down.

She wasn't nearly so bold, and wrote "Imogene" on his stomach. As she was writing it, in penmanship far better than anything she'd ever written for Miss Reynolds, she did manage to glance further south. She'd never seen anything like it.

Is it heavy? she wanted to know.

Okay, Silver Beach behind the Bamboo Gardens with Benny.

It sounded to her a lot like when she'd played that game, what was it, Clue? Probably with Benny. Silver Beach behind the Bamboo Gardens with Benny and . . . Didn't the game say there had to be a weapon?

And a rope.

The rope had been around Benny's dog's neck. The dog was named God. Benny had named the dog and thought himself the only one to reverse letters ever. It was a good name, thought Imogene, especially on Sundays when the dog went missing. She and Benny would wander the woods and the field next to the church. The sign, for as long as Imogene could remember, said, "Ye Must Be Born Again." This, at the corner into Willow Junction. Did it mean, she wondered growing up, that every time her father, Ray, drove to work, and every time he came home, that he had to imagine his birth all over again? That was twice a day, almost three hundred and sixty-five days a year, because he hardly ever missed work. And what if someone couldn't remember their birth?

Imogene couldn't remember hers, though she'd been told often enough that she was fast and that she'd tried, in her hurry, to come out left leg and right arm first. The doctor liked to tell her every time she went for a checkup that he'd had to reach in and turn her around. He said it was like trying to get a pop out of one of those new machines. If it wasn't turned the right way, like on its side, you couldn't get the can out. Imogene couldn't quite follow what he was talking about, and couldn't connect why her mother turned red each time Dr. Wilson said these things, but she smiled at the man anyway.

The dog would go missing while church was in. Sunday evening, the two of them would be in the woods, calling for God. Inevitably, a kid would get up from where he sat in the pews and look out the window. Was this part of the service? Could they all go outside to look for God?

Late at night, back then, Imogene would hear Benny's voice calling God.

I'm on a beach, Imogene thought, her head still on the steering wheel. We're walking God, and Benny is kissing me.

Someone knocked on her head.

Oh, sorry, I thought your window was up.

It was Benny, standing beside the Mustang.

If you steer, I can push you into the station.

Sure enough, there was a blue and red gas station right beside the car. But where had Benny come from? Did I imagine him? Imogene asked herself.

Imogene was trying to steer and to fix her face in the rearview mirror. Instead, she just kept seeing the brown torso of Benny. His open flannel shirt was brown too, plaid. And it was stained with grease.

She looked at her watch: 5:20.

I was just leaving, said Benny, when I saw the line of cars. And the steam. It's probably your rad.

It was as if they'd never stopped talking. As if they'd seen each other every day. As if neither had ever married.

There were no willows in Willow Junction. Lots of poplar, pine and spruce. Some maple. But no willows. The first one Imogene saw was in her aunt and uncle's back yard one Christmas. Imogene, her sisters and her parents had driven to Toronto for the holiday in their new blue station wagon. A Chrysler, she remembered from staring at the dash from the very back all that time. She had no idea what a Chrysler was, but it felt good in the mouth when she said it.

Chrysler, she went around saying the night they got it. It was after ballet class. Ballet was her mother's idea. Imogene didn't mind, she liked to swing from the barre like an ape. After class, when she walked out to the car, her father wasn't the only one picking her up. The whole family was there.

What's going on? Imogene asked as she climbed into the front seat, crawled over her mother and flipped into the back seat on top of Janis and Peggy-Leigh. The back doors hadn't opened for months. Peggy-Leigh helped her over into the way-back as they called it, pushing her bum hard and heaving her dance bag on top of her.

A surprise, said Ray, her father. He tossed his cigarette into the winter night. It was only half smoked, which made Imogene wonder what could be so special.

The car lot lights made the cars look like liquid. Shiny blots of Kool-Aid. She liked the red ones best. She counted them as her father sat at a desk inside with a man in a purple blazer. Her mother didn't say anything; she just looked out the passenger-side window at the trucks.

And then they went to A&W. In the new blue station wagon. The way-back had plush blue carpeting that her father didn't want to get dirty. So don't spill your rootbeer, he said. They sat in front of the drive-in with all the windows down, even the one in the back. Her father had put that one down for Imogene. They'd never had electric ones before.

They waited. The waitresses in their orange and brown short dresses chatted happily inside near the counter. Outside, Imogene thought breath rising from the car looked like the stuff from the hospital chimney on cold nights.

Should we go in, Ray?

It's a drive-in, Iris.

But they're not coming out, honey. Maybe we should go in?

Peggy-Leigh tossed Imogene's dance bag back. It had only made it as far as the back seat during the transfer. They'd all been a bit distracted by the free trip to Florida. It turned out that anyone buying a new Chrysler in December, the week before Christmas, got a free trip to Florida in March. Imogene's father said he hadn't known and wasn't that a special surprise. Her mother had simply stared with part of her lip gone into her mouth.

Honey?

What?

Let's go in. Maybe it's too cold for the waitresses to come out.

It's a drive-in, for chrissakes, that's the point, Iris.

Imogene tried to cheer them up. Will they have A&Ws in Florida?

Her father laughed and opened his door. Ah, a sign, she thought, and plopped down on top of Peggy-Leigh.

Hey, get off me!

And then they were inside ordering Baby Burgers, a Teen Burger, a Mama Burger and two Papa Burgers. Imogene's mother even let them order onion rings. The best part, they all agreed, was the ice on the mugs. Imogene could hardly lift hers but that didn't matter.

The first thing Imogene noticed about her aunt and uncle's place was the tree. It was a long and twisted thing, skinny, almost artificial, she decided. There were long ropes where branches should have been. And the trunk was a trail to be followed. Imogene and her sisters rolled out of the station wagon and immediately climbed the tree. When Aunt Ed walked out, the girls squawked, pretending to be exotic birds.

Their snowsuits were intentionally different colours so that their mother could readily tell them apart. Peggy-Leigh's suit was bright green. Janis had a pink and orange one. Imogene's was yellow. She hated yellow, and imagined her suit was red.

The girls stayed in the tree a long time, swaying the rope branches back and forth the same way they'd played with the skin under their aunt's arms the last time she'd visited. Their mother warned them this time not to do that, as Aunt Ed didn't seem to like it. What wouldn't you like? thought Imogene. Wouldn't it feel good?

The next morning was Christmas. The girls had just dumped out their stockings when there was a knock at the front door. Uncle Keith answered it. A big policeman wanted to know who the blue station wagon belonged to.

Imogene threw up. She had eaten too much chocolate too fast, and then had eaten half of the red jelly beans before drinking two glasses of orange juice. And she was scared. As her mother led her to the kitchen to clean her up, Imogene cried, What's wrong? Is Daddy going to jail?

It turned out that someone had hit the back of the car. It had been parked behind the house, in an alley. The officer figured it had happened in the middle of the night.

I'm pregnant, said Imogene.

She'd hoped not to say it like that. She'd imagined a nice quiet dinner at the back of Rosetta's Restaurant. Some garlic bread, ravioli, maybe they could share a dessert.

But things hadn't worked out.

It was the wine. Benny had wanted to order some red wine as soon as they arrived. She said no to a bottle, perhaps he could just have some by the glass?

Bottle's cheaper, he said.

Not if I'm not drinking any, she said.

Since when have you turned down wine? he said, winking at Imogene and then at the waitress in red gingham.

I'm pregnant, Imogene said.

The waitress looked up from her small yellow pad and click pen, then moved away.

What?

Pregnant, said Imogene. You know, with a baby?

Benny had this look. This look she couldn't read. His eyebrows went flat like the brim of the caps he wore, John Deere or Evinrude.

He stretched his leg out, towards Imogene, and it hit her foot. She left her foot there, touching him. She needed some kind of contact.

Does it hurt? she asked.

She meant his leg, the one he'd injured.

No, he said.

But she knew he was lying. His leg often hurt. Ever since that accident with his dirt bike, he'd had pain. They said the bike hit something in the sand, tossed Benny, and then drove over him.

He'd been riding too fast on Silver Beach. When she was finally allowed to see him at St. Mary's, he was still covered in sand. When he nodded his head to say, Yeah, I'm okay, sand rained down onto the hospital sheet. She could see it under his nails. The traction chains and bolts and handles glinted in the sun.

He spent the summer that way. And in the fall, they learned his leg was shorter. By a good inch. And he wasn't the kind to wear special shoes.

Okay, he said, so it hurts.

She wondered which he was talking about and hoped it was his leg.

I thought you were on the pill?

I am, she said. It happens.

The baby wasn't the problem. Imogene had wanted a child for two years. The last twenty-four periods had her in tears every single time. Each red sign broke her heart. Again and again, she hoped her period would not come. But she couldn't go off the pill. Russ didn't think the time was right, and she couldn't bear to resort to tricking him. She hoped that nature would somehow overtake technology.

And the problem wasn't that Imogene and Benny weren't married. They were. To other people.

Benny poured himself more wine even though almost none would fit into the glass. His arm paused above Imogene's glass and it was then that he realized.

I guess you'll have to leave Russ.

What?

Benny put the half-carafe down. The waitress was hovering near the cash, seemingly afraid to come closer.

Well, you will.

This wasn't really the way Imogene had imagined the conversation while she waited for the home pregnancy test to work. Home pregnancy? What a stupid name, she'd decided as she held a small wand up to the bathroom window. She guessed it couldn't be called a work pregnancy test, and imagined a thousand women in office bathroom cubicles peeing onto white wands or into little trays and then holding things up towards the flourescent lights. Outside the locked stall doors, the line-up grew and grew as more women came in to see if they were pregnant.

The blue-and-white bathroom curtains bordered the wand. It was blue she was waiting for, she thought. Or was it not blue?

This is nuts.

What? said Benny.

This, sitting here in Rosetta's talking about how I'm pregnant.

Imogene imagined herself in her bathroom again, that afternoon, before she'd called Benny at the garage to see if he could meet her for dinner. She wasn't supposed to call him at the garage. He didn't say that; she did. It was one of her rules. But she'd called anyway. Five o'clock, she'd said, before Rosetta's gets busy.

Martha's got to work late anyway, he said, till ten.

For three months they'd met, or tried to. It wasn't always easy for Benny. But Russ was away, and Imogene could always get there since Benny had stopped the smoking thing her car did.

It wasn't smoke, said Benny the first time they went to bed in her apartment.

It wasn't?

It was steam. Your rad. Smoke is worse, trust me.

That time she was stalled in the intersection, Benny had said he'd fix her car first thing in the morning, and did she need a ride home from the garage?

Imogene of course needed a ride home. Benny seemed to know where she lived, even though they hadn't talked since he'd climbed over her parents' fence one ancient afternoon to say that he and Martha Loach were getting married. Martha went to their high school but Imogene didn't know her well. She hadn't known Benny did.

Why? Imogene had wanted to ask there by the fence. Instead she'd asked, Do you want a Coke?

Looking back, as she often did, she realized this had probably seemed like a rude thing to say. But what the hell, she thought, was Benny doing?

Where's Russ? Benny asked as he opened his Coke and wobbled a loose fence board.

Up north, said Imogene. Surveying.

Lots of bugs there.

Yeah, I guess so.

You haven't talked to him?

Not really, not for a while. He left after . . . She hadn't wanted to finish her sentence.

Graduation? said Benny.

Right.

Graduation always seemed to fuck you up, thought Imogene. She'd seen it happen to her older sister, Peggy-Leigh, the year before. Peggy-Leigh's best friend Pam had asked Derek to graduation. Derek had been Peggy-Leigh's boyfriend for two years. It had been ugly. It was the first time Imogene really noticed her sister's habit of chewing the inside of her cheek when she was upset.

Not to mention, Imogene continued remembering, the car accident the captain of the basketball team had, driving his graduation gift, a red convertible, into the lake. And one of the cheerleaders had a kid nine months later.

Why Imogene had ended up going to graduation with Russ, she didn't know. He'd asked her, not knowing about her and Benny, and anyway, she thought at the time, against her locker, with Russ looking right at her, what was there to know?

She'd never been able to hurt anyone. At least not deliberately, she thought.

Sure, she said, I'd love to go with you. She tasted metal in her mouth.

Martha's dad owned the bait store. It was a thriving business, what with the town being on a lake. People came from everywhere to fish in the summer. Martha drove the minnow van. All summer Imogene watched the van drive up to Benny's to get him. She'd wave from her lawn.

Martha always smiled and waved back. But who wouldn't be happy driving a truck with Benny on the seat beside her? thought Imogene as she read another postcard from Russ.

Bugs are bad. Hot as hell. Having a great time. The guys are super. Why don't you come visit? Love Russell Innes, it was signed.

He still signs his last name, thought Imogene, turning the card over in her hand, like I won't remember which Russ.

The other side of the card showed evergreens and rocks. Russ was hoping to study geology at university. Imogene was hoping to avoid university. Benny was working in his father's garage. Martha drove a van full of minnows.

And gradually, Imogene and Benny had stopped talking. They both had work, they said, where did the time go? Imogene taught all those classes at the dance studio for Mrs. Valente now that the woman's back wouldn't let her really instruct any more. She still tried to lead the class, but more often than not, she retired to a chair in the corner and yelled out the steps as Imogene, in front of the girls, demonstrated. Eventually Mrs. Valente retired completely to the other side of the one-way mirror.

What will you tell Russ? Benny said now.

Imogene sighed and longed for some red wine. She sipped her water. The truth, she said.

Which is?

At first this seemed like a really stupid question to Imogene. But as she tried to talk, she realized how brilliant Benny was and that she'd always loved him. She started to cry.

Jesus, said Benny, leaning over the table and wiping Imogene's face with his napkin.

Don't, said Imogene, pulling away. My mascara will ruin the cloth.

That's what I love about you, said Benny.

Imogene couldn't be certain what he was referring to. Could it be that she wore mascara, never leaving the apartment without it? Ballerinas never went without make-up, she'd learned from Mrs. Valente when she was ten and auditioning for summer classes at the National Ballet School in Toronto.

Marry me.

Imogene stared at him.

You're married, she said. Martha, remember? And looked at her watch.

That's been over for ages.

Imogene put down her water.

Benny continued talking with his eyes down, looking in the direction of the fettuccine the waitress had brought.

She can't have kids.

Imogene looked at her ravioli. She'd ordered it out of habit. In high school they'd had a dance where the girls had to ask the guys to it, and had to take the guys to dinner before. Imogene had asked Benny and had taken him to an Italian restaurant that went under shortly after. Imogene had ordered spaghetti and realized her mistake even before it arrived. The strands were suddenly lethal to her white blouse. And she knew pasta wasn't supposed to be cut. How can I talk and eat? Why are things between males and females so difficult, she wailed in her mind while pouring more parmesan to kill time.

We tried for a year. Then she went to see a doctor. Impossible, he told us. That was it. It's her, not me, he added. Then he blushed. Obviously, it's not me.

He put his hand over Imogene's. Hers was covering a stain on the tablecloth.

Anyway, we kind of couldn't get over it. We'd never counted on just being the two of us. In fact, I think we got married because we both wanted kids. Not because we were in love.

Benny poured more wine.

Does this bother you? he asked.

No, no. I just can't believe we're talking like this.

I meant the wine, said Benny. Does it bother you if I drink and you can't?

I love you.

Benny's hands still had grease on them in places. Imogene stared at the black patterns. She wondered if they could be read like tea leaves. She imagined Benny washing his hands the way he did before they made love. They'd sit in the bathtub in the house he shared with Martha. Dark turquoise. They'd soak and talk and not talk about some things. As Imogene was drying off with a towel that more often than not said Benny and Martha, Benny would wash his hands again in the sink. Again and again.

It's okay, Imogene would say.

But Benny would say, I want you to know they're clean.

I do.

They were not like Russ's hands, thought Imogene in bed as she waited for Benny. Russ's hands often had small cuts in them from rocks he'd picked up. He was always talking about samples. Sometimes Imogene felt like she was one. Like he would slice her through the middle to see where the lines went.

I'm fool's gold, she'd think, lying alone in their bed when Russ was away. And he's out looking for the real thing.

He was away more than he was home. And he was happy. She'd never met anyone happier. Why was I afraid to say no to you, she thought. You could have handled it. Better than Benny.

She had thought about Benny a lot. And she knew he was still around. She assumed he knew she was still around. And neither tried to contact the other. Her father, Ray, had got them back together by giving her his old Mustang. Her father had given her a one-arm hug that said, Come on, kid, get your life in gear. But she hadn't. Except she did stop reading the postcards Russ sent to the apartment from foreign countries. Or the north. What was the point? Still, she couldn't call Benny. There was Martha to think about. All those minnows.

Martha, said Benny, as the waitress wrote down coffee for Benny and herbal tea for Imogene, always figured it was something I brought home from the garage. All that oil and gas, she'd say, can't be good for a body. You poisoned me.

People could say the cruellest things to each other without even knowing what they'd done, thought Imogene. She and Peggy-Leigh had said some pretty horrible things growing up. It was funny, she thought, that Peggy-Leigh was the first person she thought of telling, other than Benny, when the home pregnancy test turned positive. She will be happy and she will help me, Imogene thought. This is good.

Peggy-Leigh had moved away the second she could after graduation. Who could blame her? And her letters were like those from someone Imogene had never met. They wrote often. Peggy-Leigh was married, and she and her husband lived in downtown Toronto.

I called Peggy-Leigh, said Imogene. She says hello.

She knows?

Everything. And she said Martha was never good enough for you and doesn't graduation fuck up lives?

Benny laughed.

I can make this man happier, thought Imogene.

Moments later Benny said, With you, in a winterized cottage on the lake, with our daughter. And we're sitting on the bed watching the snow and eating ice cream.

Either I told him this long ago, Imogene thought, or this is for real.

Lesley-Anne Bourne has published three books of poetry, The Story of Pears, Skinny Girls *and* Field Day, *with Penumbra Press. She received the 1994 Air Canada Award for a writer under thirty. She teaches at the University of Prince Edward Island and is completing a novel.*

Larissa Lai

The Peacock Hen

The Peacock Hen was not the kind of place Artemis normally went into. It doubled as a café and bar and was frequented mostly by fly young stockbrokers and film industry types. She passed it on her way to the bus stop where she was to catch a bus to Mercy's house. She didn't even bother to look up when someone rapped on the window from the inside. It was only when a man on the street nudged her and said, "I think someone's trying to get your attention," that she turned her head and saw Diane grinning and beckoning her with a quick, playful hand. The grin was warm, the kind you don't turn away from, the kind that promises mischief or a juicy revelation. Artemis went round to the wide, glass double doors and grasped a thick brass handle cool from the air conditioning inside. The purple carpeting was plush under her tattered hightops. The clothes that had been hip and urban on the street became suddenly straggly and cheap. She slid into the booth across from Diane. The leather upholstery felt cool against her bare arms.

"Want to go shopping?"

"I don't have money."

"Me neither. I'll get us some." Her eyes glittered. "Stay here and watch my stuff."

Only Diane could look so smashing in a lime-green spandex dress as she shimmied up to the bar and drew her legs over a high chrome stool, donning a forlorn look. Artemis waited. The pause grew uncomfortably long. A waiter came to the booth.

"Waiting for someone?"

"Yeah."

"Would you like a drink while you're waiting?" Out of the corner of her eye, Artemis saw a stately-looking man go up to Diane. She ordered an iced tea quickly to get the waiter out of the way. The man was jacketless. He wore a well-ironed white shirt and a tie in tastefully aggressive colours, turquoise blue and yellow. Artemis slid to the outside edge of the booth so she could hear.

"No, no. I just finance them," the man was saying.

"I would have pegged you for an actor," said Diane. "You don't have those kinds of aspirations?"

"No, I'd like to write and direct, if anything."

"And why don't you, then? You must have ideas, a story you want to tell?"

"Oh, of course. I've got this idea for a western, about a homesteader who falls in love with an Indian woman. But he has killed her brother and she doesn't know." He laughed. "But I don't know if I would fund it myself." The bartender slid martinis across the counter. "Run a tab, will you, Allan?"

"Come on, now. You've got to have more faith in yourself, in your own creative process."

He shrugged. "I have my own little creative outlets. I'm a photographer."

"Oh?"

"It's a little sideline I've had since I was in college. I do boudoir photography. Would you believe women pay me to take pictures of them? They're dressed, of course. It's sexier that way, don't you think, when you can imagine what's underneath instead of having it all laid out in the open?"

"Absolutely."

"Sometimes I do it for friends, just for the hell of it. Now that money isn't really an issue any more."

"I just finished doing some work for a photographer."

"I'm sure you looked lovely. Are you a model, then?"

She grinned that mischievous grin. "I do it sometimes when I'm invited. But I'm studying to be a singer."

"What kind of music?"

"Opera."

"Opera?!"

"My mother was an opera singer as a young woman in Tokyo."

"She must have made a charming Madame Butterfly."

"Not at all. In Tokyo they like *Tristan*. My mother would sing Isolde."

The image of a small Asian woman battling the octaves through two and a half hours as a tragic Germanic blonde must have been too much for the man. A confused grin bloomed across his face. "You'll excuse me. I have to go to the john."

"I should be going anyway." She opened her purse.

"Oh, please, no. I'm getting this. Here." He snapped open his wallet and placed a credit card on the bar. He leaned close to her and whispered, "I'll be right back." Then he disappeared around the corner.

"Good-bye, Allan!" Diane called sweetly to the bartender. She slid off the high chrome stool, sweeping the countertop with her hand and deftly palming the credit card. "Marshall is going to pick up the tab when he gets back from the can." The bartender, busy with other customers, turned his head, nodded and smiled.

"Come on, let's go!" Diane quickly gathered her things from the booth and hurried Artemis out the door.

"Shit, Diane!"

"Shit nothing. Come on."

They caught a cab at the corner.

"How did I do?"

"That man's going to be a woman-hater for life."

"Nah. He was drunk. I don't think he'll even notice for another hour or two. And how much can he mind, really? A man like that must know by now that pretty girls come only at a price. That opera line was risky, though. Those are the only two operas I know."

"This isn't right."

"Just creatively balancing one of society's more glaring inequalities."

The driver put them down in the centre of a fashionable area of town. Diane paid him with the card.

"This is crazy. He'll have put a stop on it by now. We'll get caught."

"I figure we have a good two hours. You need a new dress."

"I don't wear dresses much."

"We'll find something. Come on."

Diane pulled her into a shop that sold suits for men and women. She rifled through the racks, choosing items quickly but judiciously.

"Try these."

"Diane . . . "

"Go on."

Artemis stepped into the dressing room with two jackets, three silk shirts and two pairs of pants. She tried them one by one. "I look like a gangster girl."

"Planning your career. That's good."

She stepped out.

"Perfect," said Diane, placing the card on the counter. "This too," she said to the saleswoman, taking a grey fedora off the rack and squaring it on Artemis's head at a roguish angle.

In the next shop, Diane pulled a dress off the rack, outrageous in red satin and vinyl. "So expensive for so little fabric, but a girl deserves a treat every now and then, don't you think?"

Out on the street, she looked at her watch. "Half an hour before the bomb drops. Do you like cologne?" They went to a counter. Diane requested the largest bottle of Opium available, while Artemis sniffed at a number of exquisitely shaped bottles, with curves that suggested but did not mimic the lines of the body.

"You've got to spray it on, or you can't tell," said Diane.

"Will this be all?" asked the clerk, a heavyish, elegantly made-up woman in her fifties. She had succeeded in tricking the eye to diminish the size of her nose, drawing attention instead to her lovely green eyes with their large, carefully sculpted lids.

"No. It's my friend's birthday, and I need to get a scent for her. But she doesn't know what she wants."

The woman gazed thoughtfully at Artemis's unmade-up, slightly terrified face. "Something clean and simple," she pronounced, and produced several uncomplicated-looking bottles. She sprayed one on each of Artemis's wrists and a third on one of Diane's. Artemis lifted each of her wrists to her nose. All that she noticed was that her pulse was racing. She lifted Diane's wrist to her nose to sample the third scent, accidentally hooking her lip against Diane's smooth palm as she did so. The smell was a little too chemical to be pleasant, but there was something green and smoking about it that appealed to her.

"This is it," she said to the saleswoman.

"The largest bottle you have," said Diane.

She put the card down.

The woman looked at it, and ran it through the authorizing machine. "Anderson's an unusual name for an Asian woman."

"I'm married."

"So young!"

"I think nineteen is old enough."

"Young," said the woman. "But then I suppose you'll look the same at fifty. You Orientals never age." She smiled and pushed the slip and a pen towards Diane.

Diane picked up the pen and paused over the slip for a moment. Then, with a quick and determined hand, she signed and pushed it back. The clerk glanced back and forth between the signature on the card and that on the slip. Artemis looked at the floor. The woman tore the top copy off and gave it to Diane.

"Have a nice day."

"Can I have the carbons?" said Diane.

They fled to the lobby of a hotel attached to the mall. There was no reason to flee, really, except that it filled a need for the sensation of escape. Diane checked her watch and declared them out of time. In the elegant empty waiting room of the women's washroom, they opened their bags to gloat over their loot. Diane produced a small pair of folding scissors from her purse, cut the credit card in half, took it into one of the toilet stalls and flushed.

Larissa Lai was born in La Jolla, California, and grew up in St. John's, Newfoundland. Currently she lives in Vancouver where she works as a writer, curator, critic and activist. "The Peacock Hen" is an excerpt from her novel, When Fox Is a Thousand, *which was nominated for the 1996 Chapters/ Books in Canada First Novel Award.*

Jenna Newman

Duets

From up in the branches of the oak tree, Devon teaches me how to spit for distance. We come to the river a lot. It's calm, it doesn't cost anything, and there's nowhere else to go. There are shrubs and smaller trees separating us from the path, and this one old oak growing out on the edge of our clearing gives us privacy and a bit of shade.

Other days, I show Devon how to skip stones. Or we do nothing. I am memorizing the curve of the river; the view from this spot is pretty good.

Colin and I discovered the clearing one day when we were looking for a shady place. We sat at the base of the tree, but then we heard two other voices, muffled, coming from the bushes and obviously unaware of our presence. Colin and I were both trying not to giggle. We stood up, but before we were quite away, I could no longer help myself and I laughed. Then Colin had to laugh too, and a head surfaced from a bush. He saw us; we were running then, but it was hard to get through the branches and stuff. *Oh my God,* he said, embarrassed. *What?* the woman asked, still hidden. *Two kids* . . . By then, we were gone. We come back often to this place, but we never see anyone else.

This is where I met Jules, I tell Devon. She is suntanning in her bra, lying on her stomach with a blade of grass in her mouth. She raises one eyebrow. I smile. *Well, not really,* I explain. *We came here after, though, and talked. Then we went back to the house he was staying at . . .* She is interested, but she laughs. *Okay, Mel, listen. Men are like brooches,* she says, with a smile. *You've got the perfect outfit, and they're just a dynamite finishing touch. But if you don't find one, well, you've still got your perfect outfit and you'll knock 'em dead.* Devon gives very good advice. She doesn't have a boyfriend right now, and likes it that way.

So far, I haven't found that peace of mind, but I want to. I think she will teach me.

While Colin is in Iceland, I spend a lot of time alone. Not the best thing to do, given my state of mind. We have just broken up, for the first time, and I take it badly. People tell me stories of the after-effects of first love, and I begin to think any other relationships will be pointless, if not impossible. I believe them when they say, *You'll never really get over him.* And at first, they're right.

A couple of friends take me to a gay bar, just for kicks. None of us has ID saying we're older than we are, so the expedition is a failure. We walk around the city instead, loud and obnoxious. I can tell my friends think they're being funny, and in other circumstances they would be, but I'm thinking of Colin. I stop listening to them after a while. The next voices I hear are strange ones, and I don't quite understand what they're saying. An angel tells me to wake up before I self-destruct. He is so sweet, and so beautiful. I listen because he's the only one making any sense.

Colin and Jules have never met, but I think of them together because they happen at the same time. Their duet begins halfway through a hot, dry summertime. The night before he leaves for Iceland to visit his father's family, Colin says he doesn't love me. Numbly, calmly, I begin to cry, which makes him unsure of himself, as always. He tries to explain, and I wonder if he's rehearsed this. *I don't know if I want to be in this relationship if we're not in love. I want some time to think. And you could think too, about what you want to do. Maybe we'll decide to stay together, maybe not.* It's well planned. I know what's coming. I know how this will end.

It doesn't matter any more that I love him, or that I already know what I want; I'm on trial in his mind, in a far-off country. There's nothing I can do but wait for him to come back with his verdict, my sentence.

Jules is my first act of rebellion, although he doesn't know it. He is only visiting; he lives in Halifax. I show him around town. My angels are with us, fretting nearby, but binding us together. Prairie summers are hot, so I take him to the river. We sit in the shade and talk for hours, becoming friends. I decide Jules is beautiful. Later we walk home together. We hold hands. In my mind I am amused, calmly surprised because I am about to cheat, to betray Colin, so to speak. I choose to let it happen. Curiosity may tend to kill, but that's why cats have nine lives.

Everything about Jules is delicate and fine; he reminds me of an elf, dreamed and transient. He has long curly dark hair and thin lips. There's not enough flesh on him to hide all his bones. Best of all, he's a few years older than me and very intriguing. It's summer, so I can forget that I'm still in high school and that compared to him, all my friends are children, nowhere near as interesting. When we kiss, it is slow, without the desperate abandon I'm used to. I like that.

After we make love, and Jules is drawing his fingers across my back, I begin to realize what has happened. *Congratulations,* I say to myself, *you've now officially slept around behind his back. Be proud—you're an independent woman.* But Colin left me up in the air. It's not really cheating. I sigh, confused that I don't feel guilty.

What are you thinking about? Jules asks. *Nothing,* I answer, and I kiss him to change the subject. Devon rolls her eyes when I tell her about this, later. *Men always fall for that,* she says. I think she's right, but I'd fall for that, too.

I decide to love him, and do so from a distance because we never talk about it. My little rebellion seems to be a one-time-only quick fix. That's fine, for some reason. We promise to write, and I almost believe he will.

I dream of Colin once while he is gone. It is in Iceland, and it is cold and snowy, which I imagine is appropriate. I know it's farther north than where I live, and in the dream I equate that northernness with greater height too. Jules is there, radiant, his huge frost-covered wings delicate as a butterfly's. The air, their skin, everything is cast over with a pale-blueness, as if seen from behind tinted glass. I see Colin sleeping in a high-ceilinged room, his face frozen into a mask. I have no place in this dream, no actual presence; I can only watch. Jules comes down. He is translucent. He whispers in Colin's ear, his wings rustling like silk and flute music. I know he is telling Colin that he should leave me.

Just before Jules goes back to Halifax, Colin comes home. I tell him everything, of course. Well, almost everything—I let him think he is still my only lover, and that a few stolen kisses are all I needed to satisfy my creative experiments. He's not as upset as I thought he would be. Or maybe I've just given him an excuse.

He says he still doesn't know if he wants to break up for real. We spend a week talking about what we want from each other. I am, incredibly, happy. I feel closer to him than I have for a long time. It takes a few hours for me to slip back into our habits, partly because I haven't seen him for weeks, mostly because I have been pretending to be at least twenty years old and now I have to act my age: bittersweet sixteen.

Then one night, Colin decides, and it's over. I was lying when I thought I was prepared for this. We say little, both of us uncomfortable; soon, suddenly, we are saying good-bye.

I force myself from tears in record time, and Colin and I still spend a lot of time together. In fact, my life is mostly the same, because I'm pretending we haven't broken up. It's easy. Especially since there's no one to stop me—few people know we broke up at all. I know I am fooling myself, but it hurts less than admitting the truth. It's confusing because I know everything's wrong, and I have no idea what the right thing to do is.

Often, when I am not with Colin, I hang around with Devon. She's great. She gets away with anything because she's so confident, and she's got this wonderfully dismissive way of looking at boys. Besides, my circle of friends is mostly couples, and I feel lonely. I think of Jules sometimes. He hasn't written. I miss having a boyfriend.

Devon and I skip class together and go down to the river. *Cheer up*, Devon says. *Men aren't worth it, so forget about them and tell me a joke. In French. I want to hear your cute little accent.* She stands up, and pats me on the head as she walks by. *You know how much I like to be cute,* I say sarcastically. I turn to watch what she is going to do. She hikes her skirt up, and climbs the oak tree. The leaves are beginning to turn, and some fall off as she goes higher. I laugh. Often, if she's bored, she sits up in the branches and recites Shakespeare to me until I agree to do something else. Today, I beat her to it, with my best shot at melodrama. *Out, out, brief candle!* I begin. *Life's but a . . . something, a shadow! A poor player that struts his stuff on stage . . .*

I don't think those are quite the words, she teases. Then she moves out a little farther on the branch. She jumps.

At first, I am paralyzed with shock. She rises to the surface of the river, spitting water, her short hair plastered down. She laughs and swims towards me. *Don't just stand there, come help me out.* I offer her my hand. *You idiot,* I yell, but I am laughing too. She shakes water onto me.

Expect the unexpected, she says. *Let's go change, I'm a little wet.*

I send Jules a postcard of the seaside. The moon is rising, and the sand seems silvered. The water is black glass, the sky is not quite as dark, and there are stars above and stars below. I have never seen the ocean. *Dear Jules,* I write. I feel it is important to say the exact right words, so I have to be careful. *How are you? I am going mad—it is so hard to concentrate, on life, at school. Especially since it's nice out . . . Come sweep me off my feet, take me away from this desert island.* I think I am being coy, subtle. *Colin has come home & we are no longer together. It's lonely. Write me. Love, Melanie.* After the card is sent, I wish I hadn't written it. I worry that it is childish.

I do get a letter back, though. *Hi, Melanie. Too bad about Colin. I know how it feels. I could tell you a few sob stories, but you probably need a mirror, not a picture of me. It's funny. You can either be in control of your life, or you can be in wild and crazy love, and you have to choose. At least it's like that for me, and hellishly confusing. I just had a fucked-up fight (telephone) with my west-coast lover. What fun. Avoid long-distance relationships if you can, they're murder.*

I am dreaming almost every night of the most divine music but as I wake it fades too quickly to catch. What's the point of inspiration if you can't hold it? I wish angels sang slower. At least I know they'll be back, my recurring dreams are pretty dependable that way.

My roommate cut my hair yesterday. Very crazy. You should see it. We're wannabe trilinguals, so we have a rule that I can only speak German to her, and Ruby can only speak French. It's a good way to learn the language, but I had to sacrifice my beautiful locks because I couldn't describe what I wanted her to do. Now I look like I put my finger in an electrical socket, so I get some pretty weird looks from the innocent bystanders. But it gives me some licence—I can act strange, if I want, in the streets. People almost expect it, and in a way it's fun, but I'm not sure that it's worth it.

Tomorrow we're going busking. Ruby found a great new place, and so far no one's kicked us off or made a fuss. Music is frustrating for me these days. I guess I'm at an impasse—I haven't written a note for weeks. So my barely remembered dream songs are damn annoying. Anyway, it's late. I'm going to sleep. Have fun. Love, J.

I read his letter twice. I am jealous of his lover, though I knew about her already. I realize I don't have any pictures of him; and I can't remember his face exactly. I want to see him, to make him real. Our first time was just me proving myself. I want Jules to know that.

I come home one night, still a little drunk from a stress-free, no-boys-allowed party, and find a message: *Call Colin. Whenever you get in.* He can't sleep, and convinces me it would be okay to come to his house, even though it would mean sneaking out, since it's now nearly two. But he's offering me his body, and I can't refuse. I am willing to forget that he doesn't love me because this may be my only chance.

He lets me in, gives me a hug. I realize how much I've missed his arms. Little things I'd forgotten I once noticed overwhelm me with a sad sort of desire. The still-smoothness of his face, the scar on his forehead from someone's fingernails in a soccer game. *This is being friends,* he whispers, as we hold on to each other. I know we're lying, but I convince myself it's not wrong to have just this much. *This isn't,* he whispers; and we kiss, on his bed, legs tangled, as lovers' should be; and for an hour it's like nothing's changed. I go home before the sun is up, and when I see Colin the next day, he avoids my eyes. I decide I will tell no one about this; it was a mistake, although one I've been longing for. You're not supposed to sleep with someone after they dump you, everyone knows that.

There will be no second time, he tells me simply. Otherwise we will have to break up all over, if one of us falls in love. "One" means him, since I haven't fallen out of love yet.

Before Colin, I had thrown myself in love with people I didn't really know. I imagined their "true identities," and after they proved to be not quite what I had thought, the infatuation wore off. It was all relatively painless, though silly; pathetic, even, when I think about it now. Most of my boys were shy enough, and generally we would do nothing more than tremble in each other's presence.

Most, but not all. Before I met Colin, I was involved with this boy named Eric. He was thrilling to my naive standards, but had his peculiarities. He imagined who I was as much as I imagined him. In that respect, we were a perfect match, both content to be in love with a fantasy. Once he said to me hopefully, *If we were ever to have sex, and if I got you pregnant, and if you decided to have the baby, would you let me suck your milk?* I think I was shocked. *I'm only fourteen years old.* That's not what I said, though; all I could manage was a weak *I don't know.* I am a bad liar to everyone but myself, so even while Eric continued to propose strange pastimes for us, and while he asked me every few days if I was ready to let him make love to me yet, I believed I really, really liked him. One day, it wasn't worth it any more, and I stopped calling him. I don't think he cared much, or noticed.

I learned where to draw the line. I promised not to cover my boys in quite so many imaginings. I didn't speak to Eric again, and he left me no wounds. In the end, he was the least confusing guy I've known. I don't regret him, but he's not something I'd like to repeat. His version of our ending is that he got bored because I wasn't "putting out." I was marginally annoyed.

I wrote off the experiment with Eric as good practice. When Colin and I got together, I had some experience and some expectations. Much later, he told me I took him by surprise: he had less of both.

The third time Colin and I break up is the worst, although by now you'd think I'd know how to deal with it. It's at a party at Devon's. We are talking in the kitchen, about my apparent inability to let go. He is crying, which is unusual, and that makes it hard for me to explain myself. I want to hold him, and tell him he's wrong, that he misunderstands. The next thing he says just makes me mad, though. *You're obsessed. You have to accept it: we're not going out together any more. Go seduce that Jules person or something.*

You don't even know what you're talking about. Obsessed? Do you think I'm crazy? I begin to scream. *You don't have the slightest idea how I feel, or what I think. You never did. Go fuck yourself, okay?*

That's really mature, Melanie. That must be why you have a twenty-year-old boyfriend now, right? Us high school kids just aren't good enough for you. He walks out.

I lose touch then. *Fuck you,* I scream over and over. I am scaring everyone there. I storm to the door and find my shoes. Someone comes and holds me, rocks me, calms me down. We sit on the floor for a long time and I tell her I am frustrated, hurt, angry. When I stand up, she is the only one who looks at me.

You're okay, Mel, Devon pronounces. I'm grateful to hear her say this. *I want to hurt him back,* I manage, not screaming any more. She nods. *No, you don't.* She walks me home, humming softly but not speaking. In the morning, I will ask her what has just happened; now, I prefer our silence and her song. The wind in the leaves sounds like a thousand wings flying over my head. I wonder if a wing can exist without a pair.

A long time later, I unlock my door, and tiptoe up to bed.

Hey, Melanie. Guess what. I'm going to be in town. I got a job there to set up a friend's computer stuff (he's technologically inept) on my way home for the holidays. I'll only be there for a few days. Save an afternoon for me. Love, J.

I walk around in a state of intense happiness, which people notice. *I'm glad to see you're feeling better,* my mom says one morning. I am singing while I make the toast because I'm seeing Jules later on. *We were worried, since you were taking that thing with Colin so hard . . . The first one is always the worst. You're more in love with the idea of being in love than with the other person.* She sighs, and shakes her head. *You're so young, and already there's so much pain . . .* I stop singing, and look at her in a certain way, so she knows I want her to be quiet, although part of me suspects she's right. *Relax, honey, and I'll spare you the "he's too old for you" lecture. I'm just happy for you, okay? Thanks, Mom,* I say through clenched teeth.

Jules is here for a week and a day. He is feeling sad: his west-coast lover has rejected that title, and opted for "acquaintance" instead. He doesn't talk about her much. I can feel myself developing a crush on him. Jules is expressing an interest in me, too, but I know he's acting out of loneliness. Me, I'm just trying to forget Colin, a bad reason to fall in lust, so I let Jules take all initiative. From the first, neither of us expects any commitment. I am surprised that I have become so shallow, but I comfort myself with an ulterior motive: I imagine that I will love him, one day. I know very little of who Jules is, but I like falling for strangers. He knows me equally slightly, so I pretend I am mature and sophisticated. He pretends to believe me.

I begin to hate my age. When I'm with him, I'm older. When he leaves again, I become endlessly impatient with my friends, my school, my little girl's life.

He sends me a strange letter soon after. It is filled with drawings of snowscapes. He has drawn people holding trumpets, singing, in all the corners. I think of my dream of Iceland. *I have found solace in the calm clarity of a winter's morning,* he writes. *Do you remember the angels who were with us when we met? Who introduced us. Mel, I think I am falling in love with them. They are staying with me here in the apartment. I have noticed sometimes they sing, just under their breath, and it is the music I see in my dreams. Which I never remember in the morning. They are here, though; they're not leaving. I think they will teach me.*

An odd feeling spreads over me as I read the letter. Devon comes over later on, and I show it to her. While she reads, I drink the tea I have made us, hot and sweet, and I burn my tongue. *If I were his age,* I say, *we could've had a real relationship.* She looks straight at me. *Darling, he is falling in love with imaginary people. Didn't you tell me the "angels" who brought you two together were just voices you heard, as in they're all in your head? And he says he's living with a hallucination? Your hallucination. You can't be serious about him—he's either crazy, or he's playing with your mind.* I think of a third possibility, for everything comes in threes, but it is even less desirable. She waits for me to agree. *Anyway, you barely know him.*

I know, I tell her after a minute. *I know.* I am whispering, and I sound so quiet I think she can hear the wish underneath my words. I want that angelic state of being. I want the comfort of a lullaby. I wish that I was all grown up, that Jules and I could run away somewhere simple. And I wish that he would let me love him, but I know that's unlikely.

From Devon's kitchen we can see the back yard, snow covered. It's one of those sunny Saturday mornings, with everything made hard and bright by winter. *Jules sent me flowers,* I tell her, smiling. *The card said, J'ai perdu ma maîtresse, sans l'avoir mérité, pour un bouquet de roses que je lui ai refusé.* Lines from a French folk song. Devon considers them.

"*I lost . . . something . . .*" Her French is at a bare minimum to pass in school. *No,* I correct her, "*I lost my lover, for no reason . . .*"

Oh, of course. It's that accent of yours, she finally replies, and pauses again. *That's good. Flowers in February are always cheerful.* I nod. She doesn't ask, so I don't tell her, but the card also says that those lines are part of a lullaby the angels sing to him. Devon asks me if he really exists, and I don't know what to say. *You yourself say you're good at self-deception. Maybe you're dreaming.* I think of snow angels, and look up at the clouds and the hard, blue sky.

Up till now, I have successfully avoided Colin. I haven't seen or spoken to him at all since our final fight, or even asked about him, though I am incredibly curious. I am proud of myself. Devon and I have tacitly agreed not to mention his name until the subject is no longer painful for me. The post-mortem discussions are done now, and Devon thinks dwelling on him isn't helpful.

One night, Devon and I play dress-up. We give each other make-overs and borrow Devon's mother's high heels; she won't mind, she's out of town. We take the bus downtown, and pay the adult fare as practice for what we are about to do. A band Devon likes is playing at the Cauldron, a bar that doesn't always ask your age despite the sign at the door. I am nervous, and hope it doesn't show. Devon is very cool about it all, though, and we walk in no problem. It's fun. We don't drink much, we dance till closing time, and when unsteady men try to pick us up, we refuse outright, smiling only at each other.

When the bar closes, we go out for coffee at a greasy all-night café. My parents think I'm sleeping at Devon's, but we don't go home; instead I take Devon to the river. In the summer, Colin and I came here to watch the sunrise. We raced our bikes down the semi-dark streets to watch the mist burn off. Sometimes we stayed until the rest of the world woke up, and sometimes we walked home while the streets were still empty. We took turns making breakfast after. I have suggested doing this with Devon before, but she always says, *I'm not getting up at 5:00* A.M. I've never done it in the wintertime. We're cold, despite the coffee, but we don't have to wait long. The sun surfaces from the frozen field across the ice, and we are silent as the frost is lit up like silver, like glass. Everything begins to shine.

We catch the bus and get to school early. I trade the snow-stained heels for my gym shoes. Devon tells me they look silly with a skirt. The make-up washes off, but we have no other clothes, so we stick out a bit when we walk down the hallways. We can't stop laughing, because we are somewhat deaf—Devon says an unimaginative drummer will not leave her head. My ears are ringing, and occasionally I hear a faint four-part choir. Both of us are yelling *What?* at everything anyone says.

Jules sends me another letter. *Melanie—Life is ecstasy, don't you think? Pardonne-moi, but I am in a good mood these days. Just a note, between phrases . . . Yes, I am able to write music again, and it is an amazingly wonderful feeling. There are just not enough superlatives. I swear. And talk about your divine muse—the angels guide my hand, and the piece is practically writing itself. It's a choral work. I don't remember if you said you could read music, but I'll send you a copy. Ruby (roommate/hairdresser, 'member?) got married, finally, can you believe it. I can't really afford this place by myself, so the angels and I are moving a week Saturday. I'll send the address soon (with the music). So if you've got an urgent letter, send it quick, or you'll have to wait till we're all settled. Come visit us, we'll have a housewarming party. Catch you later. Love, J.* The margins are filled with drawings of little people, and bizarre flowers, and things I don't quite recognize. The products of an overactive imagination, maybe.

I am always inspired when I get mail, so the next day I make him a card. It's an abstract-type thing, mostly just shapes of colour. It takes me all of ten minutes to paint, but I am pleased with how it turns out. *Dearest Jules,* I begin, not bothering any more to weigh each word as if it were life and death. *I think I have been hearing your piece already. I was at the river, where the ice is just beginning to break up, and with the sound of running water in the background, I heard this beautiful singing. Out of nowhere. Maybe your angels speak to me too. After all, it was them who brought us together, right, so we've all met . . . Congratula-*

*tions (on writing). I don't think I'll come to see you just yet, but a week
with you would be good, we could refuse to use English—Devon says my
accent is funny. Good luck with your move. Don't hurt yourself. M.*
I seal it with a kiss, and decorate the envelope. As I walk home
from the mailbox, I pass Colin's house. I decide not to look over,
but then I hear him call my name. He has his bike with him. I used
to think he was brave, for riding all year long. *I'm on my way to the
library,* he explains. His hair is long enough now that it curls out
from under his hat. *How are you these days?* he asks, and it's a loaded
question. I smile. *Fine,* I say. I am trying for flippancy. *Devon and I
are celebrating springtime next week. Jules is writing music again. At least
one of us is crazy. How 'bout you?*
He laughs, a strange sad laugh. *I'm okay. I . . . I don't know. I'll see
you around.* Yeah, I tell him, with the same tone of voice. *See you
later. And be careful—it's icy.*

Devon and I are running away together. We're hitchhiking, hopefully to Montreal, for a holiday. Just an experiment. Neither of us
has done something this drastic before, but it doesn't seem to be too
hard, so far. Anyway, we are both getting bored with our afternoons
by the river. She says we've exhausted its possibilities, since she's
already jumped in and everything. It will change shape while we are
gone, once the snow melts and the spring flooding goes down. When
we get back, there will be a different curve to watch from our oak
tree.
Before we go, I send one more postcard to Jules. I found one
with a road on it; it seemed appropriate. But with a twist: the road
is running through some sky place. Surreal. I don't know if he'll get
it, though, because he's moving any day now. *Darling: You'll never
know how close I came to racing off to join you. It's hard to tell with these
sorts of things, I find. But I'm jealous of the angels you always talk about.
(I thought they were mine.) It's a chance, I know; I'm not exactly sure what
happens after death. But there are other ways of getting there. So much to
see, and there's not enough time. I know this is cryptic as all hell, but it's
just so damn fun, too. See you soon. Love, M.* I go to mail it, and buy
a loaf of bread and some chocolate for the trip. I have already packed.
I call Devon when I get home. *I'll pick you up in fifteen,* she says.
We can take the bus to the city limits. My backpack is at the door. I

leave a note for my parents, but they will kill me when I get home. I promise to call when I get somewhere, and that will have to do for now. I go up to my room one more time. I take all the letters and postcards and pictures from the shelf where I kept them, to be avoided or forgotten. Colin's and mine. I arrange them chronologically and put them in a large envelope.

The night before he went to Iceland, I remember, Colin tried to explain why he wanted to break up. *It's just semantics,* I tell him. *Your and my definition of "love" are different, yours is harder to say.* No, he says, *I need to know what love is. I'm not sure that you're it.* He didn't mean to be harsh, but it couldn't be helped. I offered him an excuse and he refused it. Maybe my definition is the odd one, but definitions aren't always the most important things. It's not what you say, it's what you do that matters; it's what you hang on to and remember; it's what you learn to see. Maybe I'll see the ocean, once, before I come back.

I rip a page from my notebook for a cover letter. *Colin: Here. I'm so confident I could shoot myself. Love, M.* I put that one on top of the stack, and seal the whole thing. I wonder if he'll understand.

Devon is knocking, and so I grab the envelope and the notebook and go down to her. I shove the book in my bag, and we lock the door behind us. I think of throwing away the key, but that would be excessive. *Can we drop this off first?* I ask, holding up the envelope. *Sure. What is it?* I smile, and answer, mysteriously I hope. *Letters.* We walk to Colin's. I drop my package in his mailbox. He will find them. Let him think what he wants, the more fantastic the better. There will be time to explain later, when we come back, if I want.

I look at Devon, one eyebrow raised. I'm not sure what she's thinking, until she smiles. So we run out of Colin's yard, laughing in the noontime sun, towards the highway. It's spring, and our duet begins.

Jenna Newman wrote "Duets" while attending high school in Winnipeg, Manitoba. She now lives in Vancouver where she is studying English and creative writing at U.B.C. Jenna's work has also been published in Roots Literary Magazine.

Andrea Galbraith

Outrunning

Geography you learn out the back-seat window. Math I teach you every night when we figure out how much moolah we've got to take us on down the road. You get history in the rearview; don't look too long."

It was the two of us, no one else, but I sat in the back anyway. Now and then she'd pick up a dusty traveller. He'd wedge his backpack, smelling of road oil and sweat, in beside me. It was summer, it never ended, as she kept pointing the car south. I thought she'd stopped time; there would never be any more seasons.

One day we drive through some pine trees, a break in the desert, and come to stop beside a big open space. From the car I can see the edge, and the far side, but nothing below. It is the Grand Canyon, and I think it will be like other holes, empty and musty, with grey dust farther down sucking up all the light.

She walks me to the edge, hand in hand for once, and presents it to me. I see a lizard, red and blue, running for some kind of cover. She chases it around the edge, closer than I want to see. She wants to take it with us, stow it in the back with the suitcases and me, as if we were on holiday, and it was a souvenir. But we don't know where we're going. There was once a fold-out map with a horseshoe line across it in red magic marker, but I haven't seen that map since we got to the place where people started to talk with accents.

I see yellow and orange rounded cliffs, stretching for ten miles, she tells me. It is hot; she sticks her chubby hand back into mine.

"If you're going to walk, walk. If you're going to look, stop. Stop and look."

She doesn't see that I'm not going anywhere. I am watching a thin curve of blue as far down as the view goes. It curves away from my eye. From where we stand, it looks level and calm.

"There," she says finally, and points. "That's the Colorado River. That caused all this." And although I don't believe her, I feel full of power, and slide out from her slick grasp and press my face against the chainlink barrier.

"Where do you think you're going, little imp?"

So angry she makes me, I kick at the fence, and scare somebody's dog out of a picture they're trying to take. The pet is happy to be free, anyway, chases a little lizard, barks it under a rock. Bored, chews on an aloe plant, starts barfing. More people look, and that's when the dog people say "brat" and haul their own kids away. All the time, she looks over my head, over the fence, past the people on the flowerpot lookout.

"Have you seen enough?" she asks politely, in a while.

"No."

"Good. I'm not raising a kid who grows up to turn away from every amazing thing in this world." But soon she has a hand on my shoulder. "Come on. It has to be sometime."

"Can we come back tomorrow?"

"No."

"Why not?"

"Don't whine, kiddo. We've got someplace to get to."

"I don't want to."

"Come on. No lip. I'll take you to Niagara Falls tomorrow." She laughs and walks to the car. "God in Heaven, it's ten to eleven. I promise I will see the Light, if you will see me home tonight." Then she turns the key. The car always starts.

She takes the phone in the bathroom and tells me to turn the TV up. I bounce my butt on the end of the double bed, and wonder if this call means she'll be away tonight. But the more numbers it is, the farther away it calls, I know, so I think she might be talking to someone from the place we left.

She probably forgot to do something, leaving so quick. Pulling me out of bed, a bath towel twisted around her head and neck, sunglasses on. I thought she was trying to make me laugh with her funny outfit, but she yanked my arm till I wanted to cry but didn't. She pulled until I slid to the floor, blankets and all. She grabbed my little knapsack and dumped the schoolbooks out on my mattress. She didn't take shirts from my dresser, but grabbed the pile of dirty clothes near the door and stuffed them in. I couldn't keep up as she ran down the stairs. I grabbed onto her waist, and she didn't slow down at all. She left me in the car, parked halfway down the street, and flew back to the garage. She came back carrying two pieces of black hose. They looked like they came from inside a car. She hadn't said anything, so I didn't either. I turned my face to the door, pretended to sleep. In a town I didn't recognize, she pulled into a convenience store. Gave me a dollar, said, "Get me a pop, and spend the rest." I took a long time over the candy, decided we must be going on a trip. I couldn't remember going away without Dad before. When I got back to the car, her towel-hat was gone and a long scarf was wound around her head. She leaned against the steering wheel, shaking like she was cold. Mom's tired, I thought. Later on, she stopped at a drugstore, bought some pinky-coloured powder, and came back from the bathroom with her glasses finally off.

Oceans end all roads, she says. Sooner or later. "What I'd give to be standing by the ocean again. What's stopping us, anyway? We can go as far as we like." She looks in her purse, but what she's looking for isn't there. Soon all she talks about are the hurricanes pounding the eastern shores.

"I know what those are. That's when it rains cats and dogs."

"You're smart. You don't want to see a thing like that, eh?"

"No, it would hurt."

"So it would. Give you a big lump on the head."

"It would hurt them when they hit the ground."

So I'm happy enough when she turns the car north again. I know right away, and she says, "Boy, do you have a sense of direction. That's something I never had. Never knew which way I was going . . ." All the time, I could just smell Canada. Feel it push against the sides of the car, like a hurricane wind, pulling us one way, then another.

When I remembered the house I had come from, I remembered it white, with two little front windows like eyes flanking the door. I saw this house in every town, though, with stunted trees, and neat flowerbeds hugging its walls. I soon wasn't sure who my memories belonged to, or where.

She leans on the horn and pulls to the left as a boy runs into the roadway after a rolling Frisbee. I feel the toy squash under the front wheel, and he looks at us, keeps looking at us, as we leave the town behind. Two others stand behind him. Maybe they wonder where we're going, always in a hurry. Then it's into a pothole and we're jolted up, my insides hurt. I fling myself against the back seat recklessly, moving with the car, as its belly absorbs the shock. I'm crying and she talks to fill up the space.

"I didn't see a cow back there. Was that a cow we ran over? Had to be. Felt like the car was coming apart . . . Some suspension we got in this baby, eh? It wasn't always like that, till you-know-who, who thinks he's some kind of mechanic or something, said he'd fix it for me . . . I tell you, you can't count on people, you can only depend on yourself."

"When are we going back?"

"Back? Back where?"

"Home!"

"Home? Where's that? Which way?"

"You know which way. It's not fair you won't take me."

"What's the name of the place?"

And what was it, the last place we moved to? Now that I've seen so many places, it seems too far away.

"I want to go to Canada."

"Canada's a big place."

"We used to live in Saskatoon," I say finally.

"A+ for your memory, tyke. Maybe we'll be there again."

The X on the map that had disappeared had been marked with the name Jenny. I had met Aunt Jenny once, on her way back from Australia. She was golden and laughing, and I thought she was too young to be my mom's sister. My mom was dark and quiet, smoking a cigarette. She drank two thick, green bottles of something when Jenny left to catch a plane, and started to talk in short little gasps. She would try to laugh but start to choke instead.

"The things we did when we were young . . . Always on the go.

I saw every part of this country, and I remember every day of it, even if I couldn't find the places on a map."

Jenny flew to Missouri that day to meet a man she had climbed pyramids with in Mexico.

"The two of them together—she'll never be tied down. Send me a postcard, I said, from every place I'll never get to." My mother laughed and said, "Boo hoo, boo hoo, poor me." Pulled her hair and pretended to wipe tears from her eyes. She made me laugh, then smiled, satisfied.

"We're in a good spot, you and I. We've got wall-to-wall carpeting, that's not something everybody can say." Laughing. "Things are good. We only go 'round once." Then she bit her lip, told me to go see what was on the tube.

She keeps lifting her coffee cup and not drinking. Nodding and listening to that man at the counter. I am falling asleep in the booth on the other side of the café. Why doesn't she want to be going? She is getting quieter these days; sleepier, too. I play with the twenty-five cents on the table—a dime and three nickels. We went through a time zone today, and now her face is sad and settling back into its old drooping lines.

"More coffee for y'all?" the waitress asks them, and Mom waits for him to make an answer. He waves the coffee away, leans close to her, letting his hand slide along the counter to her arm. She nods, gets up looking more tired than ever, and comes over and hands me a dollar bill.

"You know better than to leave, or to spend that all on Coke, or you'll be mighty hungry tonight. I'll be back as soon as I can."

I have an old comic book with me that I've read before. It says the usual things. It isn't even funny. I open it and lay it in front of me when the noise around me quietens, and two men, big and warmly dressed, stuffed like bears, turn and look at me like they have something to say. There is a bear in my story, saying "y'all" like the people in the diner. "Y'all better behave, or ah'll be back to teach you a lesson."

"What the hell's going on here?" someone asks. I am not listening, I am reading, but I forget to turn the pages. Where is my other

book, the one she tells me to read when I'm bored, so I won't turn
into an illiterate?

Ed and Fred, she named them to me when we first walked into
the diner and she spotted them at the counter. Probably got nothing
else to do all day but sit there, she said. Now Ed and Fred have
turned around on their stools, feet pressed into the floor, and they
stare at me. One of them, I don't know which is which, gets up and
steps towards me. He should see I'm reading. But he doesn't care if
he's rude. Men do just what they like, she said to me once.

"How old are you?"

I hold my place in the book with my finger and look up at him,
look him in his squinty bear eyes.

"I'm eleven." Hope he can't tell I'm lying.

"Who's that you're with?"

"My mother."

"Not much of a mother, I'd say, to just leave you sitting here."

"She'll be back."

"Used to this, are you? That's what I call just plain sick. What
are you two doing travelling all alone?"

I don't like him. I turn back to my book.

"She's just a kid," the waitress says, as she walks by with the coffee
pot.

"Oh, yeah? Maybe we should see about that." The other one laughs,
gives Ed a shove. I can see him from the edge of my eye as he comes
closer, sits his big butt down on the end of the booth right beside me.
I scramble over to the far corner. He grins and begins to slide over.

"You afraid of me?" he mocks. I slide out of the booth onto the
floor, bite at the bare leg that shows above his sock and roll into the
aisle. I dart out the door. She always takes the keys, so I can't get
into our car. I pull and pull at the handle, and he's in the doorway,
puffing out his nose and mouth like a bull. A car pulls up between
us, and my mother opens the door and hops out, brushing her clothes
all over, smiling tightly. She thinks I might be just playing, but she
follows my eyes back to the restaurant, and stiffens. There is a sound
like a growl in her throat.

"I could have you arrested," he bellows. But he isn't coming any
closer. She lets me into the car, and I huddle in the bucket seat.

"You just clear on out of here," a voice yells from outside as my mother climbs in beside me, starts the engine. My eyes are closed. My head rolls to one side, then the other, as she backs out to face the street. She doesn't tell me to get in the back, stretch out and give her some room. She asks if I'm feeling okay.

"Sure."

"Did you have lunch?"

I didn't eat anything, I realize. I left the dollar bill sitting on the table, on top of the silly book of funnies.

"I'm sorry."

"Sorry! Don't you say that to me! I'm going to find us a nice room and cook up your favourite meal."

"Hot dogs."

"If that's your favourite. Then we're both going to get to sleep, because we're getting an early start tomorrow."

And after she puts water on to boil, she goes to her suitcase, pulls a map out of an inside pocket and begins to unfold it.

"You remember the name of this town, pumpkin?"

"Abbotstown."

She nods and runs a finger over the paper for a while until the water starts to boil over. I pick up the map and look at the index of place names.

"Do you see that anywhere?"

In a moment I point it out to her, a tiny grey dot on the border of Missouri and Oklahoma. She nods as if she half believes me.

"How about that?" she murmurs.

A dog comes around from the back of the house and leaps at the car. My mother pulls a worn piece of paper from her purse and studies it, then looks again at the number on the front door. The inside door opens, and a woman stands in front of the screen, peering out.

"Bulldog!" this woman calls. "You get back in your yard." When the dog whimpers away, my mother opens the car door, tells me to wait, she won't be long. She walks up the steps solemnly. Driving here, Mom had said, "There'll be so much hooting and hollering when her and I get together again." But Aunt Jenny doesn't move, and I think someone is about to cry, someone must have died. The house is white, with yellow creeping up from the basement like the bubbly fungus that grows on trees and kills them. Uncle's lived here all his life. He was born here.

The dog comes back and snuffles around the car. He is not a bulldog, he's small, brown and white. He's got a funny name; Jenny always said funny things. I throw half my ham sandwich to Bulldog, and he's happy, he doesn't pay attention to me any more. I get out of the car and walk around to one of the side windows.

"It's absolutely impossible, Chrys."

"Isn't this your house, too? Your own sister can't visit you?"

"It's not just a visit . . . But I'm telling you, people have funny ideas down here. There's religion, and I don't know what all. Family is family. No one messes with it."

"This is between you and me."

"He's in a rage over it. If only I'd answered the phone when Earl called, but Terry talked to him for half an hour . . ."

"Course he'll hate me after listening to Earl's stories. Earl's good at stories."

"Chrys, you don't know how things are. He started in on me, asking if I had bad blood too."

"Bad blood? What the hell? I never would have thought it of Terry. I know you told me things had changed—"

"You should have listened when I said don't come."

"What the hell happened?" she says after a while. "To our plans?"

Sound of a metal spoon clacking against coffee cups.

"Years go by. We go to church, every day's Sunday, it seems. When he said he had to stay here for a year until his contract ended, I could believe that. Then his sick mom, try and sell the house . . . Goddamn house. I said I'd paint it orange, just to have something interesting to look at. But they don't sell orange paint in this town. Man said they don't sell orange paint anywhere, but I knew that was a goddamn lie."

"Jenny! Jesus, cut it out now."

"I get on about things. He's always saying so. Saying things don't turn out like you think. Ditto, I say."

"Get in the car with me and the kid. Just stand up from this table and we'll be on the road again."

"I'm just as broke as you, and we're out of family."

"I can get money."

"Sssh. The answer is, you've got to go back. Don't you know they're out looking for you? Don't you see, when they stand back and look at you out there, and don't know any better, what they call you?"

"I don't give a shit."

"You should." She moves away from the window, speaks over the sound of water running. "I wish I was older, and could have said, look at me, don't let this happen to you . . . But there wasn't any time."

We are driving at night. She keeps banging on the dashboard, trying to keep the left headlight lit. We pass a bearded man with his thumb out. He looks like a statue, standing there so long into the night. She slows down, then presses hard on the gas, pushing us both into the hard vinyl upholstery.

"What's he doing out on a night like this? I keep thinking I'm still young, but times have changed."

There are no radio stations to find. I start trying as soon as she begins talking this way, as if she's lost something expensive. I don't know what it is. Maybe I've lost it, too.

"I'm going to tell you one more story," she says after a while. "Do you understand what love is?"

"No," I say, after considering. "But people always talk about it."

"You sound like me, just like me when I was young. Somebody started the rumour, and everybody else joined in. Well, kiddo, I was one of them once. Twice, if I was still pretending, but I'm past that . . . This guy came to Canada to walk in fresh air, he said. Groovy, I thought. What a sap your mom is, eh? I knew some crazy people back then. The truth was, he ran away so he wouldn't have to go to war, which is a better reason, probably . . . This one summer we stayed at a cabin on a lake. Some old cabin, at the end of an old trail. Dony, he'd talk and talk, and I'd read books about the forest, and go dig up roots and weeds—you wouldn't think it, but you could eat them. He had stuff to say, enough to fill up two lifetimes. We said we'd never go back to a city or town. 'Enough marches and speeches and anger and hate, enough spitting into a goddamn

hurricane,' he'd say. 'I can't believe that peace is something I have
to argue for.'

"But it got to be September, and started getting cold at night.
We stole an axe and cut some wood, but we didn't know better,
we cut live wood, green as the grass, and we'd lie in bed all day,
arguing over who'd get up and start a fire. So we packed up finally,
and stuck out our thumbs, but there was no more holiday traffic. I
was feeling bad, I couldn't walk all day. We got to a town, one of
those little B.C. towns: a mill, a few restaurants and a motel. He was
restless, but I had to stop. See, I'd figured it out; it was what my
parents called 'consequences' when they yelled at me over the phone.
It was you, knocking on the door. Dony thought he had the answer,
but it was his answer, not mine. He bulldozed around our tiny room,
started walking right into the walls. He had to keep on keeping on,
he said. There were things to be done, governments to smash, wars
to stop. It was all bigger than him and me."

She twists the steering wheel to the right and coasts too quickly
into a rest area. She switches on the roof light, her face too bright
in the shadowy glow. I am scared of her.

"I'm talking over your head now, aren't I?"

I don't answer. I want her to act like a mom again. I wonder
where we are, are we near a town? Maybe tomorrow we can go for
ice cream, or to a movie, the zoo.

"The upshot's this: your dad isn't really your dad. You watch TV,
you know these things happen. But this is a really big secret,
understand? Even from your dad. I'm just telling you so it might be
easier for you to make a decision someday, when you have to."

I howl, tears streaming down my face. She shakes me.

"Listen to me! I don't have anything left in me to deal with you
now. If you love me, you'll stop crying."

She's mean, she's cruel, it feels like I can never stop. I take big
gulps of cold air, dig my nails into my leg skin. After a while, she
puts an icy hand on mine.

"Good. I'm proud of you. You're such a good kid, you know.
You just keep your eyes and ears and brain open, and you won't get
shanghaied." She reclines her seat and takes her sleeping pose. "Keep
your arms folded around you like this," she says, hugging herself
tightly.

"Big day tomorrow," she says, sleepily. I watch her for a long time.

Out the window, the hills are low and trees are small. There are some farmers' fields, but nothing growing. I woke up shivering this morning and haven't been able to stop. I am not happy to be going home, because she is so sad. Soon you'll be back in school, she says. School seems like a big, empty hallway, and I don't know which room I belong in.

"Your mother's done a very bad thing," she says, finally. I feel the seatbelt move in against my tight belly. "They'll all be telling you so, so you might as well hear it from me . . . All this we've done, all the places we saw, the talks we had, it was all bad. I'm a bad influence. What's good is you back home with your dad, going to school every day, coming home to a good home-cooked meal, four food groups, visually appealing." She laughs; it sounds like crying, but my mother doesn't cry. She drives me all around the country; she can fix the car when it breaks. "You want to go home, don't you?"

Since she says it that way, I say yes, and we don't talk any more. From out of the forest come a lot of buildings, a high arch, parked tractor trailers. She turns into a parking lot, asks again if I have everything packed into my bag. I nod, and she leans back against her door with a sigh.

"You're a smart kid, and I'm going to ask you to follow some directions now. You have to follow this road till you get to that archway. Don't go where the cars are going, look for a narrow walkway and go in there. Inside there'll be a man wanting to ask you some questions . . . You know what your birth certificate is? Let him see that, but don't let him keep it. Here—this is your address. They'll probably take it and phone your dad. You might have to wait a little while in there, and they're not very nice to talk to. I'm sorry. Here's a book for you. Don't look helpless, and you'll be okay."

"Why can't I drive through with you?"

"Don't you want an adventure?"

"Not any more."

She nods. "Truth is, kiddo, I'm not coming over right away. I've got a couple of things to do."

"When?" I ask.

"You want to see your dad, don't you, pumpkin?"

I have to nod, although I'm thinking that I hope there's someone else there, too, when he sees me. Someone to stand in between us.

She turned the back end of the car towards me, while I was still standing there. As soon as I took a few steps, she drove away. She had to get away, I guess, her heart must have been pounding. But she drove away from me, and I tried to watch the car all the way, until I couldn't see the number plate, or the tires, or the colour, anything at all. I couldn't be sure of what it had looked like. Was it green like a golf course, or a tree, or a dollar bill? That's a silly thing to try and remember. Now remember what she said about the archway . . . But I didn't want to. I didn't want to talk to anyone, anyone, anyone. Ha, ha, she always said, at the end of everything. This won't hurt because you can hear me laughing.

I took dusty steps down a two-lane highway that was quickly coming to an end. I heard her voice in my head, and began to rehearse it.

Andrea Galbraith grew up in rural Ontario and Saskatchewan and now resides on the West Coast. She studied writing at the University of Victoria and the Banff Centre for the Arts. As a playwright, she writes fact-based scripts exploring Canadian history.

you can go to sleep now, nana,
I'm here

_____

Janis McKenzie

Saturday Night, August

O f course Edie leaves early, when she's hardly even drunk yet, and Carla and Michele just watch her, a shadow darker than the trees, walking away.

"Does she always do that?" Eric asks. He's on the tire swing, moving slowly, more than halfway through his mickey of rum now.

"Always," Carla says.

"She's supposed to be home at eleven," Michele says, and Eric and Carla and Steve all make sounds of disgust.

"But she *is,*" Michele insists, before she realizes that they're laughing at her. Then she's quiet. For a minute they're all quiet, Carla and Michele swinging their legs over the edge of the platform where the rope bridge begins, Eric on his swing, Steve a little way away, at the top of the slide.

"D'you got any Bacardi left?" Steve asks.

"Dream on," Eric tells him, and tips the bottle up to his mouth until it's empty.

"You're crazy," Carla says.

"Pig," Steve says. "You could at least share."

Eric doesn't answer, just pulls his arm back and then throws the bottle in the direction of the school. He waits for the sound of glass breaking before he says, "Hey, so now it's two guys and two chicks, right, Steve? All *right.*"

"Yeah, Eric the stud," Carla says, "I bet."

"Wouldn't you like to know," Eric says, but then suddenly leans forward and vomits. From across the playground, in this dark, Michele and Carla can't see much, but they hear the spilling sounds.

"Oh god, I'm going to be sick too," Michele says.

"No you're not," Carla tells her.

Steve lets himself go down the slide. "We'd better take him home," he says.

"He can't go home like this," Michele says.

Eric makes some coughing noises.

"Oh, he'll be fine," Carla says. "But let's get out of here—I can't stand the smell of puke."

So they walk, back towards the school and the street, Carla and Steve helping Eric while Michele follows, carrying his jean jacket.

"The drunk leading the drunk," Carla says, pretending she doesn't think it's funny. They're all stumbling, and Eric is so bent over that even with two arms around him he can hardly walk.

"Michele," he calls out plaintively. "Michele, are you gone?"

"She's right behind you, moron," Carla tells him.

"Michele, I love you," Eric calls. "Michele, where are you?"

Carla groans and lets Eric slip a little, as if she'll drop him, but Michele can't help smiling.

"I'm right here," she says happily, and looks up at the first streetlamp ahead of them making a puddle of light between trees and spread-out houses.

They leave Eric in his back yard. The sprinklers must have been on earlier because the grass is wet, but Eric lies down without making a sound, just lets his muscles relax and lower him onto the soft moist lawn, and falls asleep. Gently, Michele tucks the jean jacket under his smooth cheek, and then they start walking again.

The whole neighbourhood is asleep. Sometimes a dog barks far away, but that is the only sound. They follow Cedar Drive, Cedar Way, Cedar Crescent, and no one drives past them. They walk down the unmarked centre lines of the streets, Steve in the middle stretching his arms out to Carla and Michele, and when they laugh the sharp sound of their voices bounces off the dark houses and comes back broken and distorted.

At last they hear the creek and come to where Cedar Way crosses it, the creek with its forest on both sides stretching away in both directions like another kind of road, but here reduced to just a trickle through a culvert under the street.

"Come on," Steve says, and hops down to some rocks.

Carla and Michele follow, and Michele slips, one of her feet landing ankle-deep in slow cool water. Carla grabs her arm roughly and pulls her out, gesturing with her chin at Steve up ahead jumping from rock to rock unsteadily but fast.

"You leave him alone," Carla whispers through her teeth. "This one's for me."

Then she follows, and Michele does too, careful now to check each rock for stability before she puts her weight on it. And very soon she falls behind, so that she is following the sound of Carla and Steve laughing up ahead. And then she can't even hear them, just the creek and the rocks shifting under her feet.

The stones are mostly pale coloured, but still hard to see in the dark, especially with the trees blocking off most of the sky. Michele concentrates on where to step and tries not to think of how far away Steve and Carla might be. She'll catch up with them, sooner or later. Right now she just feels tired, maybe as tired as Eric, and her foot is itchy in her wet running shoe.

"Oh, *there* she is," Carla says in a loud voice. Michele can just make out the two of them, sitting on a log at the edge of the creek, Steve's arm across Carla's shoulders, but both their faces are dim. All that's clear is the lit end of Steve's cigarette.

"I don't understand why they all fall in love with Michele," Carla says, still loud enough for Michele to hear, and Michele can see that they have a mickey of gin now, and are passing it back and forth.

"Oh, do they?" Steve asks.

Michele just stands still, wondering what they're going to do.

"Yeah, they always fall in love with her," Carla says. "They think she's beautiful or something."

Steve throws his soft voice across to Michele. "Michele," he says, "come sit here with us." He puts the bottle down carefully between some rocks.

And Michele walks over carefully, then sits down on the long sloping log a few feet from Steve.

"Come on," Steve says, and pats the rough bark closer to him. "I won't bite."

Michele slides over a little and almost immediately feels Steve's arm around her, the warmth of the cigarette in his fingers near her ear.

"Does everybody really fall in love with you?" he asks her. "Does everybody really tell you you're beautiful?"

"What about *you*?" Carla asks from the other side of Steve. "What do *you* think?"

Steve tosses his cigarette into the water with a small movement of his wrist. "Let me get a better look," he says, and moves his arm up to Michele's shoulder, pulls her closer.

Michele tries not to pull away. Steve's face is almost touching hers, and his eyes are moving up and down as he looks at her, her hair, her eyes, her mouth, her neck, down to her T-shirt.

"Yeah, you're a pretty girl, all right," he says at last, then turns back to face Carla, keeping his arms firmly around both of them. "But *you*," he says to Carla, "*you* are something else."

"Something else?" Carla asks. "What's that supposed to mean?"

"It means you're . . . sexy," Steve says. He leans over and kisses Carla on the mouth. Michele feels herself being pulled with him, then Steve sits back again.

"You're a real woman, you kiss like a real woman," Steve says.

"Well, I'm a lot more experienced than Michele," Carla tells him.

"Oh really?" Steve asks. He turns back to Michele and kisses her now. The kiss starts out soft, then pushes her back against the arm around her. He pulls away again, and Michele feels a smear of wet all around her mouth.

"I guess you're right," Steve says to Carla. "She won't even open her mouth."

"She's just a tease," Carla says.

Michele feels her face getting hot. She bends down and picks up the gin.

"Panty remover, huh?" Steve asks, and laughs.

"It'd take more than *that*," Carla says.

Michele takes a drink and then puts the bottle down again. She can feel herself blushing. Steve leans towards her.

"You're not really as innocent as Carla says, are you?" he asks her.

"No," Michele says, shaking her head.

"I knew you weren't," he says. He takes her hand and puts it in his lap, fits it under his palm into a curve against the bulge inside his jeans.

"Can you feel it?" Steve asks, and Michele does, a kind of twitching, unfolding under her hand. She looks up at Steve but he's turned towards Carla, kissing her again. This time Michele can hear them. She starts to pull her hand away but Steve presses down on it with a sudden strength. With his hand and her hand under it he jerkily moves to get his fly undone, then pushes Michele's hand inside. She hears him moan softly into Carla's mouth.

"Mmm," Carla says back, and Michele feels Steve's hand forming her fingers into the shapes he wants, pushing them into movements.

Then Steve pulls his head away from Carla. "Put it in your mouth," he says to Michele.

Michele shakes her head to keep a mosquito out of her nose. For some reason, she thinks of Edie and Eric, both asleep somewhere.

"She's afraid of it," Carla says.

"But there's nothing to be afraid of," Steve says to Michele. "What are you afraid of?"

"Nothing," Michele answers, too fast. But still she is pulling away with her hand, pulling against Steve's fingers around her wrist.

"I told you," Carla says to Steve. "She's a tease."

With a strong tug Michele pulls her hand free. Steve leans towards her, reaches for her arm, but she stumbles away, into the creek. For a moment both feet are in the shallow water, but then she splashes up onto a rock and turns back to see if they are following her. Steve half gets up but Carla pulls him back onto the log.

"Go ahead," Steve calls. "You weren't turning me on anyway."

Michele jumps to another rock, slips again, this time falls in a pool up to her calf before she gets up. But the log is getting farther away. She gets over a few more rocks before she hears Steve shout out, "Slut."

On the other side of the creek a branch is hanging down over the water, and Michele grabs it with both hands. It bends, but not far, and for a moment she stands still, feeling the hard worn bark, listening to the water. Michele can just see the thick dark shape of Steve and Carla on their log, but can't hear what they're saying.

Michele holds the branch and listens to her own breathing as it slows down. In a little while she will be ready to find a spot where she can sit down. Then she'll wait for Carla, letting the sound of the creek put her into a kind of a dream. And then, much later, Carla will walk back to their street with her, and at last Michele will climb up quiet carpeted stairs to her own soft bed.

Janis McKenzie sings and writes songs for two bands, Violet and the Touch & Gos, *and is a regular guest on* CBC FM's Nightlines. *Her stories have appeared in* Grain *and the 1994 anthology* The Air Between Us.

Karen Connelly

Esmeralda

She had an outlandish name, and her appearance was outlandish, too. Esmé, she was called, although on the inside of her exercise books *Esmeralda* was printed in small green letters. Had her face not been so striking, people might have thought she was ugly because her body was heavy, almost ungainly. If she walked quickly, her limp was very pronounced; one knee seemed to have a permanent kink. She'd broken her leg as a child and the village doctor botched the delicate setting of the bones. Her eyes were the same amber and honey colour as her hair. In contrast to her round body, her face was narrow, sometimes painfully sharp. A long, aquiline nose. If you were sitting close to her, you could see the complex latticework of veins in her ears. When she played, her nostrils flared and her face flushed. Even those who didn't care for her thought she was beautiful then.

She leaned very close to the piano and did not coax it to life but demanded that it rise up and make itself heard. Her way of speaking and dealing with people was gentle, although most people never knew it because she spent so much time alone. She loved to sing, and once, after we had become close, I managed to persuade her to sing for us. This surprised the people who thought her aloof, even unkind; her voice was deep and warm as flesh. During the final great snowstorm of the year, when we all gathered to say good-bye and feel the heat burst out of the fireplace for the last time, Esmé told the story of her song, then sang it in a language none of us could understand. It was a time we all have occasionally, fleetingly, when we feel close to the human beings around us, and are filled with hope for them and for ourselves, when we pray quickly and silently, even if we don't believe in a god, that something will keep us safe and help us to become ourselves. The painters, musicians, sculptors, piano tuners, kitchen staff: gathered in a ragged circle of firelight, faces warm under the red shadows, we listened to Esmé sing as though we were hearing a hymn we had loved since we were children.

Before I went to the colony in the mountains, I visited the piranhas at the bank, paid off my loan, and put a thousand down on my Visa card. I flicked paint out from under my fingernails while a woman in pointed shoes thanked me for being such a good customer. As I left, she urged me to continue doing business with the bank. Ha! I thought, and whistled myself through the shiny doors. That very afternoon, free at last, I boarded a bus with a duffel bag stuffed full of paints, pastels, brushes and a bag of powdered graphite, which is used to simulate illumination. I was interested, at that time in my life, in making light come out of the canvas.

As soon as I arrived at the colony, I lugged my bag out to my high-ceilinged studio in the woods; I wasn't interested in seeing my room in residence because I was only going to sleep there. It was the first time in my life I hadn't had a money-grubbing job to do while I painted, and I was determined to take advantage of every moment of my liberation. That same afternoon, after twelve hours on a bus, I set up my rows of paints and the photographs I wanted to work from. I walked for an hour through the trees collecting pine cones and rocks and small, inspiring twigs—I'd always liked to have things to touch—then returned to my studio and sketched for two hours to loosen up my fingers. I gobbled down the stale muffin I had bought the day before in Vancouver because I thought going to supper in the cafeteria would be a waste of time. I was twenty-four and my favourite phrase was Heinrich Böll's declaration: It's a crime to sleep!

For two weeks I worked constantly, only stopping for a few hours at a time to sleep or rush off to grab something to eat. I didn't bathe; I ate nothing before noon. I ran back and forth through the snow from my studio to the cafeteria, startling hungry deer. I'd met almost no one in the colony, although I knew the place was full of other artists. Sometimes I heard wild piano music pounding through the cold air. There was a lounge and a beautiful swimming pool and a famous library, but I hadn't gone anywhere except into my studio and into the trees where the shadows of the spruce dropped sharp and dark against the snow. I ignored other people because I didn't have money to spend on drinking, and I didn't want to get roped into boring conversations or have any melodramatic love affairs.

Esmeralda changed my mind about listening to other people. I met her just as my first flush of painter's mania was subsiding and I was returning, a little, to the world of bathtubs and breakfast.

She had a strange, almost magical way of perceiving the world; people felt nervous around her, intimidated. During a master class, the principal oboist from the Boston Symphony asked, "In your opinion, what does music mean to most musicians?" He was a chubby, laughing man; the atmosphere of the class was conversational. The other musicians and composers were being witty, sharp-tongued, a little stupid, saying that music was a harmonious way to make a buck, or meet rich women in evening gowns. In response to his question, Esmé answered, "Like anything we love, music is salvation." She did not notice the lack of seriousness around her, the giggles, the restless feet.

She acquired the reputation of being too serious, high-minded, possibly miserable, but that was not true. When she was with someone she trusted, she laughed often. She had grown up in a certain darkness, a country of secrets, and only by great external seriousness was she able to get as far as she had. When I knew her, she was twenty-six, already one of the most talented pianists in the Soviet Union. She was a woman who had come from a village in Moldavia and was without connections of any kind.

At fourteen, playing in a school concert, she interpreted a piece by Prokofiev almost faultlessly, with an unrushed power rarely observed in amateur musicians. One of the people in the audience was a visitor from Moscow, himself a pianist, an instructor at the conservatory. He spoke briefly with Esmé's parents. He said he would do everything in his power . . . Esmé's father, a pharmacist, and her mother, a worker in a zipper factory, received a call from Moscow. A month later, Esmé was living in a dormitory. She could see the Kremlin walls from her window. She studied music history and theory five hours a day, and received lessons from one of the most famous piano teachers in Europe.

"It was like a huge wind tore through my life, blew everything apart. For longer than a year, I was stunned, well stunned, like a cow before slaughter. I could not believe what had happened to me. When I had time to wander around Moscow, I had to consciously keep my mouth closed, or else I would have looked like an idiot. After three months, I was allowed to go home for a week of vacation, and though I loved my little town and my people, I suddenly realized, I understood for the first time: I had escaped. I would not grow up to work in the zipper factory. I would not study chemistry. I would play the piano. I would live in music. Do you see what that is? What that means? When I returned to Moldavia, I went back to the little school where I had learned to play. The upright piano with all its chips and forever out-of-tune strings made me weep. In Moscow, I had already been assigned a huge grand piano in a room with a mirror and a window. The piano in my school looked like a broken toy. I was only fourteen years old, but I knew a miracle had befallen me. For the last twelve years, I have tried to understand why. The gifts in our lives are the greatest mysteries we ever know."

When she was twenty-three, she attended a music competition in Poland, where she heard from a playwright about a renowned "centre for artists" in Canada. He had spent four months there and told her of the musicians he'd known, how they were given freedom and space and time to work. He gave her the address.

Esmé already had a considerable reputation. She had played abroad, recorded in England, won several major competitions. She was known in Russia as "the dark angel," even though she was pale and almost blonde. Her style was marked by a severity of interpretation rare in someone so young, and her playing, though grave, was surprisingly open and deep. She had a vulnerability, an honesty that most musicians never attain: she gave.

Every few months, since her twenty-third year when she'd heard about the artist centre, she had applied for permission to leave her position at the conservatory and study in Canada. Her teachers and advisors claimed that an extended sabbatical would be the end of her career. In an unstructured program, her discipline would evaporate, people would question her dedication. She would lose a great deal of what she had worked so hard to gain. The director of the conservatory met with her several times to warn her, dissuade her from leaving, remind her of the dangers, the temptations.

But four months later, in the beginning of September, Esmé made her first unaccompanied journey out of eastern Europe. She was twenty-six years old. While flying through darkness over the North Pole, she thought how wonderful it would be if the plane crashed. "Death," she explained, "can be the most potent revenge." She knew that she was to experience freedom for the first time in her life. She could not sleep for fear of nightmares. "The idea of doing whatever I wanted for more than an hour made me very anxious. I began to suspect that they were right, that I would become lazy, lose technique, fail to play well without the pressure of a schedule."

That did not happen. If people went to the colony with a desire to work they worked. I discovered later that my flurry of creativity was not unique. The heat of creation made that mountainside warmer than others; the snow melted faster there, wildflowers opened sooner. Some of the sculptors began to work in epic proportions. At night they dreamt of bronze mountains high enough to scrape Orion's feet. Painters rushed around with paint on their elbows and foreheads. After they played and played, the musicians saw the faces of Elektra and Stravinsky in the clouds. In the evenings, we went swimming, or drank beer, or recited filthy limericks. Some of us stayed in our rooms and studios and thought about how far we were from creating anything that would live beyond us. We moaned, cried, laughed. We joked about becoming secretaries or zookeepers or engineers. I learned there that my life, and Esmé's life, all our lives, were nearly invisible fibres in a long, ancient thread. I tried to be unafraid of being so small. At the tail end of those nights when I had been thinking too hard, I often ventured up the mountain paths until I was compelled to stop and stare up at the sky with an open mouth. At first I was afraid to believe it, but I heard the stars singing.

I once asked Esmé if she had ever heard such a thing. She looked at me curiously, as if I were joking. "Jacqueline, stars don't sing. They never sing. They weep. Sometimes in sorrow, sometimes in joy. That is why they seem to tremble. They are crying."

After my first few weeks of mad painting, when my inhuman pace had slowed down, I began spending the late afternoon in the library, studying beautiful art books and sketching notes to myself. When I paused at my work, I watched the musicians who came in to listen to music. Often they were so concentrated on the storms and reveries coming out of their earphones that I could sketch their motionless faces and bodies for more than half an hour at a time. Others grew restless, though, listening to the world's great composers. They rubbed their foreheads and hands violently, trying to press comparable music out of their own skin.

I noticed Esmé because she came to the library as often as I did. I did not know she was a musician, because she rarely listened to music. She read the newspapers, then flipped through the new photography magazines and literary journals. She had bought a great deal of the turquoise jewellery so popular in those mountains; as she turned pages, her bracelets jangled and rang. Enjoying the silvery disturbance in that quiet place, I often tried to sit close behind her or off to her side, just out of her line of vision. I loved sketching her arms and hands because they were very fine, long, lightly veined and muscled. I came to expect her in the library. If she was not there I felt vaguely disappointed. One afternoon I watched her writing furiously on loose sheets of paper, copying something from one of the books on her table. She rose and disappeared between the bookshelves, I stood and walked slowly past the books: all writing by Solzhenitsyn. As she was still hidden among the bookshelves, I leaned over and looked at what she was writing in her notebook. It was in Russian.

Uneven footsteps thumped up behind me. I was caught in the act. I swung around with an apology in my mouth, but she spoke first. "A reprint of his Nobel Lecture. I am memorizing it," she said. "Incredible, isn't it? Though he wrote it in Russian, I am memorizing a translation of it in English." Solzhenitsyn had won the prize five years before, in 1970. "But I have never seen a copy of this lecture in Russian. And I have read only parts of *One Day in the Life of Ivan Denisovich*. It is very difficult to find that novel. I don't think he has been able to publish anything else in the Soviet Union."

"I didn't mean to . . . I'm sorry I—"

"No, do not apologize. It is nice to meet you finally. My name is Esmé." She put out her hand.

"And you?"

"Jacqueline."

"We seem to work here always at the same time. You are a painter, aren't you?" I nodded, I groped for a book, put my other hand in my pocket. Her eyes did not let go of my eyes. "May I ask you a question, Jacqueline?" I nodded again and returned the book to its place. "Why do you always draw just my hands?"

Even as I looked away, I felt the bright flush rising in my cheeks, my jaw. I laughed.

She leaned over and shook my hand again, smiling for the first time now. "Let's go and have a cup of coffee. I'll tell you."

Several days after I'd noticed her, I had left my sketch pads on the table and gone to the bathroom. Esmé, having felt me watching her, did exactly what I had done: she had come over to look at my work, flipped through my sketchbook, where she recognized her own hands, the blue-studded bracelets. "But you did not catch me," she said, sipping her coffee. "Russians are quick like that. I was on the other side of the library by the time you came back." We spent the rest of the afternoon together, and ate supper at the same table. Suddenly I was talking more than I had in weeks.

What is more extraordinary than the unexpected discovery of another human being? We talked so much that first night, of our work, our lives, our beliefs. She had an easy sense of humour, even though we often discussed Vietnam, governments, their abuses of freedom. She talked often of the Soviet Union, but she did not rage or wallow. She smiled. "Who understands these things? There is nothing evil in the world except for human beings. I was eleven years old when I realized that; I wanted to stop being a girl and change into a horse. Then I began to love music, and I was happy. Music, my own hands, taught me that human beings also know what is beautiful and good."

Our greatest similarity was our love of water, the freedom of motion it creates. "It's flying," Esmé said. "It's the closest we'll ever come to being free of our bodies." We began to meet in the change room before swimming, then we would leap into the pool and do lengths until we felt our arms turning to rubber. We usually swam for about forty-five minutes, then we would play for another ten, walk on our hands, turn over and over like seals in the deep end, try to swim the length of the pool underwater. We would also race.

Unless she was being kind, Esmé always won. After hopping out and rinsing off, we usually sat in the sauna for ten minutes, laughing about the swimmers who slapped about like wounded fish, or the ones who did two lengths for every one of ours. These fast, technically flawless swimmers she jokingly called "the Soviet Athletes." We came to recognize them on dry land, too; as they walked by, Esmé or I would whisper to the other, "Ahh, one of the Soviets!"

In the change room and the sauna alike, Esmé was almost careless about her body. She was not ashamed of it. She never told me exactly how she had achieved that particular freedom, having grown up in a restrictive country. She only said, "Beneath every tough comrade lives a Russian with warm blood." Even "liberated" women who had various lovers still needed to wrap a towel around themselves in the presence of their own sex. Esmé, naked and built like a well-fed Italian duchess, would have none of it.

Sweating in the wet heat, Esmé said, "The atmosphere of the earth was just like this when amoebas decided to become gazelles." She loved the sauna. We usually spent too much time in there and come out feeling light-headed. Once, when we were alone, Esmé began doing a series of elaborate stretches that embarrassed me. She was always embarrassing me in the sauna, either by stretching, or by examining her own body with her hands, or by spreading oil over herself with the careless strength of a groom rubbing down a horse. I had to turn away from watching this, or close my eyes or cross my legs. Esmé never crossed her legs; she said that it was bad for the circulation and didn't fool anybody. "Everyone knows what you have down there, Jacqueline," she once said in a thick sexy voice, and I laughed, uncrossed my legs, then crossed them again the other way. I was thankful for the heat and the half-darkness of the sauna because Esmé could never catch me blushing.

At that time, I was working steadily on studies for my painting, two of which were commissions for a wealthy doctor who had worked years before in India. He had given me a couple of black and white photographs of laughing children wearing raggedy saris, and he wanted two paintings of these same photographs in colour. "I've never seen it since," he said, "the colour I saw there. It made me think I had wasted most of my life by wearing navy blue and grey and hospital green. I still dream about India sometimes. It was a hell of a place to work, but it was beautiful."

I had spent weeks doing studies from the photographs and mixing oils and flipping through various books in search of Asian colours. I was saturated; I needed to begin. One evening in the sauna, I told Esmé I was somehow reluctant to go ahead on canvas. I had a perfect vision in my mind and was afraid I might not be able to release it without doing damage. "Hmmm, yes," she said, and began to braid her wet hair. "This happens also to composers. They hear the creature singing in their minds, but sometimes they believe writing the notes will silence it, kill it. Strange. When this happens to me, I just begin another work, a playful work, something that does not matter to me, what I call a little mouse piece. Then, when the little mouse comes out, I fool the lion into following it, and suddenly the mouse is devoured and my other work is roaring around the room." She poured more water onto the coals and stood naked over the hiss of new steam. Her back was broad and smooth. "Why don't you paint me first?" she asked, turning around, smiling. "I will be your mouse."

The idea of Esmé being a mouse was preposterous. She knew it, and I knew it, but I agreed to do some work with her as a model. She came to my studio the next day. She walked around touching things lightly, smelling the paint, looking in closets. It was strange to watch her do this, like a cat in a new house. She made the place her own. It was only natural that she should take off her clothes and stand naked for me. I sketched her in charcoal first, then painted in watercolours, then did indeed get some canvas and work over her skin with pale oils. I went very quickly, messily, without much concentration. A thousand times I asked if her feet were cold, if she was tired, if she wanted to change positions or rest. She always said no, and kept her body perfectly still, one arm raised, hand behind her neck, the other hand on her upper abdomen, her thumb between her breasts. A couple of times we stopped and drank tea. Esmé sat cross-legged on her feet with a blanket draped loosely around her shoulders. She wore a small enigmatic grin on her face. "What are you smiling about?" I asked her.

She raised her eyebrows. "I'm just happy," she said, standing up. The blanket around her fell to the floor. Because I was sitting on a low stool, I was suddenly looking directly at her thighs. I stood up, too. "Can I see what you've done?" She walked over to the easel and flipped through the charcoal sketches, making little sounds of approval when she came to something she liked.

It worked. That night, after spending three hours with Esmé during the day, I began the Indian paintings and stayed in my studio until two in the morning. Before leaving, I flipped through some of the studies on Esmé, looking carefully at what had been in front of me all day. She had a wonderful body, all hills and basins, roundnesses, long lines. I put the sketches up on a shelf and pulled on my boots for the short walk through the trees. That night, in a dream, she came to my studio while I was working on a portrait of her. She ran her hand through the charcoal and smeared the image of her face. "That is not my skin," she said, and reached for my hand the same way she had when we first met, not to shake it again, but to lift it and press the charcoal in my fingers against her cheek. "This is my skin." And the charcoal did not appear black on her face but turquoise blue, like her bracelets, like the water in the pool. "It's flying," she whispered. I heard the sound of her deep, easy laughter, and woke, thinking she had come into my room.

A week later, we sat in the sauna together, alone, inhaling the smell of wood and wet heat. Although I was naked from the waist up, and quelling a powerful desire to cross my arms, I still wore a towel around my hips. After lolling for a few minutes, Esmé stood up in all her pink glory and poured some more water over the coals. She glanced at me and put her hands on the backs of her hips, taking up two handfuls of flesh. "If you can't stand your own naked body, with all its flaws and beauties, then you will never be able to enjoy sex honestly." I was so embarrassed by this that I did cross my arms. Esmé laughed, unpinned her hair and let it fall over her breasts. "There," she said, looking down at herself. "You can't see mine either."

She laughed at me again and stepped up from the first bench to the second, where the air was hotter. After a few seconds of stillness—my eyes were closed—I felt her manoeuvre herself behind me. She began to massage my shoulders with one hand, then the other, then both. This surprised me at first, but I relaxed under the strength of her fingers. I swivelled my neck around, feeling oiled, pliant as an otter. I thought I felt her breath on my neck. Then she kissed me, very lightly, just under the ear. Before I could say anything, or even absorb the sensation, we were both caught off guard as two other women entered the sauna, laughing and chattering.

Esmé left almost immediately, saying good-bye to all three of us, and I stayed in the heat for ten more minutes, my mind turning somersaults. I tried to convince myself it was only the heat making me feel so dazed. I left the sauna when I felt sure that Esmé had already dressed and gone. Glowing and glazed with sweat, I immediately stumbled to the washroom taps and drank water like a draught horse, swallowing great slow mouthfuls. Through the routine of showering, drying myself, dressing, I kept thinking about having been kissed (but had I really? was I imagining it?) by a woman, on the neck. I tried to remember that sensation, that rising pressure through the centre of my body, that buoy floating up, pulling the thick net of desire through my skin. Impossible, that flush radiating from just under my belly. I was imagining it. Or I had been thinking of a man. I looked at my flushed face in the mirror, my black hair, still wet, my mouth, my eyes. I looked fine, perfectly normal.

After that, tension shifted and clicked in between us. We still went swimming together, we still sat in the sauna, but it seemed that everyone sat in the sauna, trying to escape the suddenly brutal cold outside. We were never alone for more than two minutes. We never spoke of what had happened (or not happened) that evening, but I still thought about it. Esmé and I still talked for hours together over coffee and hot chocolate, growing closer, weaving ourselves through each other's lives. Another layer existed, too, a deep, untouchable place that was also the most touchable, because it lived in our very skin, our eyes. But I did not quite believe it existed, and I was afraid to go there.

Sometimes, after talking late into the night, warming our bodies with tea and memory, we walked together down the road towards the little town at the base of the mountain. "We are in Switzerland," she said once, opening her blue-gloved hands to catch the snow. Then, a moment later, we heard someone whistle high and long for a loose dog, and heard him call, his voice lower and less powerful, barely touching us. He whistled again, spearing both wood and stone with one long note. Esmé and I stood breathless in the dark, listening, feeling the nerves pluck and quiver in the backs of our legs. Why does a high whistle through a cold night stir sadness? Without any awkward words we turned and hugged each other.

During the next weeks, she talked so much about Russia that I went back to paintings of Chagall, hoping to know the colours in Esmé's mind. I returned to graphite, hard charcoal and bright oils; flowers, mythical monsters and Indian children's faces inhabited my fingers, came rushing out whenever I worked. I did not sketch Esmé again because I was working easily from the photographs and my own vision; a model would distract me. She did not mention anything about it. I went to her evening and lunchtime concerts. After every one of these recitals, I went backstage and gave her a hug and a kiss and never once did I experience the sensation I had felt in the sauna.

Then, in the middle of December, we had a Christmas party.

Over one hundred people gathered in the common room, laughing, drinking, dancing, saying good-bye. Some artists in the photography and music studios were leaving, returning to their Canadian cities or different countries; others were only going home for two or three weeks, and would return for the second term. Esmé and I went together. When we arrived, we found people crowded around the fireplace at the back of the lounge. A British ceramicist was singing "Walking in a Winter Wonderland" at the top of her lungs, with dirty words substituted for the regular lyrics. She accompanied her song with gyrating hips and shimmying shoulders, making everyone think of nightclub acts in Las Vegas because she wore a red sequinned dress.

It was a very good party. Several conversations in the works were neither trivial nor depressing. Esmé did not have her usual mineral water but instead drank screwdrivers with plenty of orange juice, "to drown out the taste of this sad vodka," she said. We danced. I taught her the lyrics to a few Christmas carols. We even stayed after the midnight toast and had a cup of coffee laced with whiskey, chocolate and cinnamon, topped with whipped cream. A great pot of this stuff brewed in the kitchen, and the entire lounge smelled like a chocolate factory full of Scotch drinkers. The scent of cinnamon lingered in our mouths. Esmé laughed as we drank, saying, "This is dessert, dessert? I want one of these for breakfast! I will become alcoholic!" When we finally left, we were still quite drunk and very happy, leaning on each other, laughing.

Outside, between the lounge and Jackson Hall, we tried to have a snowball fight. Defeated by our poor and somewhat drunken aim, we dropped the snowballs and tried to push each other into the snowbanks on either side of the pathway. When our jaws began to feel numb from laughing in such cold air, we declared a truce and began walking together up the path. Passing a snow-laden pine tree, Esmé could not resist reaching up and shaking it over my head. I was blind with snow for a few seconds and stunned by the icy whips down my neck. I lunged for her with a scream, pushing her right over the snowbank under the great boughs of the pine tree. She disappeared completely in the hole made by the wall of snow and tree. I was breathless and laughing, still scooping snow out of the collar of my coat. "Esmé?" I leaned over the snowbank to peer into the trees. Darkness. I could see the icy soles of her boots. She had fallen upside down.

I heard a moan. "Esmé? Are you all right?" Then I was afraid that she'd banged her head at the base of the tree, or hurt her back. "Esmé! What's wrong?"

She coughed. "I'm so cold," she said, and her feet wriggled beneath my chin. "I think I'm drunk enough to fall asleep like this, but I am freezing." A few warm words of Russian came, a sputtered laugh. "I have snow in my mouth!" She struggled like a turtle knocked backwards on its shell. Kicking away snow, I reached in to pull her out. She was quite heavy; each time I pulled, her coat slid up her back, exposing bare skin. "I'm freezing!" she said a few times. "I have snow everywhere." Rising at last, encrusted in snow and ice, she jogged stiffly towards the hall. I ran along beside her. "I'm sorry, Esmé, I didn't know you were going to drown in there! I'm so sorry!"

When she opened her coat, kerchiefs of snow fell to the floor. I went with her to her room, opened the door for her, ran the bath. She was shivering. "Take off your clothes," I said. Her chattering teeth filled the room with the sound of tiny castanets. "Hop in the bath." She pulled off her damp sweater and pushed her skirt to her ankles, giggling and whispering in Russian as she fell backwards onto the bed in a heroic struggle with her tights. As soon as I drew them off her calves, she jumped up, her naked body blotched red with cold, and ran to the bathroom.

"Aye! Aye! It's too hot! You're trying to kill me." I heard the splash and dance of water as it rose up the sides of the tub. When I went in she was doing a jig, lifting up one foot and then the other. I put my hand in. "It's not too hot. It's your skin. Your skin's still cold." She rolled her eyes and, grabbing onto the enamel sides, lowered herself in. She moaned and smiled. "Will you give me the oil?" she asked, pointing to the counter. She did not pour it into the water. She poured a small pool of it into her hand and began to rub it into her chest. I left the bathroom. Beside her bed, I slowly hung up her clothes. I felt the texture of the red sweater, the black skirt, the black tights, Esmé's clothes. Esmé, in the bathtub, the sound of the water still running there, hot over her feet.

I opened the bathroom door and said, "I think I'll go to bed now." She smiled and said, "Come here first." I closed the door behind me to keep the steam in and squatted down beside the tub. She rose up out of the water a little. (The faint perfume of bath oil, the scent of wet heat, wet skin, her breath, her breasts and belly and wide shoulders rising up, an ocean opening, slipping down her hips.) Then she laid her hand on my face—it was wet and very warm—and she kissed me, my mouth. I felt the moist warmth of her lips with my own. Her hands slipped down my neck, eased away the collar of my blouse. The hair on my arms rose. For a moment, I thought I might cry, these touches were so gentle.

We did not sleep until much later, almost dawn. Many times, surfacing from a deep kiss or suddenly feeling the contours of her body against mine, I said, "What's happening?" but, as in a dream, there was no answer, only her face appearing before my own, beautiful and opened as I had never seen it before. She never stopped smiling. I kissed her the way I had kissed the older boys of my adolescence, hopefully, recklessly, in a heady state of joy. But I felt guiltless and sure of myself now, despite my external awkwardness. There was passion, and want, and the anxious way of muscles under skin flexing and tensing, but I was hardly able to name the act a sexual one. It was innocent lovemaking, not sex. I felt very young, younger than any teen-ager ever feels in her storm of flesh and emotion.

So soft, so open, so different, to feel breasts where you have always felt a hard chest. We buried ourselves under the covers of her narrow bed and hugged each other. Her hair was still wet. She smelled like flowers. The wall beyond us was speckled and darkened by the shadows of the pines. For a moment, we stopped moving and held our breath to listen to the wind rocking and teasing the trees. Esmé whispered, "The ocean. It sounds like the ocean."

I touched her neck, the white slope of her chest. "Esmé, I don't really know what to do, you know." She laughed. Her neck stretched back; the hollows of her collarbones became blue pools of shadow, I saw the brightness of her teeth as she lowered her head and traced kisses over my belly.

The sound of my own breath surprised me, as her tongue touched me, as her mouth, like wet satin folding, unfolding, rubbing, braided itself into my own flesh, Esmé's mouth, and the curve of her back rising beyond me in shadow, darkness, my own body falling into the darkness of many colours, the deepest darkness of the body, the blood, where everything disappears but living feeling, pleasure in the skin, and I cried her name.

She glided up to me again, leaned over to wipe her mouth on the covers. She was smiling. Her arms looped over me; her leg rested on my stomach. After a while, I said, "What about you?"

"We have time," she whispered. "We have time. I have been wanting to be with you for so long." We fell asleep on that single bed, holding each other, breathing the perfume of women's sex.

When I woke in the morning, she was not beside me. I sat up and looked around, thinking perhaps I was in my own room: I had dreamed the whole thing. "Esmé?" I whispered. She had made love to me the night before.

Just as I was about to get out of bed, she came in with muffins and coffee. She kissed me. "Hello. How are you? No, no, don't get up. We'll eat in bed." And we did. Then we showered together, washed each other slick and fragrant, leaned together again and again, trying to fit our bodies together. We made love with the hot spray of water pounding our backs and legs and bellies. I could not believe how happy I was, how free I felt with her.

Later we lay in bed, touching each other's backs with our fingertips. Esmé talked about what it was like for her to live in Russia. "Sometimes you can see the faint signs, a certain way of talking that no one would recognize but another lesbian. Homosexuals are considered deviant, abnormal, sick, but lesbians! Lesbians are unthinkable! Lesbians aren't even mentioned in the criminal code because it's assumed they don't exist, unless they are just two women getting together for the pleasure of a man. It is difficult in the world of culture, of restricted culture, to be what I am. And it is such an evil for the privileged, not like beating your wife or children. Much worse than that. So unspeakable. So undisciplined: the greatest of sins. By the time I was fourteen, I knew that I was different. I struggled with it, cried, made endless promises to myself. I thought about killing myself: there seemed to be no other answer. I was convinced I was the only woman on earth who loved other women. I was so lonely with my self-knowledge that I thought I might as well die. A good friend saved me, an older boy who played the cello. Drawn together because we were both loners, we became close enough to talk about sex. That was when I found out that homosexuals existed, and we convinced each other that there had to be other people like us. Finally I accepted it, accepted my desire, accepted myself. I found out what an orgasm was and nearly went crazy with joy. I watched the ballet classes in the conservatory with such lust that I had to run upstairs sometimes and masturbate under my piano.

"When I was eighteen, a new teacher came from Kiev, a very well-known pianist originally from East Germany. She was very beautiful. Tall, blonde, quite thin. Too thin. Fine, fine bones. I dreamed about her, wrote love poems to her, longed for her, wanted her. This went on for about a year and a half. When I was nineteen, she and my classmates made a trip to Warsaw for a music festival. Our hotel had somehow halved our reservations, so we ended up sleeping four or five to a room. Lena and I were assigned a double bed; there were two other students in the room, sleeping on cots. All through the evening of the first series of concerts, I was terrified that when we went back to the hotel, Lena would ask one of then other girls to sleep with her. But when we prepared ourselves for bed that evening, she just talked and joked in her usual way. We all said good night, lay down. One of the other girls turned out the light. The room was so small that if I stretched my arm out of the bed, I could touch one of the other student's cots.

"Of course I could not go to sleep. I breathed in deeply, slowly, smelling the scent of her face cream, her hair. She lay with her back to me but I was close enough to feel the warmth of her body. I could see the shape of her neck in the pillow. I lay absolutely still, trying to hear the pulse of her heart, thinking of the times she had leaned over me when I was playing to see that my posture was correct. I remembered the time I had seen the lace of her bra, the curve of her breast. I was a virgin, but I felt that I would die if I did not touch her.

"I rested my hand close to her back, felt the material of her nightdress, but not the skin beneath. I did not move for over an hour. I heard three bodies breathing regularly. Finally, slowly—it seemed so loud—I shifted, so that the whole side of my hand was pressing against her back. She did not stir at all. I thought she was asleep. I opened my hand, touched her very, very lightly, travelled up towards her neck, her hair. Tears were in my eyes, I was so happy to touch human flesh.

"When she rolled over, I felt my stomach turn in fear. I pulled my hand away and closed my eyes. Then I felt her face come close to my own, her breath on my chin, my neck. She whispered into my ear so quietly that I did not hear every word. I had to piece her sentences together from rhythm and syllable. 'Not here. Wait until we are alone. Yes. I want you.' And she kissed me very lightly. I opened my eyes to see her face but she was already turning over again.

"I did not sleep all night. My mind was full of noise and moving like a train. I imagined everything for us. I lay in bed and hugged myself so hard that I bruised my arms with my own fingers.

"We became lovers. I was dazed with glory. I ran up stairs, I sang in elevators, I stared down the ugliest streets with a foolish smile on my face. She changed my life by allowing me to love her. And she loved me back, I think, although perhaps not in the way I wanted, not as absolutely as I loved her. For a long time, I wondered if she loved her brother more than she loved me, but now I know that something like that cannot be measured or judged.

"It was the happiest time of my life. We became even better friends. My playing grew very strong, energetic, lively. I grew confident; I was placed in several important concerts. Lena's brother was a well-known violinist. I remember him telling me how wonderful it was that I was finding a style. He really liked me. Once, the three of us went to my town in Moldavia to visit my parents.

"It was because of her brother that she left. We had been together for two years when she disappeared. I was twenty-one. Lena was thirty-four. Her brother defected while on a tour of Austria. He went out to buy cigarettes and ended up at the American embassy.

"I don't know what happened to Lena. I don't think she went with him—though she did go with him on tour, because she had friends in Austria and wanted to see them. If she had defected as well, she would have been publicly denounced. And she would have gotten some message to me, somehow. She would have told someone. I still don't know what happened to her. It has been over five years. I've never been able to find out if she aided him somehow, or if she was simply punished—is being punished—for what he did. Or perhaps she is teaching piano in New York. Perhaps she is afraid to communicate with me for my sake. I don't know. I do not like to think that she is wasting her life in some Siberian desert. But I don't know.

"I was sick after her disappearance. I could not play. And then, when I was better, I refused to play. I was so angry, so alone, and no one would tell me what had happened in Austria. All the musicians who had been on the tour had seen nothing, heard nothing. I went to the director. He claimed it was a mystery; no one knew what had happened, where she was. I wrote letters to committees, heads of state, the newspapers. I risked a great deal by being so vocal, so full of questions, so furious. I contacted someone who worked for Amnesty International. I went mad with grief because I could tell no one how much I really needed her.

"That autumn recitals were coming up in Moscow. Much earlier in the year, before Lena's disappearance, I had been chosen to represent the conservatory. I told them my hands were dead. I had stopped playing. I lost over ten kilograms. I smoked. I contemplated

suicide but did not have the courage for that. I knew that if I was
sent back to Moldavia, my career as a pianist would be over. I would
become a chemist, or perhaps I would work in the factory. This
thought filled me with sadistic pleasure. I would waste my gift. Like
a perverted alchemist, I would turn gold to shit. There is a certain
kind of despair which fools you into believing that your pain will
weaken if you poison others with it. I was going to transmit my
suffering to everyone who had worked with me, encouraged me,
moulded me.

"A psychiatrist was brought in. For some reason, perhaps because
he was so ugly, I was terrified. I knew what could happen. After a
long interview, he asked me to play, surveying me with an eye that
showed how pathetic he thought I was, how pale and weak and
thin. I said to myself, fuck him, I will play so well that he will fall
down on his knees and worship me. And that is how I played. A
miserable but vengeful goddess.

"That went on for a long time. My furious interpretations were
thought to be a little strange, much too extreme, but I was working
again. I was practising for ten hours a day sometimes, straining the
muscles in my forearms. I used to crack my nails with playing so
hard, and bleed on the ivory keys. If the director and my advisors
were horrified, they were also impressed by my new power. I played
all the music as if it were a battle, or as if it were dying right there
on the page. I interpreted nothing light or glorious. I despised waltzes
and gentle pieces—they were sentimental, unworthy. My Mozart
sounded diseased. My *allegro vivace* movements were criminal, like a
war of butterflies. I loved Rachmaninoff and the lonely music of
Bartok and Beethoven's darker works. Everything I played I
transformed into the music of sorrow . . ."

Esmé told me a lifetime, several lifetimes, in the months we were
together. Her great-great-grandfather, Philippe Lassaigne Maritain,
had been a French professor of European history and literature who
taught in Moscow. As a young man in Paris, he had met Victor
Hugo many times. Each of his seven children was named after
characters from Hugo's books. Sometimes the names were adapted
to Russian, sometimes they remained as they had been in French.
Esmé's mother, grandmother and great-grandmother were called
Esmeralda, Esmerina or Esmerazia.

My Esmeralda knew nothing of her namesake's story until she came here. One evening, I came to her practice studio with an English copy of *The Hunchback of Notre Dame*. In candlelight, sitting among five down pillows, a blanket and a bottle of cheap, sweet Hungarian wine, I read everything there was about Esmeralda, the gypsy woman with her trickster goat. She laughed every time I came to a passage that described the downtrodden Esmeralda. "Aye! What a name, what a gift!" We fell in love with Quasimodo. We spilled wine on the pillows. She reached over to me with both arms, kissed my throat and whispered, "Have you ever made love under a piano?" Her mouth tasted of fruit. I looked over at the Blüthner grand, polished to a high black gleam. We blew out the candles and rolled under the piano, our mouths already open to each other's skin.

A certain sadness shadowed us now, because it was already the end of February. Esmé would leave Canada in April. We did not talk about it very much. We did not make promises as other lovers do, knowing we had no right to think of promises or pacts.

A few people knew we were in love, simply by the way we spoke to one another. In 1975, there were no other lesbians that we knew of at the colony, but there was a pair of very enthusiastic homosexuals from Chicago who looked like twins. They were photographers who took the most amazing pictures of each other. I became friends with them, but Esmé tended to draw away. Her fear of being discovered or penalized never disappeared, although it diminished while she lived here. She was still afraid of what could happen outside herself, what could be done *to* her, but she was not afraid of her heart. "I sometimes experience moments of such bitterness," she once told me, "and such anger, anger at the way my world has been, because I have not been free. And I do not even mean in a political sense, though I suppose everything becomes political eventually. It is the same for deviants here, I think. There are so many risks, so many lies, so great a denial of the self." She often called herself a deviant: "When I was learning English, I always remembered it by associating it with the word 'devil'."

In late March, Esmé announced one morning that she planned to play *Carnaval* by Schumann for her last concert. She lay beside me in bed stretching one leg, then the other, towards the ceiling.

Light poured through the curtains; our window was open. It would still snow in the mountains, but the heat and movement of spring already roiled in the sky and under the ground. The clouds were high, round sometimes, summer clouds. It was warm; new birds returned from the south. We could smell pine sap whenever the wind was blowing.

Esmé said, "*Carnaval* is romantic, full of light, soft. I haven't played a piece like it since I was with Lena. It's the last time you'll hear me play for . . . a long time. So I want to play something happy for us. We have been happy together, haven't we?" After reaching down to kiss my foot, she jumped out of bed. For a few moments, she turned around and around the room, her body naked and dazzled with sunlight, her hair lit with gold. She had the dignity of a dancer who did not know she was wounded, or simply did not care.

The concert was in April, four days before she was scheduled to go home. It was held at the old hotel on the river, a great stone chateau originally built for the elite travellers who came to the mountains in the early 1900s. Members of the orchestra from the city were going to play, and reviewers came, and most of the rich people staying at the hotel. As I walked through the plush foyer, past the velvet and leather chairs, I heard the sound of a harp, a woman singing in French. I became disoriented, took several wrong turns, circled back and came to the foyer again. The ceiling was very high, domed in places like a cathedral. I felt as if I'd lost myself in a castle. Someone had told me that the concert hall was on the third floor, close to a gallery of old paintings, but when I went up there, I met an acre of round oak tables, where old ladies clinked their wine glasses and laughed beneath enormous chandeliers. I turned and ran all the way down the stairs again, tripping on my high heels, out of breath. I began to whisper Esmé's name. I was afraid she would begin to play without me. I asked one of the busboys where the concert was. He said, "I think it's already started, on the second floor, east wing." I was in the opposite end of the hotel, going up and down the wrong flight of stairs. I ran through the gilded hallways, shoes in my hand, catching glimpses of myself in the grand mirrors. I was afraid I would miss her, or they wouldn't let me in. People turned around to look at me, point; I heard someone say, "Miss, Miss . . ." Then I was pulling my skirt up over my knees to take the stairs two at a time. I begged the doormen to let me sneak into the hall. They asked me to put on my shoes, which I did, then they slivered open the door and I slipped in. I stood at the back for her whole performance, but I could see her face. She had been playing for perhaps two minutes.

Now, years later, I listen to *Carnaval* whenever I want to remember her. I see Esmé playing gently, expansively, as though the hope hidden in the notes had stretched her fingers. No one has ever played for me as she did that night, with such faith and longing. Her hands were like doves.

I remember her beyond me, beyond this world where I live now, my life so various, so busy, so changed. I haven't become a great painter, though I am quite good. I am good enough. These days, when I swim in a river of paint, my small daughter often swims beside me, leaving her smudged fingerprints on the big sheets of yellow construction paper taped to the lower halves of my studio walls. I have been very lucky. I know what is beautiful and good. Esmé and I wrote for almost five years. Then I married. And I had Katrin. Then I left my husband . . . Everything, my life, happened. Is happening now. Time and distance. Esmé and I lost each other in the translation.

But I remember her voice as she spoke of music the day before she left, when we sat in her studio and the reality of her departure fell on us like part of a mountain. The piano faced the window and both of us sat on the bench. "If only we could *be* the music," she said, "instead of being the vessel for its power. Because it only touches us lightly. It never stays. It isn't the world. It raises us up, doesn't it? But then it finishes. It stops. We fall again, and the silence is even deeper than before.

"Doesn't every musician want to become her music? Can you imagine the freedom of a bird? That is music, Jacqueline, that is flying. But how much of it belongs to us? The notes rise up and turn to light. We can't keep them. Yet if we don't let them go, they stay in our hands and grow silent before us. *That* is why I have to play. To let something *live*."

She closed her eyes, bent herself over the piano and laid her hands on its black surface. After a while, she raised her head, but her eyes remained closed. Putting my hand beneath her chin, I turned her face to mine. Then I leaned forward and kissed her eyelids. They were very white. Her eyelashes were the colour of doeskin. I felt them against my lips. We sat for a long time, barely touching, our faces turned towards the trees outside. It was a windless day, and the pines were threaded with the flight of birds. Both of us heard the music dance and slip from their small warm throats.

Karen Connelly's award-winning books of nonfiction and poetry are The Small Words in My Body, Touch the Dragon, This Brighter Prison *and* One Room in a Castle. *Her new poetry collection is called* The Disorder of Love, *and her next book of prose will be about artists in Burma. She lives in Greece, Canada and S.E. Asia, though never simultaneously.*

Gillian Roberts

The Air Between Us

My stepdaughter, Kate, is still sleeping in the guest bedroom. She refers to it as her own room. It belonged to her until she left to go to university in Toronto. Alex and I did not expect her to be coming back for the summer. Kate had originally planned to stay the school year in residence, and the summer months with her mother in Mississauga. Instead she phoned a week after exams, told us she'd be flying home and would we pick her up at the airport?

Alex opens the pantry door, fills the dog's dish from the bag of dry food sitting there on the floor. He moves to the sink and washes his hands.

"How far along is she?" he asks, looking not at me but at the window.

"Three months," I answer.

He takes a deep breath. "Have you thought about what she said last night?"

"Of course I have."

Now he turns to face me. "So what do you think?"

I don't know. And I tell him so, that nine hours—seven of which have been occupied by sleep—isn't enough time to come to any sort of conclusion.

Kate has come home because she is pregnant and wants to give us her baby. I am flattered and I am upset. Kate asked her mother if she would take the baby, and Doreen said no. Alex has told me many times that Doreen is not good with children. Kate was three when her parents divorced, and Doreen willingly gave custody to Alex. Two years later, I became Kate's stepmother. Doreen never mentioned having any problems with my raising her child.

Before Alex and I were married, we discussed what kind of wedding we should have. At one point, I made the mistake of mentioning to

242

Kate that perhaps she could be our flower girl. It was ultimately decided that there would be no big ceremony, that Alex and I would take vows by ourselves. We broke the news to Kate as gently as we could, sitting out on the porch of their house, drinking her favourite Kool-Aid. She rose from her chair, cool and poised as a ballerina.

"Excuse me," Kate said quietly and walked into the house. She slowly slid the screen door into place and we could hear her footsteps through the house.

"She took that remarkably well." Alex was frowning, too bewildered to be relieved.

Then an incredible shriek let loose, so painful that Alex and I both jumped up, thinking Kate had broken a limb. We stumbled through the family room and kitchen, rounding the corner to the hallway. And then we stopped. Kate was lying on her back, pounding the floor with her fists, kicking her feet against the wall. The picture that hung there shuddered back and forth while she wailed, her face red.

Alex covered his mouth with his hand, shaking with laughter, and pulled me back into the kitchen. Because Alex and I had been dating for over a year, I knew Kate well, but I had never seen her unleash behaviour like this over such a seemingly little thing. I could not see how funny this was after Kate's composed exit.

We reached a kind of compromise. On the day of our wedding, before we left for the church, Kate scattered rose petals in the front entrance of the house. As Alex and I drove away, she waved good-bye from the door, her grandmother smiling behind her.

While I'm sitting at the kitchen table working on the newspaper's crossword puzzle, Kate walks into the room. She is wearing a U of T T-shirt and plaid flannel pyjama bottoms. I am surprised at the shirt—Kate is not one to celebrate institutions through her clothing.

She finishes weaving her dark red hair into a long braid, wraps an elastic around the end.

"Good morning, Elaine," she yawns.

"Morning." I put on a smile. "What's with the shirt?"

Kate grimaces. "My mom bought it for me for Christmas."

I nod slowly, tapping my pen against the page.

"I feel guilty if I don't wear it once in a while," she explains. For a moment, neither of us says anything, and Kate seems a little lost.

She glances quickly around the kitchen, looking for something to grab onto to break the silence.

"Where's Dad?" she asks.

"In the den. He has some marking to do. How did you sleep last night?"

"Great. I was so tired, especially with the time change. It feels like I should be eating lunch."

It is nine o'clock. Noon in Toronto. Kate didn't arrive until ten last night. In fact, we'd only half-believed she would get here. Kate never flies alone. Alex and I went with her at the beginning of September to help her get settled. She took tranquillizers before the flight, something we hadn't thought of her using before.

The summer Kate was nine, she and I flew out to Toronto. I went to see my sister's new baby, and Kate came to visit Doreen. It was not Kate's first flight, but she hadn't been on a plane in several years. I remember her grabbing hold of my hand as soon as the takeoff began, my fingers almost crushed by the grip of her little ones, the sweat of her palm soaking mine. For five long hours, she kept her eyes shut, tears squeezing under the lids. By the end of the flight, my throat was sore from singing quiet lullabies, and the man beside me had moved to an empty seat at the back of the plane.

So Alex and I were quite amazed when Kate appeared last night at the baggage claim, neither drugged nor accompanied.

"Are you going to have breakfast?" I ask.

Kate shrugs. "I don't feel very hungry." She drums her fingers lightly on her abdomen.

"Have you been having morning sickness?" I feel strange asking, as though it is not my right.

"No," she replies. "Mom said she didn't have it at all with me."

Kate pours herself a glass of water, then sits down at the table. I am concentrating on my crossword. When I raise my head, Kate is looking at me.

"What are you thinking?"

"Got a synonym for 'pacifist'?" I evade. Kate frowns, shakes her head.

After another silence she asks, "Are you angry with me?"

I put down the pen, rub my forehead with my fingers. "Your father and I told you last night, Kate. No."

She sighs, frustrated, as though it would be easier for her to be screamed at. But I will not yell and carry on.

Last night, by unspoken agreement, Alex and I both kept calm and reasonable, though I could see my husband's stony face was on the verge of cracking.

"Does your mother know?" he asked Kate.

"Yes," she answered. "I asked her if she would take my baby. Adopt it. She isn't going to." In the quiet that followed, Kate inhaled deeply. "Will you two consider raising my baby?" Her question was confident, sounded almost adult.

"Why do you want us to do it?" Alex asked her.

"Because." Kate sighed, as though she'd already explained this many times. "If you are the baby's parents, I'll feel safer about him. Or her. If strangers adopt the baby, how can I be sure everything will be okay?"

"You can't." I hadn't planned to say this, but there it was, hanging in the air between us.

"I'll make some coffee." Alex rose from his chair, trying to distance himself from his daughter, from this situation. This is his tactic when he marks essays. Stand back, try to be objective. At the coffee maker, he worked slowly, every movement precise.

I reached for Kate's hand across the table. She swallowed quickly, a sign that her bravery was failing her.

"Honey, are you sure you even want to give this baby up?"

"Yes." Her voice was firm. "I want to finish university. The baby should be born in October, and then I can go back to school in second semester."

"But what if you change your mind later?" I wanted to know. "What if you want the baby back?"

"That's not going to happen, Elaine," she said.

Last night, we decided nothing. Kate was so tired she kept slumping forward on the table, catching herself just before she could collapse. We went to bed leaving much unresolved, and none of us had any of the coffee Alex made.

"What does Eli think?" I ask, realizing we haven't discussed the baby's father. Kate met him in one of her classes soon after the school year had started. When she came home for Christmas, she showed us a picture of him. Dark hair, curly and a little long. Blue eyes and a tanned face. Twenty years old. Kate told us with pride that he'd spent the summer canoeing in lakes throughout Ontario.

Her lips tighten. "He couldn't believe I completely ruled out abortion. He thought I was too much of a feminist, that I wanted the whole thing quick and easy."

"You're still together?"

She nods. "Of course he didn't offer to marry me or anything stupid like that. We're trying to be as realistic as possible."

"Does he want children at all?"

"No, not right now." Kate starts to play with the end of her braid, avoids having to look at me.

"Really," is all I can say. In the den, Alex has put on Dvořák's New World Symphony; we can hear the music faintly from where we sit.

"Does he need to be inspired when he's marking?" Kate asks. "Not that this piece is inspirational. Certainly not cheerful, at any rate." Having said this, she looks down, taps her fingers against the table as though playing notes on a piano.

"Mom cried when I told her I was pregnant," she says.

I choose my words carefully. "Out of curiosity, Kate, why did you ask your mother to take the baby?"

She waits a few seconds before answering. "I thought maybe this could be her second chance. Because she didn't have me for very long. I thought she might want it."

Guilt again, like the T-shirt. Kate is always trying to make amends. "Do you know why she said no?"

Kate clears her throat. "She just said she didn't want to." Her forehead creases, something it's done far too often in the last few hours.

"What about you?" she suddenly demands.

"What?"

"You haven't said whether you want the baby or not." Kate pushes back her chair, and stands. She folds her arms over her chest as she has done all her life, in preparation to defend herself.

"It's just not that easy, Kate," I tell her. She bites her bottom lip to stop it from quivering. We both know she will be angry if she starts to cry.

When she says she is going for a walk, I have a ridiculous urge to tell her to be careful. Instead I say, "It's warm out," and she nods before slipping out the door.

Early in our marriage, Alex and I decided we wanted more children. We thought it would be healthier for Kate to have brothers and sisters than to be raised an only child. But mostly, I just wanted to have babies. Women's liberation was not lost on me. I knew I was equal to any man, but I considered the ability to bear children a privilege, not a burden. I loved my job at the newspaper, and I would love my children too.

Alex and I tried very hard to conceive a child, holding our breath each time my period was a little late, consulting this doctor and that specialist. Ten per cent was their magic number, the occasional fifteen adding that much more hope. When I became pregnant a few months after Kate's seventh birthday, I felt Alex and I had accomplished an amazing feat. I could believe in even the smallest of numbers.

"We'll try again," Alex said when I miscarried at six months. It was hard explaining to Kate why we hadn't kept our promise of a brother or sister, why the paper we'd so painstakingly chosen for the nursery never went up on the walls.

We did not try to adopt. It didn't seem fair to; we had Kate, but other couples had no children. Now there is a strange irony in the fact that this one child has reopened the option we refused. Except that I am no longer in my twenties, trying to be the woman who has it all. I am two years away from forty, having survived all this time only because of my husband, my career, my stepdaughter. It was a long time ago that Alex dismantled the crib set up in the spare room. We ended up getting rid of it in a garage sale, unused.

My mind has wandered far from the crossword puzzle. Our black lab, Jones, scratches against the back door. I slide it open to let him in, wonder why I didn't suggest Kate take him with her. Jones moves to his dish in the corner, begins crunching on the food.

I wait for the Dvořák music to stop. When it does I walk down the hall to the den, knock lightly on the door.

"Come in," Alex calls.

"Sorry to bother you," I say as I open the door. Alex scratches his head, puts down the paper he is reading, clears a space on the desk where I can sit.

"Where's Kate?" he asks.

"Out for a walk."

Alex takes my hand. "Did you talk to her?"

"Some."

After a silence, he sighs. "How can we fix things for her unless we say yes?"

"Is it up to us to fix it?" The question is as much for myself as for my husband. But there is no right answer.

"Why on earth did she ask Doreen?" he asks the ceiling.

"Because," I tell him, "she doesn't know what she wants." Once I have said this, I know it is the truth. And I know, too, what our answer will be. We will tell Kate we will do this for her, that we will raise her child. Because she needs help, but does not know how to get it, does not know the questions to ask.

I remember feeling a baby's body inside my own. Soon Kate's child will start to move. I know she will change her mind, because I know the nature of Kate's love. It is fierce and complete. If she manages to hand me her baby in six months, soon afterward she will be back to reclaim it, regardless of Eli, regardless of school.

I tell Alex these things, and he agrees. The sooner Kate feels safe, the better it will be for her and her baby.

We hear a door open and shut from the other end of the house, a sign that Kate has returned. Her footsteps come closer down the hall but stop before she reaches the den. She has gone into the living room, must have sat down at the piano.

She starts to play Bach. *Sinfonia Number 15.* B minor, and hardly cheerful. Perhaps she is trying to illustrate a point. Or maybe she is unaware of what she is doing.

Soon we will tell her what she wants to hear, but for now we won't interrupt.

Gillian Roberts has published work in the Claremont Review *and* sub-TERRAIN. *She is currently completing a B.A. in English at the University of Victoria.*

Nick Nolet

Bonfire Angels

I

We have our heads encircled with angels, with angels of multicoloured voices, like Gabriels flown from the right hand of God. Later they tell us that we cannot see screams, or feel the ions of death crush us like retribution, but it remains the same.

I lie on my stomach on a yellow patch of grass, my skirt spread like an open mouth around my legs. Even my skirt has secrets to tell and they are long-legged, the anxious whites like a breeze. I am fragile on this patch birthed from a line of middle children, children with edges drawn in tough and their insides replaced with malice and cast iron.

Mother sold her birthright for a clean pressed kilt and knee socks, a clean piece of Canadian winter, a photo album to fill with teddy boys. Yet she still picks up her Star of David sewn in the autumn sky like brazen daffodils, and she stakes claim to the ink brand of the soap thin persecuted. On the walls of my house of association, there is a portrait of tissue-paper screams. The persecuted have mouths like jazz singers, red whore mouths, mouths spilled open like purses; mouths like picked locks. My red whore mouth is like a sulfur strip from a matchbook. I could strike my mouth with dipped-in-secrets sticks.

When Mother called in the priests to cleanse the house of spirits, it was her own malevolence that permeated the walls like the smell of sex on the fingers of a pedophile. Mother, wear the uniform of a Nazi. It already hugs close the fullness you give to shadows and memory. It is so easy to remember the nightmares wrapped in skin, my own name is tattooed across the forearm like *Beware of Trespassing*. And forgive us our trespasses—

The sun is roasting my small bones and Serax is drying my mouth. I will wash everything I ingest with water like a raccoon. I can taste the sun like a dry, red leaf. I spread myself open in the heat like a bonfire angel. I will burn up to God and he will catch me in his great hands and stroke the hair from my brow and I will bleat repentance. A bonfire angel.

II: Cloud

I taste the setting sun, feel the heaviness drop from my limbs. I stand up and dust myself off, parts of me scatter into the grass. Now my daily slow march back into the building.

I pass the Monkey woman who is telling secrets to the Cunt man. He told me on my first day that women were the life-support systems for cunts. I hope the Monkey woman will sing today. She knows the old war songs that turn the air into a newsreel of the Battle of Britain, red lipstick, V for victory, "keep mum," "loose lips sink ships," radio programs, dancehalls, Betty Grable and glamour. Last time she sang, I was smoking in front of the lobby doors and I watched her rock back and forth on her vinyl chair, tongue lolling, spittle crawling like a transparent caterpillar down her chin, whining in her indistinguishable way. She continued swaying as shit ran down her stubby legs. Somebody said she used to be a nurse. I buried my chin in my shirt, and rocked back and forth, moaning to myself. A dance of the inmate, not of the patient. A dance overflowing with irrevocability, the footwork moving in time to the arthritic beat of the human heart.

The Serax had worn off. I wasn't stoned but clearly receptive to these melancholias of US, the ones inside.

I float past the watchman, past the gift store, to the elevators. I float like a cloud to a place where even the sun wouldn't shine. Here, inside, I am the ice princess. I do not have the gift of tongues, but of silences like icicles. My eyes are carved from winter.

III: The Dark Lands

When I was a child, I had to stuff the nightmares back down my throat or the demons would escape and cut through the night to my bed by the beacon of my screams. The nurse has come by twice with her flashlight. She locked the shower door so no one will suicide in the night. I want to curl up in the bathtub and suck my thumb. I want my daddy to hug the little girl he once protected, the same little girl who cries behind all my laughter, speaking strange words from the bottom of my gut. She screams so loud I cannot sleep. *You promised you'd protect me but you didn't. You hurt me. You let them hurt me so badly. Help me.* She has her red hair in askew pigtails, and her lip is pouted down. She is the little beggar girl who sells matchsticks in a fairy tale, the little girl who survived the holocaust and will never forgive me for wiping away her tears.

I start to cry, and panic. The smell of tiger lilies and butterscotch pudding will always be the scent of fear for me: Mommy is a Nazi. She should have drowned but the waves I have painted didn't quite reach her. This is my paintings come to voice.

My skin is trying to wander from my bones and I am afraid of sleep because sleep takes me to the dark lands where every shadow has fingers like keys, where the bogeyman is also made of shadows of men with erect penises; where hell is filled with children cutting out paper dolls and eating candy stained with sex. This is a montage of explanation, a film reel of answers, of justification. This is the why.

IV: Mimosa

Linda comes.

I have been whipping my head like a dog shaking off droplets of water. Watch the front entrance. Watch the side. Make sure she sees me here on the slope of lawn.

She comes in pink. She is Glinda the Good Witch with a bag full of magic. She wears pink regally, like I wear a hospital uniform. She brings me peppermint Laura Secord chocolate bars, Hires rootbeer and a copy of one of her own books. A book of pastel truths with an unhappy ending that always makes me cry. She is not like ordinary people who bring me flowers I end up killing. Perhaps the bouquets suicide on me. Even the plants suicide because, like me, they won't take food. My room has become an inverse garden of Eden, plants full of Eve. But Linda can poeticize my being here, she gives me a symbol-less paean to chaos.

She tells me of the psychologist who lives downstairs from her, whose daughter made a sculpture of a monster based on a photograph of her father. She tells me of the women waiting with the air full of mimosa. She harbours these experiences in the fragile framework of poems, whose skeletons become thick and cast iron like survivors themselves. She wants to make poems, make mimosa from my memories. I tell her I will incinerate the dead bodies and plant a rose garden instead. Flowers grow out of the eyes of dead things.

I give her my small poems, huddled skinless and veined in my palm on sun-bleached yellow paper. She puts on her spectacles and reads them with her lips moving. She is so quick. She pretends not to see me cry then tells me that they are crying poems. I see a thin flame, my hair, reflected in her glasses.

V: Bloody Mary

I am in the green bathroom.

Mother is on the other side of the door. Mother is holding the locks firm.

Her tough voice and her tuned ears are waiting for me to perform the mantra. Mother's mantra is clogged in my throat of quicksand and vowels are sinking, consonants are caught in my teeth. The whole alphabet is hidden in my mouth like hieroglyphs petrified from fear.

I see flames in the mirror, and armour hooked on stone walls, thrushes struggling from hunter's hand, and a dim figure too far away to materialize into recognizable form. But I know it is her.

I know because Mother has told me about her. She has told me of the Bloody Queen. The Queen who washes her food with blood, not spit. The door can only be opened with the key of my blood, my bones. The folklore girl who cut off her pinky to make a key to open the door to release . . .

This is not fair. This is too much to thrust upon a girl, a child, and innocent. We cannot make sacrifices of belief, and we are still too malleable to offer pieces of ourselves. We can only offer these pieces blind.

Years later, I tell this: She made us recite *Bloody Mary* three times in the locked washroom and inside the silver light Bloody Mary was supposed to appear and . . .

The bathroom is the museum of screaming walls. Putting your ears to the wall, you can hear the catching of breath, the cries, the questions. This is Mother's room of choice. This is the sight room, where sight is a handicap. This is where I would not look into the mirror to see my body.

VI: Kitchen

The lights are dimmer controlled. Each hour I sit at the table at the cold plate in front of me, the lights are dimmed further. I pleat the corner of the burlapy green placemat. The chandelier lightbulbs hum.

It's Belgian. Like Mother.

I won't I won't I won't I won't I won't eat this goulash.

Mother made it because she was jealous we came back from our stepfather's apartment liking his cooking better than hers. This is her act of power, of revenge, of the balancing of the sexes. This is warfare.

I'm not cooking another goddamn thing until the whole pot is eaten. You're only punishing yourself.

But . . .

Don't talk back. Don't you dare.

She is full steam now, cutting the air in two like Moses parting the Red Sea. I feel the bile rise like a snake seduced by the black music of the snake charmer. Don't let the snakes escape. Snakes twist in my eyes, like her snake-words. This is applying an image to fear so I can claim it as my own.

VII: Children

The ceiling pipes are exposed. Like vein-work or arteries. Or things that should best remain hidden, like men in overcoats with hairy legs. Like the tube-work of dreams transecting the brain into a subway of neurotransmitters. I am small in this room of easels, cupboards, paints, egg cartons, jars, clays, shelves, paper and art smocks.

When I pull the full-length mirror up to my easel, I feel I could be drawn better, I look too wavy, too old, too real. If I can draw myself real. My physical being becomes an art challenge. I am confused, isolated to image and solid being. Move though the layers of subcutaneous fat to find . . . if I can float.

The art therapist tells me I was highly recommended by the staff psychiatrist. I don't have to go but it will be advantageous. They don't know what to do with me.

Dr. Turrey says you are very intelligent. A great visual sense.

Oh that's nice, I like him a lot. He doesn't patronize me, he treats me like an adult, like a colleague. I'm not a child.

No.

She wears lilac jumpsuits and plays Enya or Nat King Cole on the cassette player. I don't feel like I want to bolt, or slink away, or pout at her like a belligerent child. I want to try to let the child inside me paint.

Close your mind and dream. Dream your mind open.

I use watercolour on expensive paper. Halfway through my throat hitches and I cry like a pig-tailed girl who wonders how the night came so fast. My hand does not stop painting. The art therapist rushes over.

Could you stay after the group?

Uh-huhh.

The child has shown me what happens when you don't wipe away the tears—they collect, transmogrify, frighten with renewed power—the sum of all the parts previously hidden.

VIII: Village

My sister and I are roller-skating in the carport.

April skates as if she were walking except with a long glide to it. She is living up to the nickname I have given her, *Clodhopper*. April is going through adolescence like a chuffing, steam-spewing train knocking aside animals that have wandered onto the track. She is all sebum and lank brown hair. And swelling large breasts. And tangy-smelling menstrual pads in a brown paper bag under the bench in her closet. No one mistakes her for a boy any more. She is solid. Unlike me.

I have frilly, curlicued hair, curlicued blouses, knock knees, jutting bony elbows and a penchant for the colour white. My eyes peer anxiously round. My nose is a small freckled knob, my smile waterily transparent. In short, I am insubstantial, half-sketched, jaggedy-lined, related to a third-world child from an Amnesty poster.

I sing as I spin round and round in circles with my arms in a cradle. I am pretending to be a Disney heroine even though I am bored by the cartoon characters on TV. Soft-spoken, so breathily sweet that birds alight on their fingers. I want to be graceful, figure-eighting through the Heavens.

April won't look at me. She skates by me without meeting my eyes. She chews her lips, she stares off into the cul-de-sac and almost skates into the garbage cans. Startled, she swerves and stumbles. I skate to her and put a hand on her shoulder.

Are you all right, April?

She lifts her shoulders, then lowers them. She bows her head at my concern. It isn't servility. It's shame. When she raises her head, tears slip down her cheeks like worms of rain. Her great blue eyes are shining like a husky dog's. She releases her breath in a pop.

What's wrong?

Oh, God, I feel so bad. I'm so sorry.

What are you talking about?

You know that book Mother was talking to us about? The one about growing up, puberty. You know. The special book.

Yes.

She gave it to me to read but told me not to tell you. She says you're too immature, you're still a baby, that's what she said. You're not . . . developed enough.

I don't need boobs to understand things. I don't need boobs to understand that I'll never grow boobs. There are some things that there are hiding places for and there are some things that there are no hiding places for. There are whole villages of wounds behind words.

IX: Razor

Thunder and spit of howl and white.

My anger is a target, a constellation of targets. The rain is piped in above my head, this shower head is suffusing me in dreams. Can one, is it safe for one to operate aquatic machinery while under the influence of sedatives?

I take baths a lot. The nurses do not care that I lock the door. Perhaps they think suicide is a way of life, not an alternative to life, which is why they left me with an arsenal of personal belongings, although I did sign a promissory note in exchange as currency. But this sly cleaving of the razor blade to my flesh, this small sudden slice isn't a dress rehearsal.

I dress hastily in a blue and yellow dressing gown with a Velcro fastening. The nurse comes running when she hears me scream. She sees the blood pouring from my calf. Too much blood. Fifteen minutes later, when the blood is finally slowing, my doctor arrives. I am trembling. He examines the half-inch cut. I know it is nothing, but carries more significance than statistics. I haven't seen my own blood in five months.

When the doctor leaves, I phone Linda from a pay phone in the hall and offer her my wound like King Herod offered John the Baptist's head to Salome. My blood cannot clot easily because of the weight I've lost. Iron deficiency, low hemoglobin, low blood pressure. It's bleeding through the bandage. Little spores of blood. I smile at all the nurses. I reward myself with a piece of banana bread and three cups of hot chocolate. I eat on the couch and know the nurses won't say anything.

X: Freezer

The packages are always carefully wrapped in tinfoil first, then in freezer bags. Mother has me take them to the deep freeze. She always tells the story of the deep freeze, how she bought it for only one hundred dollars from a man who soon after went to jail for dismembering his wife. The associations are frozen in the thick ice on the insides. There is no fear, no symbolism, no clear thought of questionable function, no hesitation on Mother's part. This is a story attached to a functional object. For me, it is different. Not lurid in her narrative, but lurid in my own private narrative.

Food is gathering in the deep freeze. Months of lasagnas, steaks, pork chops in tomato sauce, minced beef, meat pies, bologna, hams, frozen peas, bread, and aloha cookies on trays.

The women from the church bring most of it; most is there too long to remember its origin. The women come with recriminations about Stepfather, grace for Mother and sidelong, questioning looks for us children. The women are all curled hair and bright coats, like Joseph's coat of many colours I learned about in Sunday school. The Sunday women could teach me about manna, about fishes and loaves. Perhaps they had miracles in the food they brought. I was still too young to know that hope is abstract, and that the packages would remain in the freezer, getting duller and duller with frost, almost vanishing.

XI: Mirrors

It's not about mirrors. It's about using mirrors.

XII: Bed

Laundry day is every Thursday morning. We must strip the beds.

This stay, they do not mention this at all to me. I know the routine from last year. So I don't bother to change the bed but I pile up more yellow, pink and brown blankets until I can burrow on top of them in a good reading position. I drag a finger across the spines of the books, like my spine now erect in a thin veil of flesh, then hesitate on the huge one. It's the only book that isn't mine. It's the book everyone else wants, no, *needs*, and I must share, the nurses tell me, other patients may want to benefit. Half of them look as if they don't know how to read.

A plate of rotted food, a sheet of saran over it, balances on top of the books. Sometimes, after I've had my sedative, I open my ears as wide as the wind and hear the scuttering of the fruit flies. Out of the garden of tiger lily, tulip, carnation, I can pick out browning bananas, tangy Spam, mayonnaise, butterscotch. Other smells join them until finally I have a garden de mal.

If I want to read, or sleep, or find a patch of grass to reform the memories, I must hurry. When I am asleep, I will not wake until the patients are back in the beds, smelling of gravy and ice cream. There are strategies here for surviving outside of rules.

XIII: Scream

In this damp painting I am. In this damp painting I have a mandala around my head. My mouth is open, red. My dress is a blue network of veins and a heart. My arm floats above my Eve's rib like a veined science lab skeleton. What my hand reaches into is a burning bush. Below my arm is a thick oak door, like Mother's furniture, and there is a picked lock over my vagina, blood seeping down the carpet of my thighs.

You want you want you want you want yes . . . but it's painful.

XIV: Mouse

I get real scary dreams and Mommy don't come and get me. I hid in blanky. Night is real dark like the bogeyman, ummmm. And I remember the hoxpital. And oni oni with cheese when I was there, my arm hurt, and my legs.

I get fections and sick and puke. I sleep with my blanky cos he is magical. He saves me. I love him better than anyone. Except my Real Daddy. My Real Daddy is skyscraper tall and can talk to God. My Real Daddy hates when Mommy dresses me in my red dress with a ducky on the front. Red red red as mad. She calls me Ugly Duckling. She made me not tell Daddy, cos it's a secret. I hate I hate I hate secrets.

Daddy told me about death when I was in the kitchen, when we emptied the traps from under the sink. I am too big for traps. When I carried mousey home in a box I got caught showing it to Mommy's friends. I want a mouse.

I steal Oreos cos we are hungry and we can't find Mommy. I steal Oreos cos we are hungry and I'm the only one who can fit in the cupboards. I know the secrets in the kitchen. I am a mousey.

XV: Carpet

I pee in the corner of my room. The carpet is already yellowy there. I feel the heat against my bottom, smell the ammonia. I crawl back into bed and strike my ankle against the post. Cannot turn on the light. I hear my own heart pounding in my ears, not my mother pounding up the stairs. I crouch waiting, like last night, like last week, like last month, hoping the stain dries before she sees it. When it's bedtime, the door stays shut.

Let the stain dry before she smells it. Or else I'll have to blame it on the cat.

I blame it on the cat and the cat disappears.

He ate too much food, Mother says.

XVI: Float

I'm floating on one Serax, two Serax and a Tylenol 3 from an hour earlier. Lights are out. On the ceiling, pink dinosaurs and wilted cats, the flashlight comes. I want to float now. Tissue-paper body, and wings of fly eyes, wings of ocean colour and Icarus-proof. Burning orange haloes, and my arms like white streamers, I'll fly in a curl of autumn smoke up to God. Spring, what was the colour of the angel's wings in spring?

And this is the hardest part. This is match-letting to tinder. It's easy to collect tinder, but lighting it to smoke is a quest.

Somewhere drinking a doctor-prescribed milkshake is a small kitchen angel at fifteen. She has a feathery body, and the shakes. There are angels getting stabbed in the hands with forks and they are dreaming of ceilings, of ceilings as a start to sky, as the rudiment of wishing.

There she is in her milky, cold bath, afraid to move, afraid to disturb the thin membrane of dirt and urine.

There she is in a blizzard of flesh and recriminations; with small lips she says *float*, as the blows continue to fall.

XVII: Flesh

Flesh isn't beauty! It's escape.

XVIII: Perfect

Mother hasn't even taken off her coat, her socks are slipping off like snakeskins, and she shakes her keys at April, who is crouched sullen on an immense throw pillow.

Goddamn you, she spits at April. *Mister Fancyass Johnston said you don't work in his class. What does that mean?*

April scowls, shaking her greasy head. *I got a G.*

Mother stalks towards April. *That was in drama. You got S's and U's.*

I cower behind April and put a hand on her knee. April squares her shoulders and says mutinously, *Last time I got G's and you said marks are the only thing that matters.*

Mother narrows her black eyes. *Don't back talk.*

And to me, *I see you cowering, little Miss Perfect. You want to know what Mister Smeath said about you?*

I don't want to know. I peer from behind April's shoulder, my stomach in knots, my nerve in one leg goes and my leg starts vibrating.

He said you work yourself too hard. That you will have a breakdown at fourteen.

But I got all A's and one A+. I look at the ground like a dog who's been shown the place it just urinated and expects to get her nose ground in it.

He thinks I'm pushing you too hard. He said you gave him that impression. What have you told him?

Nothing.

Can't you do anything right? Why can't you be

Perfect?

XIX: Elves

We get the Elves Club Christmas carton. Inside are two green knitted toques with orange stripes and an orange pompom on top. Mother isn't home yet so I rifle through the box unearthing tins of Spork; flat red tins of cranberry sauce, four of them; two small cans of no-name peas; one tin of stewed tomatoes with a dent in the side; a black and white tin of sauerkraut; one floppy bag of powdered milk; and a frosted bag of bulk-style pretzels. I repack the cardboard box as efficiently as I can, just like, I imagine, the ladies at the Elves Club. My hands are shaking. I hop up and down on the spot, turn and confront the Christmas hamper with a kick that numbs my toes.

Mother makes a goulash with most of the tins, stewed tomatoes, peas, Spork and sauerkraut. The cranberry sauce is spooned onto bread for dessert. The powdered milk Mother pours on top of the puffed wheat already in our bowls for when we wake. All we have to do is add water and devour. Mother munches on the pretzels as she stirs the saucepan of goulash. She calls it manna from Heaven.

XX: Bathroom

I blame the stuffed pink pig named Piglet. I blame the thought of beer, an elegant glass of wine, a snifter of sherry. I blame all the ruses used to gain those three pounds to get an overnight pass, to keep my breasts, small as they are, from shrinking into my rib cage. I blame the vanity of flesh. I blame waking up at seven-fifteen to make fresh coffee at eight; the two 250-ml glasses of orange juice, the bruised banana, the soggy slicelet of toast. I blame the blood trickling over the swollen flesh of my rectum, the solid black missiles of waste digging, tearing their way out, the push of muscles, the pain. The tissue paper glued to my flesh with a dab of Vaseline. I blame the unexpected fullness of flesh, of tubes, inner pipework that once had been fallow.

XXI: Coal

I sit on the counter with one leg on the floor, the other swinging. I crane my neck to read the private notices pinned up to the corkboard. One letter regarding patients' personal belongings, another with staff parking information, another about rules and regulations. All are well thumbed and hang limply from a corner punctured with numerous thumbtack holes. I look out through the small window in the upper door to see if I'm noticed peering about by the day nurses. They are bent over big blue binders, patients' personal histories. Mine has my name in block letters with red felt marker, and my room number—C 204, 3B.

I read the nurses' names over their cubbyholes, a gestalt of mail and memos. Sharon, Denise, Ron, Theresa, Rozema, Collette, Eva, Nicholas, Susan, Dave, Pat and Carmella. There is something very efficient about these names, as if their service were weighed and measured in every consonant and vowel. A hodgepodge of names collecting a hodgepodge of duties in their framework.

Through the ear holes of the telephone, a tinny voice is rattling on into my confidence. I have been given permission by the head psychiatrist to use the phone because my long distance call is not collect but charged to my home phone number on the outside.

The tinny voice beckons, demands my concentration. The voice belongs to April, who hasn't heard from me in months. Being long distance, I cannot afford to call. No, the truth is, I do not want to call because she is the living reminder, the talisman through which we conjure up the past. Besides, she is too healthy for me to talk to unless I am in some sort of admirable danger in which she loses her gloating position, and I, like in the childhood games, become the King of the Castle, and she is in the loathsome position of dirty rascal. Yes, disease rises as something to be veiled in robes, and crowned, a royal bargaining power. This is how we communicate now, and I suppose it is how we've always communicated.

She is crying, and this dissolving of borders make me succumb to the tight pulling ball in my throat. Over and over she cries like a dirge:

There is something more underneath.

There is something more underneath.

And I add, *Yes,* like a lump of hard coal growing older and older under strata of different permeabilties, there is something more that needs to be mined. But a question remains: Where are the tools and what do they look like?

XXII: Swings

Where have you been? Where have you been? The voices call.

In the park, across the old wooden bridge, down from the school, and on the playground, I was in the heavens, pumping my legs up to God to see if I could fly even for a second, even for the briefest suggestion of flight. This is how it will feel without flesh on, without my skin contouring my bones. This is how it will feel to whistle through the fingers of God. I pump my legs higher and feel terrified of earth colliding with my bones. Distance becomes fear. Height becomes fear. Motion becomes fear. As youth recedes into the background, lining the brain as pictures in a photo album, an amalgamation of class pictures and counting rhymes, first steps, first teeth, etc.—so does the paradise of pure fantasy, the ability to read more into clouds than mere clouds, the ability to project yourself into the fairy robes, into the crown, into the wedding procession.

I say, *I cannot swing this high*. I enter wave after wave of nausea until my feet are on the ground. I throw up spittle only, clear, acidy, induced from a raw throat and bucking stomach.

When I get back, dragging my feet, scuffing my shoes, the nurse comes to me like an alert bee. They worry I might find a more permanent alternative to psychotherapy.

You think too much, they say.

XXIII: Grass

I burn on this patch of grass shaped as a shadow's angel now. Every frond is yellow and bends its knees as if in a bow. My face is mercury. My body heat is recorded on this ball of fierce red. My head, the head of a match, my body, easy tinder. I will snap or I will burn up like a bonfire angel.

XXIV: Red

It takes two doctors to restrain me. I am thrusting my head down to my knees and flinging it back up. Air is wooshing in harsh gasps from my mouth. I feel as if every prick of light has rushed into my eyes and blinded me. The moaning continues until my doctor comes.

Emergency, they said, *hurry!*

At first when I whispered what was wrong, through groaned syllables, I was greeted with skepticism. Now they repeat, like a mantra, *We've never seen anything like this before*. And they haven't. Hadn't. They all clustered around the 3B station and took turns finding medication, water, anything to alleviate the pain. I bled through seven maternity pads in a day. I went through forty-two. I went through two Motrin every three hours for the duration. I dreamed dreams that would have rivalled the dream that Joseph struggled to interpret.

I gained two pounds.

I've lost ten.

I was suddenly terrified of my own blood and had to be dragged out of the washroom by a nurse.

XXV: Finger

It takes a harder jab than the ones that preceded it. My esophagus burns with a strip of liquid heat. I drool onto the toilet. My fist is slimy, not merely wet but slimy. I jab and dig hard as far down, as into the flesh as I can. My eyes hitch with tears and in the mirror this face looks like an Egyptian death mask.

The Kentucky Fried Chicken, all twelve pieces, skins and all, have no right to be in me. They have to leave. They are weighing my flesh down. I feel every pore struggling with the grease, the weight.

The twenty-four pack of mini Mars Bars have to—

My heart begins to burn, and the coloured ferris-wheel lights of the mirror whirl fragments of me around the room. Who will collect the pieces? My skin is vibrating and the sounds of the walls are too baritone, too ponderous.

She'll be all right. She had a sugar rush.

They find me with my hands around my throat, passed out in the hallway by the pop machines. Someone had urinated on my legs and it spread in an ugly gash on the cool white floor.

XXVI: Polish

Someone has given me a gift. It was wrapped in lilac tissue paper with my name delicately scrawled in gold across the wrap, shadowed by the big gold bow and card. It was on the nurses' station with my cut-up celery and carrots, butterscotch pudding and yellow apple with my name on masking tape stuck to the skin like a Band-Aid.

The plastic white Chanel bag has a blue drawstring. Opened, it releases smells like secrets and fear like Pandora's box: a papery smell of unopened strawberry scented nail-polish remover, Santa Monica beach peach hand cream, Brucci red nail polish and a bar of pink Fa soap.

The card reads, *Get Well.* There is no name. I should know? If it were so easy.

I lacquer each nail with ultra-bitch red, and even my toenails stand out like drops of raspberry blood. I cover my hands with the female smell of peach. I decide to dig in my cupboard drawer and unearth my make-up kit, which I brought with me through force of habit but haven't used yet. I decide to do my face. Mirrors are used for this. With every feather of the brush, time floods from my pores, days of bathrobe wandering, of winter carved into the eyes, of screaming in the soft room, of painting, of laughing with the nurses, of singing with the others, of sitting at the dining tables with ease, of diving deeper and deeper under the surfaces, of unearthing half time-rotted clues like an archaeologist.

I look like a girl whoring with her flesh.

I look like an actress whose face I cannot remember.

I feel like Borgia wishing that discretion hadn't stopped his hand from poisoning the emissaries of God.

XXVII: Street

The gift comes from a secondary friend, one I see perhaps every three months. What is important is not her, but her function.

She comes to see me on a brittle-hot day. She joins me on the grass and instead of lying down she sits, *You get a good view of the road from here.*

I arrange myself so I am facing away from the noise of traffic. She talks to me in a soothing stream of words that slide over my sticky skin. She talks to me about her job dancing, about drinks she's bought, the party she went to where everyone asked where I was, the new leather jacket she bought, and it is soft, yes it's soft, and the long, stoned walks down Fisherman's Wharf and Dallas Road Beach, and how my plants have all died in my apartment, *oh yeah,* and somebody broke in but it is no big thing, and when the hell am I getting out? and would I like to smoke just a pinner with her, if I still do that sort of thing?

We smoke it on the playground like fugitives, our heads pressed close, our hands involved in a secret manner of communication. I feel her words, and the world within them, sticking to my skin.

Yes, I say, there is a good view of the street.

XXVIII: Shark

It's for you, it's for you. You better answer it.

I translate: It's for me. I better answer it, and I do. The receiver is warm and sticky with sweat and jam. I pick it up and hello into it. The voice is Linda's.

Hey, kiddo, sorry I couldn't visit but I was busy rushing around. Linda includes her husband in her "I," which I think is exceptional. There are too many people in my "I."

No problem. I'm okay.

You'd say that even when you're near death.

Yeah I know.

I tell her about my bleeding. She thinks I sound wistful, spaced out. She says there is something that makes me very sad but I don't know what it is.

Every day is different. You've had quiet days and days where you screamed or laughed.

I tell her about the latest memories to surface, like plankton on a boundless ocean housing bigger and bigger units of the food chain. Sharks can smell blood miles away, I tell her.

So, when are you getting out?

I don't know. Maybe in a week or two.

Are you ready?

That's what I'll find out.

There is no guarantee you can avoid or survive a shark attack. This is where I need the wings.

XXIX: Bonfire Angels

This is where I need wings. This is where autumn comes into play, the burning of sun like an eyeglass. The heat focusses on skin, and I burn, and my bones are left charred smoothly from bone, smoke forms wings, and a dress, a halo, and this is where I leave.

This is where I can burn, fly, float weightless to God who will not crush me in his palm like an insect, but say, *It took you long enough to get here.*

And I'll say, Only as long as it takes.

Welcome home, Bonfire Angel, welcome home.

Featured as an emerging writer in Boulevard *magazine, Nick Nolet has published two chapbooks of poetry,* Dangerous Aphrodisiacs *(Iris Press) and* Collecting Mirrors *(Reference West). She reads regularly in Victoria and Vancouver, most recently with poet/editor Lynn Crosbie at Open Space.*

Erin Soros

Home Free

She watches me through the glass. As I walk up the pathway to her house, I can see her body small and still, framed by blinds and orange curtains. One palm is pressed against the window, fingers spread, but she doesn't wave. Her hand is tense, as if she is holding up the pane.

I flip the car keys over and back across my thumb. Over and back, waiting for her to open the door. I hear her footsteps inside. The paper rasp of slippers, the hurried snap of boots. "Coming, coming," she shouts frantically, as if I'm going to leave without her.

"Don't worry, we've got time. I hope it's not in black and white." She doesn't respond. Leans her forehead into the door as she closes it, rattling the knob to check the lock.

I slip my arm through hers, lead her down the steps. Her other hand grips the edge of the banister Colleen and I had slid down, backwards, on late September afternoons, racing to see who could reach the grass first. We used her as our referee, to make sure there was no cheating, kicking, pulling hair or pushing each other off.

"I don't like scary movies in black and white. They remind me of when I was a kid." I keep talking, uncomfortable touching her, the bones in her arms. "Remember the one where the parents get a letter saying their son will be coming home and when the doorbell rings they run all excited and it's their son at the door only he's dead? Standing there held up in a box, dead?"

"Yes," she says, nodding. "Of course. I watched that whole series. One man got pushed onto railway tracks when the train was coming. I was looking after you kids. You sneaked out of bed and hid behind the couch to watch. I pretended like I couldn't hear you breathing behind me."

I lower her into the Pinto, pull the safety belt across her narrow shoulders. The belt doesn't arch over her. It stretches straight across her hips. As if she isn't there, as if I'm belting an empty seat.

The car smells comfortable, of heated rubber and wet wool. Old sand and crushed seashells line the cracks in the fake leather. Raindrops begin to tap at the windshield. Her eyes watch my hands on the wheel. Her knuckles whiten on the door handle. She is perched for escape.

We are not going that far, Commercial to Cambie. She doesn't get out much any more. I had planned for dinner and a movie, but when I called she said restaurants are too noisy. Besides, she added sharply, doing two things in one evening is bad for her nerves. She has this way of expressing surprise and disdain. She closes questions or suggestions by stating something about herself she thinks I should already know. Implying I'm rude or selfish for expecting her to do something she didn't want. I'd like to yell back that I only take her out to be nice. But I never do it. Instead, I act as if she's doing me a favour. It was the same when she came to visit, when I still lived at home. One of us had to drive down to meet her at the loop, but then through the whole weekend she never stopped cleaning the house. I used to feel guilty for not wanting to pick her up.

"Look at that corner. There was a dancehall there. Danceland, it was called. It's gone, though. You can't see it." The windshield wipers squeak and whine. "Pearl went there every Saturday night when she was your age. She loved to dance, your mother did. She met your father there. He was short, see, and when she saw him she thought to herself, wouldn't he be a good dance partner for that right tiny friend of hers. That's why she danced with him, when he asked her. To match him up with her friend. She was always doing things for other people, your mother was. He was nice enough though—then."

She rarely speaks to me like this. When other relatives are around, our roles are more rigid. She gives me Easter candy, tells me not to swear, hands me knives and forks for the table, spits on Kleenex to wipe my face. Though she doesn't look like grandmothers do in books, I forget she has not always been old. To think of her as a young mother is embarrassing, improper somehow. Like that time we found half a pack of Players in her freezer. It was *high schoolers* who smoked. Leaning in a row against the graffiti-covered concrete outside Fay's, they blew doughnuts and inhaled them back in through their nostrils or lips, looking down at Colleen and me as we collected bottles to trade in for licorice and sour soothers. I couldn't imagine Nana's lips sucking at a cigarette. Or being kissed. It was even hard to watch her eat. She stuck her tongue out to catch the food and bring it in, never letting the fork enter her mouth.

"He didn't take to music much, not like your mother. Before they went and got married she'd dance with anyone. Her girl-friends—they did that back then. Dancing round the kitchen, on her own, even. I'd come home from work and there'd she be. Spinning and spinning by herself."

She lifts both arms up and sways them in the air. I turn at an intersection and her hand snaps to the door. Her mouth is pinched. She looks as if she's been caught.

When I lived at home I sat on the dining room floor and listened to Nana through the walls. We didn't have a table or chairs or cabinets in the dining room. It was completely empty. It wasn't really a dining room at all. I liked it that way because when I did homework I could lie down and spread my notes across the floor. The papers covered the carpet like uneven white tiles, a different pile for each paragraph or problem. There was a window, but all I could see was the glazed glass of the neighbour's bathroom. Sometimes I scared myself by staring at the window and imagining I saw someone crawling through.

I didn't want to see a face looking in. I didn't know what would be worse, that someone might be there or that I might see him.

I felt safe when Mom and Nana were talking in the kitchen. They drank sweet milky tea and laughed. Nana let hers sit for a long time, stirring it or twirling the cup. She didn't mind cold tea. She didn't even mind cold toast. Mom said that's how English people eat it. But Nana wasn't English. When Mom and Nana told stories about Prince Edward Island—back home, they called it—they talked funny. Mom said "boight" instead of "bite." "Well, Lord knows I don't need it but I suppose a boight of cake won't hurt." Or "Please—just try to get down one more teensy little boight."

They sat kitty-corner at one end of the table, on the edge. Facing each other. Both leaned forward, but didn't let their weight fall into the table. Its legs branched out from a single pole in the centre, which meant they had to be careful sitting like that together on one end. If they forgot to hold themselves back it would tip.

They only talked about things that were already familiar. One supplied the beginning of a line and the other picked it up, as if they were knitting something, taking turns to untwist tangles. "No, no, this one *had* to get married." Or, "That was no accident. That was gangrene." They appeared to anticipate these corrections, mutually nodding, mirroring each other's sighs. They knew the stories too well to make genuine mistakes.

But from the other side of the wall, I got the names and events confused. Not only was the genealogy complicated, but the family history was full of disguises, practical jokes, lies. A story started out in one direction and then flipped on me halfway through. Like a trick. Like opening what looks like an ordinary book or an innocent box of candy and one of those snakes leaps out at my face.

When the war began, Nana's brothers lied about their ages to get enlisted. When they were sent home in winter their bodies were left on the snow to wait for the dirt to thaw. Even after spring arrived, Nana said, the memory of them lying like that stayed with you. They could never be buried deep enough. Her brother-in-law wasn't allowed to enlist because he only had one eye. Or maybe the story was he lost the eye in the war. There was some kind of connection. His glass eye looked real enough, though. I'm sure he could have fooled them. Adults were usually too polite to ask about those kinds of things and I could only tell it was fake when he hugged me up too close.

Whenever Nana saw a crepe on a well-off family's door, she made sure to attend the wake, even if she'd never known the person who died. She planted the children in front of the buffet table, told them to eat more meat than cake and act shy when adults asked them who they were. She nibbled and mingled, getting any mourners she met to discuss what relationship they had with the deceased. If they said they were friends, she answered she was family. If they were family, she was a friend. When in doubt she explained she took in laundry. They would nod, assume she once worked for the deceased, and shuffle away. No one wanted to think about a dead person's dirty clothes.

She never crashed parties or weddings. At festive occasions people are more particular about their guests, they ask questions. You have to eat politely and wear the right kind of clothes. It wouldn't be worth the trouble.

I didn't understand where her husband fit in her stories. Our name for him never matched with "Nana." "Grandad," we called him, spelled missing a "d" in the middle, as if the word "dad" had begun to eat away at the word "grand."

I could tell when Mom and Nana were going to talk about Grandad. They closed the door between the dining room and kitchen, leaving me alone with my books and my window. It was a sliding door that slipped into a hole in the wall, so even when I couldn't see it, it was there all the time. Closing it made a spooky hollow sound like the wind does late at night. The sound made me feel sick inside, even after I discovered it was only the wheels the door rolled on. I saw how it worked one day when Dad had to take it apart—I had hidden things in there and they jammed the door until it wouldn't come out at all.

If I leaned against the wall I could hear them talking. The kitchen ceiling was high so their voices echoed. But all they said was "the bad time" or "this one" or "you know." Since I didn't know, I made up things to put inside their words. I'm sure my stories were better than theirs. Nana slipped up sometimes and said "Phil," so I had something to go on, a name to root my inventions and their floating "he's." It was shocking to hear him called a real name, not Grandad or Daddy or Your Father.

We asked Mom over and over why Nana and Grandad didn't live together like normal people. She just told us to go play or clean up our room. Then once on the way to the doctor's she told me Nana had to leave Grandad because he fooled around on her. I thought she meant he acted silly, like the time Colleen and I spat toothpaste on the wall and Dad yelled at us to get to bed and stop fooling around. Teachers used those words too, but I didn't get in trouble much at school. Grandad fooling around didn't seem like a good reason to leave him and move across the country. I was sure Mom was lying or at least not telling me the whole truth.

But then I started thinking about what Mom had said. Grandad fooled around *on* Nana. I knew how one word can change things. I saw Grandad holding her down, fooling around, thinking it was all a joke. She would be afraid and angry while he just acted silly, tickling her like Dad did to me when we played roughhouse. And she couldn't stop laughing when she yelled at him to stop. She would hate him when he made her say uncle and admit he'd won. She couldn't get up unless he wanted it. That feeling stuck with you.

As I got older the story changed. I heard things. How she buried her savings in the hard red dirt. How she dropped their clothes through the window, keeping watch as the bags hit the grass. How it was all arranged so that when she took each child by the hand and walked out the front door, there was nothing on her. No one could tell, no one could follow her from the Island to Vancouver. The longest line in Canada.

I can grasp it now, but need her to fill in the gaps. The train ride across the country, the jobs bussing tables and hanging laundry, the short nights in a Prior Street attic apartment. Mother and daughter and son spooned into a single bed. Nana up before dawn to scrub the floor. Hands cracking in the bleach.

But I don't ask questions. I keep my fingers locked to the wheel and try to look like I'm concentrating on the road ahead. She's a stubborn woman and resents intrusion. Headstrong, people say about her, with awe or insult. I can't tell her which stories to tell or how to tell them.

She always called the bus loop by our house "P-hibbs Exchange," pronouncing the *p* and the *h* separately. "It's Phibbs, Nana," we'd correct her. "Like a lie. You know, to tell a fib. Or like Phyllis. Phibb. Like that." But the next week it would be the same, the letters becoming even more distinct. "I'm at P-hibbs Exchange," she'd say on the phone. "I'm here, waiting." She was there, and we weren't, and she'd say things as she saw them.

"Then the summer Pearl turned eighteen," she continues, and I realize I haven't been listening. "She and a few other girls had it all planned to go stay at the Blue and White, in Penticton. Each night for weeks she'd be pinching a record from Ricky's collection and hiding it away in her suitcase. She thought he'd never notice if it was done gradual-like. You know how protective Ricky is. No one can so much as breathe on his records. He knew what she was up to all right. But he plays along with it, lets her go ahead and steal them. Then the night before she's off, what does he do but creeps into her room and takes all his records back. So the next day she hurries on that bus, see, all happy, thinking like she done got away with it. And as soon as she gets there, don't you know, she opens her suitcase and them records are gone. Gone, every last one. There she was, poor thing. It ruined her holiday. She thought someone stole them."

I stop the car in front of the theatre to drop her off before I park. She lifts herself up, suddenly strong. She marches through the rain to the awning, turns around, waves. Not good-bye, but hurry up. Traffic is bad and someone is waiting for me to pull out.

When I meet her in line, she looks annoyed that there are other people in the lobby, milling around. It's a gangster film, rated Restricted, but we are surrounded by teen-agers. Hoodlums, she calls them. When I was a child I thought all teen-agers were evil. Not an age group but a shameful passage. I didn't expect to become one.

"They fought, then, those two, Pearl and Ricky, but they weren't like you and Colleen. They were never like that. No, not like you."

I find myself at the front counter pulling out quarters and bills for popcorn. I'm not hungry but I need to crunch at something.

"No, no. I'm fine. I don't want nothing." She hunches over to pick up the coins I've scattered across the carpet. Clutching pennies and bits of fluff, she scans the floor once more, then tugs my palm down so she can cup hers over mine. "Here. You left this." I pocket the change, dig my fist back in the popcorn.

She doesn't flinch during the movie. Instead I reach for her hand in the dark. "It's all pretend," she whispers, contemptuous as I cover my face. A machine gun rips a man's stomach into hamburger and her eyes never leave the screen. She mutters occasionally, to me or herself, "It's not really happening. It's all pretend."

When the movie ends I want to get outside, but stepping through the theatre doors I become disoriented. The street looks new. No, not new, different. Still wet and dark, but tilted somehow. The lights on Grouse Mountain move closer to me in the rain and the sidewalk warps. Walking down the street, holding keys in my hand, I'm suddenly too tall.

She's talking again and I try to hear her but the movie is following me. People hurry by, hunching. She stops and lets go of my arm to pull a plastic rain cap from her purse, crinkled like a cellophane fan. She stretches it out, releasing the wrinkles to the rain. Wraps it around her head and ties it under her chin.

"Keeps my hair in place," she says, expecting criticism. "At least I don't wear them black overshoes like old ladies do." She's right. Her black leather boots, silver buckles on the side, snap as the heel hits the pavement. Click, click. They're not old lady's shoes. "Sharp," Mom would call them. "Aren't those boots sharp?" she'd say. Or "smart." As in, "She's a real smart dresser." Meaning fashionable, up to date, not secondhand. Meaning she's not letting herself go. But when Nana stayed with us the first thing she did was take her boots off on the front landing. Left them by the door and stole socks from my father's drawer, the brown wool gathering around her ankles.

"I get my hair done still. Once a week. The rain'd ruin it." Her voice has an edge now, though I haven't said anything. I've seen her plastic hat before. Her face like a cabbage in a grocery bag.

She is always wrapping herself in something. A-line dresses and skirts meant to suggest depth, if not curves, falling outward in a triangle from her neck or her waist. But the skirts merely exaggerate the thinness of her legs, which poke out under the hem like a rickety Christmas tree trunk. Hard to say if she has a body under all that material.

We used to share a bunk bed. Nana stayed with us on weekends, on holidays, and when I got sick. I would wake to the creak of the ladder and watch her nightgown flap through the rungs as she climbed to the upstairs bed. She carefully slid each socked foot along the wood, her right hand clinging to the banister, her left to her rosary. The beads knocking against each other. Her hair wrapped in a turban of yellow toilet paper.

"It's me, Ellen." Rustle of fabric and paper and feet. "Just me. Go back to sleep."

If I woke in the middle of the night and called her name, or even whispered it so quietly I could barely hear myself, she always answered me right away. Quick and sharp in the dark. "Yes yes dear, what's wrong?" Lying flat and rigid, braced for something. Her eyes half-open as she slept.

Now she is looking at my hair. Obviously a disgrace, wet and ragged in the rain. I pull my hood on, tucking tangles inside where they rub against my neck and drip beads of water down my spine.

"No, your father don't like dancing." She sounds more like she is talking to herself than to me. "I never said a thing against him though. He was stable enough, most times. Not like your grandfather. Not like what he . . . No, I never said nothing against him. Even after, when she had you kids. Even when he would . . . I'd just keep quiet and clean up your room so he wouldn't get all mad at you. He'd start in, and I'd just hide away your toys. Sweep. Tried once to . . . But I couldn't . . ."

I open the car door for her and try to meet her eyes, but she is looking intensely at the floor mat. She refuses my hand and lowers herself into her seat, still staring. When I start the engine she reaches again for the door handle. Taps the plastic with her fingers, over and over.

She used to tap me like that, the back of my head, my shoulder, my hand. I often tried to pinpoint the tune or rhythm she made, but it was never recognizable. When there was a fight she sat all hunched at the table, carefully folding and unfolding a paper napkin along imaginary lines. Once I came into the kitchen to find her like that, folding and unfolding, brushing away crumbs. I repeated something that Dad had just said to Mom. I don't remember what I said or why. Nana stood up and started choking. Sucking at air. I screamed and hit her on the back. She spat toast and tea on the table, then Mom and Dad ran in and told me not to touch her. "Don't you worry," she said, after a few sips of water. "It just went down the wrong way. It's happened before."

Mom demanded we all drive to emergency. I didn't tell them it was my fault. Neither did Nana, even though she hates hospitals.

"I'd never say it to Pearl," her voice farther and farther away. "But I wish she'd married someone else. Back then. She liked to laugh, your mother did. So much life in her. Light in her eyes, you know. Always running away to skate. Dance. Laughing. And he just . . . He . . . Don't you tell your mother about this. I just . . . don't think she felt like she deserved much. Don't think she did."

"What about you, Nana?"

"Me? Oh well, don't know about that. Maybe you're right. It

was my fault. Own fault. Worked too hard, I guess. Always cleaning. I got kind of funny. Cleaning. My hands and knees. They'd bleed, see. Always cleaning. I got funny. It . . . It wasn't good, that. For your mother."

She stops herself, as if surprised, and begins smoothing out an invisible crease in her skirt, both palms open and down. She smiles.

"What wasn't good, Nana? What do you mean by 'funny'?"

"Oh, I don't know. I mean what I said."

"But I don't understand."

"No. No, dear. You do."

I park in front of her house. The engine idles urgently. The whole car shakes along with her hands.

"It's all past now. We got each other. That's what's important. We still have each other."

I know she is not talking to me. She pats my hand with hers and gets out of the car, her head still wrapped in plastic.

She walks alone up to her house. I won't drive away until she has locked herself in, searched each room, and waved from the kitchen window to let me know she's okay. After watching the car disappear, she'll shuffle to the living room and watch *Twilight Zone* reruns. She'll wait until I call to let her know I'm home. Safe and sound.

"Hello? Ellen, is that you? Did you check the doors?

"Yes, yes, it's all locked up. You can go to sleep now, Nana, I'm here."

Erin Soros is writing a novel funded in part by an Explorations grant from the Canada Council. Her work has appeared in Fireweed *and* Tessera.